Wild Fire

NOVELS BY NELSON DEMILLE

By the Rivers of Babylon
Cathedral
The Talbot Odyssey
Word of Honor
The Charm School
The Gold Coast
The General's Daughter
Spencerville
Plum Island
The Lion's Game
Up Country
Night Fall

WITH THOMAS BLOCK

Mayday

Available from Warner Books

Nelson DeMille

Wild Fire

WARNER BOOKS

NEW YORK   BOSTON

Copyright © 2006 by Nelson DeMille
All rights reserved. Except as permitted under the U.S. Copyright Act of 1976, no part of this publication may be reproduced, distributed, or transmitted in any form or by any means, or stored in a database or retrieval system, without the prior written permission of the publisher.

Book design by Ellen Rosenblatt/SD Designs, Inc.

Warner Books
Hachette Book Group USA
237 Park Avenue
New York, NY 10169
Visit our Web site at www.HachetteBookGroupUSA.com

Warner Books and the W" logo are trademarks of Time Warner Inc. or an affiliated company. Used under license by Hachette Book Group USA, which is not affiliated with Time Warner Inc.

Printed in the United States of America

Originally published in hardcover by Warner Books
First International Trade Paperback Edition: November 2006
First International Mass Market Edition: April 2007

10 9 8 7 6 5 4 3 2 1

AUTHOR'S NOTE

When fact and fiction are combined in novels, it's not always clear to the reader which is which. Early readers of the manuscript for *Wild Fire* have asked me what is real and what is a figment of my imagination, so I thought I'd address that here.

First, the Anti-Terrorist Task Force (ATTF) represented in this and other John Corey stories is based primarily on the actual Joint Terrorist Task Force (JTTF), with some literary license taken.

In this book, specifically, there is a lot of information on ELF, which is an acronym for something you'll discover in the story. All the information about ELF is accurate, to the best of my knowledge.

As for the secret government plan called Wild Fire, this is based on some information I've come across, mostly online, and can be taken as rumor, fact, pure fiction, or some blend thereof. I personally believe that some variation of Wild Fire (by another code name) actually exists, and if it doesn't, it should.

Other subjects in the book that people have asked me about, such as NEST, Kneecap, and other acronyms, are factual. If what you're reading sounds real, it probably is. Truth is indeed stranger than fiction, and often scarier.

(cont'd)

The most frequently asked question I've gotten so far is, "Are BearBangers real?" Yes, they are.

The time period of this story is October 2002, a year and a month after 9/11/01, and the *New York Times* headlines and stories I use are real. Similarly, any mention of government security procedures, or lack of same, was true as of the time the story is set.

A few of my readers who work in law enforcement think that Detective John Corey has some problems with the limits of his power and his jurisdictional authority. I admit to taking some dramatic liberties for the sake of entertainment. A John Corey who plays by the rules and goes by the book is not what any of us wants in a hero.

Early readers of this book have told me that *Wild Fire* kept them awake long after they put the book down. Indeed, this is a scary book for scary times; but it's also a cautionary tale for a post-9/11 world.

Best wishes,
Nelson DeMille

— PART I —

Friday
NEW YORK CITY

The FBI investigates terrorism-related matters without regard to race, religion, national origin, or gender.

—*Terrorism in the United States*
FBI Publications, 1997

CHAPTER ONE

I'm John Corey, former NYPD homicide detective, wounded in the line of duty, retired on three-quarter disability (which is just a number for pay purposes; about 98 percent of me still functions), and now working as a special contract agent for the Federal Anti-Terrorist Task Force.

The guy in the cubicle facing me, Harry Muller, asked, "You ever hear of the Custer Hill Club?"

"No. Why?"

"That's where I'm going this weekend."

"Have a good time," I said.

"They're a bunch of rich, right-wing loonies who have this hunting lodge upstate."

"Don't bring me any venison, Harry. No dead birds, either."

I got up from my desk and walked to the coffee bar. On the wall above the coffee urns were Justice Department

Wanted Posters, featuring mostly Muslim gentlemen, including the number one scumbag, Osama bin Laden.

Also included in the nearly two dozen posters was a Libyan named Asad Khalil, a.k.a. The Lion. I didn't need to memorize this man's photo; I knew his face as well as my own, though I'd never formally met him.

My brief association with Mr. Khalil occurred about two years ago when I was stalking him, and as it turned out, he was stalking me. He escaped, and I got away with a grazing wound; and, as the Arabs would probably say, "It is destined that we meet again to settle our fates." I look forward to that.

I drained the dregs of the coffee into a Styrofoam cup and scanned a copy of the *New York Times* lying on the counter. The headline for today, Friday, October 11, 2002, read: CONGRESS AUTHORIZES BUSH TO USE FORCE AGAINST IRAQ, CREATING A BROAD MANDATE.

A subheading read: *U.S. Has a Plan to Occupy Iraq, Officials Report.*

It appeared that war was a foregone conclusion, and so was the victory. Therefore, it was a good idea to have an occupation plan. I wondered if anyone in Iraq knew about this.

I took my coffee back to my desk, turned on my computer, and read through some internal memos. We are now a mostly paperless organization, and I actually miss initialing memos. I had an urge to initial my computer screen with a grease pencil, but I settled for the electronic equivalent. If I ran this organization, all memos would be on an Etch A Sketch.

I glanced at my watch. It was 4:30 P.M., and my colleagues on the 26th floor of 26 Federal Plaza were dwindling fast. My colleagues, I should explain, are, like me, members of the Anti-Terrorist Task Force, a four-letter agency (ATTF) in a world of three-letter agencies.

This is the post-9/11 world, so weekends are, in theory, just another two workdays for everyone. In reality, the honored tradition of Federal Friday—meaning cutting out early—has not changed much, so the NYPD, who are part of the Task Force, and who are used to lousy hours anyway, man the fort on weekends and holidays.

Harry Muller asked me, "What are you doing this weekend?"

This was the start of the Columbus Day three-day weekend, but as luck would have it, I was scheduled to work on Monday. I replied, "I was going to march in the Columbus Day Parade, but I'm working Monday."

"Yeah? You were going to march?"

"No, but that's what I told Captain Paresi." I added, "I told him my mother was Italian, and I was going to push her wheelchair in the parade."

Harry laughed and asked, "Did he buy that?"

"No. But he offered to push her wheelchair."

"I thought your parents were in Florida."

"They are."

"And your mother's Irish."

"She is. Now I have to find an Italian mother for Paresi to push up Columbus Avenue."

Harry laughed again and went back to his computer.

Harry Muller, like most of the NYPD in the Mideast Section of the Task Force, does stakeouts and surveillance of Persons of Interest, which, in politically correct speak, means the Muslim community, but I do mostly interviewing and recruiting of informants.

A large percentage of my informants are total liars and bullshit artists who want either money or citizenship, or who want to screw someone in their close-knit community. Now and then, I get the real deal, but then I have to share the guy with the FBI.

The Task Force is comprised mostly of FBI agents and NYPD detectives, plus retired NYPD, like me. In addition, we have people assigned from other Federal agencies, such as Immigration and Customs Enforcement (ICE), plus state and suburban police, Port Authority Police, and so forth, too numerous to name or for me to remember.

Also included in our collegial group are people who, like ghosts, don't actually exist, but if they did, they'd be called CIA.

I checked my e-mail, and there were three messages. The first was from my boss, Tom Walsh, special agent in charge, who had taken over the ATTF when my old boss, Jack Koenig, died in the World Trade Center. The e-mail read: CONFIDENTIAL—REMINDER—IN THE RUN-UP TO POSSIBLE HOSTILITIES WITH IRAQ, WE NEED TO GIVE SPECIAL ATTENTION TO IRAQI NATIONALS LIVING IN CONUS.

"CONUS" meant "Continental United States." "Hostilities" meant "war." The rest of it meant "find an Iraqi we can link to a terrorist threat against the U.S. so we can make life easier for the folks in Washington before they bomb the shit out of Baghdad."

The message went on: PRIMARY THREAT AND

EMPHASIS REMAINS UBL WITH NEW EMPHASIS ON UBL/SADDAM LINK. BRIEFING ON THIS NEXT WEEK—TBA. WALSH, SAC.

For the uninitiated, "UBL" is "Osama bin Laden," which should be "OBL," but long ago somebody transliterated the Arabic script into Latin letters as "Usama," which is also correct. The media mostly uses the "Osama" spelling of the scumbag's name, while intelligence agencies still refer to him as "UBL." Same scumbag.

The next e-mail was from my second boss, the aforementioned Vince Paresi, an NYPD captain assigned to the ATTF to keep an eye on the difficult cops who sometimes don't play well with their FBI friends. That may include me. Captain Paresi replaced Captain David Stein, who, like Jack Koenig, was killed—murdered, actually—one year and one month ago today in the World Trade Center.

David Stein was a great guy, and I miss him every day. Jack Koenig, for all his faults and for all our problems with each other, was a professional, a tough but fair boss, and a patriot. His body was never recovered. Neither was David Stein's.

Another body that was never recovered, along with two thousand others, was that of Ted Nash, CIA officer, monumental prick, and archenemy of yours truly.

I wish I could think of something nice to say about this asshole, but all I can think of is, "Good riddance."

Also, this guy has a bad habit of coming back from the dead—he's done it at least once before—and without a positive body identification, I'm not breaking out the champagne.

Anyway, Captain Paresi's e-mail to all NYPD/ATTF

personnel read: YOU ARE TO STEP UP SURVEIL-
LANCE OF IRAQI NATIONALS, REACH OUT TO
IRAQIS WHO HAVE BEEN HELPFUL IN THE PAST,
AND BRING IN FOR QUESTIONING IRAQIS ON
WATCH LISTS. YOU ARE TO PAY SPECIAL ATTEN-
TION TO IRAQIS WHO ASSOCIATE WITH OTHER
ISLAMIC NATIONALS, I.E., SAUDIS, AFGHANIS,
LIBYANS, ETC. STAKEOUT AND SURVEILLANCE
OF MOSQUES WILL BE STEPPED UP. BRIEFING
NEXT WEEK, TBA. PARESI, CAPT. NYPD.

I think I see a pattern here.

Hard to believe, but it wasn't so long ago that we were
trying to figure out what we were supposed to be doing
every day, and memos were more carefully worded so as
not to appear that we disapproved of Islamic terrorists or
that we were upsetting them in any way. That changed real
quick.

The third e-mail was from my wife, Kate Mayfield,
whom I could see at her desk across the NYPD/FBI great
divide of the 26th floor. My wife is a beautiful woman,
but even if she weren't, I'd still love her. Actually, if she
weren't beautiful, I wouldn't have even noticed her, so it's
a moot point.

The message read: LET'S KNOCK OFF EARLY,
GO HOME, HAVE SEX, I'LL COOK YOU CHILI AND
HOT DOGS, AND MAKE YOU DRINKS WHILE YOU
WATCH TV IN YOUR UNDERWEAR.

Actually, it didn't say that. It said: LET'S GO AWAY
FOR A ROMANTIC WEEKEND OF WINE TASTING
ON THE NORTH FORK. I'LL BOOK A B&B. LOVE,
KATE.

Why the hell do I have to taste wine? It all tastes the same. Also, bed-and-breakfast places suck—cutesy run-down hovels with nineteenth-century bathrooms and creaky beds. And then you have to eat breakfast with the other guests, who are usually yuppie swine from the Upper West Side who want to talk about something they read in the Arts and Leisure section of the *Times*. Whenever I hear the word "art," I reach for my gun.

I typed my response: SOUNDS GREAT. THANKS FOR THINKING OF IT. LOVE, JOHN.

Like most men, I'd rather face the muzzle of an assault rifle than a pissed-off wife.

Kate Mayfield is an FBI agent, a lawyer, and part of my team, which consists of another NYPD guy and another FBI agent. Plus, now and then, we add a person or two from another agency, as needed, such as ICE or CIA. Our last CIA teammate was the aforementioned Ted Nash, who I strongly suspect was once romantically involved with my then future wife. This was not why I disliked him—it was why I *hated* him. I disliked him for professional reasons.

I noticed that Harry Muller was cleaning up his desk, locking away sensitive material so that the cleaning people, Muslim and non-Muslim alike, couldn't photocopy or fax it to Sandland. I said to him, "You got twenty-one minutes before the bell."

He looked up at me and replied, "I have to go pick up some Tech stuff."

"Why?"

"I told you. I'm doing a surveillance upstate. The Custer Hill Club."

"I thought you were an invited guest."

"No, I'm trespassing."

"How did you catch this one?"

"I don't know. Do I ask? I own a camper, a pair of boots, and a hat with earmuffs. So, I'm qualified."

"Right." Harry Muller, as I said, is former NYPD, like me, retired with twenty years in, the last ten in the Intelligence Unit, and now hired by the Feds to do stakeouts and surveillance so that the Suits, as we call the FBI, can do the cerebral work.

I asked him, "Hey, what's with this right-wing stuff? I thought you were with us?" "Us" meaning the Mideast Section, which makes up about 90 percent of the ATTF these days.

Harry replied, "I don't know. Do I ask? I just have to take pictures, not go to church with them."

"Did you read the e-mails from Walsh and Paresi?"

"Yeah."

"You think we're going to war?"

"Duh . . . let me think."

"Does this right-wing group have any Iraqi or UBL connections?"

"I don't know." Harry glanced at his watch and said, "I need to get to Tech before they lock up."

"You got time." I asked him, "You going alone?"

"Yeah. No problem. It's just a non-invasive surveillance and stakeout." He looked at me and said, "Between us, Walsh says this is just killing trees—file building. You know, like, we're not just up the Arabs' asses. We're on the case of domestic groups, too, like the neo-Nazis, militia, survivalists, and stuff. Looks good for the media and

Congress, if it ever comes up. Right? We did this a few times before 9/11. Remember?"

"Right."

"Gotta go. I guess I'll see you Monday. I need to see Walsh first thing Monday."

"He's working Monday?"

"Well, he didn't invite me to his house for a beer, so I guess he'll be here."

"Right. See you Monday."

Harry left.

What Harry said about file building didn't make too much sense, plus we have a Domestic Terrorist Section for that kind of stuff. Also, snooping on rich right-wingers with a club upstate was a little odd. Also odd was Tom Walsh coming in on a holiday to debrief Harry on a routine assignment.

I'm very nosy, which is why I'm a great detective, so I went over to a separate, stand-alone computer where I could access the Internet, and did a Google search for "Custer Hill Club."

I didn't get any hits, so I tried "Custer Hill." The counter at the top showed more than 400,000 hits, and the mix on the first page—golf courses, restaurants, and several historical references in South Dakota having to do with General George Armstrong Custer's problem at the Little Bighorn—indicated that none of these references would be relevant. Nevertheless, I spent ten minutes scanning the hits, but there were no references to New York State.

I went back to my desk, where I could use my ATTF

password to access internal files on the ACS—the Automated Case System, the FBI's version of Google.

The Custer Hill Club came up, but apparently I had no need to know about this file, and below the title was row after row of Xs. Usually you get something, even on restricted files, such as the date the file was opened, or who to see about getting access to the file, or at least the classification level of the file. But this file was completely Xed out.

So all I managed to do was alert the security goons that I'd been inquiring about a restricted file that had nothing to do with what I was working on, which was Iraqis at the moment. But just to mess with their heads, I typed in, "Iraqi Camel Club Weapons of Mass Destruction."

No hits.

I shut down my computer, secured my desk, grabbed my coat, and walked over to Kate's desk.

Kate Mayfield and I met on the job when we both worked the case of the aforementioned Asad Khalil, a nasty little shit who came to America to kill a lot of people. He did that, then tried to kill me and Kate, then escaped. Not one of my better cases, but it brought Kate and me together, so the next time I see him, I'll thank him for that before I gut-shoot him and watch him die slowly.

I asked Kate, "Can I buy you a drink?"

She looked up at me and smiled—"That would be nice"—then went back to her computer.

Ms. Mayfield is a Midwestern girl, posted to New York from Washington, and originally unhappy about the assignment, but now deliriously happy to live in the greatest city on Earth with the greatest man in the universe. I asked her, "Why are we going away for the weekend?"

"Because this place drives me crazy."

Great cities can do that. I asked her, "What are you working on?"

"I'm trying to find a B and B on the North Fork."

"They're probably all booked up for the holiday weekend, and don't forget I have to work Monday."

"How could I forget? You've been complaining about it all week."

"I never complain."

She thought that was funny for some reason.

I studied Kate's face in the glow of the computer screen. She was as beautiful as the day I met her nearly three years ago. Usually, women I'm with age fast. My first wife, Robin, said our one-year starter marriage seemed like ten years. I said to Kate, "I'll meet you at Ecco's."

"Don't get picked up."

I walked through the cube farm, which was nearly empty now, and entered the elevator lobby, where colleagues were piling up.

I made small talk with a few people, then noticed Harry and went over to him. He was carrying a big metal suitcase, which I assumed contained cameras and lenses. I said to him, "Let me buy you a drink."

"Sorry, I need to get on the road ASAP."

"You driving up tonight?"

"I am. I need to be at this place at first light. Some kind of meeting going down, and I need to photograph car plates and people as they arrive."

"Sounds like the mob surveillance we used to do at weddings and funerals."

"Yeah. Same shit."

We crowded into an elevator and rode down to the lobby.

Harry asked, "Where's Kate?"

"On her way." Harry was divorced, but he was seeing a woman, so I asked, "How's Lori?"

"She's great."

"She looked good in her photo on Match.com."

He laughed. "You're an asshole."

"What's your point? Hey, where is this place?"

"What place? Oh . . . it's up near Saranac Lake."

We walked out onto Broadway. It was a cool autumn day, and the streets and sidewalks had that Thank-God-It's-Friday feeling.

Harry and I bid each other farewell, and I walked south on Broadway.

Lower Manhattan is a tight cluster of skyscrapers and narrow streets, which insures minimum sunlight and maximum stress.

The area includes the Lower East Side, where I was born and raised, plus Chinatown, Little Italy, Tribeca, and Soho. The major industries down here are diametrically opposed: business and finance, represented by Wall Street, and government, represented by Federal, state, and municipal courthouses; City Hall; prisons; Federal Plaza; Police Plaza; and so forth. A necessary adjunct to all of the above are law firms, one of which employs my ex-wife, a defense attorney who represents only the best class of criminal scum. This was one of the reasons we got divorced. The other was that she thought cooking and fucking were two cities in China.

Up ahead was a big patch of empty sky where the Twin Towers once stood. To most Americans, and even to most New Yorkers, the absence of the towers is noted only as a gap in the distant skyline. But if you live or work downtown, and were used to seeing those behemoths every day, then their absence still comes as a surprise when you walk down the street and they're not there.

As I walked, I thought about my conversation with Harry Muller.

On the one hand, there was absolutely nothing unusual or remarkable about his weekend assignment. On the other hand, it didn't compute. I mean, here we are on the brink of war with Iraq, waging war in Afghanistan, paranoid about another Islamic terrorist attack, and Harry gets sent upstate to snoop on some gathering of rich right-wingers whose threat level to national security is probably somewhere between low and non-existent at the moment.

And then there was Tom Walsh's nonsense to Harry about file building in case anyone in Congress or the media wanted to know if the ATTF was on top of the homegrown terrorists. This may have made sense a few years ago, but since 9/11, the neo-Nazis, militias, and that bunch have been quiet and actually thrilled that we got attacked and that the country was shaping up pretty good, killing bad guys and arresting people and so forth. Then there was the holiday Monday debriefing.

Anyway, I shouldn't make too much of this, though it

was a little odd. Basically, it is none of my business, and every time I ask too many questions about things that seem odd at 26 Federal Plaza, I get into trouble. Or, as my mother used to say, "John, Trouble is your middle name." And I believed her until I saw my birth certificate, which said Aloysius. I'll take Trouble over Aloysius any day.

CHAPTER TWO

I turned onto Chambers Street and entered Ecco's, an Italian restaurant with a saloon atmosphere—the best of both worlds.

The bar was crowded with suited gentlemen and ladies in business attire. I recognized a lot of faces and said a few hellos.

Even if I didn't know anybody there, being a good detective and an observer of New York life, I could pick out the high-paid attorneys, the civil servants, the law enforcement people, and the financial guys. I bump into my ex here sometimes, so one of us has to stop coming here.

I ordered a Dewar's and soda and made small talk with a few people around me.

Kate arrived, and I ordered her a white wine, which reminded me of my weekend problem. I asked, "Did you hear about the grape blight?"

"What grape blight?"

"The one on the North Fork. All the grapes are infected with this weird fungus that can be transmitted to human beings."

She apparently didn't hear me and said, "I found us a nice B and B in Mattituck." She described the place based on some tourist website and informed me, "It sounds really charming."

So does Dracula's Castle on the Transylvanian website. I asked her, "Did you ever hear of the Custer Hill Club?"

"No . . . I didn't see it on the North Fork website. What town is it in?"

"It's actually upstate New York."

"Oh . . . is it nice?"

"I don't know."

"Do you want to go there next weekend?"

"I'll check it out first."

Apparently, this name didn't ring any bells with Ms. Mayfield, who sometimes knows things she doesn't share with me. I mean, we're married, but she's FBI, and I have a limited need-to-know, lower security clearance than she does. On that note, I wondered why Ms. Mayfield thought that the words "Custer Hill Club" referred to a place to stay, and not, for instance, a historical society, or a country club, or whatever. Maybe it was the context. Or maybe she knew exactly what I was talking about.

I changed the subject to the memos about Iraq, and we discussed the geopolitical situation for a while. It was Special Agent Mayfield's opinion that war with Iraq was not only inevitable, but also necessary.

Twenty-six Federal Plaza is an Orwellian Ministry, and the government workers there are very attuned to any slight change in the party line. When political correctness was the order of the day, you would have thought the Anti-Terrorist Task Force was a social service agency for psychopaths with low self-esteem. Now, everyone talks about killing Islamic fundamentalists and winning the war on terror—grammatical correctness would be "the war on terror*ism*," but this is a newspeak word. Ms. Mayfield, a good government employee, has few politics of her own, so she has no problem hating the Taliban, Al Qaeda, and UBL one day, then hating Saddam Hussein even more when a directive comes out telling her who to hate that day.

But perhaps I'm not being fair. And I'm not totally rational on the subject of bin Laden and Al Qaeda. I lost a lot of friends on 9/11, and but for the grace of God and heavy traffic, Kate and I would have been in the North Tower when it went down.

I had been on my way to a breakfast meeting there in Windows on the World on the 107th floor. I was late, and Kate waited in the lobby for me. David Stein, Jack Koenig, and my former partner and maybe best friend in the world, Dom Fanelli, were on time, as were a lot of other good people and some bad people, like Ted Nash. No one in that restaurant survived.

I don't get shaken up very easily—even getting shot three times and nearly bleeding to death on a city street didn't have any lasting effect on my mental health, such as it is—but that day shook me up more than I realized at the time. I mean, I was standing right under the plane when it hit, and now, when I see a low-flying plane overhead—

"John?"

I turned to Kate. "What . . . ?"

"I asked you if you wanted another drink."

I looked down into my empty glass.

She ordered me another.

I was vaguely aware that the news was on the TV at the end of the bar, and the reporter was covering the congressional vote on Iraq.

Back in my head, it was 9/11 again. I had tried to make myself useful by helping the firemen and cops evacuate people from the lobby, and at the same time, I was searching for Kate.

Then, I was outside the building carrying a stretcher, and I happened to look up and see these people jumping from the windows and I thought Kate was up there and I thought I saw her falling. . . . I glanced at her standing beside me, and she looked at me and asked, "What are you thinking about?"

"Nothing."

And then the second plane hit, and later I could hear this odd rumbling sound of collapsing concrete and steel, unlike anything I'd ever heard before, and I can still feel the ground shaking under my feet as the building fell and shards of glass rained down from the sky. And like everyone else, I ran like hell. I still can't remember if I dropped the stretcher, or if the other guy dropped it first, or if I was actually carrying a stretcher at all.

I don't think I'll ever remember.

In the weeks following 9/11, Kate became withdrawn, couldn't sleep, cried a lot, and rarely smiled. I was reminded of rape victims I'd dealt with who lost not only their innocence but part of their soul.

The sensitive bureaucrats in Washington urged anyone who'd been involved with this tragedy to seek counseling. I'm not the type to talk about my problems to strangers, professional or otherwise, but at Kate's insistence, I did go see one of the shrinks hired by the Feds to handle the large demand. The guy was a little nuts himself, so we didn't make much progress in the first session.

For my next session and subsequent sessions, I went to my neighborhood bar, Dresner's, where Aidan the bartender gave me sage counsel. "Life's a bitch," said Aidan. "Have another drink."

Kate, on the other hand, stuck to her counseling for about six months, and she's much better now.

But something had happened to her that was not going to completely heal. And whatever it was, it might have been for the better.

Since I've known her, she has always been a good company girl, following the rules and rarely criticizing the Bureau or its methods. In fact, she used to criticize me for criticizing the Bureau.

Outwardly, she's still a loyal soldier, as I said, and she goes along with the party line, but inwardly, she realizes that the party line has done a 180-degree turn, and this realization has made her a little more cynical, critical, and questioning. To me, this is a good thing, and we now have something in common.

Sometimes I miss the starry-eyed team cheerleader I fell in love with. But I also like this tougher and more experienced woman, who, like me, has seen the face of evil, and is ready to meet it again.

And now, a year and a month later, we are living in a state of perpetual color-coded anxiety. Today is Alert Level Orange. Tomorrow, who knows? For damn sure, it's not going to be Green again in my lifetime.

— PART II —

Saturday
UPSTATE NEW YORK

It does not do to leave a dragon out of
your calculations, if you live near him.

—J.R.R. Tolkien

CHAPTER THREE

etective Harry Muller parked his camper on the
side of an old logging road and gathered his gear
from the front seat, then got out, checked his compass,
and headed northwest through the woods, wearing an autumn camouflage outfit and a black knit cap.

The terrain was easy to navigate, with well-spaced
pine trees and ground cover of moss and dewy ferns. As he
walked, daylight began filtering through the pines, revealing a thick ground mist. Birds sang and small animals scur-
ried through the undergrowth.

It was cold, and Harry could see his breath, but the
pristine forest was spectacular, so he was slightly more
happy than miserable.

Slung over his shoulders were binoculars, a Handycam, and an expensive Nikon 12-megapixel camera with a
long 300mm lens. He also carried a *Sibley Guide to Birds*

in case anyone asked him what he was doing there, and a 9mm Glock in case they didn't like his answer.

He'd been briefed by a guy known as Ed From Tech, who'd told him that the Custer Hill Club property was about four miles long on each side, for a total of sixteen square miles of private land. Incredibly, the entire property was enclosed within a high chain-link fence, which was why the Tech guy had also handed him the wire cutters that Harry now carried in his side pocket.

Within ten minutes, he came to the fence. It was about twelve feet high and topped with razor wire. Metal signs, about every ten feet, read: PRIVATE PROPERTY— TRESPASSERS WILL BE PROSECUTED.

Another sign read: DANGER—DO NOT ENTER— PROPERTY PATROLLED BY ARMED GUARDS AND DOGS.

From long experience, Harry knew that warning signs like these were usually more bullshit than reality. In this case, however, he'd take the signs seriously. Also, it troubled him that Walsh either didn't know about the dogs and armed guards or knew and didn't tell him. In either case, he would have a few words for Tom Walsh on Monday morning.

He took out his cell phone and switched it from ringer to vibrate. He noticed that his phone had good signal strength, which was a little strange up in the mountains. Impulsively, he dialed his girlfriend Lori's cell phone. After five rings, his call went into voice mail.

Harry said softly into the phone, "Hi, babe. It's your one and only. I'm up here in the mountains, so maybe I won't have good reception for very long. But I wanted to say hi, I got up here last night about midnight, slept in the camper, and now I'm on-duty, near the right-wing loony lodge. So don't call back, but I'll call you later from a landline if I can't reach you by cell phone. Okay? I still need to do something at the local airport later today or tomorrow morning, so I might need to stay overnight. I'll let you know when I know. Speak to you later. Love you."

He hung up, took the wire cutters, sliced a gap in the chain-link, and squeezed through onto the property. He stood motionless, looked, listened, then put the wire cutters back in his pocket. He continued on, through the woods.

After about five minutes, he noticed a telephone pole rising between the pine trees, and he approached it. Mounted on the pole was a telephone call box, which was locked.

He looked up and saw that the pole was about thirty feet high. Approximately twenty feet up the pole were four floodlights, and above that were five strands of wire running along a crossbeam. One wire obviously powered the telephone and another powered the floodlights. The other three were actually thick cables that could carry lots of juice.

Harry noticed something unusual and focused his binoculars toward the top of the pole. What he'd thought were evergreen boughs from surrounding trees were actually boughs protruding *from* the telephone pole. But these boughs, he knew, were the plastic kind that cell-phone companies used to camouflage or beautify cell-phone towers in populated areas. Why, he wondered, were they here in the middle of the woods?

He lowered his binoculars, raised his Nikon, and snapped a few shots of the pole, recalling that Tom Walsh had said to him, "In addition to cars, faces, and plate numbers, photograph anything else that looks interesting."

Harry thought this seemed interesting and good for the files, so he took his Handycam and shot ten seconds of tape, then moved on.

The terrain began to rise gradually, and the pines gave way to big oaks, elms, and maples whose remaining foliage were brilliant hues of red, orange, and yellow. A carpet of fallen leaves covered the ground, and they rustled when Harry passed over them.

Harry did a quick map-and-compass check and determined that the lodge was straight ahead, less than half a mile away.

He broke out a breakfast bar and continued on, eating, enjoying the fresh Adirondack mountain air while staying alert for trouble. Even though he was a Federal agent, trespassing was trespassing, and without a warrant, he had no more right to be on private, posted land than a poacher.

And yet, when he'd asked Walsh about a warrant, Walsh had said to him, "We have no probable cause for surveillance. Why ask a judge if the answer is no?" Or, as the NYPD liked to say about bending the law, "It's better to ask for forgiveness later than to ask for permission now."

Harry, like everyone else in anti-terrorism, knew that the rules had changed about two minutes after the second tower had been hit, and the rules that hadn't changed could be broken. This usually made his job easier, but sometimes, like now, the job also got a little riskier.

The forest had thinned out, and Harry noticed a lot of stumps where the trees had been felled and carted away, maybe for firewood, maybe for security. Whatever the reason, there was a lot less cover and concealment than there had been a hundred yards back.

Up ahead, he could see an open field, and he approached it slowly through the widely spaced trees.

He stopped under the last standing maple and surveyed the open land with his binoculars.

A paved road ran through the field and downhill to the entrance gate, where he could see a log-cabin gatehouse through his binoculars. The road was lined with security lights mounted on metal poles, and he also noticed wooden telephone poles with five strands of wires coming out of the woods, crossing the field and road, and disappearing again in the woods on the far side of the road. This, he assumed, was a continuation of what he'd seen near the fence, and it appeared that these poles and wires circled the property, meaning the whole sixteen-mile perimeter was floodlit. He said to himself, *This is not a hunting lodge.*

He scanned the road as it traveled uphill to a huge two-story Adirondack-style mountain lodge that sat on the rising slope in front of him, about two hundred yards away. On the front lawn of the lodge was a tall flagpole from which flew the American flag and, beneath that, some sort of yellow pennant. Beyond the lodge were some utility structures, and at the top of the hill was what looked like a radio or cell-phone tower, and he took a telescopic photo of it with his Nikon.

The lodge was made of river stone, logs, and wood shingles, with a big columned portico out front. The green-shingled roof sprouted six stone chimneys, all of which billowed gray smoke into the air. He could see lights in the front windows and a black Jeep in the big gravel parking lot in front of the house. Obviously, someone was home, and hopefully they were expecting guests. That's why he was here.

He used the Nikon to take a few telescopic photos of the parking lot and lodge, then he turned on his Handy-cam and took some establishing footage of the lodge and his surroundings.

He knew that he'd have to get a lot closer if he was going to photograph arriving cars, people, and license plates. Ed From Tech had shown him an aerial photo of the lodge and pointed out that the terrain was open, but that there were lots of large rock outcroppings for concealment.

Harry looked at the outcroppings rising up the hill, and he planned his route to sprint from one rock formation to another until he could reach a vantage point about a hundred feet from the lodge and the parking field. From there, he saw he could photograph and videotape parked cars, and people going into the lodge. He needed to stay there until late afternoon, according to Walsh, then get over to the local airport to check out arriving-passenger manifests and car rentals.

He recalled the time he was on the case of a bunch of Irish Republican Army guys who'd set up a training camp not far from here. The Adirondack Forest Preserve was as big as the state of New Hampshire, a mixture of public and private land with a very small population, making it a good place to hunt, hike, and try out illegal weapons.

This surveillance was a little different from the IRA bust, in that no crimes had apparently been committed and the people who lived in that big lodge probably had some pull someplace.

Harry was about to make his first rush toward an outcrop when suddenly three black Jeeps appeared from behind the lodge and started traveling cross-country at high speed. In fact, they were traveling straight toward him. "Shit."

He turned and moved back into the tree line, then heard dogs barking in the forest. "Holy shit."

The three Jeeps came right up to the trees, and two men exited from each vehicle. They carried hunting rifles.

Out of the trees around him came three men with German shepherds straining at their leashes and growling. The men, he noticed, had sidearms strapped to their hips. Harry now saw a fourth guy coming out of the trees who walked as if he were in charge.

Harry realized the only way his position could have been fixed so accurately was if there were motion or sound detectors planted in the area. These people *really* liked their privacy.

He felt an unaccustomed sense of anxiety, though not fear. This was going to be messy but not dangerous.

The security guards had formed a circle around him but kept a distance of about twenty feet. They were all dressed in military-type camouflage fatigues with an American flag patch on their right shoulders. Each man wore a peaked cap with an American eagle on it, and each had a wireworm sprouting from his left ear.

The man who was in charge—a tough-looking, middle-aged guy—stepped closer, and Harry saw he had a military-type name tag that said CARL.

Carl notified him, "Sir, you are on private property."

Harry put on a dumb face. "Are you sure?"

"Yes, sir."

"Oh, geez. Well, if you'll point the way—"

"How did you get through the fence, sir?"

"Fence? What fence?"

"The fence that surrounds the property, sir, and is posted with 'no trespassing' signs."

"I didn't see any—. Oh, *that* fence. Sorry, Carl, I was following a woodpecker, and he flew over, so I found a hole in the fence and—"

"Why are you here?"

Harry noticed that Carl's tone had become a little less polite, and he'd forgotten the "sir" word. Harry replied, "I'm a bird-watcher." He displayed his guidebook. "I watch birds." He tapped his binoculars.

"Why do you have those cameras?"

"I take *pictures* of the birds." *Asshole.* "So, if you'll point me to where I can exit the property—or, better yet, drive me out—I'll be leaving."

Carl didn't reply, and Harry sensed the first sign of possible trouble.

Then Carl said, "There are millions of acres of

public land around here. Why did you cut a hole in the fence?"

"I didn't *cut* any fucking hole, pal. I *found* a fucking hole. And by the way, Carl, fuck you."

Harry, and everyone around him, realized that he was not sounding like a bird-watcher any longer.

He was about to flash his Fed creds, stand these bastards at attention, and tell them to give him a ride back to his camper. His second thought, however, was not to make a Federal case of this. Why let them know he was a Federal agent sent here to snoop? Walsh would have a total shit fit. Harry said, "I'm outta here." He took a step toward the forest.

All of a sudden, rifles were raised and pistols came out of their holsters. The three dogs growled and pulled at their leashes.

"Stop, or I'll let the dogs loose."

Harry took a deep breath and stopped.

Carl said, "There are two ways to do this. Easy or hard."

"Let's do hard."

Carl glanced around at the other nine security guards, then at the dogs, then at Harry. He spoke in a conciliatory tone. "Sir, we are under strict instructions to bring any trespassers to the lodge, call the sheriff, and have the individual transported by a law enforcement person off the property. We will not press charges, but you will be advised by the sheriff that if you trespass again, you are subject to arrest. You may not, under the law or under our insurance policy, exit the land by yourself on foot, and we will not drive you off the land. Only the sheriff may do that. It's for your own safety."

Harry thought about that. Though the assignment was belly-up, he could pull out a little win by seeing the inside of the lodge, and maybe getting a little info there, and a little 411 from the local sheriff. He said to Carl, "Okay, sport, let's go."

Carl motioned for Harry to turn and walk toward the Jeeps. Harry assumed they'd put him in one of the vehicles, but they didn't, so maybe their insurance policy was real strict.

The Jeeps did stay with him, however, as he was directed to the road and up the hill toward the lodge, accompanied by the whole contingent.

As he walked, he considered these ten armed security guards with the dogs, the gatehouse, the chain-link fence, the razor wire, the floodlights and call boxes, and what were most likely motion and sound detectors. This was not your everyday hunting and fishing club. He was suddenly pissed off at Walsh, who'd barely briefed him, and more pissed at himself for not smelling trouble.

He knew he shouldn't be frightened, but some instinct, sharpened by twenty years of police work and five years of anti-terrorist work, told him that there was an element of danger here.

To confirm this, he said to Carl, who was walking behind him, "Hey, why don't you use your cell phone to call the sheriff now? Save some time."

Carl didn't respond.

Harry reached into his pocket. "You can use my cell phone."

Carl snapped, "Keep your hands where I can see them, and shut your fucking mouth."

A cold chill ran down Harry Muller's spine.

CHAPTER FOUR

CHAPTER FOUR

arry Muller sat across a desk from a tall, thin, middle-aged man who had introduced himself as Bain Madox, president and owner of the Custer Hill Club. This, explained Mr. Madox, was not his day job, only a hobby. Bain Madox was also president and owner of Global Oil Corporation (GOCO for short), which Harry had heard of, and which also explained two of the photographs on the wall—one of an oil tanker and another of a burning oil field in some desert or another.

Madox noticed Harry's interest in the photographs and said, "Kuwait. The Gulf War." He added, "I hate to see good oil burning, especially if no one is paying me for it."

Harry didn't reply.

Mr. Madox was wearing a blue blazer and a loud plaid shirt. Harry Muller was wearing his thermal long johns. He'd been subjected to a humiliating strip search by Carl and two other security guards, who had cattle prods and promised to use them if he resisted. Carl and one of those two guys stood behind him now, cattle prods in hand. So far, there was no sign of the sheriff, and Harry didn't think the sheriff was on the way.

Harry watched Bain Madox sitting quietly behind his big desk in the large pine-paneled office on the second floor of the lodge. Through the window to his right, he could see the rising slope behind the lodge, and at the top of the hill, he noticed the tall antenna he'd seen from the woods.

Mr. Madox asked his guest, "Would you like some coffee? Tea?"

"Fuck you."

"Is that a no?"

"Fuck you."

Bain Madox stared at Harry, and Harry stared back. Madox looked about sixty, Harry thought, very fit, unseasonably tanned, swept-back gray hair, a long, thin, hooked nose like an eagle's with gray eyes to match. Harry also thought this guy looked rich, but not stupid rich. There was something about Madox that signaled strength, power, and intelligence. Command and control. And Madox didn't seem one bit nervous about having abducted and detained a Federal agent. This was not good, Harry knew.

Madox took a cigarette from a wooden box on his desk and asked, "Do you mind if I smoke?"

"I don't give a fuck if you burn. Call the sheriff. Now."

Madox lit the cigarette with a silver desk lighter and

puffed thoughtfully, then asked, "What brings you here, Detective Muller?"

"Bird-watching."

"I don't mean to be rude, but that seems like a sissy hobby for a man involved in anti-terrorism."

"You're about one minute away from me placing you under arrest."

"Well, then, let me use that minute wisely." Madox examined the items strewn across the desk: Harry's cell phone and pager, which were now shut off, his key chain, the Handycam, the Nikon digital camera, the binoculars, the Sibley bird guide, a terrain map of the area, the compass, the wire cutters, Harry's credentials, and his 9mm Glock 26, the so-called Baby Glock that was easier to conceal. He noticed that Madox had removed the magazine, which was smart of him.

Madox asked Harry, "What am I to make of this?"

"Whatever the fuck you want to make of it, pal. Give me my shit, and let me the fuck out of here, or you'll be looking at twenty years to life for kidnapping a Federal agent."

Madox made a face, suggesting he was annoyed and impatient. "Come on, Mr. Muller. We're well beyond that by now. We need to move forward."

"Fuck you."

Madox suggested, "Let *me* play detective. I see here a pair of binoculars, a small video camera, a very expensive digital camera with a telescopic lens, and a bird guide. From that, I can conclude that you are an enthusiastic bird-watcher. So enthusiastic, in fact, that you also have these wire cutters in the event a fence comes between you and a bird. Plus, a 9mm handgun in case a bird won't stay still long enough for you to photograph it." He asked Harry, "How am I doing?"

"Not too good."

"Let me keep trying. I also see here a U.S. geological survey map on which is drawn in red the perimeter of my property, plus the gatehouse, and this lodge and other structures. This suggests to me that an aerial photograph was taken of my property, and these man-made features were transferred to your map. Correct?"

Harry didn't answer.

Mr. Madox continued, "I also see here on my desk this badge and a card that identifies you as a retired New York City police detective. Congratulations."

"Eat shit and die."

"But what interests me most is this other badge and ID card that say you are a Federal agent with the Anti-Terrorist Task Force. *Not* retired." He stared at the photo ID, then at Harry Muller and asked, "Working today?"

Harry decided to try the cover story one more time, just in case this guy wanted a reason to cut him loose. "Okay, let me tell you again what I told your paranoid rent-a-cops. I'm up here for the weekend camping. I watch and photograph birds. I'm also a Federal agent, and by law I have to carry my credentials and my piece. You shouldn't put two and two together and come up with five. Understand?"

Madox nodded. "I do. But put yourself in my position. And I'll put myself in yours. I'm Federal Agent Harry Muller, and I'm listening to a man who tells me that all the circumstantial evidence I see in front of me—evidence of surveillance—can be explained as bird-watching. So, do I let you go? Or do I demand a more logical and truthful explanation? What would *you* do in my position?"

"Sorry, I can't hear you over your loud shirt."

Mr. Madox smiled, then opened the Sibley guide, put on his eyeglasses, and selected a page. He asked Harry, "Where are you most likely to encounter a loon, Mr. Muller?"

"Near a lake."

"That was too easy." He flipped a few pages. "What is the color of a cerulean warbler?"

"Brown."

Mr. Madox shook his head. "No, no, Mr. Muller. Cerulean *means* blue. Sky blue. One more. Two out of three is passing." He flipped through the book again. "What color is the male—?"

"Hey, take that book, put a coat of K-Y jelly on it, and shove it up your ass."

Mr. Madox closed the guide and threw it aside. He turned to his computer screen. "Here are your digital photos. I don't see any birds in them. I see, however, that you seem interested in one of my utility poles . . . and let's see . . . here's a telescopic shot of the tower behind my lodge . . . close-ups of my lodge . . . ah, there's a bird perched on my roof. What is that?"

"A shit-seeking hawk."

Madox picked up the Handycam, switched it to Replay, and looked through the viewfinder. "Here's the pole again . . . you noticed the plastic boughs, I assume . . . here's the lodge again . . . nice views from where you were standing . . . that bird is flying away. What was that? Looks like a great blue heron, but he should have migrated south by now. It's been unusually warm this fall. Global warming, if you believe that crap." He put down the camcorder and asked, "Do you know what the solution is to global warming? No? I'll tell you. Nuclear winter." He laughed. "Old joke."

Madox sat back in his chair and lit another cigarette. He blew perfect smoke rings and watched them as they rose and dissolved. "That's a lost art."

Harry Muller glanced around the room as Bain Madox practiced his lost art. He could hear the breathing of the two men behind him as he shifted his gaze to a wall that was covered with framed certificates of some sort. Harry thought that if he could get a handle on who this guy was, it might be helpful.

Madox noticed Harry's gaze and said, "The one on the top left is my certificate for the Silver Star. Next to it is the certificate for the Bronze Star, then the Purple Heart. Then there's my commission as a second lieutenant in the United States Army. Next row are the usual service medals, including the Vietnam Campaign Medal and a Presidential Unit Citation. I served in the Seventh Cavalry Regiment of the First Air Cavalry Division. The Seventh Cav was General Custer's old unit. That's part of the reason for the name of this club. I might tell you the other part later, but if I do, then I'll have to kill you." He laughed. "Just joking. Hey, *smile*. Just joking."

Harry forced a smile. *Asshole.*

"The last row is the Combat Infantry Badge, my Expert Rifleman Badge, my Jungle Training School diploma, and, finally, my Army discharge. I left the service after eight years with the rank of lieutenant colonel. We made rank fast in those days. Lots of dead officers opened up the promotion list. Did you serve?"

"No." Harry decided to play along. "I was too young, then they ended the draft."

"Right. They should bring it back."

"Absolutely," Harry said. "They should draft women, too. They want equal rights, they should have equal responsibilities."

"You're absolutely right."

Harry was on a roll and continued, "My son still had to register for the draft in case they ever bring it back. But my daughter didn't. What's that all about?"

"Precisely. You have a son and daughter?"

"Yeah."

"Married?"

"Divorced," Harry replied.

"Ah, me, too."

"Women will drive you crazy," Harry said.

"Only if you let them."

"Well, we let them."

Madox chuckled. "We do. Anyway, you're here on surveillance for the Federal Anti-Terrorist Task Force. Why?"

"How long were you in Vietnam?"

Madox looked at Harry Muller for a few seconds, then replied, "Two tours of one year each, then a third tour that was cut short by an AK-47 round that missed my heart by an inch, nicked my right lung, and broke a rib on the way out."

"You're lucky to be alive."

"I tell myself that every day. Each day is a gift. Have you ever been shot at?"

"Five times. Never got hit."

"*You're* lucky to be alive." Madox stared at Harry. "It changes you. You're never the same again. But it's not necessarily for the worse."

"I know. I've got friends who've been hit." He thought of John Corey, but he was fairly sure that Corey was the same wiseass both before and after getting hit. He said, "Sometimes, I think I should have volunteered. Vietnam was over, but I could have still served. Maybe I would have caught the Grenada Invasion or something."

"Well, don't be hard on yourself. Most American men have never served. And to tell you the truth, war is a damned scary thing. And now we're engaged in this war on terrorism, and you, Mr. Muller, are apparently on the front lines. Correct?"

"Uh . . . yeah."

"And by terrorism, we generally mean Islamic terrorists. Correct?"

"Yeah . . . but—"

"So, are you looking for Islamic terrorists here? Can I help?"

Harry was forming a thought, but Mr. Madox went on, "If there's anything I can do, Mr. Muller, just let me know. There's no one who feels more strongly about winning the war on terrorism than I. How can I help?"

"Uh . . . well . . . here's the thing. About five years ago, I was on this case of Irish Republican Army guys— terrorists—only about fifteen miles from here. They had a training camp." Harry filled in Madox on the case and concluded, "We sent eight guys to Federal prison for terms ranging from three to twenty years."

"Ah, yes. I remember that because it was so close to here."

"Right. So, this is the same thing. We're checking a lot of private preserves to see if there's any suspicious activity involving the IRA. We've had intelligence reports that—"

"So, this has nothing to do with Islamic terrorists?"

"No. Not today. We're doing IRA."

"Seems like a waste of time and resources in light of 9/11."

"Well, I think so, too. But we need to keep on top of everything and everybody."

"I suppose." Madox thought a moment, then asked, "So, you think the Custer Hill Club is . . . what? A training camp for the Irish Republican Army?"

"Well, the bosses had a tip about activity in this area, so I got picked to take a peek. You know, in case people were using your property without you knowing."

"No one can enter my property without me knowing, as you just found out."

"Yeah, I see that. I'll report—"

"Certainly not people engaged in paramilitary training."

"Yeah, I—"

"And that doesn't explain why you were taking pictures of my *lodge*. You should be out in the woods looking for these IRA people."

"Yeah. I got turned around."

"You certainly did. The point is you *are* on surveillance."

"Well, yeah. I need to check about a dozen properties in the area."

"I see. So, I shouldn't feel singularly honored?"

"Huh?"

"I shouldn't feel picked on?"

"No. Just routine stuff."

"That's a relief. By the way, do you have any sort of government warrant for these activities?"

"I do . . . but not with me."

"Aren't you supposed to carry the warrant with you?" He waved his hand over the desk and said, "We didn't find anything, even when we looked up your rectum." Mr. Madox smiled.

"Hey, fuck *you*! Fuck *you*!" Harry stood. "You motherfucking scumbag piece of shit!"

"Excuse me?"

"Shove it up *your* ass. I'm walking the fuck out of here—" He reached for his things on Madox's desk and an explosion of pain ripped through the right side of his body. He heard a crashing sound and a thump, then nothing.

He realized he was lying on the floor, and a cold sweat covered his body. His eyes were blurry, but he could see Carl standing over him, tapping the cattle prod into his palm as if to say, "You want another jolt?"

Harry tried to stand, but his legs were rubbery. The other guard got behind him, lifted him under his arms, and dropped him back into his chair.

Harry tried to steady his breathing and his quivering muscles. His eyes were still unfocused, and everything sounded tinny in his ears.

One of the guards gave him a plastic bottle of water, which he could barely hold.

Mr. Madox said, "It's amazing what electricity can do to a person. And there's almost no visible evidence. Where were we?"

Harry tried to say, "Fuck you," but couldn't get the words out.

"I think you were trying to convince me that you were on a routine assignment looking for IRA training camps. I'm not convinced."

Harry took a deep breath and said, "It's true."

"Well then, let me reassure you there are no members of the Irish Republican Army on my property. In fact, Mr. Muller, my ancestry is English through and through, and I have no fondness for the IRA."

Harry didn't reply.

Madox said, "Okay, let's cut the IRA crap and go right to the heart of this matter. What, exactly, do your superiors think is going on here?"

Again, Harry didn't respond.

"Do you need electrical encouragement to answer my question?"

"No . . . I don't know. They didn't tell me anything."

"But they must have said something like, 'Harry, we suspect that the Custer Hill Club is . . .' what? How did they characterize this place and its members? This is really important to me, and I want you to tell me. You're going to tell me now or later. Now is easier."

Harry tried to clear his head from the electrical jolt and think about his situation. He'd never been on the wrong side of an interrogation desk, and he'd never had the experience or training that would guide him in a situation like this.

"Mr. Muller?"

He couldn't figure out if he should stick to the IRA story, or if he should just tell this bastard the little he knew. The goal, obviously, was to get out of here alive, though he could hardly believe that his life was in danger.

"Mr. Muller? We did bird-watching, then the IRA—which is actually a good story. But not the true story. You seem a bit confused, so let me help you. You were told that the Custer Hill Club was made up of a bunch of rich, old right-wing crazies who are conspiring to do something that may be illegal. Correct?"

Harry nodded.

"What else did they tell you about us?"

"Nothing. I have no need to know."

"Ah, yes. Need to know. Did they mention that several of our members are very highly placed and influential people in society and government?"

Harry shook his head. "I have no need to know that."

"Well, I think you *do* need to know. That's why you're here, whether you know it or not. Fact is, the members of this club hold a lot of power. Political power, financial power, and military power. Did you know that one of our members is the deputy secretary of defense? Another is a top national security adviser to the president. Did you know that?"

Harry shook his head.

"We don't appreciate some government agency conducting an illegal surveillance of our activities, which are entirely legal. We hunt, fish, drink, and discuss the world situation. The Constitution itself protects our right to assemble, to free speech, and to privacy. Correct?"

Harry nodded.

"Someone in your agency has overstepped his bounds and that person will be made to answer for his actions."

Again, Harry nodded. He believed Madox. This wouldn't be the first time one of his bosses screwed up and ordered surveillance on some group or some person who wasn't guilty of anything. On the other hand, that's what surveillance was for—to see if a suspicion of criminal activity was accurate or justified. Harry said, "I think they screwed up."

"Oh, I *know* they did. And you just got caught in the middle."

"Right."

"You're not an FBI agent?"

"No."

"Or a CIA officer?"

"Hell, no."

"You're . . . what? A contract agent?"

"Yeah. Retired NYPD. Working for the FBI."

"Low level," suggested Mr. Madox.

"Well . . . yeah."

"I'll make sure you're not punished."

"Yeah, and thanks for the jolt."

"I don't know what you're talking about." Mr. Madox checked his watch and said, "I'm expecting company." He stared at Harry. "Did you know I was expecting company?"

"No."

"You just happened to be here on this particular day?"

Harry didn't answer.

"Talk to me, Mr. Muller. I have a busy morning."

"Uh . . . well, I was told to . . . see if anyone . . ."

"You were told to observe arriving guests, photograph them, take down their license-plate numbers, note their arrival times, and so forth."

"Yeah."

"How did these people you work for know there was a meeting here today?"

"I have no idea."

"Why did you take a photograph of my utility pole?"

"Just . . . saw it. Ran into it."

"When did you get here?"

"Last night."

"Is anyone with you?"

"No."

"How did you get here?"

"I drove my camper up," Harry replied.

"And these are the keys?"

"Yeah."

"Where is the camper?"

"On the logging road south of here."

"Near where you entered the property?"

"Yeah."

"Are you supposed to make a telephone report?"

He wasn't, but he replied, "Yes."

"When?"

"When I leave this property."

"I see." Madox picked up Harry's cell phone and

turned it on. "I see you have a message." He added, "In case you wondered why you have such good service here in the middle of nowhere, I have my own cell-phone relay tower." He gestured toward the window. "Now you know what that tower is, and you can label your photograph. You can also indicate that it has a voice scrambler so that no one can listen to my calls." He asked Harry, "Isn't it nice to be rich?"

"I wouldn't know."

"What's your voice-mail code?"

Harry gave it to him, and Madox dialed voice mail, punched in the code, and put the phone on speaker.

Lori said, "Hi, honey. Got your message. I was sleeping. I'm going shopping today with your sister and Anne. Call me later. I'll have my cell with me. Okay? Let me know if you have to stay over. I love you, and I miss you." She added, "Be careful of those right-wing loonies. They like their guns. Take care."

Madox commented, "She sounds very nice. Except for that part about the right-wing loonies and the guns." He observed, "She apparently thinks you may be staying here overnight. She may be right." He turned off the power to the cell phone, and said to Harry, "I guess you know these things send off a signal that can be tracked."

"Yeah, that's my job."

"That's right. Amazing technology. I can call my children anytime, anyplace. Of course, they never answer, but they call back after five messages, or when they need something."

Harry forced a smile.

"So," said Mr. Madox, "you seem to be who and what

you say you are. To be quite honest, Mr. Muller, I thought you might be an agent of a foreign power."

"What?"

"I'm not being paranoid. The people who are members of this club have enemies around the world. The right kind of enemies. We are all patriots, Mr. Muller, and we've caused some problems for the enemies of America around the globe."

"That's good."

"I thought you'd agree. And these same people are your enemies. So, to use an old Arabic expression, 'The enemy of my enemy is my friend.'"

"Right."

"Sometimes, however, the enemy of my enemy is also my enemy. Not because he wants to be, but because we have a difference of opinion about how to deal with our common enemy. But that's a discussion for another time."

"Yeah, I'll call you next week."

Bain Madox stood, looked at his watch, and said, "I'll tell you what. Since you and your agency seem so interested in this club and its members, I'm going to do something that I've never done before. I'm going to allow you, an outsider, to sit in on the Executive Board meeting, which will take place this afternoon after a welcome lunch for our arriving club members. Would you like to join us?"

"I . . . No, not really. I think I should get—"

"I thought you were here to get information? What's your rush?"

"No rush, but I—"

"I'll even let you take pictures."

"Thanks, but—"

"I think your presence at this meeting can do both of us some good. You'll learn something, and I'll get to see your reaction to what we're discussing. Sometimes, we get into this bunker mentality, you know, where outside reality is excluded, and only our reality is heard. That's not healthy."

Harry didn't reply, and Bain Madox warmed to his idea. "I want you to feel free to comment, to tell us if we're sounding like a bunch of crazy old fools—right-wing loonies." He grinned. "We need your honest opinion about our next project. Project Green."

"What's Project Green?"

Mr. Madox glanced at the security guards, then went over to Harry and whispered in his ear, "Nuclear Armageddon."

CHAPTER FIVE

Harry Muller was led, blindfolded and barefoot, down two flights of stairs into what must have been the basement of the lodge. It was cold and damp, and he could hear sounds of mechanical and electrical motors.

He heard a door open, then he was prodded forward. The door slammed shut, and he heard a metal bolt sliding.

He stood there, then said, "Hey. You. You there?"

Silence.

He listened awhile, then pulled the blindfold off and looked around. He was alone.

Harry stood in a small room walled with concrete blocks painted the same gray enamel as the concrete floor. The low ceiling was covered with corrugated metal.

As his eyes adjusted to the glaring light of an overhead fluorescent fixture, he saw that the room held only a steel bed, which was bolted to the floor. On the bed was a thin mattress, on which were his camouflage shirt and pants, which he put on. He checked his pockets, but they hadn't given him anything back.

In a corner of the room were a toilet and a sink. The toilet had no seat and no water tank. Just like in a prison cell. The sink had no mirror over it, not even the plastic or steel mirrors they used in jail.

He went to the steel door that had no handle and no window, and pushed on it, but it didn't budge.

He searched the room, looking for anything that he could use as a weapon, but it was completely bare, except for the bed and a rusty radiator that wasn't putting out much heat.

He noticed now a small swivel eyeball camera mounted in the corner of the ceiling, with a recessed speaker beside it. He stuck up his middle finger and shouted, "Fuck you!"

No one replied.

He looked around for something that he could use to smash the camera and the speaker, but there wasn't a single loose item in the room except for himself. He took a running start, jumped, and smacked the camera with his hand. The camera continued sweeping the room, then a shrill, high-decibel sound pierced the room, and Harry covered his ears and backed away from the speaker. The painful noise continued, and Harry shouted, "Okay! Okay!"

The sound stopped and a voice said, "Sit."

"Fuck you." *Bastards. Wait until I get out of here.*

He had lost track of time, but he figured it must be

about ten or eleven in the morning. His stomach growled, but he didn't feel particularly hungry. Only thirsty. And he had to pee.

He walked to the toilet and the camera followed him. He urinated, then went to the sink and turned on the single tap. A trickle of cold water ran into the basin. He washed up, then used his hands to drink from the faucet.

There was no towel, and he wiped his hands on the sides of his pants. He went back to the bed and sat. He thought about his conversation with Bain Madox.

Nuclear Armageddon.

He said to himself, *What the hell is that asshole talking about?*

And what was this meeting that he was invited to? None of this made too much sense unless . . . unless this was all a setup.

He stood. "That's it!" *This is one of those stupid training camps.* "Holy shit!"

He thought about the whole assignment, from his ten minutes in Tom Walsh's office, to the Tech guy, to cutting through the fence, to the guards, to this prison cell in a private house—this whole thing was a test . . . one of those SERE courses—Survival, Evasion, Resistance, and Escape.

Well, he definitely didn't pass the evasion part, which was why he was in the cell. He went over in his mind the interrogation from the guy named Madox—the resistance part—*Oh shit! Did I blow that? What the hell did I say? I told him to go fuck himself and stuck to my cover . . . then I did the IRA rap, which was smart . . . right?*

He thought about the cattle prod. *Would they do that? Yeah . . . maybe.*

And later, there'd be the escape thing, then the evasion thing again and survival in the woods . . . *Yeah! That's where this is going.*

He replayed everything in his mind, slanting it toward his new belief that this was some crazy FBI or CIA thing. It *had* to be. This was just too weird otherwise.

They had their eye on him for something big, and this was the big test. They did this kind of thing to see what you could take. The Custer Hill Club was like the CIA Farm in Virginia, right?

He said to himself, *Okay, good. I passed the first test. Now, we do the meeting and see what that's all about. Keep cool, Harry. Stay pissed.* He shouted at the camera, "Assholes! I'm gonna rip your fucking heads off and shit down your necks!"

He lay back on the thin mattress and smiled to himself. He yawned and drifted into a restless sleep.

The glare of the overhead light and the cold made him dream that he was outside again, walking through the woods. He was taking pictures of birds, then he was arguing with some men, then he was talking pleasantly to Mr. Madox, who gave him back his gun and said, "You're going to need this." The men suddenly raised their rifles, and dogs were running toward him. He pulled the trigger on his Glock, but it didn't fire.

Harry sat up quickly and wiped the cold sweat from his face. *Holy shit . . .*

He fell back on the bed and stared up at the metal ceiling. Something was bothering him. It was Madox.

Something about that guy seemed too . . . real. *No. Can't be real.*

Because if this was all real, then his life was in danger.

The door opened, and a voice said, "Come with us."

— PART III —

Saturday
NORTH FORK, LONG ISLAND

If love is the answer, could you rephrase the question?

—Lily Tomlin

CHAPTER SIX

K ate and I got to the bed-and-breakfast in the hamlet of Mattituck before the lockout time of 10:00 P.M., and checked in with the proprietor, a lady who reminded me of the nice matrons who work in the Metropolitan Correctional Center downtown.

The quaint old house was everything I expected and more. In fact, it sucked.

We slept late Saturday morning, so we missed the home-cooked breakfast, and also missed meeting the other guests, two of whom we'd heard through the thin walls the night before. The woman was a screamer, but not multiorgasmic, thank God.

Anyway, we spent Saturday touring the North Fork vineyards, which have replaced the potato farms that I remember from when I was a kid. The vines are mature now and produce fine chardonnays, merlots, and so forth. We sipped a little free wine at each of the vineyards, and I especially enjoyed the sauvignon blancs, which were dry and fruity, with a hint of . . . well, potatoes.

Saturday night, we went to a floating barge restaurant, which had a great view of Peconic Bay and was very romantic, as per Kate.

We sat at the bar while we waited for our table, and the bartender rattled off a dozen local wines that were available by the glass. Kate and the bartender—a young fellow who looked like he could benefit from a few weeks of man camp—discussed the whites and settled on one that wasn't too fruity. I thought grapes *were* a fruit.

The young man asked me, "Did any of those wines sound good to you?"

"They all did. I'll have a Bud."

He processed that, then got our drinks.

There was a stack of newspapers on the bar, and I noticed the *New York Times* headline: PENTAGON PLANS SMALLPOX SHOTS FOR UP TO 500,000.

The invasion looked like a done deal unless Saddam knuckled under. I considered calling my bookie to see what today's odds were for going to war. I should have placed a bet last week, when the odds were longer, but I have inside information, so that's cheating. Also, it's not ethical to make money on a war, unless you're a government contractor.

I asked Kate, who's a lawyer, "Am I a government contractor or a contract agent for the government?"

"Why do you ask?"

"I'm struggling with an ethical issue."

"That's probably not much of a struggle."

"Be nice. I'm thinking of calling my bookie and placing a bet on the Iraq war."

"You have a bookie?"

"Yeah. Don't you?"

"No. That's illegal."

"Am I under arrest? Can we do the thing with the handcuffs later?"

She tried not to smile and glanced around the bar. "Lower your voice."

"I'm trying to be romantic."

The hostess came over and escorted us to our table.

Kate studied the menu and asked if I'd split a dozen oysters with her, reminding me with a grin, "They're an aphrodisiac."

I informed her, "Not really. I had a dozen last week and only eleven worked." I added, "Old joke."

"It better be."

Seafood was the specialty of the house, so I ordered Long Island duck. They swim. Right?

I was feeling relaxed and happy to be away from the stress of job and city. I said to Kate, "This was a good idea."

"We needed to get away."

I had a brief thought of Harry in upstate New York, and I wanted to ask Kate again about the Custer Hill Club, but the purpose of being here was to leave the job behind.

Kate was in charge of the wine menu, and after some

fascinating discussion with the waiter, she ordered a bottle of something red.

It came and she tasted it, pronouncing it full-bodied with a hint of plum, which would go well with my duck. I didn't think my duck cared.

Anyway, she raised her glass and said, "To beepers that don't go off on weekends."

"Amen." We clinked glasses and drank. Hers must have had the plum.

I held the wineglass to the candlelight and said, "Nice sleeve."

"Nice *what*?"

"Cuffs?"

She rolled her eyes.

So, we had a nice dinner in pleasant surroundings, and Kate's beautiful blue eyes sparkled in the candlelight, and the red wine made me feel all warm and fuzzy.

It was easy to pretend that all was right with the world. It never is, of course, and never was, but you have to steal a few hours now and then, and pretend that the rest of the world isn't going to hell.

On that subject, everyone I know still talks about how their lives have changed since September 11, and it's not all for the worse. A lot of people, myself included, and Kate, too, sort of woke up and said, "It's time to stop sweating the small stuff. It's time to re-connect to people you like and get rid of people you don't like. We're not dead, so we need to live."

My father, who is a World War II veteran, once tried to describe to me the mood of the country after Pearl Harbor. He's not good with words, and he was having some difficulty painting a picture of America on that first Christmas after December 7, 1941. Finally, he got it and said, "We were all scared, so we drank and fucked a lot, and we called and visited people we hadn't seen in a while, and people sent lots of cards and letters, and everybody came closer together, and helped each other, so it really wasn't that bad." Then he asked me, "Why did we need a war to do that?"

Because, Pop, that's the way we are. And on September 11, last year, my parents spent two days trying to reach me from Florida, and when they finally got through to me, they spent fifteen minutes telling me how much they always loved me, which was a bit of a surprise, but I'm sure they meant it.

And that's the way we are now, but in a year or two, lacking another attack on the country, we'll be back to our normal, self-centered, standoffish selves. And that's okay, too, because quite frankly I'm getting a little tired of out-of-town friends and family asking me how I'm doing. We've all had our cathartic moment, and our re-evaluation of our lives, and it's time to get on with whatever we were doing, and go back to being whoever we were.

I do, however, like the excessive drinking and fucking thing, and we should hold on to that awhile longer. My bachelor friends tell me . . . well, that's another topic for another time.

Meanwhile, I said to Kate, "I love you."

She reached across the table and took my hand. "I love you, too, John."

And that's one good thing that came out of that day. I wasn't the most attentive husband on September 10, but the next day, when I thought she was dead, my world collapsed with those towers. And when I saw her alive, I realized I needed to say "I love you" more often, because in this business and in this life, you never know what's going to happen tomorrow.

— PART IV —

Saturday
UPSTATE NEW YORK

Power always thinks it has a great soul and vast views beyond the comprehension of the weak, and that it is doing God's service when it is violating all His laws.

—John Adams

CHAPTER SEVEN

Harry Muller sat blindfolded, with his ankles shackled, in what felt like a comfortable leather chair. He smelled burning wood and cigarette smoke.

He could hear people speaking in low tones, and he thought he heard Bain Madox's voice.

Someone slid the blindfold down around his neck, and as his eyes adjusted to the light, he saw that he was sitting at the end of a long pine table. Also sitting at the table were five other men: two on each side, and at the head of the table, facing him, was Bain Madox. The men were speaking to one another as if he wasn't there.

In front of each man were legal pads, pens, water bottles, and coffee cups. Harry noticed a keyboard in front of Madox.

He looked around the room, which was a library or a den. The fireplace was to his left, flanked by two windows whose drapes were drawn so that he couldn't see out, but he knew from his blindfolded walk from his cell that he was on the ground floor.

Standing near the door were Carl and another security guard. They were wearing holstered pistols but not carrying cattle prods.

He now noticed a very big, black leather suitcase sitting upright in the middle of the floor. It was an old suitcase, strapped to a wheeled caddy.

Bain Madox seemed to notice him for the first time and said, "Welcome, Mr. Muller. Coffee? Tea?"

Harry shook his head.

Madox said to the other four men, "Gentlemen, this is the man I told you about—Detective Harry Muller, NYPD, retired, currently working for the Federal Anti-Terrorist Task Force. Please make him feel welcome."

Everyone acknowledged their guest with a nod.

Harry thought two of the guys looked familiar.

Madox continued, "As you know, gentlemen, we have a few friends on the Task Force, but apparently none of them were aware that Mr. Muller was going to drop in today."

One of the men said, "We'll need to look into that."

The others nodded in unison.

Harry tried to see through this bullshit, to reinforce his hope that this was an elaborately staged test. But somewhere in the back of his mind, this hope was fading, though he clung to it.

Madox motioned to the guards, who left the room.

Harry looked at the men along the table. Two were about Madox's age, one was older, and the one to his right was younger than the rest. They all wore blue blazers and casual plaid shirts like Madox, as though this were the uniform of the day.

Harry focused on the two men who looked familiar; he was sure he'd seen them on TV or in the newspapers.

Madox noticed Harry's stare and said, "Forgive me for not formally introducing my Executive Board—"

One of the men interrupted, "Bain, names are not necessary."

Madox replied, "I think Mr. Muller recognizes a few of you, anyway."

No one responded, except Harry. "I don't need any names—"

"You need," said Madox, "to know what august company you are in." Madox indicated the man to his immediate right—the oldest person in the room and the one who had made the objection. "Harry, this is Paul Dunn, adviser to the president on matters of national security and a member of the National Security Council, whom you probably recognize."

Madox turned to the person sitting next to Dunn, near Harry, and said, "This is General James Hawkins, United States Air Force and a member of the Joint Chiefs of Staff, whom you may also recognize, though Jim is a low-profile guy."

Madox indicated the man to his left. "This is Edward Wolffer, the deputy secretary of defense, who likes the cameras. Never stand between Ed and a news camera or you'll get knocked over." Madox smiled, but no one else did. Madox added, "Ed and I graduated from Infantry Officer Candidate School together, Fort Benning, Georgia,

April 1967. We served in Vietnam at the same time. He's made quite a name for himself since then, while I've made a lot of money."

Wolffer didn't smile at what Harry thought must be an old joke by now.

Madox continued, "And to your right, Harry, is Scott Landsdale of the Central Intelligence Agency, who is definitely camera shy, and who is also the CIA liaison to the White House."

Harry glanced at Landsdale. He seemed a little cocky and arrogant, like most of the CIA guys Harry had had the misfortune to work with.

Madox said, "This is the Executive Board of the Custer Hill Club. The rest of our members—about a dozen men this weekend—are hiking or bird-hunting, which I hope doesn't upset you." He explained to the other men, "Mr. Muller is a bird-watcher."

Harry wanted to say, "Fuck you," but remained silent. He understood now that the guys in this room had not come here from Washington to participate in a test of Harry Muller's qualifications for a bigger and better job.

Madox told Harry, "This holiday weekend was to be a regularly scheduled gathering to discuss world affairs, to exchange information, and to just enjoy some camaraderie. But your presence here has made it necessary for me to call this emergency meeting of the Executive Board. I'm sure that means nothing to you now, but it will later."

Harry said, "I don't want to hear any of this."

"I thought you were a detective." He stared at Harry and said, "I've had a little time to check you out with our friends in the ATTF, and you appear to be who you say you are."

Harry didn't reply, but he wondered who Madox's friends were in the ATTF.

Mr. Madox informed him, "If you were an FBI agent, or CIA, we'd be very concerned."

Scott Landsdale, the CIA man, said, "Bain, I can assure you that Mr. Muller is not a CIA officer."

Madox smiled. "I suppose it takes one to know one."

Landsdale continued, "And I'm fairly certain that Mr. Muller is not FBI. He is what he appears to be—a cop, working for the FBI, on surveillance."

"Thank you for that assurance," said Madox.

"You're welcome. Now, *I'd* like some assurance, Bain. You weren't very clear about when Mr. Muller will be reported as missing in action."

Madox replied, "Ask Mr. Muller. He's right next to you."

Landsdale turned to Harry. "When do they start wondering where you are? No lies. I know how they work at 26 Fed. And what I don't know, I can find out."

Harry thought, *Typical CIA bastard, always pretending they know more than they actually know.* Harry replied, "Well, then, find out yourself."

Landsdale resumed without comment, like a trained interrogator, "Will anyone call you?"

"How do I know? I'm not psychic."

Madox interjected, "I'm checking his cell phone and beeper every half hour or so. The only message was from Lori. That's his girlfriend. I'll send her a text message later from Mr. Muller's cell phone."

Landsdale nodded. "God forbid anyone on the Task Force would interrupt their holiday weekend." He asked Harry, "When are you supposed to get back to 26 Fed?"

"When I get there."

"Who gave you this assignment? Walsh or Paresi?"

Harry thought this guy knew too much about the Task Force. He replied, "I get my orders on an audiotape that self-destructs."

"Me, too. What did your audiotape say, Harry?"

"I already answered that. IRA surveillance."

"That's really lame." Landsdale said to the others, "Mr. Muller's assignment probably came from Washington, and in the hallowed tradition of intelligence work, no one tells anyone more than someone thinks they need to know. That, unfortunately, is how 9/11 happened. Things have changed, but old habits are hard to break, and sometimes they're not bad habits. Mr. Muller, for instance, can't tell us what he doesn't know." He added, "I'm fairly sure we're okay for at least forty-eight hours. His girlfriend will probably miss him long before his supervisor does." He addressed Harry. "Is she connected to law enforcement or to the intelligence business in any way?"

"Yeah. She's a CIA officer. Former prostitute."

Landsdale laughed. "I think I know her."

Madox said, "Thank you, Scott, for your assistance." He said to Harry, "Your visit here, even as a low-level surveillance person, has given us some concern."

Harry didn't reply but looked around at the other men, who did seem a little concerned about something.

Madox continued, "However, some good may come of this. We've been planning a long time for Project Green, and I'm afraid that the planning has become procrastination. This often happens when a momentous decision needs to be made." He stared at his Executive Board, two of whom nodded and two of whom seemed annoyed.

Madox went on, "Harry, I think that your physical presence in this room is a strong reminder that there are forces in the government that are too curious about who we are and what we're doing. I think time has run out." He looked at the other four men, who nodded, almost reluctantly.

Madox said, "So, gentlemen, if you have no further objections, Mr. Muller stays with us so we can keep an eye on him." He looked at Harry. "I want to make it perfectly clear to you that although you have been detained here, no harm will come to you. We just need to keep you here until Project Green begins. Perhaps two or three days. Understand?"

Harry Muller understood that he might be dead in less than two or three days. But on another level, looking at these men, who in his world of police work were not the murdering type, he thought that Madox might be telling the truth. He couldn't believe—or make himself believe—that guys like this would go ahead and kill him. He glanced at Landsdale, who seemed like the only one in the room who might actually be dangerous.

"Mr. Muller? Do you understand?"

Harry nodded. "Yeah."

"Good. Don't let your imagination get the best of you. What you're going to hear in the next hour or so is so far beyond your wildest imagination that you'll forget about yourself anyway."

Harry looked at Madox, who still seemed cool and smart-mouthed, but Harry could also see that Madox was a little hyper and worried about something.

Harry regarded the other four men, and he thought he'd never seen guys who were so powerful looking so worried. The older man, Dunn, the president's adviser, was pale, and Harry noticed that Dunn's hands were trembling. Hawkins, the general, and Wolffer, the defense guy, looked pretty grim. Only Landsdale appeared relaxed, but Harry could see he was putting it on.

Whatever was going on here, Harry thought, it was real, and it was something that was scaring the shit out of these guys. Harry took some comfort in the fact that he wasn't the only one in the room who was scared shitless.

CHAPTER EIGHT

Bain Madox stood and said, "I call this emergency meeting of the Executive Board of the Custer Hill Club to order."

Still standing, he continued, "Gentlemen, as you know, because of the one-year anniversary of 9/11, the Office of Homeland Security has put the nation on Alert Level Orange. The purpose of this meeting is to decide if we should go ahead with Project Green, which will reduce the alert level to that color. *Permanently.*" Madox looked at Harry. "You'd like that, wouldn't you?"

"Sure."

"Might put you out of a job."

"That's okay."

"Good. Now, if the Board will bear with me, I'd like to get Harry up and running on this. In fact, we can all benefit from some perspective before we make any decisions." He looked at Harry and asked, "You've heard of Mutually Assured Destruction?"

"I . . . yeah . . ."

"During the Cold War, if the Soviets launched nuclear missiles against us, we would, without debate, launch our arsenal of nuclear weapons against them. Thousands of nuclear warheads would rain down on both countries, assuring mutual destruction. Remember that?"

Harry nodded.

Madox continued, "Paradoxically, the world was actually safer then. No hesitation on our part, and no political debates. This strategy had a beautiful simplicity to it. The radar images of thousands of nuclear missiles headed our way meant we were dead. The only moral question—if any—was, Do we kill tens of millions of them before we all die? You and I know the answer to that, but there were fuzzy-headed people in Washington who thought that revenge was not a justification for us destroying a big part of the planet—that no purpose would be served by obliterating the innocent men, women, and children whose government had just assured our obliteration. Well, the doctrine of Mutually Assured Destruction—MAD—removed any such questions by making our response automatic. We didn't have to rely on a president who lost his nerve or had a moral crisis, or who was out playing golf or getting laid somewhere."

There were a few polite chuckles.

Mr. Madox continued, "The primary reason that MAD worked was that it was unambiguous and symmetrical. Each side knew that a nuclear first strike by one would set off a counterstrike by the other of equal or overwhelming force, which would destroy the very civilization of both nations." He added, "That would leave places like Africa, China, and South America to inherit what was left of the Earth. Pretty depressing, don't you think?"

Harry remembered how the world was before the collapse of the Soviet Union. Nuclear war was pretty scary, but he never really believed it was going to happen.

Madox seemed to be reading his mind and said, "But this never happened, and never would. Even the most insane Soviet dictator could not contemplate this scenario. Despite the rantings of left-wing pacifists and pinhead intellectuals, Mutually Assured Destruction actually assured that the world was safe from nuclear Armageddon. Right?"

Harry thought, *What the hell is this guy getting at?*

Bain Madox sat down, lit a cigarette, and asked Harry, "Have you ever heard of something called Wild Fire?"

"No."

Madox looked at him closely, then explained, "A secret government protocol. Have you ever heard these words used in passing, or in any context?"

"No."

"I wouldn't think so. This secret protocol is known only at the highest levels of government. And by us. And now by you—if you pay attention."

Paul Dunn, the presidential adviser, interjected, "Bain, do we need to talk about this in front of Mr. Muller?"

Bain Madox stared at Dunn and replied, "As I said, this is a good exercise for all of us. Very shortly, we're going to make a decision that will change the world as we know it, and the history of the world for the next thousand years. The least we can do is explain ourselves to Mr. Muller, who represents the nation we say we are going to save. Not to mention explaining ourselves *to* ourselves at this critical juncture."

Landsdale, the CIA man, said to everyone, "You have to let Bain run it his way. You should know that by now."

Edward Wolffer added, "More important, this is a transformative moment in the history of the world, and I wouldn't want Bain, or anyone, to ever think we didn't give it the time that's equal to its importance."

Madox turned to his old friend. "Thank you, Ed. No one may ever know what happened here today, but we know, and God knows. And if someday the world does know, then we need to justify ourselves to God and to man."

Landsdale commented dryly, "Let's not tell God."

Madox ignored him and drew on his cigarette. "The first Islamic terrorist attacks began in the 1970s, as you recall."

Bain Madox began with the Munich Olympics Massacre, and then rattled off a list of thirty years of airplane hijackings, bombings, kidnappings, executions, and mass murder by Islamic jihadists.

The men in the room remained silent, but a few nodded in remembrance of one or another terrorist attack.

Harry Muller, too, recalled almost every attack that Madox mentioned, and what surprised him was how many there were over the last thirty years. He was surprised, too, that he had forgotten so many of them—even the big ones, like the car bomb attack on the Marine barracks in Lebanon that killed 241 Americans, or the bomb on board Pan Am Flight 103 over Lockerbie that killed hundreds of people.

Harry felt himself getting angrier as each attack was chronicled, and he thought that if a terrorist—or any Muslim—were brought into the room, the guy would be ripped apart by everyone there. Madox knew how to inflame the crowd.

In fact, Madox looked around the table and said, "Every one of us here had a friend, or knew someone, who was killed in the World Trade Center or the Pentagon." He addressed General Hawkins. "Your nephew, Captain Tim Hawkins, died in the Pentagon." Next he spoke to Scott Landsdale. "You had two CIA colleagues who died in the World Trade Center. Correct?"

Landsdale nodded.

Madox turned to Harry. "And you? Did you lose anyone that day?"

Harry replied, "My boss . . . Captain Stein and some other guys I knew died in the North Tower . . ."

"My condolences," said Madox, who then concluded his recitation of the atrocities, brutalities, and violence against America and the West. "This was all something new under the sun, and neither the world nor the United States knew how to react. Many people thought it would just go away. Obviously, it did not. It just got worse. In fact, the Western world wasn't equipped to counter these terrorist attacks, and we seemed to lack the will to respond to these people who were murdering us. Even when the United States was attacked on its own soil—the 1993 bombing of the World Trade Center—we did *nothing*." He looked at Harry. "Correct?"

"Yeah . . . but that changed things—"

"I hadn't noticed."

Harry said, "Well, 9/11 changed everything. We're more on top of—"

"You know, Harry, you and your ATTF friends, and the whole FBI, CIA, Defense Intelligence, British MI5 and MI6, Interpol, and the rest of the useless European intelligence services could spend the rest of their fucking lives chasing Islamic terrorists, and it wouldn't make much difference."

"I don't know—"

"*I* know. Last year, it was the World Trade Center and the Pentagon. Next year, it will be the White House and the Capitol Building." Madox paused, blew smoke rings, then said, "And one year, it will be an entire American city. A nuclear bomb. Do you doubt that?"

Harry didn't reply.

"Harry?"

"No. I don't doubt that."

"Good. Neither does anyone at this table. That's why we're here." He asked Harry, "How would you prevent that from happening?"

"Well . . . actually, I sometimes work on the NEST team—the Nuclear Emergency Support Team. You know about that?"

Bain Madox smiled. "Harry, you're sitting here with

the deputy secretary of defense, a top national security adviser to the president of the United States, a member of the Joint Chiefs of Staff, and the CIA liaison to the White House. If there's anything we don't know, I'd be very surprised."

"Then why do you keep asking me questions?"

Madox seemed a little annoyed. "Let me tell *you* about NEST—known as the volunteer fire department of the nuclear age. Very quaint, and about as effective. A thousand or so volunteers from the fields of science, government, and law enforcement who sometimes disguise themselves as tourists and businesspeople. They walk or drive around American cities and other sensitive targets, such as dams, nuclear reactors, and so forth, carrying their gamma-ray and neutron detectors hidden inside briefcases, golf bags, beer coolers, and whatever. Correct?"

"Yeah."

"Did you ever find an atomic bomb?"

"Not yet."

"And you never will. There could be an explosive nuclear device or a dirty bomb sitting in an apartment on Park Avenue with the timer going, and the chances of NEST or Harry Muller discovering that bomb is near zero. Correct?"

"I don't know. Sometimes you get lucky."

"That's not very reassuring, Harry." Madox said, "The question is, How does the American government prevent a weapon of mass destruction—specifically, a nuclear device, planted by terrorists—from obliterating an American city?" He looked at Harry and said, "I want you to draw a lesson from the Cold War strategy of Mutually Assured Destruction, and tell me how we can keep terrorists from planting and exploding a nuclear bomb in an American city. This is not a rhetorical question. Answer me, please."

Harry replied, "Okay, I guess like with the Russians—if they knew we were going to nuke them, then they wouldn't nuke us."

Madox replied, "True, but the nature of the enemy has changed. The global terrorist network is not like the old Soviet Union. The Soviets were an empire with a government, cities, hard targets, and soft targets. All laid out in a strike plan drawn up by the Pentagon and known to the Soviets. Islamic terrorism, on the other hand, is very amorphous. If an Islamic terrorist organization detonates a nuke in New York or Washington, who do we retaliate against?" He stared at Harry. "Who?"

Harry thought a moment. "Baghdad."

"Why Baghdad? How would we know if Saddam Hussein had anything to do with a nuclear attack on America?"

Harry replied, "What difference does it make? One Arab city is as good as the next. They'll all get the message."

"Indeed, they would. But here's a better plan. During the Reagan administration, the American government devised and put into place this secret protocol named Wild Fire. What Wild Fire is, is the nuclear obliteration of the *entire* Islamic world by means of American nuclear missiles, in response to a nuclear terrorist attack on America. How does that sound to you?"

Harry didn't respond.

"You can speak freely. You're among friends. Wouldn't you, deep in your heart, like to see Sandland turned into a sea of molten glass?"

Harry looked around the table, then replied, "Yes."

Bain Madox nodded. "So, there you have it. Harry Muller, who is an average American in most respects, would like to see Islam eradicated in a nuclear holocaust."

Harry Muller was happy to go along with Madox's bullshit—and it was just that. Bullshit. Right-wing loony fantasy talk that probably gave these guys hard-ons. He couldn't see any connection between what Madox was saying and what Madox was able to do. It reminded him of his days in the NYPD Intelligence Division, when he'd interrogate left-wing radicals who talked about world revolution and the rising of the masses, whatever the hell that was. His boss used to call it pinko wet dreams. He looked around the table again. On the other hand, these guys didn't seem like they were jerking themselves off, or jerking him off. In fact, they looked serious about something, and they were important guys.

Madox broke into Harry's thoughts and said to him, "How do we get the United States government to put a quick end to terrorism, and to this clear and imminent nuclear threat to the American homeland? Well, I'll tell you. The government has to launch Wild Fire. Right?"

Harry didn't answer, and Bain Madox informed him, "There are about seventy suitcase-size nuclear weapons missing from the inventory of the old Soviet Union. Did you know that?"

Harry replied, "Sixty-seven."

"Thank you. Did you ever wonder if any of those suit-case nukes has gotten into the hands of Islamic terrorists?"

"We think they have."

"Well, you're right. They have. I'll tell you some-thing you don't know—something that fewer than twenty people in the world know—one of those suitcase nukes was discovered last year in Washington, D.C. Not by a NEST team having a lucky day, but by the FBI acting on a tip."

Harry didn't respond, but thought about that, and a cold chill ran down his spine.

Madox continued, "I'm sure there are a few more suit-case nukes that have been smuggled into the country, prob-ably through our non-existent border with Mexico." He smiled at Harry. "There's probably one sitting in an apart-ment across the street from your office."

"No, I don't think so. We've swept the area."

"Well, I'm just making a point. Don't take me lit-erally. The question is, Why hasn't a missing Soviet nuclear suitcase bomb been detonated in an American city? Do you think Islamic terrorists would have any moral or ethical qualms about obliterating an American city and killing a million innocent men, women, and children?"

"No."

"Me, neither. And neither does anyone else after 9/11. But I'll tell you why it probably hasn't happened and won't happen. Because for Wild Fire to be a reli-able deterrent, as Mutually Assured Destruction was, it cannot be kept a complete secret. In fact, since the Wild

Fire plan was implemented, the heads of all Islamic governments have been notified by succeeding administrations in Washington that an attack on an American city with a weapon of mass destruction would automatically ensure an American nuclear retaliation against fifty to one hundred cities and other targets in the Islamic world."

Harry said, "Good."

Bain Madox continued, "As these gentlemen here can attest to, Harry, Wild Fire is seen by the American government as a very strong incentive for these countries to control the terrorists in their midst, to induce these countries to share information with American intelligence agencies, and to do whatever they need to do to keep themselves from being vaporized. In fact, the tip about the nuke in Washington came from the Libyan government. So, it seems to be working."

"Great."

Madox added, "Something like NEST is a pathetic defensive response to nuclear terror. Wild Fire is a pro-active response. It is a gun to the heads of Islamic countries— a gun that will go off if they fail to keep their terrorist friends from going nuclear. Undoubtedly most, if not all, terrorist organizations have been warned of this by the Islamic governments that harbor, aid, and have contact with them. Whether the terrorists believe this or not is another question. So far, they seem to believe it, which is probably why we haven't been attacked by weapons of mass destruction. What do you think, Harry?"

"Makes sense to me."

"Me, too. The Islamic governments have also been informed that Wild Fire is hardwired—that is, no sitting American president can alter or cancel this retaliation against Islam. This keeps our enemies from trying to analyze each president to see if he—or she—has any balls. The president is pretty much out of the equation after a nuke goes off in America. Just like during the Cold War." He turned to Paul Dunn and asked, "Correct?"

Dunn replied, "Correct."

Madox looked at Harry. "You seem lost in thought. What are you thinking about?"

"Well . . . I'm sure somebody in the government thought about this, but wouldn't fifty or a hundred nukes in the Mideast kind of fuck up the oil thing?"

A few men smiled, and Madox grinned as well. He glanced toward Edward Wolffer and said, "The deputy secretary of defense has assured me that there are no oil fields on the target list. No refineries, and no oil shipment ports. They will remain intact, but will come under new management." He smiled. "I've got to make a living, Harry."

"Yeah, right. But how about the environment and all that? You know, nuclear fallout, nuclear winter."

"I told you, the answer to global warming is nuclear winter. Just kidding. Look, the effects of fifty or even a hundred nuclear explosions detonating across the Mideast have been studied extensively by the government. It won't be that bad." He added, "I mean, for them, it's lights-out.

But for the rest of the planet, depending on what computer model you like, life will go on."

"Yeah . . . ?" Something else was troubling Harry Muller. "Well, it's not going to happen anyway because, like you said, if the terrorists know about this . . . I mean, do you think, or have you heard, that they're going to nuke us?"

"I haven't heard anything. Have you? Actually, my colleagues here think that Wild Fire is such an effective deterrent that the likelihood of an American city being attacked with a nuclear device by Islamic terrorists is very small. That's why we have to do it ourselves."

"Do *what*?"

"We, Harry, the men here in this room, have devised Project Green—the plan to detonate an atomic device in an American city, which will in turn trigger the Wild Fire response—which is the nuclear obliteration of Islam."

Harry wasn't sure he'd heard correctly and leaned toward Madox.

Madox made eye contact with Harry and continued, "And the beauty of this is that the government doesn't even have to be certain that the nuclear attack on America has come from Islamic terrorists. There exists a very strong presumption of guilt toward Islamic jihadists so that conclusive evidence is not required to launch Wild Fire. Brilliant, isn't it?"

Harry took a deep breath and said, "Are you *crazy*?"

"No. Do we look crazy?"

Harry didn't think the other four guys looked crazy, but Madox was a little nuts. Harry took another deep breath and asked, "You got a nuke?"

"Of course we do. Why do you think we're here? We actually have four nukes. In fact . . ." Madox stood, walked over to the black leather suitcase, and patted it. "Here's one of them."

CHAPTER NINE

Bain Madox suggested a short break, during which everyone, except Scott Landsdale and Harry Muller, left the room.

Landsdale stood at the end of the table, away from Harry, and they sized each other up. Landsdale said, "Don't even think about what you're thinking about."

"I can't hear you. Come closer."

"Cut the macho bullshit, Detective. The only way you're getting out of here is if we let you out."

"Don't bet your silk CIA panties on that."

"If you answer a few questions for me, we can work something out."

"That sounds like what I used to say to suspects. I was lying, too."

Landsdale let that slide and asked, "When Tom Walsh gave you this assignment, what did he tell you?"

"He told me to dress warm and save my gas receipts."

"Good advice. And thanks for confirming that it was Walsh." He asked, "What were you supposed to do with your digital disks?"

"Find a CIA guy and shove them up his ass."

"Were you supposed to go to the Adirondack Airport as part of this assignment?"

Harry realized that Landsdale was good at what he did. CIA guys were pricks, but they were highly professional pricks. Harry replied, "No, but that's a good idea. I bet I'll find your name on the arrivals manifest."

"Harry, I've got more IDs than you have clean socks in your drawer." He asked, "Who else at 26 Fed knows about your assignment?"

"How the hell do I know?"

"I didn't mention this before, but one of my friends at 26 Fed tells me you were talking to your cubemate, John Corey, in the elevator lobby, and you were carrying a metal suitcase from Tech. Did Corey ask you what you were doing?"

"Why don't you go fuck yourself?"

Landsdale ignored this suggestion, and said, "I'm trying to help you, Harry."

"I thought you were CIA."

He asked, "Do you want a piece of this, Harry?"

"Yeah, sure. I'm with you."

"You may not mean that now, but after this is over, you'll see that this was the only way to go."

"Don't you have to go take a piss or something?"

"No, but here's a question for you to think about: Do you think you might have been set up?"

"What do you mean?"

"I mean, Walsh was told by somebody, probably in Washington, to send a guy up here—an NYPD surveillance guy—to take pictures of people arriving at this club. It sounds like no big deal, right? But the people who ordered this—and maybe Walsh himself—knew you weren't going to get within a mile of this lodge before you were caught."

"I got a lot closer than that."

"Congratulations. So, what I'm thinking, Harry, is that you're the sacrificial lamb. Follow?"

"No."

"I mean, this is so clumsy that the only reason you could have been sent here is to scare the hell out of us and make us put Project Green on hold. *Or* maybe put it on the fast track. What do you think?"

"I've worked with CIA, and what I think is that you people see a conspiracy in everything, except the things that *are* a conspiracy. That's why you've been fucking up."

"You may have a point. But let me share my paranoia with you. You were sent here by higher-ups, through Walsh, for the purpose of spooking us into action *or* for the purpose of the FBI's getting a search warrant to come looking for you and finding four atomic suitcases that they might believe are here."

Harry didn't reply, but he thought about that.

Landsdale continued, "Let's assume, first, that someone wants to spook us into action. Who could that be? Well, maybe my people. Or, maybe the White House itself wants an excuse to launch Wild Fire."

Harry thought about that, too, but again didn't respond.

Landsdale went on, "But it could be the other thing—that you were sent here to disappear so that the FBI could swoop down on this place with probable cause and a search warrant. Actually, the only really incriminating things here at the club are the four nukes and you, and neither the nukes nor you will be here much longer. The ELF transmitter is not illegal, just hard to explain. Right?"

Harry Muller felt as if he'd stepped into one of the upstate psychiatric hospitals, and that he'd arrived ten minutes after the patients took control. And what the hell was an elf transmitter? How do you transmit an elf? And why would you want to . . . ?

Landsdale asked him, "You know about ELF?"

"Yeah. Santa's helpers."

Landsdale smiled and stared at Harry. "Maybe you don't." He explained, "Extremely Low Frequency. ELF. Does that mean anything to you?"

"No."

Landsdale started to say something else, but the door opened, and Madox and the other three men entered the room.

Landsdale caught Madox's eye and nodded toward the door.

Madox said to the others, "Excuse us a moment."

He and Landsdale left the room, and Madox said to Carl, who was standing near the door, "Keep an eye on Mr. Muller."

Carl went into the room and shut the door.

Landsdale moved down the corridor, and Madox followed. Landsdale said, "Okay, I spoke to Muller, and he seems honestly clueless about anything, except his assignment. Muller was not briefed by Walsh or anyone, which is standard procedure when sending a low-level surveillance guy on a sensitive assignment."

Madox replied, "I know that. What are you getting at?"

Landsdale paused, then said, "I have no doubt that whoever sent Harry Muller here fully expected him to be caught. Correct?"

Madox didn't reply.

Landsdale went on, "I'm fairly sure that the CIA knows what you're up to, Bain, and so does the Justice Department and the FBI."

"I don't think that's true."

"I think it is. And I think—based on my information— that Justice and the FBI are about to shut you down." Landsdale looked at Madox and continued, "But you have fans and friends in the government. Specifically, the CIA, who want you to go for it. Follow?"

"I don't think *anyone* in the government, except the people here, know a damn thing about Project Green, or—"

"Bain, deflate your fucking ego a little. You're being manipulated and used, and—"

"Bullshit."

"Not bullshit. Look, you've got a great plan. But you've been sitting on it too long. The do-gooders in the Justice Department and the FBI have gotten on to you, and they want to do the right thing and bust this conspiracy. The CIA sees it quite differently. The CIA thinks your plan is absolutely fucking terrific, and absolutely brilliant, and taking entirely too fucking long."

Madox asked Landsdale, "Do you know all of this for certain? Or are you speculating?"

Landsdale considered his reply, then said, "A little of both." He added, "Look, as the CIA liaison to the White House, I'm not fully in the Langley loop. But I used to work in a Black Ops branch, and I heard about you long before you heard about me."

Again, Madox didn't respond.

Landsdale continued, "Every covert branch of the intelligence establishment has its legendary members, men and women who are looked on as bigger than life, almost mythical. I worked with a guy like that, and this guy once briefed me about Wild Fire, and that's when your name came up, Bain, as a private individual who had the capacity to trigger Wild Fire."

Madox seemed uneasy with that information, and asked, "Is that how and why I got to make your acquaintance?"

Landsdale did not answer directly but said, "It's how and why I got posted to the White House." He added, "Your little conspiracy here has triggered a similar conspiracy among certain individuals in the CIA and also the Pentagon . . . and maybe in the White House itself. In other words, there are others in Washington, aside from your Executive Board, who are helping. I'm sure you understand that. And understand, also, that if you didn't exist, then the people in government who want to trigger Wild Fire would need to plant their own nukes in American cities." He forced a smile and said, "But we like to encourage private, faith-based initiative."

"What's your point, Scott?"

"The point, Bain, is that whoever sent Harry Muller here wants to bring this to a quick conclusion. If it was the FBI, then you're about to be busted. If it was the CIA, then they're telling you to move fast." He added, "I have no doubt that both organizations know what the other is up to, and it's become a race to see whose idea of safeguarding American security is going to win out."

Madox stared silently, then said, "All I need is about forty-eight hours."

"I hope you have that much time." Landsdale added, "I have a contact in the Anti-Terrorist Task Force where Muller works, and my guy tells me that Muller is a Mideast guy, and he doesn't work in the Domestic Terrorist Section, so it's unusual that he'd be picked for this job. But he further tells me that a guy named John Corey, former NYPD like Muller, and also in the Mideast Section, was the one originally picked to do this surveillance. Specifically picked. Why? That's the question. What difference would it make who was sent here as the sacrificial lamb?" He lit a cigarette and continued, "Then, I recalled that the CIA guy who originally told me about Wild Fire was once attached to the ATTF, and while there, he'd gotten into a major pissing match with this guy Corey. Actually, worse than a pissing match—they really wanted to kill each other."

Madox glanced at his watch.

Landsdale continued, "One of their many problems with each other seemed to be Corey's present wife, an FBI agent assigned to the Task Force." He smiled and said, "There's always a woman involved."

Madox, too, smiled and said, "Sexual jealousy is the wild card of history. Empires have been destroyed because Jack was fucking Jill, and Jill was also fucking Jim." He asked, "But what's your point?"

"Just that I see more than a coincidence here that Corey was supposed to be sitting where Muller is now sitting, waiting to die."

Madox observed, "Sometimes, Scott, coincidence is just coincidence. And what difference does it make?"

Landsdale hesitated, then responded, "But if it's *not* coincidence, then I see the hand of the master here—the guy who originally told me about Wild Fire and who also got me my job in the White House, and who got me introduced to the Custer Hill Club . . . but that's not possible because this guy is dead. Or supposed to be dead." He added, "Died in the World Trade Center."

Madox pointed out, "People are either dead, or they're not."

"This guy is the ultimate spook. Dead when he needs to be, alive when he needs to come back. The point is, if it's this guy who's behind Muller's being here, then I feel much better about our chances of getting Project Green going in the next forty-eight hours, and much better about the government initiating Wild Fire as the response."

Madox stared at Landsdale and said, "If that makes you feel better, Scott, then I'm happy for you. But the bottom line, Mr. Landsdale, is not what's going on in Washington, but what's going on *here*. I have worked on this plan for nearly a decade, and I *will* make it happen."

"Not if they shut you down in the next day or two." Landsdale said, "Be grateful that you have friends in Washington, and be very grateful if my former mentor in Black Ops is alive and looking after you."

"Well, if you say so . . . maybe, when this is over, I can meet this man, if he's among the living, and shake his hand." Madox asked, "What's his name?"

"I couldn't tell you his name, even if he was actually dead."

"Well, if you ever see him—alive—and if he was my guardian angel on this project, then thank him for me."

"I will."

Madox indicated the door. "Let's continue the meeting."

As Landsdale walked toward the door, Madox nodded, happy in the knowledge that this mystery man was so well thought of. In fact, the man in question had not died on September 11, as Madox knew, but was actually on his way to the Custer Hill Club. In fact, Mr. Ted Nash, an old friend of Bain Madox's, had called right before the meeting of the Executive Board to see if John Corey was in Madox's custody. When Madox said they had a Mr. Harry Muller in the net instead, Nash seemed disappointed and said, "Wrong fish," but he was optimistic, adding, "I'll see what I can do to get Corey to the Custer Hill Club . . . You'd like him, Bain. He's an egotistical prick, and nearly as smart as we are."

Bain Madox followed Landsdale into the room, walked to the head of the table, and began, "The meeting will come to order." He pointed to the black suitcase in the middle of the floor and said, "That thing, which you are seeing for the first time, is a Soviet-made RA-155, weight about seventy-five pounds, containing about twenty-five pounds of very high-grade plutonium, plus a detonating device."

Harry stared at the suitcase. When he'd worked with NEST, they'd never told him what to look for—small atomic devices came in different shapes and sizes, and as the instructor had said, "There won't be an atomic symbol on the device, or a skull and crossbones, or anything. Just rely on your gamma-ray and neutron detectors."

Madox continued, "That little thing will yield about five kilotons, about half the explosive power of the bomb dropped on Hiroshima. Because these devices are old, and need constant maintenance, the explosion could be smaller. But that's not a lot of consolation if you happen to be sitting next to one." He chuckled.

Landsdale pointed out, "Actually, we *are* sitting next to one." He joked, "Maybe you shouldn't smoke, Bain."

Madox ignored him. "For your information, gentlemen, that little thing would level Midtown Manhattan and cause about half a million instant deaths, followed by as many as another half million in the aftermath."

Madox walked over to the big suitcase and put his

hand on it. "Incredible technology. You have to wonder what God was thinking when He created atoms that could be split or fused by mortal men to release such supernatural energy."

Harry Muller, with great difficulty, took his eyes off the nuclear bomb. He seemed to notice the bottled water in front of him for the first time, and with an unsteady hand, he drank from it.

Madox said to him, "You're not looking well."

"None of you are looking too good yourselves, and where the hell did you get that bomb?"

"Actually, that was the easy part. It was just a matter of money, like everything else in life, plus my private jets to fly these here from one of the former Soviet republics. I paid—out of my own pocket—ten million dollars, if you're interested. That was for all four bombs—not each. You can imagine how many suitcase bombs people like bin Laden have already bought."

Harry finished his water, then took Landsdale's bottle along with Landsdale's ballpoint pen, which he put in his pocket. No one noticed as Madox continued speaking.

Madox turned to Harry and said, "We're not monsters, Mr. Muller. We're decent men who are going to save Western Civilization, save our families, our nation, and our God."

Harry, against his better judgment, asked, "By killing millions of Americans?"

"The Islamic terrorists are going to kill them anyway, Harry. It's just a matter of time. It's better if we do it sooner. And *we* get to pick the cities—not *them*."

"Are you all out of your fucking minds?"

Madox snapped, "Hold on, Harry! A little while ago you had no problem with the idea of wiping out the world of Islam—men, women, children, plus Western tourists and businesspeople, and who knows who else is in the Mideast next week—"

"Next week?"

"Yes. And as I said, you can thank yourself and your organization for that. Today, it was just you snooping around. Tomorrow or the next day, it will be Federal agents and perhaps troops from Fort Drum swarming all over this place, looking for you . . . and finding *this*." He slapped the suitcase.

Harry almost jumped in his seat.

"So, we have to hide you and deliver the suitcases to their final destinations." He said to the Board, "Meanwhile, we will proceed with the business at hand. First . . ." He walked back to the table and hit a key on his console. The lights dimmed as a flat screen monitor brightened on the wall, illuminating a color map of the Mideast and East Asia. "We will take a look at the world of Islam, which we are about to destroy."

CHAPTER TEN

B ain Madox began, "There, gentlemen, is the land of Islam, stretching from the Atlantic coast of North Africa, through the Mideast, into Central Asia, all the way to East Asia, ending in the most populous Muslim country of Indonesia, which is the latest battlefront in the war on terrorism."

He paused for effect and said, "There are over one *billion* Muslims living in these countries today. By sometime next week, there will be a lot fewer."

Madox let that sink in, then turned on a reading lamp and said, "Ed has provided us with a list of Islamic cities targeted under Wild Fire . . ." He glanced at the paper in front of him and joked, "This looks like my Christmas wish list."

No one laughed, and Madox said, "Ed will give us some details of Wild Fire."

The deputy secretary of defense, Edward Wolffer, explained, "There are actually two lists—the A-list and the B-list. The A-list includes the entire Middle East— the Arabic heart of Islam—plus some specific targets in North Africa, Somalia, Sudan, Muslim portions of Central Asia, and a few targets in East Asia. The list has basically stayed the same for the last twenty years, but now and then we add a target, such as the northern portion of the Philippines, which has become a hotbed of Islamic fundamentalism. Note, too, that we occasionally delete targets. For instance, as a result of our occupation of Afghanistan, we've removed most of Afghanistan from the target list as well as certain places in the Gulf region, Central Asia, and Saudi Arabia, where American troops are presently stationed."

Everyone nodded, and a few men jotted notes.

Wolffer continued, "We've also acquired new targets in southern Afghanistan, specifically the Tora Bora area and the adjacent border areas of Pakistan, where we believe bin Laden is hiding." He added, "If that sonofabitch survives this, he'll be king of the Nuclear Wasteland."

A few men laughed politely.

Scott Lansdale asked, "Why two lists?"

Wolffer explained, "There are two possible retaliatory responses under the Wild Fire plan. The A-list is always included, and the B-list is added, depending on the level and type of terrorist attack on America. For instance, if the attack is biological or chemical, then only the A-list targets will be destroyed. If the attack is nuclear, and it destroys one or more American cities, then the B-list is added to the retaliatory response—without debate."

Madox said, "Well, we know the attack on America will be nuclear, because we're the ones setting off the bombs."

There was silence in the room, then Paul Dunn said, "Bain, you don't have to sound so enthusiastic about it."

"Sorry, Paul. But this isn't a polite meeting of the National Security Council. Here, we can actually say what we're thinking."

Paul Dunn didn't reply, and Wolffer continued, "There has always been some concern about the level of radioactive fallout as well as climatic changes . . . thus, the existence of a primary list and a supplementary list. Plus, of course, not all Islamic countries are harboring terrorists, or are unfriendly to the U.S. But Wild Fire removes much of that debate by calibrating the response to the nature of the attack on the U.S. So, if a chemical or biological weapon killed only, say, twenty thousand people in New York or Washington, then our response would be to take out only the sixty-two targets on the A-list." He added, "We don't want to appear to have overreacted."

Landsdale laughed at the absurdity of that statement, but no one else seemed to see the humor.

Wolffer went on, "As of today, both lists together total one hundred twenty-two targets. We would expect initial casualties of about two hundred million people, and probably another hundred million dead within six months as the radiation takes its toll." He added in a matter-of-fact tone, "After that, it's hard to gauge the effects of disease, exposure, starvation, suicide, civil strife, and so forth."

No one commented.

Ed Wolffer said, "The people who created Wild Fire

understood that it was necessary to ensure that any future president, and his administration, did not have to make any strategic or moral choices. If X happens, we respond with List A. If Y happens, we add List B. Simple."

Harry Muller turned away from the illuminated map and looked at the four men on either side of the table. In the reflected light from the monitor, these four guys, who had seemed a little nervous a half hour ago, now seemed pretty calm. It was like, *Okay, it's here. Pay attention and get on with it.*

He glanced at Madox, who was staring at the TV monitor, and saw that Madox had this weird grin on his face, like he was watching a skin flick. Madox caught Harry's eye and winked at him.

Harry turned around in his seat and stared at the screen. *Jesus Christ Almighty. This is real. God help us.*

Wolffer continued, "Wild Fire is simply a version of MAD. Actually, Wild Fire was proposed, developed, and put in place by a group of old Cold War warriors during the Reagan administration."

He stayed silent a moment, then said in a reverential tone, "These were men with balls. They stood eyeball to eyeball with the Soviets, and the other guys blinked first. They have passed on to us a great lesson and a great legacy. To be worthy of these men who have given us a world free of Soviet terror, we need to do to Islamic terrorists what these Cold War warriors were prepared to do to the Soviet Union."

Again, there was silence in the room, then General Hawkins noted, "The Russians, at least, had some honor and a healthy fear of death, and it would have been a shame to destroy their cities and their people. These other bastards—the Islamics—deserve everything they're going to get."

Madox said to Edward Wolffer, "Tell us what they're going to get."

Wolffer cleared his throat and said, "What they're going to get is one hundred twenty-two nuclear warheads of varying kilotons, delivered primarily from Ohio-class nuclear submarines stationed in the Indian Ocean—plus, some ICBMs fired from North America." He added, "The Russians will be notified, as a courtesy and a precaution, about a minute before launch."

General Hawkins informed everyone, "These warheads represent a very small percentage of our arsenal. There will be thousands of warheads left, if we need them for a second strike on Islam, or if the Russians or Chinese get any stupid ideas."

Wolffer nodded, then continued, "Included on the A-list are almost all the capital cities of the Mideast—Cairo, Damascus, Amman, Baghdad, Tehran, Islamabad, Riyadh, and so forth—plus other major cities, known terrorist training camps, and all military installations."

He glanced at his notes and said, "Originally, Mogadishu in Somalia was on the B-list, but since Black Hawk Down, it's moved to the A-list to avenge that shameful debacle. Same with the port city of Aden in Yemen—the USS *Cole* will also be avenged."

Madox commented, "I'm glad this list has kept up with the changing times. We have a lot of payback to accomplish."

Wolffer replied, "Indeed, we do. But as much as we'd

like to avenge the Marine barracks bombing in Beirut, that capital city is not on the list. Half the population is Christian, and Beirut will become a bridgehead for us into the new, improved Middle East. Note, too, that Israel will no longer be surrounded by enemies—it will be surrounded by wasteland."

Landsdale asked, "Do the Israelis know about Wild Fire?"

Wolffer replied, "They know what our enemies know. It was presented to them as a possibility. They're not too thrilled with the thought of being covered with radioactive dust, but they have good civil defense programs in place, and they can ride it out until the air clears."

Scott Landsdale inquired with a smile, "Ed, do you think I should book an Easter trip to the Holy Land?"

Wolffer responded, "We're talking about a whole New World, Scott. A world where airport security will return to the level of the 1960s. A world where your family and friends can once again see you off at the gate, and where luggage lockers are not a thing of the past. A world where every airline passenger is not treated as a potential terrorist, and where aircraft safety has to do with mechanical issues, not terrorists on board or shoe bombs. A world in which every American tourist or businessperson is not a potential terrorist target. In this New World, gentlemen, every American will be treated with courtesy, respect, and a little awe—the way our fathers and grandfathers were who liberated Europe and Asia from evil. So, yes, Scott, plan on going to the Holy Land for Easter. You'll be treated well, and you won't have to worry about suicide bombers in crowded cafés."

The room was quiet as Wolffer continued his briefing on the subject of holy sites. "The primary targets also include Muslim holy sites, such as Medina, Fallujah, Qum, and so forth. This alone will take the heart out of Islam. Their holiest site, Mecca, is to be spared—not out of any sensitivity to that religion but as a hostage city that will be destroyed if any surviving terrorists threaten or carry out a retaliation." He concluded, "The governments in the Middle East know this and asked us to also spare Medina if the worst happens. Our answer was no."

"Good answer," said Madox. He added, "I've had a lot of unpleasant dealings with the Saudi royal family. Next week, they're history, and the only good thing about that place—the oil under the sand—will be waiting for us."

Edward Wolffer ignored that and continued, "The other Muslim holy site that will not be destroyed is, of course, Jerusalem, which we as Christians and also the Jews revere as our holiest site. We expect that, post–Wild Fire, the Israelis will kick the Muslims out of Jerusalem, Bethlehem, Nazareth, and other Christian holy sites under their control. If they don't, we will."

Madox commented, "On the subject of cities to be spared, I see a number of Turkish cities on the target list, but not Istanbul."

Wolffer explained, "Istanbul is a historic treasure, located geographically in Europe, and it will again become Constantinople. The Muslims will be expelled." He added, "In fact, gentlemen, there is a political plan for the post–Wild Fire world that redraws some lines on the map and moves people out of places where we don't want them.

Jerusalem, Beirut, and Istanbul come to mind, though I'm not completely familiar with the political plan."

Madox noted, "Whatever it is, we can leave it to the State Department to screw it up."

General Hawkins said, "Amen," then observed, "With Baghdad and most of Iraq gone, we won't need to go to war with Saddam Hussein."

Wolffer replied, "Actually, we won't need to go to war with Syria either, or Iran, or any other hostile country which will no longer exist."

Madox said, "I like the sound of that. Don't you, Harry?"

Harry hesitated, then replied, "Yeah, if you like the sound of mass murder."

Madox stared at Harry and said, "I have a son, Harry—Bain Junior, who is a reserve officer in the United States Army. If we go to war with Iraq, he will be called to active duty, and he may die in Iraq. Bottom line on that is I'd rather see everyone in Baghdad dead than to be notified that my son is dead in Iraq. Is that selfish?"

Harry didn't answer, but thought, *Yes, that is selfish.* Also, Madox was conveniently forgetting the American sons and daughters he was going to nuke in America.

Bain Madox said to Harry, and to the others, "Sometimes a joke illuminates a truth that people won't admit to. So let me tell you a joke, Mr. Muller, which, in your line of work, you may have already heard." Madox smiled in the manner of a person about to tell a good one. "So, it seems that the president—Mr. Dunn's boss—and the secretary of defense—Mr. Wolffer's boss"—he smiled again and went on—"are having a disagreement over some policy issue, so they call in a junior aide, and the secretary of defense says to the aide, 'We've decided to A-bomb a billion Arabs and one beautiful, blond-haired, blue-eyed, big-breasted woman. What do you think?' And the young aide asks, 'Mr. Secretary, why would you bomb a beautiful, blond-haired, blue-eyed, big-breasted woman?' And the secretary of defense turns to the president and says, 'See? I told you no one cares about a billion Arabs.'"

There was some polite and restrained laughter around the table, and Harry, too, smiled at the old joke, which he'd heard a few times.

Madox asked Harry, "Point made?"

Edward Wolffer returned to his subject and said, "Regarding Iraq, ground wars are costly in terms of men, matériel, and money. And ground wars always have unintended consequences. I can tell you from firsthand knowledge— and Paul can verify this—that this administration is hell-bent on provoking a war with Iraq, then Syria, and eventually Iran. In principle, none of us, I think, are opposed to this. But for those of us here who fought in Vietnam—Bain, Jim, and I—we can say with some authority that when you let loose the dogs of war, those dogs are out of your control. The beauty of a nuclear attack is that it is quick and cheap. We've already bought and paid for a huge atomic arsenal— we presently have about seven thousand nuclear warheads— that is sitting around doing nothing. For a small fraction of the cost of those warheads, we can achieve monumental results. The results of a nuclear strike are unequivocal." He grinned and added, "The *New York Times* and the *Washington Post* won't have to agonize over whether or not we're winning the war on terrorism."

Everyone laughed, and Bain Madox asked, rhetorically, "You mean, I won't have to read some bleeding-heart story in the *Times* about some little girl and her grandmother who were wounded by American fire?"

Again, everyone laughed, and Wolffer said, "I don't think the *Times* or the *Washington Post* are going to send any reporters into the nuclear ash to get a so-called human-interest story."

Madox chuckled, then looked again at the map on the screen. "I see on the list the Aswân High Dam." He moved a cursor to Egypt and the southern Nile. "That, I assume, is the mother of all targets."

Wolffer replied, "Indeed, it is. A multi-warhead missile will take out that dam and send billions of gallons of water rushing down the Nile, which will, in effect, wipe out Egypt, killing perhaps forty to sixty million people as it floods the Nile Valley on its way into the Mediterranean. This will be the largest single loss of life and property— and there are no oil fields there. Unfortunately, we have to accept the loss of thousands of Western tourists, archeologists, businesspeople, and so forth, along with the loss of historical sites." He added, "The pyramids should survive."

Madox said, "Ed, I see that several Egyptian cities along the Nile Valley are on the list to be hit with nuclear warheads. Considering that the Aswân waters will sweep away those cities, aren't the missiles redundant? Or are they biblical?"

Wolffer glanced at his friend and replied, "I never thought about that." He considered a moment, then said,

"I suppose the floodwaters will put out the fires in the burning cities."

Madox commented, "That's too bad."

Wolffer went on, "Some bad news, as I've alluded to, is that a great number of Westerners will be killed in this attack. Tourists, businesspeople, expats, embassy people, and so forth. That number could easily reach a hundred thousand, many of them Americans."

No one commented on that statement.

Wolffer continued, "Unfortunately, too, we can't predict when these areas will again be habitable or socially stable enough to get the oil flowing. A Defense Department analysis, however, predicts that there will not be much shortfall in global or national needs because these countries which produce the oil will no longer be using any. Therefore, oil from other sources, along with reserves, should be sufficient to meet any short-term demands in America and Western Europe." He added, "The Saudi oil will probably be available to us first—within two years."

Madox interjected, "You government people should speak to us in the private sector. My analysis is that Saudi oil will be on board tankers and coming this way in about a year. I think we can get a hundred dollars a barrel, if we exaggerate the post-nuclear-war problems of pumping and shipping."

Wolffer hesitated, then said, "Bain, the Defense Department is thinking more in terms of twenty dollars a barrel, since we'd be controlling all aspects of pumping and shipping. The idea is that we'll need cheap oil to help revive the American economy, which we predict will go into a severe slump after two American cities suffer nuclear devastation."

Bain Madox waved his hand and said, "I think that's also an exaggeration. You'll see a stock-market slump of a few thousand points for less than a year. Some cities will experience a population flight for a few months, the way New York did post-9/11. But after it becomes clear that the enemy is dead and buried, you will see an American renaissance that will amaze the world." He said to Wolffer, "Don't be pessimistic. If the collapse of the Soviet Union was the dawn of the American century, then the obliteration of Islam will usher in the millennium of American peace, prosperity, and confidence. Not to mention unrivaled power. The American millennium will make the Roman Empire look like a third-world country."

No one commented, so Madox continued, "Things will be different. The last global threat to America will be gone, and the entire nation will rally around the government, as it did post-9/11 and post–Pearl Harbor. The internal enemies of America, including the growing Muslim population, will be dealt with without protest. And you won't be seeing any anti-war demonstrations in America, or anywhere in the world. And those bastards around the world who danced in the streets after 9/11 will be either dead or kissing our feet."

He took a breath and spoke rapidly. "And the Europeans will shut their mouths for a change, and then it will be Cuba's turn, then North Korea. And the Russians will keep their mouths shut as well. Because after we go nuclear once, everyone will understand that we will do it again. And when the time is right, we will smother the China problem in its cradle before it grows up to challenge us."

Harry Muller watched the other men as Madox continued his tirade. It seemed to Harry that the other guys were a little uncomfortable now that Madox had taken off from the Islamic terrorist problem and was finding new enemies to kill. And then there was the oil thing, which Harry thought was at least as important to Bain Madox and Global Oil Corporation as getting rid of terrorists. Harry already knew this guy was nuts, but now he was *seeing* how nuts—and so were Madox's buddies.

Madox stood, and his voice became strident. "And as a Vietnam veteran, I tell you, we will also redeem our lost honor when American troops march into Saigon and Hanoi without a peep from China or anyone."

He looked at his four colleagues and concluded, "For us *not* to go nuclear—for us to continue this fight against our enemies by conventional and diplomatic means, to waste lives and treasure in this battle, to prolong it without a clear victory in sight—is morally wrong. We have the means to end this quickly, decisively, and cheaply through the use of nuclear weapons that we already possess. To *not* use these weapons against people who would use them against us if they could would be national suicide, a strategic blunder, an affront to common sense, and an insult to God."

Bain Madox sat down.

The room was still.

Harry Muller studied the faces in the dim light and

said to himself, *Yeah, they know he's nuts. But they don't care because he's just saying what they're thinking.*

Bain Madox lit a cigarette and said matter-of-factly, "Okay, let's talk now about which American cities need to be sacrificed, and how and when we're going to do that."

— PART V —

Saturday
NORTH FORK, LONG ISLAND

Nassau Point, Long Island, August 2, 1939
F. D. Roosevelt, President of the United
States, White House, Washington, D.C.

Sir . . . it may become possible to set up a
nuclear chain reaction in a large mass of
uranium, by which vast amounts of power
and large quantities of new radium-like el-
ements would be generated . . . by which,
my dear Mr. President, it might be possible
to unleash an immense destructive force.

—Albert Einstein

CHAPTER ELEVEN

After dinner at the barge restaurant, Kate and I drove out toward Orient Point on the eastern tip of the North Fork of Long Island.

The sky was partly cloudy, but I could see stars, which I rarely see in Manhattan.

The North Fork is a windswept spit of land, quite beautiful in a stark sort of way, surrounded by the Long Island Sound to the north, Gardiner's Bay to the south, and the Atlantic Ocean to the east.

Because the surrounding water holds its summer heat, the autumns are unusually warm for this latitude. In fact, this microclimate, plus maybe global warming in general, was the reason for the newly planted vineyards, and the resulting explosion of tourism, which has changed the feel of the land.

As a kid, I summered out here with my parents along

with other hardy and less affluent families who could not afford the Hamptons, or who specifically wanted to avoid the Hampton crowd.

One such hardy soul was Albert Einstein, who summered here at a place called Nassau Point in 1939; and since there wasn't much to do, he probably had a lot of time to think. So one day, at the urging of other physicists, he wrote a letter to Franklin Roosevelt—now called the Nassau Point Letter—in which he strongly advised the president to get moving on the atomic bomb before the Nazis built one of their own. The rest, as they say, is history.

Regarding microclimates and the warming weather, I said to Kate, "Let's go for a skinny-dip."

She glanced at me and replied, "It's October, John."

"We should take advantage of global warming before everyone else does. In ten years, this place will have palm trees instead of vineyards, and thousands of people will be coming here in October to soak up the sun."

"Then let's come back in ten years for a swim."

I continued east on Route 25, an old colonial-era road, formerly known as King's Highway when the British were in charge here before the Revolution. Along the road, in the bluffs to the north, I could see old white clapboard houses and recently built summer houses of cedar and glass. I never really wanted to be rich, but now and then I think about starting a new revolution so I can appropriate some stockbroker's summer house on the water. I mean, I'd give it back after a few years, and everyone would benefit from the experience.

We were close to Orient Point now, and up ahead was the terminal for the ferry to New London, Connecticut, and beyond that, the restricted area where the government ferry went to the top secret Animal Disease Center on Plum Island.

This, of course, made me think back to that summer when I was recuperating from my gunshot wounds out here, and I got involved with a bizarre double homicide when I was supposed to be watching my bullet holes closing up. I also got involved with a lady named Emma Whitestone, whom I still think about too often.

Subsequent to the case, I also became involved with a lady named Beth Penrose, who was the county homicide detective assigned to that case—Beth preceded Kate, or perhaps they overlapped a bit—so the Plum Island case and the name Beth Penrose didn't come up too often when Kate and I were talking about old cases.

Also while working that case, I first met Mr. Ted Nash of the Central Intelligence Agency, and this meeting was to have a profound influence on my life, and as it turned out, on his as well. His life ended before mine, so he doesn't think about me much anymore, though I still think about him now and then.

And, in another weird twist of fate, Ted Nash knew Kate before I did, and I really think they had something going before I came along.

Therefore, I sometimes have this fantasy that Nash actually survived the World Trade Center, and that he and I meet again. Then, the fantasy continues with a verbal confrontation that I win, of course, followed by a physical confrontation—no guns—in which I throw him off a cliff, or a skyscraper, or sometimes I just snap his neck and watch him twitch.

Kate asked me, "What are you thinking about?"

I came out of my happy reverie and replied, "About what a beautiful place this world is."

She asked, "What did you say your name was?"

"Be nice. I'm trying to get in the mood of . . . whatever."

"Good." She suggested, "Let's go back to the B and B and make love."

I made an immediate two-wheeled U-turn on the deserted road and hit the accelerator.

"Slow down."

I eased off on the gas pedal. As the old expression goes, "Women need a reason to have sex; men need only a place." So, in that spirit, I hung a quick left at a sign that said: ORIENT BEACH STATE PARK.

"Where are you going?"

"A romantic spot."

"John, let's go back to the B and—"

"This is closer."

"Come on, John. I don't like to do it outdoors."

I didn't care *where* I did it as long as I did it. And my pocket rocket had clearly pointed to this road.

I continued on the dark, narrow road that ran through bulrushes and sea grass along a narrow peninsula. The land widened, and I saw an opening in the vegetation to the left and turned onto a path that went down to the water. I put the Jeep in four-wheel drive, continuing through some boggy ground until we reached a small sand beach on Gardiner's Bay.

I shut off the ignition, and we got out of the Jeep,

took off our shoes and socks, and walked to the edge of the water.

To the east, we could see the mysterious shore of Plum Island, and to the south was Gardiner's Island, which had been in the Gardiner family since the 1600s, and where Captain Kidd had supposedly buried his treasure, which may be true, but the Gardiners weren't talking about it.

Further south across the bay were the lights of the Hamptons, whose summer residents had more treasure than any pirate could hope to steal in a lifetime of pillaging and plundering.

But, I digress from the subject at hand, which was my extreme horniness. I said, "Let's skinny-dip." I took off my jacket and flung it back on the sand.

Kate put her toe in the water. "It's *cold.*"

"It's warmer than the air." I took off my shirt and pants. "Come on." I slipped off my boxer shorts and stepped into the water. *Jeez.* My stiffy dropped like a cold noodle.

Kate noticed and said, "Maybe you do need to cool down." She pushed me. "Go ahead, Tarzan."

Well, this was my idea, so, remembering the Polar Bear Club's annual January dip into the Atlantic Ocean at Coney Island, I let out a bloodcurdling scream and charged into the water, then dove under.

I thought my heart stopped, and for sure my testicles headed straight up into my groin, while my formerly stiff member shrunk to the size of a comma in a telephone book.

I stayed under as long as I could, then popped my

head up and treaded water. I called to Kate, "It's okay once you're in!"

"Good. Stay in. I'm going back to the B and B. Bye!"

I shouted back, "I thought FBI agents were tough! You're a pussy!"

"You're an idiot. Get out of there before you freeze to death."

"Okay . . . oh . . . jeez . . . I'm getting cramps . . ." I went under, then came up again, spit water, and yelled, "Help!"

"Are you joking?"

"Help!"

I heard her say, "Damn," or maybe she said, "Drown." She pulled off her clothes, took a deep breath, and ran into the water up to her waist, then dove in and began swimming toward me.

I filled my lungs with air and floated on my back, looking up at the magnificent night sky. I think I saw Pegasus through the skimming clouds.

Kate reached me and treaded water a few feet away. "You asshole."

"Excuse me?"

"If you're not drowning now, you will be in a fucking minute from now."

"I didn't say I was drowning." I suggested, "Float on your back. I'll show you Pegasus."

"I cannot fucking believe you did that. I'm *freezing*."

"The water's warmer than—"

She put her hand over my face and pushed my head underwater. And held it there. For a long time.

I swam away underwater and came around her from

behind. Her beautiful naked butt was right in front of me—so how could I resist giving her right cheek a little love bite?

She shot straight up, and when I surfaced, she was swimming in a circle, trying to see into the black water.

I called out, "I just bit a white-butt shark."

She turned toward me and screamed a lot of words that didn't sound nice. I did, however, catch the words "Fucking idiot."

Well, enough foreplay. I said, "I'm going back. Are you staying in?"

She didn't reply and headed for shore using a strong overhand stroke.

She was fast, but I caught up, and we raced each other to the shore. I think we're both very competitive, and this is what keeps our relationship so interesting. Also, one of us is an immature idiot, and the other is not, so we sort of complement each other, like an alpha male baboon and his female trainer.

Anyway, I think Kate was a little angry with me, so I let her beat me to the shore, and when I walked onto the beach, she was drying herself with my pants and sports jacket.

It was really cold out of the water, with a little breeze blowing, and my teeth were chattering. I said to her, "That was refreshing."

No response.

I tried another approach. "Hey, you're a hell of a swimmer. Do you want to have sex?"

She was gathering her clothes from the sand and didn't seem to hear me.

"Kate? Hello?"

She turned toward me. "I have never in my life been with a grown man who is so infantile, so stupid, so *moronic,* so harebrained, so reckless, so—"

I interrupted, "So I guess a blow job is out of the question."

"A *what*? Are you kidding?"

"Well . . . I thought you said—"

"Don't speak to me."

"Okay."

So we both stood there on the little beach, naked, and I mean, she really looked *good,* not withstanding her wet hair and blue lips. She has this incredibly athletic yet voluptuous body, with breasts that defy the laws of gravity, and a tummy as flat and firm as a bar top, long legs that are as beautiful as any I've ever seen, including my own, and a patch of blond pubic hair that drives me crazy. Plus, she has a butt that is so firm I could barely get a good bite out of it.

She was looking at me, too, and I knew she was getting a little steamy despite the air temperature. We're really physically attracted, and we click sexually, so even when she's not speaking to me, which is about twice a week, we can still make love. To tell the truth, I sometimes like it that way.

Anyway, I made the first move toward her, and she hesitated, then dropped her clothes and took a step toward me.

I felt some warm blood making its way back into my shriveled weenie.

We stood a few feet apart, face-to-face, then our hands

reached out, and we caressed each other. Big John perked up a little more, then she took it in her hand and said, "That's *hot*."

I put my fingers between her legs. "It's hot in there, too."

By now, we were both hot as pistols, proving once again that when you're having a disagreement with your partner, just skip the conversation and get down to the sex.

We came closer, and I could feel her breasts on my chest, and her thighs against mine, and her hands on my butt, pulling me closer.

I dropped to my knees and kissed her blond bush, and I was about to drop onto my back so she could get on top, but she suddenly turned and said, "Kiss it where you bit me."

Okay. I didn't remember where I bit her, so I covered the whole field.

Then she turned around and demanded, "Tell me you're sorry."

So, still on my knees, I said, "I'm sorry."

"Kiss my toes."

Well, all right. I kissed her sandy toes.

"Lie on your back."

I rolled back and lay on the sand.

Kate knelt between my legs and took Big John in her hand, commenting, "This guy needs some work." She put her other hand on my scrotum. "Where did they go?"

"Someplace warm."

She put her head down between my legs, and within a few minutes, testicles A and B had dropped into their proper position, and Big John was standing straight up, pointing to Pegasus.

Kate lowered herself on me, stretched out, and moved her hips at her own pace until she had one of her quietly intense orgasms.

She rolled off, stood, and began getting dressed.

I felt a little used. "I think you forgot me."

She shook the sand out of her bra. "You're much nicer to me when you're horny."

"Actually, I get real mean when I'm horny."

She smiled. "No, you're a total puppy dog."

I sat up. "I'm really close. I just need a minute of your time."

She slipped on her skirt and sweater and said, "If you can wait until we get into a nice warm shower, I'll make it worth the wait."

"Deal." I stood quickly and got dressed in my damp clothes.

We got back into the Jeep, and Kate turned the heater up full blast.

We drove out of the state park, then headed west back toward the B&B.

Kate said, "If I get pneumonia, it's your fault."

"I know. I'm sorry."

"I really thought a shark bit me."

"I know. That was stupid. I'm sorry."

"And you should *never, ever* pretend you're drowning."

"I know that was unforgivable. I'm sorry."

"You're a total jerk."

"I know. Wanna fuck?"

She laughed.

So we drove along the lonely highway, holding hands and listening to some Connecticut station that was playing Johnny Mathis, Nat King Cole, and Ella Fitzgerald.

We got back to the B&B, and the stupid key didn't seem to work, and I almost kicked the door down, but Kate got it unlocked, and we charged up the stairs like two teen-agers who'd just discovered sex an hour ago.

Bottom line, the hot shower was better than the cold bay, and Kate, true to her word, made the wait worth it.

— PART VI —

Saturday
UPSTATE NEW YORK

America, with the collaboration of the Jews, is the leader of corruption and the breakdown of values, whether moral, ideological, political, or economic corruption. It disseminates abomination and licentiousness among people by way of the cheap media.

—Suleiman Abu Ghaith
Spokesman for Osama bin Laden

CHAPTER TWELVE

The members of the Executive Board and Harry Muller remained silent as Bain Madox gathered his thoughts. Then, Madox began, "First, we need to establish a time frame for Project Green. Suitcase nukes"—he motioned toward the upright suitcase—"need periodic maintenance to ensure detonation and maximum design yield. It's all very complex, having to do with the plutonium core, but the good news is that I have a nuclear physicist in my employ who has been performing this function. The gentleman's name is Mikhail, a Russian working in America. I've contacted him, and he will be here sometime tomorrow. By tomorrow night, if there are no problems, the devices will be hot."

Scott Landsdale inquired, "Does Mikhail know anything about Project Green? Or Wild Fire?"

"Of course not," Malox replied. "He thinks these devices are to be planted in cities in the Middle East, which makes sense to him and is all he needs to know."

"Where is he now?"

"He lives on the East Coast and works for an American university. That's all *you* need to know. He understands that this is urgent." Madox smiled and said, "For fifty thousand dollars a visit, I think he'll get here as soon as possible."

"And you trust this guy?" Landsdale asked.

"Not at all. But I offered him a million dollars if and when the nukes detonate. Prorated, of course, based on how many detonate and the approximate yield." He added, "Mikhail has good incentive."

Landsdale asked, "And when they go off in American cities—rather than Middle Eastern cities—how will Mikhail react to that?"

"I have no idea. And does it matter?"

"What happens to Mikhail after the detonations?"

Madox commented, "You ask a lot of questions, Scott."

"I'm very security conscious. I have this unsettling thought of Mikhail having one vodka too many and telling someone that his part-time job is maintaining nuclear devices at the Custer Hill Club."

"I don't intend for that to happen."

"Does that mean you're taking care of Mikhail?"

Madox glanced at the other three Board members, then said to Landsdale, "Don't worry about it."

Harry Muller listened to a gentlemen's discussion of murdering a witness. If Mikhail, who only knew a piece of this, was going to get whacked, then he, Harry Muller, didn't stand much of a chance, though he knew his chances had been around zero anyway.

Madox continued, "Obviously, this is all on a fast track since Detective Muller's unannounced visit, but I see no reason why we can't get Project Green in place in the next few days." He glanced at Landsdale and went on, "In fact, gentlemen, our hand has been forced, and we have no choice but to move forward."

Paul Dunn, the president's adviser, said, "Bain, I'm thinking we could hide those nuclear devices until a better time—"

"The time, Paul, is *now*. I believe—from recent information—there are people in the government who are beginning to suspect something, and we have to go forward before they show up here. Those nukes need to be at their destinations in a day or two, and you need to be back in Washington, close to the president, so that when *we* initiate Project Green, *he* will initiate Wild Fire." Madox asked Paul Dunn, "What does the president's schedule look like on Monday and Tuesday?"

Dunn glanced at a piece of paper in front of him. "The president will be in the White House Monday morning— Columbus Day—then he flies to Dearborn, Michigan, arriving at Oakland County International Airport at about three-thirty. Election Day is less than three weeks away, as you know, so the president will make a speech in support of Dick Posthumus for governor of Michigan. Then, he motorcades to the Ritz-Carlton in Dearborn, where he'll make a dinner speech in support of Thaddeus McCotter for congressman of that district. Then, he leaves on Air Force One and should be back at Andrews Air Force Base about ten P.M., then he helicopters to the White House and arrives on the South Lawn about ten-thirty."

Madox thought about that, then said, "Monday, Columbus Day, might be a day that Islamic terrorists would decide to detonate nuclear bombs in American cities."

Paul Dunn said, "Bain, for a variety of reasons, a holiday is not a good day to . . . to do this." He explained, "For one thing, neither I nor Ed will be with the president when he's on the road Monday, and Scott will not be at the White House, either." He looked at Landsdale for confirmation.

Scott Landsdale said, "I have a company picnic and softball game on Monday."

Madox laughed. "Well, then, we have to postpone the nuclear attack on America." He turned to Edward Wolffer. "Maybe we need some information on JEEP to help us make this decision."

Wolffer nodded and replied, "You probably all know a few details about JEEP—the Joint Emergency Evacuation Plan. During the Cold War, the plan called for the president and a select group of military and political leaders to be taken as quickly as possible—by vehicle or helicopter—to either Andrews or National Airport, whichever is closer to where the president happens to be." He continued, "At the designated airport is an E-4B jet aircraft ready for takeoff at a moment's notice. This aircraft is called the National Emergency Airborne Command Post—NEACP—known by its code word of Kneecap, sometimes referred to as the Doomsday Plane."

Wolffer glanced around the room and continued, "The president, of course, would have the nuclear football with him, and he could launch a retaliatory attack from the airborne command post. But there is a post-9/11 variation of JEEP and Kneecap, which goes into effect when the attack on America is not from intercontinental ballistic missiles. If it's determined that the attack was initiated by terrorists, then it's assumed that we don't have the ten or fifteen minutes' warning that an inbound ICBM would give us, and that a hidden nuke could be detonated in Washington at any second. Therefore, the response is different—the president needs to get on the Marine helicopter on the White House lawn as soon as possible, and he'll be flown by helicopter to a secure location, far away from Washington, which, of course, is a potential terrorist target."

Madox said, "Well, *we* know it's not one of the cities on our target list for obvious reasons of national survival." He smiled and added, "Not to mention that you gentlemen will all be there at zero hour. You can all look like heroes by staying at your posts during the panic and confusion that will follow the nuclear detonations. You three men— Ed, Paul, and Scott—will need to influence events."

Wolffer noted, "In fact, we've already done that by pushing for this variation on JEEP." He explained, "The Marine helicopter is not as well equipped as Air Force One or the E-4B Doomsday Plane to handle large volumes of communication or certain types of encrypted messages, so that time between attack and response will be largely eaten up by the evacuation procedures, and there's less likelihood of the president receiving any messages or getting bad advice that might cause him to think about interfering with Wild Fire." Wolffer concluded, "The time the president spends on the Marine helicopter is always a period of less-than-ideal command, control, and communication."

Madox responded, "That's actually quite ideal for us." He asked Paul Dunn, "So, what does the president's schedule look like on Tuesday?"

"The president," Dunn replied, "will be in the White House all day. At two P.M., he is hosting a White House conference on Minority Homeownership. The rest of the day, he will be in the Oval Office. Dinner is with friends, select staff, and the first lady." Dunn added, "Scott should be working late that day in his West Wing office, and Ed should be as close to the secretary of defense as possible all day. Jim should be in the Pentagon, keeping track of the movements of the Joint Chiefs." Dunn concluded, "I will be dining at the White House."

Bain Madox seemed lost in thought, then said, "All right . . . Tuesday seems like the best day to initiate Project Green. That gives us a comfort zone to accomplish what needs to be done." He explained, "First, Mikhail needs to be here, and he may need some time to service the nuclear devices. Second, I need to be certain my aircraft are here and ready for departure. Third, I need to have the diesel generators serviced to power up the ELF antenna. Then, the ELF transmitter needs to be checked out, which I'll do myself . . . and then there are the logistics of the two flights to the designated cities."

Harry listened to Madox, but he wasn't quite sure what the guy was talking about, though everyone else seemed to know.

Madox continued, "So, let's say Tuesday, early evening. I know the president retires early, and I don't want him dragged out of bed and put on the Marine helicopter in his pajamas." He grinned. "Let's say sometime during the dinner hour when Paul and the first lady are with him, which will make the helicopter evacuation much easier for everyone. Exact time to be determined by me, and passed on to Scott and Ed, who will be working late that night in their offices." He looked at General Hawkins and said, "And you, Jim, will be working late in the Pentagon."

Hawkins nodded.

Madox finished, "So, gentlemen, the New World begins Tuesday evening—three days and about three hours from now. And you will all stay in touch with one another. And you, Scott, will calm down the situation by announcing that you have hard intelligence that the cities that have experienced a nuclear attack are the only cities that will suffer this fate."

Landsdale nodded. "I'll do my best, but not many people are believing the CIA these days."

"The White House believes you about the weapons of mass destruction in Iraq. Which, by the way, I don't think exist."

Landsdale smiled and replied, "Maybe they do, maybe they don't. In any case, post–Wild Fire, that will be a moot question, which is good for everyone."

Madox nodded and turned to Wolffer. "How does Wild Fire actually go into effect? Take us through this."

Edward Wolffer explained, "After it is reported and confirmed that an American city or cities have been attacked with a weapon of mass destruction—which in this case will be nuclear—then the secretary of defense sends a coded message to Colorado Springs that says simply, 'Wild Fire is go,' followed by the response level: the A-list, or the A- and B-lists." He looked around the table and continued, "If Washington itself has been destroyed, and/or there is no message from the secretary of defense or the president, then Wild Fire goes into effect anyway."

No one commented, so Wolffer went on, "The protocols and safeguards are similar to the ones in place for MAD, and although Wild Fire is less of a hair-trigger response than MAD, this is one of those rare cases when common sense prevails. In other words, as soon as the people in Colorado Springs know—from *any* reliable source—that an American city has been nuked, they will send out an encoded message to the missile silos that have been designated as Wild Fire response sites, and to naval operations in Norfolk and Pearl Harbor, who will contact the submarine fleet. These subs and silos will be given a pre-launch command. Wild Fire calls for a thirty-minute interval between pre-launch and launch."

Wolffer made eye contact with each man. "During this time, the people in Colorado Springs will await any encrypted message from the president that may modify or cancel the launch."

Landsdale said, "I thought the president couldn't cancel the Wild Fire response."

Wolffer replied, "He can, but only if he has overwhelming evidence that the nuclear attack did not originate from Islamic terrorists. And he's got only thirty minutes to come up with this. And if he's on the Marine helicopter, flying to a secure location, there is less chance of him receiving such information. As we discussed earlier, there is a strong presumption of guilt against Islamic terrorists, especially since 9/11. In effect, these nuclear devices will appear to have Al Qaeda's fingerprints all over them. Lacking any other evidence, such as that the attack was initiated by North Korea, for instance, or, as wildly improbable as this sounds, some domestic group that knows of Wild Fire"—he smiled—"Wild Fire targets the land of Islam. In effect, we shoot first and ask questions afterward. If we were wrong about the source of the attack, we've still accomplished a worthwhile goal."

Madox said, "It's my understanding from Paul that this president will not attempt to cancel Wild Fire."

Paul Dunn responded, "The president was again briefed on Wild Fire, right after 9/11, and very recently on the one-year anniversary. He seems comfortable with this and understands that all he has to do is nothing."

Wolffer said, "If Colorado Springs has heard nothing from the president after thirty minutes, then that silence is an order to launch. So within, say, an hour of the nuclear attack on America, we will have accomplished the nuclear obliteration of those responsible."

Landsdale pointed out, "I hope not. *We* are responsible."

Madox didn't see the humor and replied, "No, Scott, the Islamic extremists are ultimately responsible for the destruction of their homeland. They've been fucking around with us for too long, and if you play with fire, you get radiation burns."

Landsdale commented, "Whatever makes you feel

good." He asked Madox, "What are the logistics of getting these suitcase bombs to where they belong?"

"I have two Citation jet aircraft, which are unfortunately not here at the moment, but I've contacted the pilots, and the aircraft are inbound to the Adirondack Regional Airport. Sometime tomorrow, or Monday the latest, when Mikhail tells me that the nukes are hot, the pilots and co-pilots will transport the four suitcases in two Jeeps to the airport and put them aboard my two aircraft." Madox glanced at the black suitcase and said, "They're called suitcase bombs, but, as you can see, they don't look like anything you've ever seen from American Tourister or Samsonite, so before they're out in public, we'll put each of them in a wardrobe trunk with a carbon steel padlock." He continued, "Then, the pilots and co-pilots will fly to two different cities, where they'll take a taxi to designated hotels—with their suitcases—and await further instructions."

Landsdale asked, "Can you trust these guys?"

"They've been with me for a long time, and they're all former military. They follow orders."

"Will they be told when to leave their rooms?"

Madox replied, "Unfortunately, they'll still be in the rooms when the suitcases detonate. Obviously, they don't know what's in the suitcases, but they know the contents are valuable and can't be left unattended."

Harry Muller listened to all this. He'd lost track of the body count a while ago, but he knew his chances of getting out of there alive just dropped a few more points below zero.

He stretched his ankle shackles, then pushed his foot down on the chain. He realized he wasn't going to break the shackles, but his hands were free, and assuming none of these men were armed, maybe he could break out. Harry glanced furtively at the door, then the curtained windows.

Madox noticed and said to him, "Are we boring you? Do you have someplace to go?"

Harry replied, "Fuck you."

Paul Dunn said, "Bain, we don't need him here any longer, if we ever did."

Madox replied, "I'm afraid this is the best place for Mr. Muller for now. We don't want him speaking to the guards and upsetting them with crazy talk about nuclear bombs." He looked at Muller, then said to the others, "I have a sedative on the way here. Mr. Muller needs to be asleep until Tuesday."

No one responded, except Harry, who said to the other four men, "This bastard is going to kill me. You understand that?"

No one spoke, or looked at Harry, except Scott Landsdale, who patted Harry on the shoulder. "No one is going to hurt you."

Harry pushed Landsdale's arm away and snapped, "You're all fucking murderers."

Madox interjected, "Harry, you're getting yourself worked up for no reason. Maybe you need that sedative now. Or do you want to shut up and hear the rest of this?"

Harry didn't answer, and Madox said to his Board, "As I was saying, the pilots and co-pilots will remain at their posts, and sometime on Tuesday, when Paul tells me the president and first lady are dining in the White House, I'll activate the ELF transmitter here and send the coded radio signal that will detonate all four nuclear devices." He continued, "By the time the president has finished his salad, he'll have gotten the terrible news, and the clock will begin ticking toward Wild Fire as the president and the first lady are flown by helicopter to a secure destination." He asked, "Are any of you designated to be evacuated with him?"

Paul Dunn replied, "I am, but only if I happen to be close by."

"Well," Madox observed, "you can't be much closer than at the same dinner table."

General Hawkins cleared his throat and said to Madox, "I know we once discussed the placement of the nuclear devices, but now that the time is here, I'd like to know specifically what you have in mind. You mentioned two cities, but we have four nuclear devices."

Bain Madox said, "As I indicated, these are low-yield weapons, and perhaps not as reliable as we'd like. So, in consultation with Mikhail, the plan is to place two suitcases in each of two cities. This is so that if one doesn't detonate, we still have the other to rely on. If both detonate at maximum yield, we have a nicer explosion."

He looked around the table and continued, "So for instance, if we pick, say, San Francisco as one city, then the pilot checks into one hotel with one suitcase, and the co-pilot checks into another nearby hotel with the other suitcase. Now we have two ground zeros, which will be within the total destruction radius of each other so that if only one device goes off, it will obliterate the hotel of the other. This is important so that afterward an unexploded suitcase—and a stunned pilot—are not found in a hotel room that can be traced back to . . . well, me. In other words, one explosion will destroy the evidence of a possible dud bomb—and the pilot—in another location. If neither device detonates, then I will call my pilots with further instructions."

General Hawkins asked, "How reliable, exactly, are those devices?"

Madox replied, "Mikhail has assured me that each device is over ninety percent reliable as to detonation. Regarding their maximum design yield, we won't know until they detonate." He explained, "As I said, they're old—about 1977 vintage—and because they're mini-nukes, they're actually more sophisticated and complex than, say, a one-megaton atomic warhead. But they have been maintained by Mikhail, who tells me the design is good, and the detonating device and plutonium core are in excellent condition."

General Hawkins commented, "Weapons, especially nuclear weapons, are the one area in which the Soviets excelled." He smiled and added, "During the Cold War, we used to joke that we didn't have to worry about Soviet suitcase nuclear bombs because the Soviets didn't have the technology to build a suitcase."

A few men chuckled, and Madox glanced at the suitcase. "It *does* look a little ratty." He laughed, then stared at each man. "And now, perhaps the most difficult decision we need to make—one that we've never really discussed in any detail—but the time has come. What two American cities need to be sacrificed so that America and the world will be free of Islamic terror? Gentlemen?"

CHAPTER THIRTEEN

Bain Madox hit a button on his console, and the map on the screen changed from the world of Islam to a map of the United States. He said, "Forget that you are Americans. Put yourselves into the mind of an Islamic terrorist. You are able to destroy two American cities. Which two will most please Allah?"

Madox lit a cigarette and watched the smoke rise in front of the illuminated map of the United States.

He said, "Well, then, I'll begin. If I were an Islamic terrorist, my first and second choices would be New York and Washington. *Again.* But I'm not really an Islamic terrorist, so Washington is not on our list. And New York will not be on our list either because of the stock exchanges, and its vital importance to the world economy, plus the fact that I believe we all—including Mr. Muller—have friends and family in the New York area."

Landsdale said, "And don't forget your Park Avenue apartment, Bain."

"Scott, I have many assets in many cities. That's not a consideration. The only thing we will consider are loved ones in the cities which we target. If necessary, we may need to get some people out of a targeted city on some pretext. But we'll cross that bridge if we come to it."

Landsdale inquired, "Where does your ex-wife live?"

Madox replied in an annoyed tone, "Palm Beach. Not a likely Islamic target for nuclear destruction."

Landsdale smiled and pointed out, "If I was paying *your* alimony, I could make a strong case for it."

Madox said, "All right, I think we need to remove *all* East Coast cities from the potential target list. A nuclear detonation in any city along the Boston-Baltimore corridor would have serious consequences for the national economy, which is something we need to avoid. On the other hand, as I said, we need to give the illusion that this is an Islamic attack."

Harry Muller listened as the five men spoke about what two American cities were to be nuked. As they got into it, they started to sound like businessmen thinking of closing a plant in one city or another. This was so unreal that Harry himself began to forget what they were actually talking about.

Bain Madox said, "I think we have to seriously consider Detroit. The city is dead anyway, it has a large Muslim population, and it's right next to Canada, which has become a pacifist and socialist pain in our ass. This might be a good signal to send to our Canadian allies."

Edward Wolffer responded, "Detroit may be high on *our* list, but for the reasons you just pointed out, Bain, it would not be high on the list of any Islamic terrorist group."

"I know, but it's such a tempting target."

Landsdale reminded him, "Think like a Muslim terrorist. I say Miami, with its large Jewish population. The city has some economic importance as a port and a tourist destination, but we can do without it. Also, we can make a preemptory strike against some of those confused electoral votes, before the next election."

Someone laughed, then Paul Dunn said, "There's a large Cuban population in Miami that is very supportive of . . . some of the administration's policies. They'll be helpful when we address the Cuba problem."

Everyone nodded, and General Hawkins suggested, "Disney World. Haven't there been Islamic threats against Disney World?" He looked around the quiet table and continued, "It's a perfect target. No industry, no vital economic or military value. Far from the population centers . . ."

Bain Madox stared at General Hawkins. "Are you suggesting that we kill Mickey Mouse?"

Everyone laughed.

Madox continued, "Minnie, Goofy . . . who else? Jim, that's just . . . cruel. Not to mention the children." He added, "We're not monsters."

Harry Muller wasn't too sure about that. Yet, these guys didn't fit his criminal profile of psychopaths, sociopaths, or just plain crazy and violent men. It began to dawn on Harry that these guys were mostly normal, educated, and successful guys with good jobs, families, friends, and people who looked up to them. The closest he could come to getting a handle on these guys was to compare them to Irish Republican Army men he'd had dealings with. Mostly normal, but filled with hate and all charged up for their cause. So, nothing they did was wrong—like the IRA guy he'd interrogated once who ordered a tuna fish sandwich for lunch because it was Friday during Lent. And back in Belfast, he'd shot two policemen in cold blood. Guys like this were scarier than street criminals.

Bain Madox was speaking. "Chicago is also too vital to the U.S. economy, and it has no special significance to an Islamic terrorist. Look, let's cut to the chase. I have three excellent candidates—Los Angeles, San Francisco, and Las Vegas. Sodom, Gomorrah, and . . . what?"

Landsdale said helpfully, "Babylon."

"Thank you. First, San Francisco. Some economic importance, but that's outweighed by the fact that this city is a festering, pus-filled boil on the ass of America. A left-wing loony hotbed of sexual deviancy, anti-American values, political correctness, defeatism, and pacifistic appeasement."

Landsdale said, "Why don't you tell us what you really think of San Francisco?"

Madox ignored him and asked, "Can anyone here make a case for *not* putting San Francisco on the target list?"

Edward Wolffer replied, "Well, I can. For one thing, my daughter lives there, though I can get her to fly out tomorrow on the pretext of an illness in the family. But also, it's a . . . well, an architecturally beautiful city. And

I think, in the new America, San Francisco can either be redeemed or, if not, just looked at as a curiosity—sort of a social laboratory. It would be interesting to see how that city reacts to two other American cities being destroyed, followed by the destruction of much of the Islamic world."

Everyone thought about that, then Madox said, "I'm not interested in their reaction or redemption. I'm more interested in their vaporization."

Paul Dunn warned, "That's a very egotistical and prejudiced attitude, Bain. This is not about your personal opinion of San Francisco, which would not be a high-priority target for Islamic extremists. There have been no specific threats against that city—"

"Why should there be?" snapped Madox. "If I were an Islamic terrorist, or a Marxist, or Osama bin Laden himself, the last place in the world I'd threaten is the friendly city of San Francisco."

"That," said Wolffer, "is exactly why this city should not be a target."

Madox seemed irritated that his own arguments were being turned against him, and he slapped his hand on the table and said, "San Francisco goes on the short list."

Landsdale asked, "Bain, are you chairing this meeting, or taking it over?"

Madox took a deep breath and replied, "I apologize for my management style. But this isn't a government committee. It's an Executive Board meeting that needs to make some quick, hard, and final decisions. Your contributions are valuable, and your actions on Tuesday will be invaluable to the success of Wild Fire. While I need a consensus, we also need direction and clarity." He added, "As Friedrich Nietzsche wrote, 'The most common form of human stupidity is forgetting what one is trying to do.'"

Landsdale said, "Thank you. I think we know what we're trying to do—start a one-sided nuclear war by giving the illusion that we were attacked. This shouldn't be too difficult." He added, "If you recall, many people in Sandland accused us of attacking the World Trade Center and the Pentagon so we could retaliate against them. They get the concept, even if they were wrong that time. This time, they're going to be right. But we need to pick the targets that are just right so that hopefully no one—at least for a few hours—will believe that we did this to ourselves so that we could do it to them. So, let's be rational and smart about the targets." He smiled. "That's what Nietzsche would say."

Bain Madox ignored this and continued, "The next two cities to consider are Los Angeles and Las Vegas. Let's look at LA first. It's an economic powerhouse, but the city is so huge that I don't think two five-kiloton nuclear devices will cause much more damage or dislocation than one of their periodic earthquakes or riots. Therefore, I'd like to specifically target the area of Hollywood and Beverly Hills. Do I need to give my reasons?"

General Hawkins said, "I think we're all on the same page with this one."

Madox nodded. "And keep in mind that there have been very specific threats and public statements made by the Islamic jihadists against Hollywood. They seem to think the place is a cesspool of moral corruption. That's not very liberal minded, and I'm embarrassed to admit I agree with them."

A few men chuckled.

Madox glanced at a note on the table and said, "A gentleman named Suleiman Abu Ghaith, an official spokesman for bin Laden, has said, quote, 'America, with the collaboration of the Jews, is the leader of corruption and the breakdown of values, whether moral, ideological, political, or economic corruption. It disseminates abomination and licentiousness among people by way of the cheap media." Madox added, "There may be something lost in the translation, but I believe he was speaking of Hollywood."

Again, there were a few chuckles.

Madox hit some keys on his console, and a map of Los Angeles appeared on the screen. He said, "This is a sprawling urban area, and if we focus in on Hollywood"— he enlarged a section of the map and continued—"and nearby Beverly Hills, we see that the blast radius of our two nukes would barely overlap. Which presents the problem of this getting back to us if one of the nukes doesn't go off. But I believe we need to take a risk here because the rewards are so great."

Paul Dunn spoke. "Somehow, I think this *will* get back to us, one way or another. Bain, we'll have one or two ground zeros that can be identified as hotels, and sometime down the road, the FBI will obtain a list of everyone who was staying at those hotels. Eventually, the guest lists of those four hotels will reveal the names of your four pilots, and further investigation will reveal their

flight plans and landings at the airports of those cities. I
don't believe the FBI—or the CIA—is going to think this
was a coincidence."

Madox thought a moment, then looked at Harry
Muller. "Harry, what do you think?"

"I think you're out of your fucking minds."

"We know that. I'm looking for a professional opinion." He added, "Please."

Harry hesitated, then said, "If I were working the
case, it would take me less than a week to put all this together. You start with the scene of the crime—the hotels
that are ID'd as ground zero—then you go to the guest
lists kept on a reservation computer someplace else, then
you work the lists twenty-four-seven, until something
starts to connect."

Madox asked, "Would it make a difference if my pilots
check into the hotels with false names and bogus credit
cards?"

"Yeah . . . but—"

"Well, that's the plan, Harry. That's the plan, Paul. I'm
not that stupid."

Harry, trying to introduce some element of doubt,
asked, "Is it a coincidence that you have two aircraft in
the cities that are nuked, and that you're missing four pilots after the attacks?"

"Do you know how many coincidences there were in
the Twin Towers?" Madox replied. "The risk, if any, of this
being traced back to us, with a million dead, is insignifi-
cant and acceptable. And you know what? If the FBI does
come knocking on my door, they'll probably be there to
congratulate me."

Harry replied, "You'll all end up in jail."

Madox ignored that and continued, "And if the FBI, or anyone in the government, concludes that the Custer Hill Club had something to do with these attacks on America that led to the launch of Wild Fire, do you think they're going to announce this to the world? What will they say? 'Sorry, we made a little boo-boo.' Followed, of course, by an expression of regret for the two hundred million dead Muslims, and a sincere apology to the shell-shocked survivors, along with a promise that it won't happen again."

That seemed to make sense to everyone, and Madox said, "Let's continue. I've done some work on targeting Los Angeles, and I've determined that the best hotels for the pilot and co-pilot to check into would be the Beverly Wilshire in Beverly Hills and the Hollywood Roosevelt Hotel." He explained, "I will reserve a room for them in each hotel with a bogus credit card, and request a room on the highest floor, which offers the best view and, not incidentally, the best altitude for detonation. Also, the higher up you go, the less likely it will be for a roving NEST team to pick up any gamma rays or ambient neutrons." He looked at Harry and asked, "Correct?"

"Yeah, don't worry about it, Bain. The NEST teams are useless anyway. Remember?"

Landsdale laughed, but no one else did.

Madox seemed about to say something unpleasant to Harry, but instead he continued, "If I calculate correctly, and if the nukes yield their maximum power, the rings of destruction should overlap. The area of complete and partial destruction in Beverly Hills will rid us of a good number of untalented movie stars, overpaid studio executives, and various other limousine liberals." He asked, rhetorically, "How good is *that*?"

Landsdale commented, "I hope Demi Moore doesn't live in the area."

"I'll get you a Hollywood star map, Scott. Okay, the second area of destruction, Hollywood, encompasses several moviemaking facilities, including Paramount Studios, Warner Studios, as well as the ABC-TV studio. And as an extra bonus, we get the headquarters of the Screen Actors Guild." Madox said, "I think we'll all be watching old DVDs and reruns for a while."

A few men smiled politely.

Paul Dunn said, "Los Angeles is one of the most vitally important cities in the country, with a metro area population of over fifteen million people. If you detonate two nuclear devices to destroy Hollywood and Beverly Hills, it will cause chaos and panic in the city. Millions of people will attempt to flee, and the results will be catastrophic."

Madox replied, "Paul, you put a pessimistic spin on everything. Be positive. Think of this as solving the problem of undocumented aliens. They all know which way Mexico is."

Dunn pointed out, "That's a racist remark."

Madox made an expression of mock contrition and said, "Terribly sorry. And I do see your point. In fact, I own extensive oil storage and refining facilities in south LA. But I'm optimistic that things will be back to what passes for normal there within a year. More important, the Islamics *really* want to destroy Hollywood. So, this target goes on the short list."

Everyone nodded.

Madox continued, "Last, but not least, Las Vegas." He hit a few keys, and an aerial view of Las Vegas at night appeared on the screen. Madox said, "To me, this is the *perfect* target. A drug-infested den of iniquity, and a moral wasteland, populated by scam artists, godless men, loose women—"

"Hold on," Landsdale interrupted. "Some of us like loose women."

Madox replied, "I'm giving you the Islamic view-point." He returned to his subject. "This is a one-industry town, and while I've been known to engage in casino gambling, I can find someplace else to lose my money. In any case, I see no downside to leveling a piece of this place. It's far from other population centers, and it's at the top of the Islamic hit list, so it should be at the top of ours."

The four men nodded.

Madox motioned toward the view of Las Vegas, an oasis of sparkling lights surrounded by dark desert and black hills. He said, "Actually, there may be an economic upside to nuking this place. The city is growing too fast, and it's using too much electricity and too much scarce water."

No one responded.

Madox continued, "What I propose is one suitcase bomb in a tall hotel along the strip—maybe Caesars Palace, right in the center of the strip—and another in the downtown area. This should take out all the casinos but leave the surrounding suburbs intact." He pointed out, "The suburbs happen to be heavily Republican." He smiled, hit a key, and the screen went blank.

The room lights brightened, and Madox said, "So, I believe we have three candidates for two positions. Shall we vote?"

Paul Dunn answered, "I think it would be difficult for us to . . . to actually choose the two cities that will suffer nuclear devastation. I mean, we've chosen three . . . but it may be easier for us if we just draw ballots for the final two."

Madox looked at each man, and each nodded in agreement. He tore off three strips of paper from the legal pad in front of him and wrote the names of each city on the strips, then held up the names so everyone could see them, and said, "So you don't think I've written San Francisco twice." He grinned, folded the papers into quarters, then put them in an empty coffee mug. He slid the mug down the length of the table and said, "Harry, you're God. Pick Sodom and Gomorrah."

"Go to hell."

"Then let's do it the other way—pick the city that *won't* get nuked." He added, "God will guide your hand."

"Eat shit."

Landsdale seemed impatient and picked up the mug. He drew two ballots, then lit them with his cigarette lighter and threw the burning papers in his ashtray. Everyone stared at the burning ashtray, then Landsdale said, "Those are the two losers in the National Nuclear Lottery." He drew the last folded ballot out of the mug and said, "The city that will escape nuclear destruction is—"

"Don't look at it," Madox instructed. "Put it in your pocket and show it to us later. I don't want anyone to be disappointed, disconcerted, or distracted during this meeting."

Landsdale put the name of the city that would be spared in his pocket and said to Harry, "Now you won't know until it's over."

Harry didn't think he'd ever know.

CHAPTER FOURTEEN

Harry Muller listened as the five men discussed the final details of Project Green and Wild Fire.

Somewhere, deep down in his heart, Harry Muller agreed that 122 nukes exploding across Sandland might not be a bad thing. It was the 4 nukes in America that really bothered him, and it seemed to be bothering Wolffer, Hawkins, Dunn, and Landsdale, too. But they were dealing with it. He heard Madox say, "If I could have picked our time, I'd have liked to nuke LA during the Academy Awards."

Actually, Harry thought, *Madox is dealing with it* too *well.*

General Hawkins returned to the happier subject of Wild Fire and said almost wistfully, "Coincidentally, at about the time of the Academy Awards, the huge lake behind the Aswân High Dam would be at full flood level."

Bain Madox nodded and said, "Well, thanks to Mr. Muller, we don't have the luxury of picking our time." He looked at Harry, then continued, "Even though the stars, the moon, and the planets will not be aligned on Tuesday, I think that Mr. Muller's arrival here was a sign from God that we needed to shit or get off the pot." He warmed to his subject and said, "Things don't have to be perfect to launch a hundred nukes. The nukes themselves create their own perfect world. They are transcendental. Divine."

Scott Landsdale asked Madox, "Bain, before you were rich and powerful, did anyone ever use the word crazy in the same sentence with your name?"

Madox poured a glass of water while he stared at Landsdale. Finally, he said, "Sometimes I get carried away on the subject of Wild Fire. I mean, it's not often in the history of the human race that an overwhelming problem has a simple solution. It's even more rare when fate has put that solution into the minds and hands of a few good men. This excites me."

No one, not even Scott Landsdale, responded.

Madox continued, "A few more operational details. First, you should all plan on leaving sometime tomorrow. The rest of the club members will leave Monday, as planned. I've arranged transportation for church services tomorrow morning—"

Harry said, "I'd like to go to church."

Madox looked at him and said, "You'll be sleeping late." He paused. "It goes without saying that no one here will discuss the agenda of this closed executive session of the Board with any other members. You must act natural and look normal. As you may know, Steve Davis lives in San Francisco, and Jack Harlow and Walt Bauer live in the LA area. Do not look at any of them like they're about to die." He added, "Actually, none of us knows yet what two cities we've chosen, so that should help you."

No one said anything.

Madox suggested, "If your acting ability is not up to the situation, say that we were talking about the coming war with Iraq, which is indeed worrisome. And please watch your drinking. Understood?"

Everyone nodded.

Madox continued, "As for communication, we all have untraceable cell phones, just as the drug dealers have, and we'll use only those phones. Plus, as you know, I have my own cell relay tower here with a voice scrambler. But call only if and when I need to hear from you." He added, "Most of what I need to know about Project Green, I can see on an all-news station." He thought a moment, then went on, "Sometime around the dinner hour, every radio and TV station in America—except for those in the two cities—will become part of the Emergency Broadcast System."

No one said anything, and Madox continued, "About an hour later, I expect to hear a news flash about the American nuclear response to the nuclear attacks on America. Is that right, Paul? Ed?"

Ed Wolffer replied, "Yes, Wild Fire will be announced to the nation and the world. There's no reason to keep it secret since it's hard to keep a massive missile launch and one hundred twenty-two nuclear detonations a secret for very long." He added, "At some point during the evening, the president will address the nation from his secure location and reveal the existence of Wild Fire. Hopefully, this will have a calming effect on the country. If nothing else, it's good for national morale."

"Well," said Bain Madox, "it's good for *my* morale. After 9/11, everyone was depressed when we didn't respond immediately, but this time, Americans can't accuse the government of being overly cautious."

General Hawkins responded, "True, but this time we'll get a lot of flack for overreacting."

"This time, Jim," Madox said, "the world and the media will sit in awed silence. You won't hear a peep. Not a fucking peep."

The Board members nodded, and so did Harry.

Madox said, "It should be an interesting night. I'll stay here, obviously, to send the ELF signal that will detonate the devices." Again, he went to the suitcase standing upright on the floor and put his hands on the black leather. He stared at each man and said, "*I*, gentlemen, will push the nuclear button, which will devastate two American cities with four nuclear devices, and when I do that, I will ask God's forgiveness. *You* will see to it that Wild Fire is launched as a retaliatory response."

General Hawkins asked, "How long after Tuesday will you stay here, Bain?"

Madox returned to his seat and replied, "I don't know. Why?"

"Well, understand that there will be a lot of panic in America when the nukes detonate in the cities. People will figure, if the enemy has a few nukes, he might have more. The cities will start to evacuate, which will cause chaos and, unfortunately, some injuries and deaths. Our family members and friends are at some risk . . . and I can't and won't be calling people I know all over America telling them to stay put and remain calm. We can only hope that the retaliatory strike—the obliteration of Islam—will calm people down. But in the meantime—"

"Jim, what's your point?"

"Well . . . now that the hour has actually arrived . . . I'm thinking . . . and I guess we're all thinking of the reality of what's going to happen."

Madox replied, "I know this is all so sudden, Jim, but it's the kind of thing you needed to think about after 9/11 when we began planning Project Green."

"Yes, I know. But I'm thinking now of you staying up here in God's country while we four are in Washington, and our friends and family are scattered all over the country, which is in a state of chaos. Where will your family be?"

"Wherever they are, they are. I'm not making any calls." He added, "My children don't return my calls anyway."

"That's your decision. But I think you need to get back to New York as soon as possible after this happens."

"Why?"

Hawkins replied, "To share the experience, Bain."

"All right . . . I'll do my best to get into New York as soon as possible. But I do need to destroy and dispose of the ELF transmitter, just in case anyone shows up here with a search warrant. That's *my* job. *Your* job, gentlemen, is to stay in Washington—or the designated secure location—to influence events. Agreed?"

Everyone nodded.

Harry again scanned the faces around the table. It seemed like reality was starting to sink in. Again, he was reminded of the radical groups he'd investigated over the years. They bullshitted everything to death because, deep down inside, most of them really didn't want to risk their lives to plant a bomb, shoot a cop, rob a bank, or kidnap anyone. Now and then—when they had a Bain Madox in charge—some of their bullshit turned into action. And in half those cases, someone in the group ratted out the plan to the cops, or turned himself in after the crime to work out a deal.

Harry looked at each face around the table. Maybe, now that the time had come, one of these guys would come to his senses before Tuesday. The president's adviser, Dunn, looked a little shaky, and he might blow the whistle. The general was a little shaky, too, but Harry knew the type—he'd go along, then maybe blow his brains out afterward. The defense guy, Wolffer, was committed to the program, and he wasn't going to budge.

And then there was Landsdale. Harry remembered Ted Nash, Corey's CIA nemesis, now deceased. Corey had once said about Nash, "The best you can say about a CIA officer is that they lie to everyone equally." If Landsdale had sat there agreeing with everything, Harry would have suspected him of being a double. But Landsdale gave Madox a lot of shit, so Landsdale was probably loyal to the program, even if he wasn't loyal to Madox. Harry thought that Madox understood this, but he must have trusted Landsdale, or the guy wouldn't be here. In fact, Harry could sense that Landsdale was actually in tighter with Madox than the others were.

And then there was Madox himself. Here was a guy who had everything, but something was driving him to risk it all. It wasn't really about oil, or money, or power. It was about hate, like it always is with these guys, like it was with bin Laden, Hitler, Stalin, and all the people Harry had interrogated and arrested since he'd gotten into anti-terrorism. And it was a little bit about crazy, too, which led to the hate. Or was it the other way around?

Madox looked at Harry as though he knew that Harry Muller was thinking unkindly of him and asked, "Did you want to say something, other than 'fuck you'?"

"Yeah. As a Federal law enforcement officer, I want to remind everyone that conspiracy to commit murder is a crime—"

Madox interrupted, "We're talking about *war*, Detective Muller, not murder. Generals sometimes sacrifice troops—and even civilians—so that other troops can live to fight again."

"Bullshit."

Madox waved his hand in dismissal and turned his attention back to his Board members. "Gentlemen, on September 11, 2001, nineteen Islamic hijackers who had no good reason to do us harm, and who were not of the caliber of you men sitting around this table, carried through with *their* plan. Not one of them deserted, or informed on the others—and they went willingly to their deaths. I'm not asking any of us to sacrifice our lives—I'm only asking that we, as patriotic Americans, do no less to our enemies than our enemies did to us." He concluded, "If *they* can do it, we *must* do it."

A few heads nodded.

Madox said, "I'd like each of you, at this time, to give a yea or a nay to Project Green." He turned to the deputy secretary of defense. "Ed?"

Ed Wolffer stood and said, "Gentlemen, what we are about to do takes courage and resolve, which is in no short supply here. And I believe that each one of us knows in his heart that what he is doing is necessary and right." He paused, then continued, "This is not a time for us to think of ourselves and the personal risks we're taking. It is a time to stick our necks out for our country—the way our men and women in uniform do every day." He concluded, "I vote to implement Project Green."

General Hawkins also stood and said, "As a military man, I have taken an oath to uphold and defend the Constitution, as you all have. I have also taken an oath to obey the commander in chief. I take these oaths seriously, and after much thought, I've decided that I can, in good conscience, vote to go ahead with Project Green."

Paul Dunn got to his feet and said, "I wish this hadn't been forced on us with so little time to fine-tune our plan, but we have to play the hand we've been dealt. I vote to go ahead."

Scott Landsdale remained seated and said, "I have a strong feeling that this is the only chance we're going to get. Harry Muller was not sent here to watch birds. Our best defense against any further government interest in our activities—and possible conspiracy charges—is to take the offensive. If we don't use the nukes, we'll lose the nukes." He said, "I vote yes."

Bain Madox stood and stared silently at the far wall, deep in thought. Then he looked at his Board. "Thank you for your courage and your loyalty. Indeed, you are all soldiers in the service of civilization."

Harry said, "Good soldiers don't murder civilians. Did you murder civilians in Vietnam? Is that what they gave you the Silver Star for?"

Madox glared at Harry and for the first time showed anger. "Shut up. You are not to speak until spoken to. Understand?"

"One last thing—fuck you."

Bain Madox ignored him and began, "Gentlemen, we few men are the small army that can and will defeat the spread of Islamic fundamentalism and terror. We are but the latest, and perhaps the last, in a long line of good Christian men and women who have defended the faith and Western Civilization against Islam. Please be seated."

Madox hit a few keys, and a map of Europe and the Middle East appeared on the monitor. "The Spanish and the French—before they lost their balls—fought the Muslims in the West. The Crusaders brought the war to the Muslim heartland. The Christians in the Balkans fought the Turks for half a millennium."

He paused a moment, then continued, "Perhaps you've heard the story of the Polish king John, who, in the seventeenth century, when the Muslim hordes were poised to drive into the heart of Christian Europe, this man, without being asked by anyone, took his army from Poland and battled the Turks at the gates of Vienna."

Madox looked around the table to make sure everyone was listening and continued, "No one has asked us to save Western Civilization, but we see the danger, and we will do what needs to be done. I believe that the Holy Spirit is guiding our thoughts and our actions, just as God guided King John, who had little to gain and everything to lose by coming to the aid of his Christian brothers at Vienna. Because King John knew, gentlemen, that if he didn't stop the Turks at Vienna, then all of Europe would fall to Islam. And remember, no one else in Europe came to the aid of the beleaguered city—all of Europe chose to bury its head in the sand and pray that they would not be next. Sound familiar? But the Holy Spirit, gentlemen, entered the mind and heart of King John and told him what he had to do, told him that it was right and necessary, and that his victory over Islam would please God. And armed with the presence of the Holy Spirit, outmanned and outgunned, King John of Poland defeated the Muslim Turks and saved Christian Europe. This man neither asked for nor received any thanks or reward for all he'd done."

Landsdale asked, "Not even an oil lease?"

Bain Madox ignored him and continued, "We, gentlemen, are like King John. We are all that stands between Western Civilization and the enemy at the gates. God has led us to this place and this time for a purpose. By sacrificing two American cities—which, like Sodom and Gomorrah, aren't worth much anyway—we can prevent the enemy from destroying other American cities at *his* time and choosing. We are, in effect, saving Washington, New York, Seattle, Chicago, Atlanta, Dallas . . . Palm Beach . . . I want you all to understand and believe that, and to sleep easy tonight, and not be troubled in your hearts, your minds, or your souls."

He looked again at each man. "If Jesus Christ himself were here, he'd say, 'Strap on your brass balls, boys, and go for it.'"

The other four men glanced furtively at one another, but no one commented on Madox's speech, or his imagined message from Jesus Christ.

Bain Madox took a swig of water, which Harry was starting to suspect was straight vodka.

Madox concluded, "Okay, I've said my piece. Now, I ask you to bow your heads in silent prayer and ask the Lord for strength, guidance, and maybe a little absolution in case He has any problems with this." He called down the table, "You, too, Harry. Pray with us."

Bain Madox bowed his head in silence, then reluctantly the others followed.

Harry Muller prayed that one of these guys would come to his senses or lose his nerve, or maybe get a better divine message than Madox was getting.

After a minute, Madox said, "Amen," then said, "Cocktails start at five in the barroom, dress is casual. Poker in the game room, if anyone is interested. We have a new dartboard with Hussein's face on it. Dinner is at seven-thirty, tie and jacket, please. Use the fireplace for your notes on the way out. This Executive Board meeting is ended. Thank you for coming."

The four men gathered their things and quietly filed out of the room.

Bain Madox and Harry Muller stared at each other down the length of the table.

Madox said, "It's just you and me, Harry."

Harry Muller sized up the situation. If he could coldcock Madox, then the window was his best chance. But if he could talk to the two goons outside, and tell them what was going on, that might be better than making a run for it.

Madox asked him, "What are you thinking about?"

"I'm thinking I like this plan."

"Bullshit. Hey, how did I do?"

"Okay."

"Just okay?"

"You lost me with the King John thing." Harry guessed he could be on top of Madox in under three seconds, even with the shackles.

Madox said, "It troubles me that you don't get this. Do you want this fucking war on terrorism to go on until your grandchildren are old?"

"Look, pal, we have to take our hits, and we hit back. They're not going nuclear, so we don't have to go nuclear. You're missing the point of Wild Fire."

"No, I'm not. The point is, it works *too* well."

"Yeah, *that's* the fucking point."

"It's like this, Harry—if the mountain won't come to Mohammed, then Mohammed has to come to the mountain. Right?"

"Yeah, whatever." He grabbed the heavy metal ashtray that Landsdale had used and flung it at Madox, then jumped to his feet as Madox ducked to avoid the ashtray.

Harry covered the ten feet in less than two seconds, but Madox was already on his feet, backpedaling toward the wall. Harry moved as fast as he could with the shackles, but Madox moved faster and drew a gun from under his jacket.

Harry lunged at Madox, who fired at point-blank range. Harry stopped, confused that he didn't feel the bullet hit him, and aware that the gun had barely made a sound.

Bain Madox moved further away and both men stared at each other. Harry took a step toward Madox, but his legs felt heavy, and the room was starting to swirl.

Madox said, "You need to calm down."

Harry felt his legs buckling, and he dropped to his knees. He noticed something sticking out of his chest and put his hand on it.

"A tranquilizer dart," Madox said, "which we use for black bears. We're not allowed to kill them off-season."

Harry pulled the dart out of his chest and saw blood on the needle.

"And I'm also not allowed to kill a Federal agent, so you have to die some other way. Probably a hunting accident."

The door opened, and one of the guards asked, "Is everything all right, Mr. Madox?"

"Yes, Carl, it is. Please take Mr. Muller down to his room."

Another security guard appeared, and he and Carl came toward Harry.

Harry could barely stay upright on his knees, and the

room was getting darker, but he took a deep breath and said, "Nuclear . . ." He knew he had to stay motionless so that the tranquilizer in his bloodstream wouldn't act quickly. "They're going to . . . blow up . . . the suitcase . . ."

The security guards lifted him to his feet, and Carl stooped and got him in a fireman's carry, then walked toward the door.

Bain Madox stood by the door and said to Harry, "I actually like you. Good balls. And you did me a great service. So, no hard feelings."

Harry could barely understand what Madox was saying, but he managed to whisper, "Fuck you . . ."

"I don't think so." He told Carl, "Keep him sedated. I'll check him later."

They left, and Bain Madox shut the door. He was annoyed by the cigarette butts on the oriental rug and tidied up.

He then went to the black suitcase and ran his hands over the smooth, shiny leather. He whispered, "Please, God, let this work."

—PART VII—

Sunday
NORTH FORK, LONG ISLAND
& NEW YORK CITY

We have the right to kill four million Americans—two million of them children—and to exile twice as many and wound and cripple hundreds of thousands.

—Suleiman Abu Ghaith
Spokesman for Osama bin Laden,
May 2002

CHAPTER FIFTEEN

Kate and I made it down to breakfast on Sunday morning, and our fellow guests turned out to be no big surprise: the usual collection of cool oenophiles from Manhattan—in this case, three couples of indeterminate gender who took everything very seriously, like they were auditioning for National Public Radio. I couldn't tell if they knew one another, or who was with whom, or if they'd recently all met at an anti-testicle rally.

They were chatting and passing around sections of the *Sunday Times* as though they'd found sacred texts rolled up in their napkin rings.

We all did the intros, and Kate and I sat at the two empty places at the dining room table. The prison matron brought us coffee and orange juice and recommended the hot oatmeal for starters. I asked, "Do you have bagels?"

"No."

"I can't read the *Times* without a bagel. Hot oatmeal goes with the *Wall Street Journal*. Do you have a *Wall Street Journal*?"

Kate interrupted. "Hot oatmeal sounds fine, thank you."

My breakfast companions were commenting on little gems from the various sections of the *Times*—art, leisure, books, travel, and so forth. Did I call this or what?

Kate and I had finished a bottle of wine après sex, and I had a slight red-wine hangover, which was making me grumpy, and I wasn't contributing to the conversation, though Kate held up her end.

I was carrying my little Smith & Wesson off-duty piece in my ankle holster, and I was thinking about dropping my napkin and bringing up my gun and yelling, "Freeze! I'm a philistine! Shut up and eat your oatmeal!" But I know how Kate gets whenever I get silly.

Anyway, the conversation got around to the *Times* headline—RUMSFELD ORDERS WAR PLANS RE-DONE FOR FASTER ACTION—and my fellow guests all agreed that war with Iraq was inevitable, given the mind-set of the present administration.

If I was a betting man—which, actually, I am—I'd bet on January, or maybe February. But I'd probably get better odds if I bet on March.

One of the men, Owen, sensed that I wasn't paying close attention and asked me, "What do you think, John? Why does this administration want to go to war with a country that hasn't done us any harm?"

The question seemed slightly loaded, like the questions I ask of suspects, such as, "When did you stop beating your wife and start working for Al Qaeda?"

I replied to Owen, truthfully, "I think we can avoid a war by taking out Saddam and his psychopathic sons with a sniper team or a few cruise missiles."

There was a momentary silence, then one of the men, Mark, said, "So . . . you're not in favor of war . . . but you think we should kill Saddam Hussein?"

"That's how I'd do it. We should save the wars for when we need them."

One of the women, Mia, asked rhetorically, I think, "Do we ever need war?"

I asked her, "What would you have done after the World Trade Center and the Pentagon were attacked? Send the Dixie Chicks to Afghanistan on a peace tour?"

Kate said, "John likes to make provocative statements."

I thought I'd shut down the conversation, which was fine with me, but Mark seemed interested in me. "What line of work are you in, John?"

I usually tell people I'm a termite inspector, but I decided to cut through the bullshit, and I replied, "I'm a Federal agent with the Anti-Terrorist Task Force."

After a second of silence, Mark asked, "Really?"

"Really. And Kate is an FBI special agent."

Kate said, "We work together."

One of the ladies, Alison, remarked, "How interesting."

The third guy, Jason, asked me, "Do you think the threat level—we're up to Orange—is that real, or is it being manipulated for political reasons?"

"Gee, I don't know, Jason. What does it say in the *Times*?"

He persisted, "How real is the threat today?"

Kate replied, "The threat of terrorism in America is

very real. However, without giving away any classified information, I can say that we have no specific information about an imminent attack."

"Then why," asked Jason, "are we in condition Orange, which means high risk of terrorist attack?"

Kate answered, "This is just a precaution because of the one-year anniversary of 9/11."

"That's past," said Mark. "I think this is just a way of keeping the country in a state of fear so the administration can push its domestic security agenda, which is really a crackdown on civil liberties." He looked at me and asked, "Would you agree with that, John?"

"Absolutely. In fact, Mark, Special Agent Mayfield and I are out here to report on anti-government subversives, and I need to warn you that anything you say may be held against you in a military tribunal."

Mark managed a weak smile.

Alison said to me, "I think you're being provocative again."

"It must be my aftershave lotion."

Alison actually giggled. I think she liked me. Also, I strongly suspected she was the Friday-night screamer.

The third woman, Pam, asked both of us, "Have you ever arrested a terrorist?"

It seemed like a normal question, but by Pam's tone of voice, and the general context, it could be taken in another way, which is how Kate took it.

Kate responded, "If you mean an Islamic terrorist, no, but—" She stood and hiked up her pullover, exposing a long, white scar that began under her left rib cage and continued down to the top of her butt. She said, "A Libyan gentleman named Asad Khalil got me with a sniper rifle. He got John, too."

My scar was along my right hip, and short of dropping my shorts, I didn't see how I was going to show this in mixed company.

Kate pulled down her sweater and said, "So, no, I never arrested a terrorist, but I was shot by one. And I was at the Twin Towers when they were hit."

The room got a little quiet, and I thought maybe everyone was waiting to see my scar. I *did* have the three bullet holes from the Hispanic gentlemen that ended my NYPD career. Two holes were indecently located, but I had one in my chest that I could *say* was from the Libyan, because I really wanted to unbutton my shirt to show Alison my wound.

"John?"

"Huh?"

"I said, I'm ready to go."

"I smell sausage cooking."

"I want to get an early start."

"Right." I stood and said to everyone, "We're off to Plum Island. You know, the biological warfare research lab. There's, like, eight liters of anthrax missing, and we have to try to figure out where it went." I added, "That could be nasty if a crop duster sprays it over the vineyards, or—" I coughed twice and said, "Excuse me. So, have a nice day."

We left the quaint house and walked to my Jeep.

Kate said, "You're not supposed to say things like that."

"What?"

"You know what." She laughed, which she wouldn't have done before 9/11 or six months after. Now, as I said, she was a different woman, and she'd loosened up a lot and finally appreciated my rapier wit and sophisticated humor. She noted, "You are so fucking immature."

That wasn't exactly what I was thinking. We both got into the Jeep, and off we went.

She spoke in a deep bass voice, which I guess was an imitation of me. "There's, like, eight liters of anthrax missing."

"Do you have a cold?"

She continued, "That could be nasty if a crop duster sprays it over the vineyards." She coughed twice. "Excuse me. I think I have anthrax."

"I didn't say that."

"Where do you get this stuff?"

"I don't know. It just pops into my head."

"Scary."

"Anthrax is very scary."

"I mean, your head."

"Right. So, where to?" I asked.

"I know a great antique store in Southold."

"Let's go to church. It's cheaper."

"Southold. Make a left here."

So, we spent Sunday morning antiquing. I'm not a huge fan of antiques, which I think are mostly verminous chunks of rotten wood and unsanitary scraps of germ-infested fabric. I'd take my chances with anthrax before antiques.

Needless to say, we didn't buy anything. In fact, Kate

commented, "Why do I need to buy an antique? I'm married to one."

We had lunch in a diner where I finally got my bagel, plus the sausages and eggs I'd missed at breakfast.

After lunch, we hit a few more wineries, where we picked up a dozen bottles of wine that we could have bought in Manhattan for the same price, and then we stopped at a farm stand.

We rarely eat at home—she can't cook and neither can I, and I don't eat fruit or vegetables—but we bought a ton of this stuff with leaves and dirt on it, plus a fifty-pound bag of Long Island potatoes. I asked, "What are we going to do with all this crap?"

"You run over a deer, and I'll make hunter's stew."

That was actually funny. Why didn't I think of it?

We collected our belongings from the B&B, settled the bill, and started back to the city.

She asked me, "Did you have a good weekend?"

"I did. Except for breakfast."

"You need to talk to people with opposing views."

"I do. I'm married."

"Very funny." She asked, "Why don't we go upstate next weekend?"

"Good idea." Which reminded me to ask her, "What do you know about the Custer Hill Club? I didn't buy your last response."

She considered the question and the statement, then replied, "I know that you almost spent this weekend there."

"Meaning what?"

"Well . . . Tom Walsh asked me if I'd have an objection to him sending you there on a surveillance."

"Really? And you said?"

"I said, yes, I would object." She asked me, "How did you know about the Custer Hill Club?"

"From Harry Muller, who got the assignment."

"What did *he* tell you?"

"I'm asking the questions. Why didn't *you* tell me about this?"

"Tom asked me not to. But I *was* going to tell you."

"When?"

"Now. On the trip home."

"Yeah. Right. Why didn't you want me to go?"

"I was looking forward to getting away with you this weekend."

"I didn't know about that either, until about four-thirty, Friday."

"I'd been thinking about it."

"You were actually scrambling to find a place to stay on short notice." I informed her, "You're talking to *me*, darling. You can't bullshit a bullshitter who's also a brilliant detective."

She considered that. "Well . . . I just didn't like the sound of the assignment . . . so I told Tom we had plans, and then I needed to make plans."

I digested all of this and asked her, "What do you mean you didn't like the sound of the assignment?"

"I don't know . . . just instinct . . . something about Tom's demeanor . . ."

"Can you be more specific?"

"No, I can't . . . but thinking back on it, I may have read

too much into what he was saying. Also, I didn't want to be alone for the weekend."

"Why didn't you volunteer to come with me?"

"John, just drop it. I'm sorry I lied to you and sorry I didn't tell you sooner."

"Apology accepted, if you tell me what is the Custer Hill Club."

"I'm not sure. But Tom said it was a social and recreational club composed of rich and powerful men."

"I might have had a good time."

"You were supposed to take photographs of—"

"I know all that. What I don't know is why these men need watching."

"I really don't know. He wasn't going to share that information with me." She added, "You can assume they're politically conservative, and maybe radically so."

"That's not a crime."

"That's all I know."

I was on the Long Island Expressway now, heading west into the sinking sun. The Jeep smelled like a Korean produce market, and the wine was rattling around on the floor behind me.

I thought about what Kate had said, but I didn't have enough facts to draw any conclusions. A few things stuck out, however, such as the political orientation of the Custer Hill Club and the upscale membership. The crazies on the right who actually engage in criminal activities are almost always of the lower-class variety. Their clubhouse, if they have one, is a gas station or a shack in the woods. This group was apparently something quite different.

And that's about all I had at the moment, and if I was

smart, that's all I needed to know, and if I wanted to know more, I could ask Harry in the morning.

Kate said, "I think you're annoyed at me for not mentioning that Tom and I discussed sending you on the assignment."

"Not at all. I'm happy that my career is in such good hands. In fact, it's sort of touching to think of you and Walsh discussing if little Johnny should go away for the weekend."

"John—"

"Maybe you should have said it was okay with you, but he should check first with *his* wife to see if it was okay with her."

"Stop being an idiot."

"I'm just getting warmed up."

"Just drop it. It's totally unimportant. Go tell Walsh that I told you, and that you're not happy with his management style."

"That's exactly what I'm going to do."

"Don't be confrontational. Try being diplomatic."

"I'll be very diplomatic." I asked, "Can I put him in a headlock?"

We drove in silence awhile. I realized I should speak to Harry before I confronted Walsh in the morning. I dialed Harry's cell number on my hands-free phone.

Kate asked, "Who are you calling?"

"My emotional-stress counselor."

After six rings, Harry's voice came on the line. "This is Detective Harry Muller. At the tone, leave me a message and a phone number where I can reach you." Beep.

I said, "Harry, it's Corey. Kate wants to make hunter's

stew. I got potatoes, vegetables, and red wine. One of us has to run over a deer for the rest of the recipe. Call me ASAP."

I hung up and said to Kate, "That surveillance could have been a career builder, if I didn't get eaten by a bear."

"Maybe that's why Tom wanted you to go."

"To help my career, or get me eaten by a bear?"

"Do you have to ask?"

I smiled. We held hands, and she turned on the radio to an easy-listening station. We made small talk on the way back to the city.

As we approached the Midtown Tunnel, the lit skyline of Manhattan came into view. Neither Kate nor I commented on the missing Twin Towers, but we both knew what we were thinking.

I remember that one of my first coherent thoughts after the towers were hit was that a man who pulls a knife on you doesn't have a gun, and I recall saying to a cop next to me, "Thank God. This means they don't have a nuclear bomb."

The cop replied, "Not yet."

PART VIII

Monday
NEW YORK CITY

In America there are factions,
but no conspiracies.

—Alexis De Tocqueville
Democracy in America (1835)

CHAPTER SIXTEEN

I t was Columbus Day, a special day to celebrate a dead white male stumbling onto a continent on his way to someplace else. I've had similar experiences coming out of Dresner's bar.

We were dressed casually today; I had on comfortable loafers, black jeans, a sports shirt, and a leather jacket. Kate was also wearing jeans, with boots, a turtleneck, and a suede jacket. I said, "Your handbag doesn't match your holster."

"Well, then, I need to buy a new handbag today."

I should learn to keep my smart mouth shut.

Kate and I exited our apartment house on East 72nd Street, and Alfred, our doorman, hailed us a cab.

Holiday traffic in Manhattan was light, and we made good time down to 26 Federal Plaza.

It was a beautiful, clear, crisp fall day, and I hummed a few bars of "Autumn in New York."

Kate asked me, "Do you know if Tom Walsh will be in today?"

"No, but if you hum a few notes, I might recognize it."

"You're a jerk."

"I think that's well established."

The taxi driver, a fellow named Ziad Al-Shehhi, was speaking on his cell phone in Arabic.

I put my finger to my lips and leaned forward. I whispered to Kate, "He's talking to his Al Qaeda cell leader . . . he's saying something about Columbus Day sales at Bergdorf's."

She sighed.

Mr. Al-Shehhi signed off, and I asked him, "Do you know who Christopher Columbus is?"

He glanced in his rearview mirror and replied, "Columbus Circle? Columbus Avenue? Where you want to go? You say Federal Plaza."

"You never heard of the *Niña*, the *Pinta*, and the *Santa María*?"

"Sir?"

"Queen Isabella, for God's sake? Are you marching in the Columbus Day Parade?"

"Sir?"

"John. Stop it."

"I'm just trying to help him with his citizenship test."

"Stop it."

I sat back and hummed "Autumn in New York."

It being a Federal holiday, the Federal Anti-Terrorist Task Force was not fully open for business, but Kate had decided to go in anyway to keep me company and catch up on paperwork. We'd have lunch together, then she'd leave to catch the Columbus Day sales.

Even when we're working the same schedule, we don't always travel to work together. Sometimes, one of us takes too long with our makeup, and the other one gets impatient and leaves.

Kate had the *Times* in her briefcase, and I asked her for the Sports section, but she gave me Section A instead.

The front page headline read: RUMSFELD FAVORS FORCEFUL ACTIONS TO FOIL AN ATTACK. The story went on to explain that the U.S. needed to act early during the "pre-crisis period" to foil an attack on the nation. It seemed to me that if Saddam was reading the *Times*, he'd call his bookie and bet on an invasion in late January.

The other big story was the car bombing of a nightclub frequented by Westerners on the Indonesian resort island of Bali. This seemed to be a new front in the war of global terrorism. The death toll stood at 184 with more than 300 injured, the largest loss of life since September 11, 2001.

The *Times* acknowledged that the attack was probably the work of Islamic "extremists." Good guess. Good *New York Times* word, too. Why call them terrorists or murderers? That's so judgmental. Adolf Hitler was an extremist.

We weren't going to win the war on terrorism until we won the war of the words.

I turned to the *Times* crossword puzzle and asked Kate, "What's the definition of a moderate Arab?"

"I don't know."

"A guy who ran out of ammunition."

She shook her head, but Ziad laughed.

Humor really bridges the gap between different cultures.

Kate observed, "This is going to be a long day."

As it turned out, she was right.

CHAPTER SEVENTEEN

Harry wasn't at his desk when we got to 26 Federal Plaza at five to 9:00, and he wasn't there at 9:15, or 9:30. As per my last conversation with him, he was supposed to see Walsh today. Walsh was in, Harry was not.

The office was quiet for a change, and I counted three NYPD at their desks, and one FBI—Kate. Also, the command post center, elsewhere on the 26th floor, would be manned by at least one duty agent monitoring the phones, radios, and Internet. Hopefully, the terrorists were leaf watching in New England for the long weekend.

I called Harry Muller's cell phone at 9:45 and left a message, then I called his house in Queens and left a message on his answering machine. Then I beeped him, which, in this business, is official.

At five after 10:00, Kate came across the floor and said to me, "Tom Walsh wants to see us."

"Why?"

"I have no idea. Have you spoken to him yet?"

"No." Kate and I walked to Walsh's corner office. The door was open and we entered.

Walsh stood and met us halfway, which is usually a sign that you're not in deep doo. He motioned us to the round table near the window and we sat. The table was strewn with papers and folders, very unlike when Jack Koenig occupied this office.

On his big picture window, about where you could once see the Twin Towers, was a black decal showing the towers, with the words 9/11—NEVER FORGET!

It was, as I said, a nice fall day, like the one a year and a month ago when the attacks happened. If it weren't for the meeting at Windows on the World, Jack would probably have been here in his office and witnessed it as it happened. David Stein, too, would have seen it from his corner office. As it turned out, they saw it from much closer.

Tom Walsh began, "John, the computer security people inform me that you used your password to try to access a restricted file on Friday."

"That's right." I looked at Walsh. He was young to be the special agent in charge, about forty, black Irish, not bad-looking, and unmarried. He had the reputation of being a ladies' man, and also a teetotaler, making him an Irish queer—a guy who preferred women over whiskey.

He asked me, "What is your interest in that file?"

"Oh, I don't know, Tom. I couldn't get into it, so I don't know if I had any interest in it."

He stared at me, showing a little impatience, I thought.

I used to think I didn't like Jack Koenig's Teutonic style, and I thought I'd like Walsh, being half-Irish myself, but this was a case of the job shaping the man—nurture over nature or whatever.

He said, "What the hell is 'Iraqi Camel Club Weapons of Mass Destruction'?"

"Just me being silly." I glanced at Kate, but she wasn't amused, only confused.

"I see." He looked at Kate, his fellow FBI straight arrow, and asked her, "Did you mention that surveillance to John?"

"I did, but not until Sunday."

Walsh said to me, "So, Harry Muller mentioned it to you."

You *never* rat out a brother cop, so I replied, "Harry Muller? What's he got to do with the custard . . . ? What's it called?"

"All right . . . it's irrelevant, anyway."

"I agree. And while I'm here, can I make a formal complaint about you asking my wife for permission to send me on an assignment upstate?"

"I wasn't asking her *permission*. I was just extending both of you a courtesy. You're married, and I wanted to see if this interfered with any personal plans you had for the holiday weekend."

"Next time, ask me."

"Fine. Point made."

"Why did my name pop into your head?"

Walsh didn't seem to want to discuss this, but he replied, "Obviously, I thought you'd be the best man for the job."

"Tom, as you may know, the last rural surveillance I did was in Central Park, and I got lost for two days."

He smiled politely, then said, "Well, I was thinking more in terms of other aspects of the surveillance."

"Such as?"

"Well, for one thing, this surveillance involved trespassing on private land without a warrant, which is right up your alley. Also, this place—the Custer Hill Club—has good security, and there was a chance of the surveillance person being stopped and questioned by private guards, and I knew you could handle that." He informed me, "The members of this club are people with some political influence in Washington."

I was beginning to see why no one wanted to ask a judge for a search warrant. Aside from that, there seemed to be a disconnect between what Harry Muller told me—routine surveillance, file building, and so forth—and what Tom Walsh just said. Since Harry would not lie to me, I concluded that Harry had not been fully briefed by Walsh.

I said to Walsh, "So, bottom line, you needed a cop to take the fall if anything went wrong."

"That's totally not true. Let's move on." Tom Walsh looked at both of us and said, "We haven't heard from Harry Muller."

I had figured that's why we were all in his office, but I had hoped it wasn't. "Were you supposed to hear from him?"

"Only if there was a problem."

"Sometimes, Tom, when there's a problem, that's when you don't hear."

"Thank you for your insight. Okay, let me tell you

what I know." He began, "Harry Muller, as you know, left here before five P.M. Friday. He went to Tech Support, got what he needed, and went to the garage for his camper, which he'd taken to work in anticipation of this assignment. Jennifer Lupo happened to see him in the garage, they exchanged a few words, and that was the last person we know who saw him." He continued, "The next time he was heard from was a cell-phone call he made to his girlfriend, Lori Bahnik, at seven forty-eight A.M. Saturday morning."

There was a recording device on the table, and Walsh hit a button. Harry's voice said, "Hi, babe. It's your one and only. I'm up here in the mountains, so maybe I won't have good reception for very long. But I wanted to say hi, I got up here last night about midnight, slept in the camper, and now I'm on-duty, near the right-wing loony lodge. So don't call back, but I'll call you later from a landline if I can't reach you by cell phone. Okay? I still need to do something at the local airport later today or tomorrow morning, so I might need to stay overnight. I'll let you know when I know. Speak to you later. Love you."

Walsh commented, "So, we know he got there, and we know he was near the subject property. At nine-sixteen A.M., she called him back and left a message on his cell phone, which we recovered from the phone company." He hit the button again and Lori Bahnik's voice said, "Hi, honey. Got your message. I was sleeping. I'm going shopping today with your sister and Anne. Call me later. I'll have my cell with me. Okay? Let me know if you have to stay over. I love you, and I miss you. Be careful of those right-wing loonies. They like their guns. Take care."

I said to Walsh, "Obviously, you've spoken to her."

"Yes. This morning. She told me that at about four P.M. Saturday, she received a text message from Harry on her cell phone which said . . ." He glanced at a piece of paper on the table and read, " 'Sorry I missed your call—bad reception here—ran into some friends—fishing and hiking—see you Monday.' "

None of us raised the obvious point that the text message could have come from someone other than Harry. But apparently Lori thought it was from him because Walsh informed us, "She was not happy. She called him when she got the text message, and he didn't answer. She continued calling and leaving messages and also paged him four or five times. Her last message to him was Sunday evening. She described to me her messages as increasingly angry and emotional. She told him if he didn't return her calls, they were through."

I asked him, "At what point did her anger turn to worry?"

"At about ten P.M. Sunday night. She had the after-hours number here and called. She spoke to the FBI duty agent—Ken Reilly—and told him about her concern."

I nodded. I've gotten calls like that from girlfriends, boyfriends, husbands, and wives. You do the best you can to determine if there actually is a cause for concern. In about 100 percent of those cases, the loved one was not dead but would be when he or she got home.

Walsh continued, "Ken tried to reassure her, but girl-friends don't get same courtesy as a wife or family member, so he didn't offer much assistance. He did take her number and told her he'd call her back if he heard anything. He actually tried Harry's cell phone and beeper but got no response." Walsh added, "He wasn't concerned."

In truth, there was no reason why he should be, except for Harry's failure to answer his beeper. On the one hand, it was the weekend, and agents have been known to forget their beeper, or to be in, say, a loud bar or quiet bed where the beeper may not be noticed or acknowledged. On the other hand, Harry *was* on-duty. I said, "Maybe the problem is just bad reception."

Walsh nodded and continued, "When I got here at eight, I pulled up the weekend duty agent's reports and saw Ken Reilly's entry about Lori Bahnik and Harry Muller. I wasn't concerned, but I called Harry's cell phone, and house, and beeped him. Then I called Ms. Bahnik and spoke to her. Then, I made a few other calls, including one to the FBI field office in Albany. I asked the SAC in Albany, Gary Melius, to begin a missing-agent response, and he said he would, though I sensed he wasn't quite sure if Detective Muller was missing in action or missing on purpose. In any case, the SAC notified the state police, and they in turn were to notify the local police, who know the area but don't have a lot of manpower. They're checking local hospitals, but so far, no admissions under that name, and no unidentified admissions."

He looked at Kate and me, trying to determine, I guess, how this was playing with us and, by extension, how it was going to play when he related his immediate responses to people higher up the chain.

He continued, "The state police ran Harry Muller through DMV, and they have the make, model, color, and plate number of his camper. As of fifteen minutes ago, the vehicle hasn't turned up . . . but it's a huge wilderness, and it may take a while even if the vehicle is still in the area."

Kate asked, "Is his cell phone or beeper giving off any signals?"

"The phone company is still working on that. As of now, the answer is no."

As per my conversation with Harry, I knew he was supposed to be here this morning, but Walsh hadn't mentioned it yet, so I asked him, "Was Harry supposed to report to you today?"

"Yes. He was supposed to drop off his equipment and his digital camera disks to Tech no later than nine a.m., then see me for a debriefing."

"And yet, you're not quite at the point where you're worried."

"I'm concerned. But I wouldn't be surprised if he called right now or walked into this office."

"I would. Harry Muller would not miss a meeting with a supervisor."

Walsh didn't respond.

I wasn't too thrilled with Tom Walsh's laid-back management style, but new guys on the job needed to be careful not to call the director of the FBI to report that the sky was falling.

And, of course, there was the other dimension to this problem, which was the Custer Hill Club itself. If Harry Muller had been staking out Abdul Salami in the woods and disappeared, the response would have been very different.

Also, to be cynical, if Harry Muller was FBI and not NYPD, the response may have been a little quicker, holi-

day weekend notwithstanding. In fact, FBI Agent Ken
Reilly may have called Tom Walsh on Sunday night. Not
that the safety of a cop is less important than that of an
FBI agent; it has more to do with the unfortunate and
partly deserved reputation of New York's Finest being
free spirits.

I asked Walsh, "Do you think Harry's disappearance
is directly related to his assignment?"

Walsh had a ready answer. "I don't want to speculate
on the nature of his disappearance, but if I did, I'd say that
it's possible that Harry Muller met with an accident. There
are millions of acres of wilderness in that area, and it's possible that he's lost or hurt. He could have broken a leg,
stepped in a bear trap, or even been attacked by a bear. And
from what the Albany SAC told me, people up there sometimes hunt off-season. Harry was most probably wearing
camouflage and may have been accidentally shot by a
hunter." He continued, "There are all sorts of dangers in the
wilderness. That's why it's called the wilderness."

Kate commented, "That's why it's not a good idea to
send someone there alone. He should have had a partner."

Walsh replied, "In retrospect, that may be true. But
I've run dozens of rural surveillances with a lone agent.
The Adirondacks are not the African jungle."

"But you just said—"

"Don't second-guess me on this. This is standard procedure, and you never raised that issue when we discussed
sending John. Let's address the immediate problem."

I thought Walsh was the immediate problem, so I addressed him. "Tom, what exactly is the Custer Hill Club?"

He considered a moment, then replied, "I don't see

how this relates to finding Harry, but if you want an answer . . . from what I know, which is not much, it's a very private and exclusive hunting and fishing club whose members are mostly wealthy, or powerful, or both."

"You also said they had political influence."

"That's what I was told. I'd say the membership is about half Washington and half Wall Street."

"Where do you get your information?"

"I was briefed. Don't ask." He added, "I'm sure the actual and complete list of club members is not public information, which is why someone in the Justice Department wanted a surveillance of this meeting."

"Who called you?"

"That's actually none of your business."

"Good answer." Regarding Harry's phone message to his girlfriend, I asked Walsh, "What was Harry supposed to do at the airport? Which airport?"

Walsh hesitated before he responded, then said, "Adirondack Regional Airport. Some of the people who were to attend this weekend gathering probably arrived by commercial carrier—they have commuter-plane service there. Harry was to go to the airport Saturday or early Sunday morning and get printouts of the passenger manifests."

I nodded. Walsh forgot to mention that airline-passenger manifests could be accessed from anywhere the airline had a computer, or even right here from 26 Fed with the airlines' cooperation. Therefore, Harry's other assignment at the airport was to find out who arrived by private or chartered aircraft. And then there were car rentals, and a copy of those rental contracts would be very useful in trying to determine who may have attended this meeting. I was starting to think I might want to follow up on this myself.

In any case, Tom Walsh changed the subject. "The state police have search aircraft with infrared sensors to locate large living—or recently dead—organisms. They're highly trained and equipped to find persons missing in the woods."

"That's good." It was my turn to change the subject, and I pointed out to Walsh, "You seem to suggest that this was a routine assignment, and yet, you're here on a holiday to meet and debrief Harry. And apparently Tech is open to receive his digital-camera disks and videotape, which I assume will be transmitted to Washington ASAP, along with whatever he came up with at the airport."

"What's your point?"

"What is the *urgency* with this surveillance?"

"I have no idea. I just follow orders like you . . . Actually, you don't follow orders, but I do." He advised me, "You need to only ask questions that will help you complete your assignment." He further informed me, "Our job is to gather intelligence. Sometimes we know why. Sometimes we don't. Sometimes we're told to act on intelligence—sometimes someone else acts on it."

"How long has this been going on?"

"Quite a while."

As always, there's a slight clash of cultures between the FBI and the police, which is frustrating to everyone, I'm sure.

Kate said to Walsh, "Tom, I've worked with a lot of NYPD since I've been on the Task Force, and I've learned a lot from them, and they've learned a lot from us."

Actually, I've learned next to nothing from the FBI, though the CIA is interesting.

Kate continued, "Since 9/11, we need to think differently, to ask *any* questions we want to ask, and to challenge our supervisors when we're not satisfied with what they're telling us."

Walsh looked at her awhile, then observed, "I think someone is setting a bad example for you."

"No. What happened a year ago is what has changed how I think."

Walsh didn't respond to that. "Let's return to the subject of the missing—"

Kate interrupted and went into her lawyer mode. "Tom, I still don't understand *why* this group is under surveillance. What illegal activity or Federal crime are they suspected of?"

"Whatever they are suspected of has nothing to do with Harry Muller's apparent disappearance, and therefore you have no need to know."

I butted into the argument. "This is a reactionary group. Correct? Right-wing loony lodge."

He nodded.

"So, considering that, and the high-level political and financial membership of this so-called hunting and fishing club, maybe we're talking about a conspiracy to take over the government."

He smiled and replied, "I think they already did that on Election Day."

"Good point. Meanwhile, we'd really like to know what Headquarters told you."

Walsh considered that for a moment. "Okay, for what

it's worth, what I was told was that this had something to do with a conspiracy to rig oil prices. The guy who apparently runs the club is Bain Madox. You may have heard the name. He owns and operates Global Oil Corporation. GOCO." He added, "That's more than you need to know."

I processed that. The name *was* familiar. And oil-price rigging was not unheard of. Still, that didn't completely explain the existence of the Custer Hill Club, or even the club members for that matter. Something was a little off here, and Tom Walsh wasn't going to put it straight, even if he could.

Nevertheless, I said to him, "I read your memo."

"That's encouraging."

I pointed out, "I thought that Iraqis were on the front burner."

"That's right."

"So? What does the Custer Hill Club have to do with Iraqis or the coming war?"

"Nothing, as far as I know. Harry's assignment came about because of the weekend meeting at this club, which I assume doesn't happen that often. Are you having trouble following this?"

"Sorry. I was all set to act on your memo and wrap a rag around my head and hang around an Iraqi coffee shop today."

"Forget that. Let's return to the problem at hand. Quite frankly, I have not yet reported this missing agent to Headquarters, but very soon someone there will inquire about the information they asked for. When that happens, I'll have to explain that I'm temporarily out of contact with the agent assigned to the job. That's not going to be a pleasant conversation, but if we catch a break between now and then, I might be able to offer some positive news."

I said, "Kate and I would like to go upstate and assist in the search."

I'm sure I wasn't Tom Walsh's first choice to take this assignment, but I was on-duty today, plus he knew Harry and I were friends. Also, he needed an FBI agent on the spot ASAP, and Kate had made the mistake of coming in for half a day on a holiday, and voilà, Walsh could tell Washington he already had a team on the way upstate.

Walsh said to me and Kate, "I thought you'd want to do that, so it's all arranged."

"Good. We'll leave as soon as possible."

He checked his watch. "In fact, you're leaving in about five minutes. There's a car downstairs to take you to the Downtown Manhattan Heliport. An FBI helicopter will take you to Adirondack Regional Airport. Travel time is about two.hours. There will be a Hertz rental car at the airport in John's name. When you get there, call me, and I'll give you further instructions."

Kate asked, "Do we have a contact person there?"

"You may." He added, "Agents from Albany and from here will be joining you tonight or tomorrow."

I inquired, "Have we gotten a search warrant for the Custer Hill Club?"

"The last I heard from our office in Albany is that they were trying to find a U.S. attorney on the holiday, who in turn needs to find a Federal judge who wants to work today."

"Have they tried the saloons?"

Walsh continued, "The U.S. attorney will need to convince a judge that this is a Federal case, and that he or she should issue a search warrant for the Custer Hill Club property—which is about sixteen square miles of land—but not the lodge itself. We're not going to get that without probable cause, and we have no reason to think that Harry Muller is in the house."

Kate said, "We don't need a warrant if there's an immediate danger that a person's life may be in jeopardy."

Walsh agreed. "I'm sure the owner, Mr. Madox, would consent to a search for a person who may be lost or injured on his property, and we'll go that route first. But if Madox is not cooperative, or just not available, and an employee of the club doesn't know what to do, then we'll execute the warrant for the property search."

I asked, "And how do you explain to Mr. Madox that you may have a Federal agent missing on his property?"

"He doesn't need to know it's a Federal agent. We'll leave the property search to the state police." He added, "Obviously we're trying to do all we can, short of alerting Madox that he's under surveillance."

I pointed out, "If Harry was detained by the security people at this club, then Madox knows he's under surveillance, Tom."

"First, there is no evidence and no reason to believe that Harry was detained at the Custer Hill Club. But if he was, then he'd certainly stick to his cover story."

"Which is?"

"A lost bird-watcher."

"I don't think that's going to fly, pardon the pun." I

asked, "And what if these security people searched him? Was he clean going in?"

Walsh hesitated, then replied, "No. But what are the chances that private security people are going to physically search a trespasser? Or that Harry would allow that?"

"I don't know, Tom. But I wouldn't want to find out the hard way. If I had gone in, I wouldn't be carrying my Fed creds and Glock." I reminded him, "Cops impersonating drug dealers don't have their gun and badge with them."

Walsh didn't seem to appreciate the lecture. He said to me, "First of all, the Custer Hill Club is not a drug den, so don't use your NYPD analogies where they're not appropriate. Also, let's assume Harry was *not* stopped, detained, or searched by the private security people at the Custer Hill Club."

"Okay, so let's assume he's lost or hurt on club property. The state and local police should be conducting a land-and-air search right now. What are we waiting for?"

"We're not waiting, John. We're taking it a step at a time, and they *are* searching the wooded area *outside* the club property." He stared at us and said, "I personally don't think we're going to find Harry on that property. And neither do you, if you think about it. Let's be rational, and let's try to balance our concern for Harry against our need to keep Mr. Madox in the dark."

I replied, "I'm not seeing much light here myself."

"This is no different than any other assignment. You get as much light as you need to take the next step into the dark."

"Sounds like bullshit to me."

"It's actually official policy."

Kate said, "John, we need to get going."

Walsh stood, and we stood with him. He said, "If anything develops on the way there, I'll radio the helicopter."

We all shook hands, and Walsh said, "If you need to stay overnight, find a room."

I replied, "Don't expect to see us until we've found Harry."

"Good luck."

We left Walsh's office, returned to our desks, shut down our computers and gathered our belongings, then took the elevator to the lobby.

A car and driver were waiting for us outside, and on the way to the heliport, Kate asked me, "What do you think?"

"I think you should never go to the office on your day off. No good deed goes unpunished."

"I was fortunate to be here." She asked, "I mean, what do you think about Harry?"

"Based on my experience and on statistics, the most probable explanation for any disappearance, especially that of an adult male, is an accident that hasn't yet been discovered, a suicide, or a planned disappearance. Rarely is foul play involved."

She thought about that and asked me, "Do you think he had an accident?"

"No."

"Suicide?"

"Not Harry."

"Do you think he's just goofing off someplace?"

"No."

"So . . ."

"Yes."

We didn't speak for the rest of the ride.

CHAPTER EIGHTEEN

A few helicopters sat on the pad, and ours was easy to spot because it had FBI markings, which most FBI aircraft don't. I prefer to travel and arrive in unmarked conveyances, but the pilot explained that this was the only chopper available on short notice. No big deal.

We climbed aboard the helicopter—a Bell JetRanger—and it lifted from its pad on the East River and followed the river north. To my left was the towering skyline of Manhattan Island, and to my right, the mysterious flatlands of Brooklyn and Queens, where I rarely venture.

We continued north over the Hudson, following the majestic river valley.

In less than ten minutes, we passed over the Tappan Zee Bridge, and a few minutes later, we were flying over open countryside on both sides of the valley as we continued to follow the Hudson River northbound.

I'm not a big fan of the great outdoors, but from up here, the landscape was a spectacular panorama of small towns, farms, and trees whose autumn leaves were glowing in the bright sunlight.

Kate said, "We should get a weekend house up here."

I knew that was coming. Wherever we go, she wants a weekend house, or a beach house, or a summerhouse, or a ski house, or whatever. We're up to, I think, fourteen houses. I replied, as I always do, "Great idea."

The Hudson River, America's Rhine, sparkled in the sunlight, and we could see mansions and castles along the high riverbanks. I said, "There's a nice castle with a For Sale sign."

She ignored this and said, "Sometimes, I think I want to chuck it all, and get a place in the country, and just live a normal life. Do you ever think about that?"

I'd heard this before, too, not only from Kate but from other people since 9/11. The media shrinks were explaining it as post-traumatic stress, war anxiety, fear of another attack, the anthrax scare, and so forth. I replied, "I was ready to pack it in last year, as you recall, but after the attacks, I knew I wasn't going anywhere. I'm motivated."

She nodded. "I understand. But . . . I keep thinking that it's going to happen again, and next time it could be worse. Maybe anthrax, or poison gas, or a radiological device. . . ."

I didn't respond.

She said, "People have left the city, John."

"I know. It's much easier now to get a cab and a dinner reservation."

"This is not funny."

"No, it's not funny." In fact, I knew people who, since 9/11, had bought places in the country, or bought boats for a quick escape, or simply moved to Dubuque. This was not healthy, though it may have been smart.

I said to Kate, "I'm older than you, and I remember a time when things were different. I don't like the way these bastards have made us live. I'd like to live long enough to see things get better, and I'd like to be part of making them better." I added, "I'm not running."

She didn't have a response for that, and we both gazed out the windows at the pleasant autumn landscape.

On the west bank of the Hudson, the United States Military Academy at West Point came into view, its tall Gothic spires capturing the sunlight. I could see a formation of cadets on the parade grounds.

Kate said, "Things are not going to get better in your lifetime or mine."

"You never know. Meanwhile, we'll give it our best shot."

She thought a moment and said, "This thing with Harry . . . it has nothing to do with Islamic terrorism, but it's all part of the same problem."

"How's that?"

"It's all about people who are engaged in some sort of power struggle. Religion, politics, war, oil, terrorism . . . the world is headed for something much worse than anything we've seen so far."

"Probably. In the meantime, let's find Harry."

She stared out the window.

Kate is physically brave, as I saw when Mr. Khalil was using us for target practice with his sniper rifle, but the last year was taking its toll on her emotional health.

Also, for those of us working in this business, it didn't help our mental health to read the classified memos we got every day concerning this or that domestic threat. That, plus the looming war with Iraq, was starting to fray the nerves of some of the people I was working with.

Kate had good days and bad days, as we all do. Today was not a good day. In fact, September 10, 2001, was really the last good day.

— PART IX —

Monday
UPSTATE NEW YORK

Given the magnitude of the federal response to a suspected WMD incident, first responders might be reluctant to initiate the mechanisms to set that response in motion.

—*Terrorism in the United States*
FBI Publications, 1997

CHAPTER NINETEEN

Two hours and fifteen minutes after we'd left the Downtown Manhattan Heliport, we flew over the upstate town of Saranac Lake. A few minutes later, three long runways forming a triangle came into view, surrounded by forest. I thought I saw bears lurking at the edge of the clearing.

As we descended, I could see some snazzy corporate jets parked on the ramp, though only one of them sported a corporate logo on the tail. In the case of corporate jets, it did *not* pay to advertise, partly for security reasons, and partly because it pissed off the stockholders. Nevertheless, I looked for a jet that was marked GOCO, but didn't see any identifying markings as we hovered lower.

The pilot spoke to someone on the radio, then put the chopper down on the pavement behind a long, wood-shingled building that looked like an Adirondack lodge.

This building seemed a little incongruous for an airport, but I knew from my infrequent trips into these mountains that the locals took their faux rustic stuff seriously, and I was surprised that the hangars didn't look like log cabins.

Anyway, the pilot shut down the helicopter's engine, and the noise level dropped dramatically.

The co-pilot jumped out of the cockpit, swung open the door of the cabin, and took Kate's hand as she jumped down. I followed without taking the fellow's hand, and said to him over the sound of the slowing rotor blades, "Did you see any bears?"

"Huh?"

"Never mind. Are you staying?"

"No. We'll fuel up, then head back to New York." As he spoke, I spotted a fuel truck coming in our direction, which is quicker service than I get at my gas station. It must have something to do with the FBI markings on the chopper.

I turned and looked around the mostly empty tarmac. The corporate jets were parked in a row on a blacktop ramp in the distance, and beyond them was a scattering of smaller light airplanes. There was no activity to speak of.

It was much colder up here, and I could see my breath, which is not what I wanted to see at 1:30 in the afternoon on a sunny day in early October.

Kate said, "Smell that air."

"I don't smell anything."

"The mountain air, John. And look at those trees, and those mountains."

"Where the hell are we?"

"In God's country."

"Good. I have a few questions to ask him."

Apparently the Adirondack lodge building was the main passenger terminal, and we walked around to the front entrance, which had a covered veranda surrounded by a rustic railing. There was a picnic table and Pepsi machine on the veranda, and a security guy was sitting there smoking a cigarette. No one would mistake this place for JFK International Airport.

Kate said to me, "I'll call Tom."

"Why?"

"Maybe someone is supposed to meet us here."

"Well, I don't see how they can miss us." In fact, there wasn't another soul around, and there were hardly more than a dozen vehicles in the parking lot, half of which were probably abandoned by people who had one-way tickets out of this godforsaken wilderness.

We entered the terminal, which was much warmer than the frozen alpine valley outside. The terminal interior was small, functional, and quiet.

As small and isolated as this place was, there was a security checkpoint, complete with a walk-through metal detector and a baggage scanner. There were no security people at the checkpoint, and no passengers for that matter, so I assumed there was no imminent departure.

Kate scanned the empty terminal and said, "I don't see anyone who might be here to meet us."

"How can you tell in this crowd?"

She ignored that and observed, "There are the carrental counters . . . there's a restaurant, and there are the restrooms. Where do you want to start?"

"Over here." I turned toward the sole airline ticket

counter, whose logo said: CONTINENTAL COM-MUTAIR.

Kate asked, "What are you doing?"

"Let's see what Harry was supposed to find here."

"That's not what Tom—"

"Fuck Tom."

She considered that and agreed, "Yeah, fuck him."

I approached the small ticket counter, where an impos-ing middle-aged woman and a young man sat on stools, watching us. They looked like brother and sister, and unfor-tunately, I think their parents were, too. The lady, whose name tag said BETTY, greeted us. "Good afternoon. How can I help you?"

I replied, "I need a ticket to Paris."

"Would you like to go through Albany or Boston?"

"How about neither?"

Betty informed me, "Sir, there are no direct flights to anywhere from here, except to Albany and Boston."

"You're kidding? How about arriving flights?"

"Same. Albany and Boston. Continental CommutAir. Two flights a day. You just missed the last flight to Bos-ton." She cocked her thumb at the arrival and departure schedules on the wall behind her and informed us, "We go to Albany at three P.M."

One airline, two cities, two flights to each city. That made my job a little easier and quicker. I said to her, "I'd like to speak to the manager."

"You're speaking to her."

"I thought you were the ticket agent."

"I am."

"I hope you're not also the pilot."

Kate seemed impatient with my silliness and pulled out her creds. "FBI, ma'am. I'm Special Agent Mayfield and this is Detective Corey, my assistant. May we speak to you in private?"

Betty looked at us and said, "Oh . . . you're the people who just landed in the helicopter."

I guess big news traveled fast here. "Yes, ma'am. Where can we go to check out passenger manifests?"

She slid off her stool, told her assistant, Randy, to hold down the fort, then said to us, "Follow me."

We went around the counter and through an open door into a small, empty office with desks, computers, faxes, and other electronic things.

She sat at one of the desks and asked Kate—I don't think she liked me—"What do you need?"

Kate replied, "I need a list of passengers who arrived here on Thursday, Friday, Saturday, Sunday, and today. Also, departing passengers for those days, plus tomorrow."

"Okay . . ."

I asked her, "Has anyone else been here, or called you in the last few days to ask about passenger manifests?"

She shook her head. "Nope."

"If someone had called or been here when you weren't here, would you know about it?"

She nodded. "Sure. Jake, Harriet, or Randy would have told me."

Maybe Kate was right, and I should do what a lot of my colleagues have done and get a job as chief of police in a small town where everybody knows everybody else's business. Kate could get a job as a school crossing guard,

I'd spend all my time at the local tavern, and she'd have an affair with a forest ranger.

I said to Betty, "Okay, can you print out those passenger lists?"

Betty swiveled around and banged away at the keyboard.

As the printer started grinding out paper, I looked at a few pages and said, "Not too many people on these flights."

Betty replied as she hit the keys, "These are commuter aircraft. Eighteen passengers maximum."

That was good news. I asked her, "And these are all the arriving and departing passengers for the days in question?"

"As of right now. I can't tell you who's actually going to depart on the three o'clock Albany flight, or any flights tomorrow, but I'm getting you the reservation lists for those flights."

"Good. Do you have a record of incoming and departing private aircraft?" I asked her.

"No, this is an *airline*. Private aircraft is general aviation, and the ramp operations office takes care of that."

"Of course. What was I thinking? So, where's the ramp operations office?"

"The other end of the terminal."

Before I could say this place wasn't big enough to have another end, Betty added, "They'd have a record of incoming or departing aircraft only if they spent the night or bought fuel."

That's what I like about this job—you learn something new every day about something you'll never use for the rest of your life.

Kate asked, "Can you get us those records?"

"I'll send Randy to get a copy for you."

She picked up the phone and said to her assistant, "Do me a favor, sweetie, and go down to ramp operations." She explained what she needed, hung up, and said to both of us, "Can I ask why you need these passenger lists?"

Kate replied, "We're not at liberty to say, and I need to ask you not to mention this to anyone."

I added, "Not even Jake, Harriet, or Randy."

Betty nodded absently while making a mental list of all the people she was going to tell about her visit from the FBI.

In a few minutes, Randy appeared and handed a few papers to Betty, who then handed them over to Kate. We both looked at the sheets. There were a couple dozen private aircraft that had been registered at the airport on the days in question, but the only information on the printout was the make, model, and tail number of the aircraft. I asked Betty, "Do you know if there's any information about who owns these aircraft?"

"No, but you can find out from the tail numbers."

"Right. Can I find out who was on board?"

"No. With general aviation—private flights—there is no record of who was on board. That's why it's called private."

"Right. God bless America." Meanwhile, Osama bin Laden could be on board a private jet, and no one would know it. And now, a year after 9/11, security for general aviation was still non-existent, while commercial aviation passengers, including babies, flight crew, and little old ladies, got patted down and wanded, even on small commuter aircraft. Go figure.

Kate gathered up the printouts and put them in her briefcase.

I asked Betty the standard question. "You notice anything unusual this weekend?"

She swiveled her chair toward us. "Like what?"

Why do they always ask that? "Unusual," I said. "Like, not usual."

She shook her head. "Not that I can think of."

"More people arriving than usual?"

"Well, yeah, you get a lot of people on holiday weekends. Summer and winter are real big up here. But fall is getting big with the leaf watchers. Then, hunting begins, and then you got Thanksgiving weekend, and then Christmas, skiing, and—"

I stopped her before we got to Groundhog Day, and asked, "Did any of the passengers look unusual?"

"No. But you know what?"

"What?"

"Some big shot flew in from Washington."

"Was he lost?"

She looked at Kate as if to say, Who is this asshole you're with?

Kate picked up the ball. "Who was he?"

"I don't remember. Secretary of something. His name should be on the passenger manifest."

"How did he arrive?"

"CommutAir from Boston. I think it was Saturday.

Yes, Saturday. He came in on the eleven o'clock flight, and one of our security guards recognized him."

Kate inquired, "Did he rent a vehicle?"

"No. I remember he was met by a guy from the Custer Hill Club—that's a private club about thirty miles from here. There were three other guys on that flight, and they seemed to be together."

"How," I asked, "did you know that the guy who met the secretary of something was from this club?"

"The driver had a uniform on that's from the Custer Hill Club. They come here now and then to pick up passengers." She added, "All four passengers got their luggage and went outside, where a van from the club was waiting for them."

I nodded. Very little escaped notice in small places. "Did this van from the Custer Hill Club pick up any more arriving passengers from other flights?"

"I don't know. I might have been off-duty."

"Did the van drop off any departing passengers?"

"I don't know. I can't always see what's going on at curbside."

"Right." I didn't want to show any further interest in the Custer Hill Club so I switched gears to a cover story and said, "What we need to know is if you or anyone else saw someone who looked . . . how can I put this without sounding like I'm engaging in racial profiling . . . ? Anyone who looked, well, like their country of origin may have been someplace where there are lots of camels?"

She nodded in acknowledgment, thought a second, then replied, "No, I think that kind of person would stand out."

I'll bet they would. "Can you do us a favor and ask around later?"

She nodded enthusiastically. "I sure can. You want me to call you?"

"I'll call you, or stop in."

"Okay. I'll ask around." She stood, and stared at us. "What's this about? Is something going to happen?"

I moved closer to Betty and said in a low tone, "This has to do with the Winter Olympics in Lake Placid. Keep that to yourself."

Betty processed that for a few seconds, then said, "The Winter Olympics were in 1980."

I looked at Kate and said, "Damn! We're too late." I asked Betty, "Hey, did anything happen?"

Kate gave me a mean look, then said to Betty, "That's Detective Corey's way of saying we're not at liberty to discuss this. But we could use your help."

Normally, this is when you give the good citizen your card, but we were doing a smoke screen now, and Kate was on top of it, so she asked Betty for her card. "We'll call you. Thanks for your help."

"Anything I can do, just ask." She added, "If those people try anything around here, we know how to handle them."

I replied in my John Wayne accent, "That's *our* job, ma'am. Don't take the law into your own hands."

She made a little snorting sound, then said to us, "While you're here, you might want to look into that Custer Hill Club."

"Why?"

"Strange things going on up there."

I felt like I was in a B movie, where the guy from the city gets warned by a local about the creepy place on the hill, then ignores the advice, which was actually what I was going to do in Act II. I responded, noncommittally, "Thanks. How's the food at the restaurant?"

"Pretty good, but a little pricey. Try the double bacon cheeseburger."

Betty looked as if she'd tried several.

She showed us out, and I said to Kate in a foreboding tone, "Whatever you do, miss, do *not* go to the Custer Hill Club."

She smiled and said, "Do not order the double bacon cheeseburger."

In fact, that was the first risky thing I was going to do today before going to the Custer Hill Club.

CHAPTER TWENTY

Out in the terminal area, I said to Kate, "I'm going to hit the men's room."

"You should. You're full of shit."

"Right. I'll meet you at the car-rental counter."

We parted company, and I freshened up and was at the car-rental area within four minutes. Women take a bit longer.

There were two car-rental counters—Enterprise and Hertz—one behind the other in a small area off to the side of the terminal. The young guy behind the Enterprise counter was sitting down, reading a book. Standing behind the Hertz counter was a young lady playing with her computer. Her big breast tag read MAX, which I assumed was her name and not her cup size. I said, "Hi, Max. I have a reservation under the name of Corey."

"Yes, sir." She found my reservation, and we went through the paperwork, which took only a few minutes. She handed me the keys to a Ford Taurus, and told me how to find the rental lot, then asked me, "Do you need any directions?"

"Do you mean in life?"

She giggled. "No. Driving directions. You want a map?"

"Sure." I took the map and said, "Actually, I need a place to stay."

She replied, "There's a rack of pamphlets over there. Lodging, restaurants, sights, and stuff."

"Great. What's the best place around?"

"The Point."

"What's The Point?"

She smiled, "I don't know, John. What's the point?" She laughed. "I get people with that every time."

"I'll bet. Got me. So, where would you recommend to stay?"

"The Point."

"Okay . . ."

"It's, like, really expensive though."

"Like what? A hundred bucks?"

"No, like a thousand dollars."

"A year?"

"A night."

"You're kidding."

"No, for real. It's, like, really exclusive."

"Really." I didn't think this was going to get past the accounting office, but I was in a reckless mood. "How do I get to The Point?"

"Stop beating around the bush." She laughed hard and slapped the counter. "Got ya."

"Hey, you're good." *What did I do to deserve this?*

Max got herself under control. "Hey, you really going there?"

"Why not? I have a rich uncle."

"You must. You rich?"

"I'm John."

She giggled politely. "Good one."

Max handed me a map, which I noticed had lots of thin, winding roads that ran through open spaces, with very few towns. I thought of Harry, who liked the Adirondacks, and I asked God to do the right thing this time.

Max put an X on the map. "The Point is on Upper Saranac Lake, about there. You should call for directions. Also, you have to call for reservations. They're, like, always booked."

"At a thousand bucks a night?"

"Yeah. Can you believe?" She pulled a phone book from under the counter, found the number of The Point, and wrote it on the map, saying to me, "You won't find a brochure on this place in the wire rack."

"Really."

I put the map in my pocket, and Max said to me, "So, you're from New York City?"

"I am."

"I love New York. So, what brings you up here?"

"A helicopter."

She started to smile, then a little light went off in her head, and she said, "Oh, you're the guy who flew in on the FBI helicopter."

"Right. Fuller Brush Incorporated."

She laughed. "No . . . FBI. Like Federal Bureau of Investigation."

Kate appeared, carrying two containers of coffee, and asked me, "You having a good time here?"

"I'm renting a car."

"I could hear you laughing from the restaurant. What's the joke?"

"What's the point?"

Max laughed. Kate did not. I said, "It's a long story."

"Shorten it."

"Okay, there's this place . . . a hotel or something—"

"A resort," said Max helpfully.

"Right. A resort called The Point. So, Max—that's this young lady—no, first I asked, 'Is there a good place to stay?' so she says, 'What's the point—?' "

"No," interrupted Max, "I said, 'The Point,' and *you* said, 'What's The Point?' and I said—"

"All right," Kate interrupted, "I get it." She put my coffee on the counter. "At what *point* are we now?"

I replied, professionally, "I was just about to identify myself as a Federal agent."

Kate beat me to it and showed her credentials. She said to Max, "I need photocopies of all car-rental contracts from Thursday to now, including vehicles that have been returned. See if you can do that in ten minutes. We'll be in the restaurant." Kate went to the next counter, Enterprise Rent-A-Car, and spoke to the young man there.

I said to Max, "That's my wife."

"Gee, I never would've guessed."

I took the coffee and went into the restaurant, which

was actually just a small café. The walls and ceilings were painted a horrid sky blue, complete with white clouds unlike any I've ever seen on this planet. Plastic models of biplanes hung from the ceiling, and photos of various aircraft added to the motif. There was a four-stool lunch counter, which was empty, and a dozen empty tables from which I could choose. I sat at a table near a picture window where I could see the runway.

An attractive waitress came over with a menu and asked, "And how are you this afternoon?"

"Great. I'm happily married. Can I have another menu? My wife will be here in a few minutes."

"Sure . . ." She put the menu down and moved off to get another one.

My cell phone rang, and the caller ID said "Private," which 90 percent of the time is the office, so I let it go into voice mail.

Kate came into the café and said, "My cell phone just rang."

"Probably Bergdorf's looking for you."

She sat down and listened to her voice mail. "Tom Walsh—wants me to call."

"Wait a few minutes."

"All right." She took the sheaf of CommutAir printouts from her briefcase and laid them on the table. I took half and started flipping through them while dialing my cell phone.

"Who are you calling?"

"The Point."

A man named Charles answered, and I said, "I'd like to make a reservation for this evening."

"Yes, sir. We have some availability."

"Do you also have rooms?"

"Yes, sir. We have the Mohawk Room in the Main Lodge, the Lookout in the Eagle's Nest, the Weatherwatch in the Guest House—"

"Slow down, Charles. What can I get for a thousand bucks?"

"Nothing."

"Nothing? Not even a cot in the kitchen?"

He quoted me some rates on the available rooms, and I got scalped by the Mohawk for twelve hundred bucks, which was the cheapest room available. I asked him, "Does this place have heat and electricity?"

"Yes, sir. How many nights will you be staying with us?"

"I'm not sure, Charles. Let's start with two."

"Yes, sir." He added, "If you're with us on Wednesday evening, black tie is requested for dinner."

"Are you telling me I need a tuxedo to eat dinner in the woods?"

"Yes, sir." He explained, "William Avery Rockefeller, who owned this property, would dine with his guests each evening in black tie. We try to re-create the experience on Wednesday and Saturday evenings."

"I might need to miss that experience. Can I get room service in my underwear?"

"Yes, sir. How would you like to secure the reservation?"

I gave him my name and government credit card, we ironed out a few other details, and I asked him, "You have any bears there?"

"Yes, sir. We have a bar in the—"

"*Bears*, Charles, *bears*. You know. Ursus terribilis."

"Uh . . . we . . . there are bears in the area, but—"

"Feed the bears tonight, Charles. See you later." I hung up.

Kate said, "Did I hear you correctly?"

"Yeah, fucking bears."

"The room rate."

"Yeah, we're in the Mohawk Room. The Weather-watch at two thousand dollars a night seemed a little extravagant."

"Are you crazy?"

"Why do you ask? Hey, after two nights in that B and B hovel you booked, we deserve a nice place."

"I think we get an allowance of a hundred dollars per diem in the Albany area." She reminded me, "We . . . you have to make up the difference."

"We'll see."

Kate's beeper went off, and she looked at it. "Tom."

"Give it a few more minutes."

"Maybe they've found Harry."

"That would be nice." I flipped through the printouts, trying to see if anything stuck out.

Kate, too, went through the printouts and said, "Here is the eleven A.M. CommutAir from Boston on Saturday . . . wow."

"Wow, what?"

"Edward Wolffer. You know who he is?"

"Yeah, he played center field for the—"

"He's the deputy secretary of defense. Very hawkish

guy, pushing for the war in Iraq. Very close to the president. He's on TV a lot."

"That's probably the guy who someone here recognized."

"Yes, and here's another one on the same flight—Paul Dunn. He's a presidential adviser—"

"On matters of national security, and a member of the National Security Council."

"Right. How did you know that?"

"It's always a *Jeopardy* question."

"Why do you like to play stupid?"

"It's a good cover for when I really am stupid." I said, "So, Wolffer and Dunn arrived Saturday, plus two other guys, according to Betty, and they all got into the van to the Custer Hill Club."

Kate looked again at the passenger manifest for the 11:00 A.M. Saturday flight from Boston and said, "There were nine other men on that flight, but none of these other names ring a bell, so we don't know who these other two guys were who got into the van."

"Right." I continued flipping through the passenger lists. "Wolffer and Dunn left on the first Boston flight yesterday, connecting to Washington."

She nodded thoughtfully, then asked me, "Does this mean anything?"

"Well, on the surface, it doesn't mean much. A lot of rich and powerful guys got together on a three-day weekend at a mountain lodge owned by an oil billionaire. It's like one of those Renaissance weekends, or a gathering of the Carlyle Group, where some people, and the media, speculate that all kinds of devious things are going on—oil-price rigging, financial and political deals, conspiracies to take over the planet, and that kind of thing. But sometimes, it's just a bunch of rich guys getting together to relax, play cards, talk about women, and tell dirty jokes."

Kate thought about that. "Sometimes it is," she said. "But someone in the Justice Department ordered a surveillance of this gathering."

"*That's* the point."

She went on, "And it's not every day that the Justice Department wants to keep an eye on the deputy secretary of defense, a presidential adviser, and who knows who else in this club."

I commented, "This is getting good." I scanned the passenger manifests. "We need to do a background check of everyone who arrived here by commercial aircraft in the last few days, and see what, if any, connection they have to one another—then try to find out what Harry was supposed to find out on his surveillance: who went from here to the Custer Hill Club."

Kate replied, "I don't think that's our job. Tom didn't mention that."

"It's good to show initiative. Tom appreciates that, and by the way, fuck Tom."

The waitress came by, and one of us ordered a double bacon cheeseburger, and the other ordered a Cobb salad, whatever the hell that is.

My beeper went off, and I looked at the number. Not surprisingly, it was Tom Walsh. "I'll call him."

"No, *I'll* call him," Kate said.

"Let me handle this. He likes and respects me." I dialed Tom's cell phone, and he answered. I asked, "Did you page me?"

"Yes, I paged you, and Kate, and I called you both. You were supposed to call me when you landed."

"We just got in. Headwinds."

"According to the pilot, you've been there almost an hour."

"There was a long line at the car rental. More important, what's the word on Harry?"

"Nothing yet." He briefed me on nothing, then said, "I want you to drive to the regional headquarters of the state police in Ray Brook. That's a few miles from Saranac Lake. Make contact with a Major Hank Schaeffer, commander of B Troop, and coordinate the search operation with him. You can offer your services and expertise, such as they are, and offer to participate in the search."

"Okay. That's it?"

"For now. Meanwhile, we're going through channels to see if we can get a few hundred troops from Fort Drum to participate in the search. That will speed it up considerably. Tell Schaeffer we're still working on that."

"Will do."

"Call me when you've spoken to Schaeffer."

"Will do."

"Okay, is Kate there?"

"She's in the ladies' room."

"Tell her to call me."

"Will do."

"What are you doing now?"

"Waiting for a double bacon cheeseburger."

"Okay . . . don't hang around the airport too long, and don't ask anyone there any questions."

"What do you mean?"

"Just get over to the state trooper headquarters ASAP. And don't even *think* about going to the Custer—"

"I understand."

"All right. Nothing further."

I hung up, and Kate asked me, "What did he say?"

I sipped my coffee and went back to the printouts. "He wants us to go to the Custer Hill Club and see if Bain Madox is there, and talk to him, and see who else is there."

"He said that?"

"Not in so many words."

"Did he want me to call him?"

"At your convenience."

She was getting a little impatient with me and said, "John, what the *fuck* did he—?"

"Here's the deal. Nothing new on Harry, Walsh wants us to make contact with the state police, help in the search, and not snoop around the airport." I noted, "Too late for that."

"I didn't hear anything about going to the Custer Hill Club."

"Why don't *you* go see the state police? I'll go to the Custer Hill Club."

She didn't reply.

I said to her, "Kate, we were sent here as a pro forma response to the disappearance of one of our guys from the Task Force. We're here to get the bad news, or the good news, if and when Harry is found. This is just protocol.

You know that. The question for you is, Do you want to take a reactive, or pro-active, role here?"

"You have a way of putting things . . . let me think about it."

"Do that."

The food came, and the double bacon cheeseburger looked like it could give you a heart attack if you touched it. The Freedom Fries had a little American flag stuck in them.

Kate asked, "Do you want some of this salad?"

"I found a slug in a salad once."

"Thanks."

Before I could get my minimum daily requirement of fat, the guy from Enterprise came into the café and handed Kate a stack of photostated car-rental contracts. He said to her, "I get off-duty at four, if you want me to show you around. Maybe we can have dinner. I put my cell-phone number on my card."

"Thanks, Larry. I'll call you later."

He left.

I said, "You put him up to that."

"What are you talking about?"

I didn't reply and called for the check so we could get moving as soon as Max showed up.

I took another bite of my cheeseburger, and Max came into the café, spotted us, and came over. She said to Kate, "Here's all the contracts from Thursday to tomorrow, including returns. There's, like, twenty-six. It's a big weekend."

Kate replied, "Thank you. And please don't mention this to anyone."

"Sure." She looked at me and said, "You're a lucky guy to have a wife like this."

My mouth was full of burger, and I grunted.

Max left, and I swallowed. "You put her up to that."

"*What* are you talking about?"

I shoved some Freedom Fries in my mouth, stood, and said, "Okay, let's go."

Kate put the papers in her briefcase, I put twenty bucks on the table, and we left the café. I said, "If you're not coming with me, go to Hertz and get yourself another car. The state police headquarters is in someplace called Ray Brook, not far from here. Ask for Major Schaeffer. I'll call you later."

She stood there, wavering between following Walsh's orders and her recently expressed opinion to him that the world had changed.

Finally, she said, "I'll go with you to the Custer Hill Club. Then, we go to the state police headquarters."

We exited the terminal, walked to the car-rental lot, and found the blue Taurus. I drove to the side of the terminal building where the general aviation operations were and parked the car. "I want to see if GOCO has a corporate jet and if they use this airport." I handed her the road map and said, "Call the county police and see if you can get directions to the Custer Hill Club."

I went into the building, where a guy sat at a desk behind the counter playing with his computer.

I asked him, "Can I get a ticket to Paris here?"

He looked up from his computer and replied, "You can go anywhere you want if you own, lease, or charter a plane big enough. And you don't even need a ticket."

"I think I'm in the right place." I held up my credentials and said, "John Corey, Federal Anti-Terrorist Task
Force. I need to ask you a few questions."

He stood, came to the counter, and checked out the
creds. "What's up?" he asked.

"Who am I talking to?"

"I'm Chad Rickman, operations officer."

"Okay, Chad, I need to know if there's a private jet
that uses this airport, registered to the Global Oil Corporation. GOCO."

"Yeah, two Cessna Citations, new models. Any
problem?"

"Are either of the jets here?"

"No . . . in fact they both came in yesterday morning,
about an hour apart, fueled up, then a few hours later they
took off."

"How many passengers got off?"

"I don't think there were any. We usually send a car out
to the aircraft, and I'm pretty sure it was just the flight crew."

"Did any passengers get on after they refueled?"

"I don't think so. They came in, topped off, and a few
hours later they flew out."

"All right . . . where did they go?"

"They don't have to tell me where they're going—
they have to tell the FAA."

"Okay . . . how do they tell the FAA? Radio?"

"No, phone. From here. Actually, I overheard both
pilots filing a flight plan to Kansas City, departing thirty
minutes apart."

I thought about that, then asked, "Why would they be
going to Kansas City with no one on board?"

"Maybe they only had cargo," Chad replied. "I remember two Jeeps met them here and put some stuff on board."

"What did they put on board?"

"I didn't see."

"These are passenger planes, right? Not cargo?"

"Right. But they'll hold a little cargo in the cabin."

"I still don't understand why two jets flew in empty and flew out with a few pieces of cargo, both of them going to the same place."

"Hey, this guy who owns the planes—Bain Madox—*owns* the fucking oil wells. He can burn all the jet fuel he wants."

"This is true." I asked, "Was Kansas City their final destination?"

"I don't know. That's the flight plan I heard them file on the telephone. That's probably about their cruising range, so maybe they're going on from there. Or maybe they're coming back here."

"I see . . . so I can call the FAA to get their flight plans?"

"Yeah, if you're authorized, and if you have their tail registration numbers."

"Well, I'm authorized, Chad." I pulled out the sheet of paper that Randy had fetched from this office and put it on the desk. "Which are the GOCO aircraft?"

He studied the sheet and checked off two numbers: N2730G and N2731G. Chad informed me, "Sequential registration numbers. A lot of companies that fly their own airplanes do that."

"I know that."

"Yeah? What's up?"

"Typical tax crap. The rich are different from you and me."

"No kidding?"

"Okay, thanks, Chad. Think more about this. Ask around for me and see if anyone else remembers anything. You got a cell-phone number?"

"Sure." He wrote it on his business card and asked me, "What exactly are you looking for?"

"I told you—tax evasion. Bags of money." I said to him, "Don't mention anything to anyone about a Federal investigation."

"Mum's the word."

I left the operations office and got back in the car. I said to Kate, "There are two GOCO corporate jets that use this airport." I filled her in as I drove toward the airport exit and told her that we'd have to call the FAA office in Washington to find out what continuing flight plans had been filed for those two jets.

Kate asked me, "Why do we want to know that?"

"I don't know yet. This guy Madox interests me, and you never know what's important until you piece it together with something else. In detective work, there's no such thing as TMI—too much information."

"Should I be taking notes?"

"No, I'll give you one of my taped lectures that I gave at John Jay."

"Thank you."

At the airport exit, I asked Kate, "Did you get directions?"

"Sort of. The desk sergeant said take Route 3 west, to 56 north, then ask around."

"Real men don't ask directions." I asked, "Which way is Route 3?"

"Well, if you're asking, turn left."

Within a few minutes, we were on Route 3, designated a scenic highway, heading west into the wilderness. I said to Kate, "Keep an eye out for bears. Hey, do you think a 9mm Glock will stop a bear?"

"I don't think so, but I hope to God you get to find out."

"That's not very loving."

She sat back in her seat and closed her eyes. "Every minute that goes by without word about Harry makes me think he's not alive."

I didn't reply.

She stayed silent awhile, then said, "It could have been you."

It could have been, but if it were me out in the woods around the Custer Hill Club, things may have turned out differently. Then again, maybe not.

CHAPTER TWENTY-ONE

We continued west on Route 3, a road that seemed to have no reason to exist, except to look at trees while you went from nowhere to nowhere.

Kate had picked up a few brochures from the airport and was perusing them. She does this wherever we go so she can enhance her experience; then, she regurgitates this stuff back to me, like a tour guide.

She informed me that Saranac Lake, the town and the airport and this road, was actually within the boundaries of Adirondack State Park.

She also informed me that this area was known as the North Country, a name she found romantic.

I commented, "You could freeze to death here in April."

She went on, "Large parts of the park have been designated as forever wild."

"That's pretty depressing."

"The area designated as parkland is as big as the state of New Hampshire."

"What's New Hampshire?"

"Much of it is uninhabited."

"That's fairly obvious."

And so forth. Actually, I could see now how someone could be lost in here for days or weeks, or the rest of their lives, but I also realized that someone could survive if they had some experience in the woods.

Route 3 was actually a decent two-lane road that occasionally passed through a small town, but there were stretches of wilderness that aroused my agoraphobia and zoophobia. I could see why this guy Bain Madox would have a lodge up here if he were up to no good.

Kate said, "This is so beautiful."

"It is." It sucked.

There were yellow signs with black silhouettes of jumping deer, which I guess were to warn the deer to jump out of the way of cars on the road.

Around a turn was a big sign that had a black painting of a bear and the word CAUTION. I said, "Did you see that? Did you see that bear sign?"

"Yes. That means there are bears in the area."

"Holy shit. Are the doors locked?"

"John, stop being an idiot. Bears won't bother you if you don't bother them."

"Famous last words. How do you know what bothers a bear?"

"Stop with the fucking bears."

We continued on. There wasn't much traffic going our

way, and only a few vehicles passed us going back toward Saranac Lake.

Kate said, "Tell me why we're going to the Custer Hill Club."

"Standard police procedure. You go to the place where you last heard from the missing subject."

"This is a little more complex than a missing-person case."

"Actually, it isn't. The problem with the FBI and the CIA is that they make things more complicated than they need to be."

"Is that a fact?"

"Yes, it is."

"I need to remind you that we don't want to alert Madox or anyone there that a Federal agent was on his property."

"I think we've discussed this. If you were on the Custer Hill property with a broken leg, no cell-phone service, and a bear nibbling on your toes, would you want me to follow orders and wait for a search warrant to look for you?"

She considered that, then said, "I know that a cop will risk his life and his career to help another cop, and I know you'd do the same for me—though you may be conflicted about my dual role as your wife and as an FBI agent—"

"Interesting point."

"But I think you have another agenda, which is to see what the Custer Hill Club is all about."

"What was your first clue?"

"Well, the stack of airline passenger lists and car-rental contracts in my briefcase, for one. And you inquiring about Global Oil Corporation aircraft, for another."

"I just can't seem to fool you."

"John, I agree that we need to push the search for Harry, but beyond that, you're getting into something that may be a lot bigger than you realize." She reminded me, "The Justice Department is interested in this man and this club and his guests. Do not screw up their investigation."

"Are you speaking as my colleague, my wife, or my lawyer?"

"All of the above." She paused for a moment, then added, "Okay, I've said my piece because I had to say it and because I really worry about you sometimes. You're a loose cannon."

"Thank you."

"You're also extremely bright and clever, and I trust your judgment and your instincts."

"Really?"

"Really. So, even though I'm technically your superior, I'll follow your lead on this."

"I won't let you down."

"You'd better not. And I also want to remind you that nothing succeeds like success. If you . . . we . . . go beyond our orders, then we'd better have something to show for it."

"Kate, if I didn't think there was more to this than oil-price rigging, we'd be sitting around the state trooper headquarters now, drinking coffee."

She took my hand, and we drove on.

About forty minutes after we'd left the airport, I saw a sign for Route 56 north, and Kate said, "Bear right."

I hit the brakes and reached for my Glock. "Where?"

"Here. Bear right. Go."

"Bear . . . oh . . . *bear* right. Don't use that word."

"Turn fucking right. *Here*."

I turned onto Route 56 north, and we continued on. This stretch of road was real wilderness, and I said to Kate, "This looks like Indian Country. What's it say in the brochure about Indians? Friendly?"

"It says that the peace treaty with the Native American population expires on Columbus Day 2002."

"Funny."

We drove for about twenty miles, and a brown sign informed us that we were leaving Adirondack State Park.

Kate said, "The desk sergeant said the Custer Hill Club is on private land inside the park, so we passed it." She glanced at the Hertz map. "There's a town called South Colton a few miles up ahead. We'll stop and ask for directions."

I continued on, and a small group of buildings appeared. A sign said: SOUTH COLTON—A SMALL TOWN WITH A BIG CHIP ON ITS SHOULDER, or words to that effect.

There was a gas station at the edge of the small bump-in-the-road town, and I pulled in and parked. I said to Kate, "You go ask for directions."

"John, get off your ass and go ask for directions."

"All right . . . you come with me."

We got out, stretched, and went inside the small, rustic office.

A wizened old guy from Central Casting wearing jeans and a plaid shirt sat at a beat-up desk, smoking a cigarette and watching a fly-fishing show on a TV that was on the counter. Reception seemed to be less than optimum, so I moved the rabbit ears for him, and he said, "Right there. That's good."

As soon as I took my hands off the rabbit ears, he lost reception again. One of my jobs as a kid used to be to act as an antenna for the family television, but I was beyond that now, and I said to him, "We need some directions."

"I need to get a satellite dish."

"Not a bad idea. You can speak directly to the mother ship. We're looking for—"

"Where you comin' from?"

"Saranac Lake."

"Yeah?" He looked us over for the first time, checked out the Taurus outside, and asked, "Where you *from*?"

"Earth. Look, we're running late—"

"Need gas?"

"Sure. But first—"

"Lady need the restroom?"

Kate answered, "Thank you. We're headed for the Custer Hill Club."

He didn't reply for a few seconds, then said, "Yeah?"

"Do you know where that is?"

"Sure do. They gas up here. Don't do no car work for them. They take their cars up to the dealer in Potsdam. Hell, I forgot more about car repair than those idiots at the dealers ever knew." He went on, "But if they get stuck in the snow or mud, who do you think they call? The dealer? Hell, no. They call Rudy. That's me. Why, just last January, or maybe it was February . . . yeah, it was that big snow in mid-month. You remember that?"

I replied, "I may have been in Barbados. Look, Rudy—"

"I got a snack machine over there and a Coke machine. You need change?"

I surrendered. "Yes, please."

So we got change, bought some petrified snacks from the machine, plus two Cokes, used the restroom, and got a few gallons of gas.

Back in the tiny office, I paid for the gas with one of my government MasterCards. Agents carry two credit cards, one for food, lodging, and miscellaneous, and one specifically for gasoline. My gasoline card said CORPORATE, and R AND I ASSOCIATES, which meant nothing, but nosy Rudy asked, "What's R and I Associates?"

"Refrigerators and Ice Makers."

"Yeah?"

I changed the subject and asked him, "You got a local map?"

"Nope. But I can draw you one."

"For free?"

He laughed and rummaged through a stack of junk mail and found a flyer advertising a moose-wrestling contest or something, and began writing on the back with a pencil. He said, "So, you got to look for Stark Road first, and make a left, but there's no signs, then you get to Joe Indian Road—"

"Excuse me?"

"Joe Indian." He went through it again in case I was stupid, then concluded, "You hit this here loggin' road with no name, and stay on for about ten mile. Now, you're looking for McCuen Pond Road on the left, and that takes you right up to the Custer Hill property. Can't miss it, 'cause you get stopped."

"Stopped by who?"

"The guards. They got a house there and a gate. The whole property got a fence around it."

"Okay, thanks, Rudy."

"Why you headin' up there?"

"We're doing a service call for the refrigerator. Problem with the ice maker."

"Yeah?" He looked at us. "They expectin' you?"

"They sure are. They can't make a cocktail until we fix the ice problem."

"They didn't give you no directions?"

"They did, but my dog ate them. Okay, thanks—"

"Hey, you want some advice?"

"Sure."

"I gotta warn you, but you didn't hear it from me."

"Okay."

"Get your money up front. They's slow payin'. That's the way the rich are. Slow payin' the workin' people."

"Thanks for the warning."

We left, and I said to Kate, "We're on *Candid Camera.* Right?"

"I'm starting to think so."

We got in the car and doubled back on Route 56, entered the park, and kept an eye out for Stark Road.

I found it and turned onto this narrow road, which ran through a tunnel of trees. "You want some beef jerky?"

"No, thank you. And don't litter."

I was hungry enough to eat a bear, but I settled for the

beef jerky, which was gross. I threw the cellophane wrappers in the rear seat, my contribution to ecology.

We were close to the Custer Hill Club, and according to Walsh, an air-and-land search was supposed to be under way around the club property, but I didn't hear any helicopters or fixed-wing aircraft, and I didn't see any police search vehicles around. This was not a good sign, or it was a very good sign.

Kate checked her cell phone and said, "I have service now, and I also have a message."

She started to retrieve the message, but I said, "We're out of contact. No messages, no calls."

"What if they've found Harry?"

"I don't want to know either way. We're going to see Bain Madox."

She put her cell phone back in her pocket, then her beeper went off, and so did mine a minute later.

We followed Rudy's directions, and within twenty minutes, we turned onto McCuen Pond Road, which was narrow but well paved.

There was a big sign up ahead that stretched above the road, fixed to two ten-foot poles with floodlights attached. The sign said: THIS IS PRIVATE PROPERTY— NO TRESPASSING—STOP AT GATE AHEAD OR TURN AROUND.

We passed under the sign, and ahead I could see a clearing where a rustic log house stood behind a closed steel security gate.

Two men in camouflage fatigues exited the house as though they knew we were coming long before we got to the gate, and I said to Kate, "Motion or sound detectors. Maybe TV cameras, too."

"Not to mention those guys are wearing holsters, and one of them is looking at us with binoculars."

"God, how I hate private-security guys. Give them a gun and some power, and—"

"That sign says slow down to five miles an hour."

I slowed down and approached the closed gate. Ten feet from the gate was a speed bump and a sign that said: STOP HERE. I stopped.

The gate, which was electric, slid open a few feet, and one of the guys walked toward our car. I lowered the window, and he came up to me and asked, "How can I help you?"

The guy was in his thirties, all decked out in military cammies, hat, boots, and gun. He also wore an expression suggesting he was very cool and possibly dangerous if provoked. All he needed to complete the look were sunglasses and a swastika. I said to him, "I'm Federal Agent John Corey, and this is Federal Agent Kate Mayfield. We're here to see Mr. Bain Madox."

This seemed to crack his stone face, and he asked, "Is he expecting you?"

"If he was, you'd know about it, wouldn't you?"

"I . . . Can I see some identification?"

I wanted to show him my Glock first so he knew he wasn't the only person carrying, but to be nice, I handed him my credentials and so did Kate.

He studied both sets of credentials, and I had the feeling he either recognized them as legitimate or was pretending he was well versed in credential recognition.

I interrupted his perusal of the creds. "I'll take those back."

He hesitated, then handed them to us. I reiterated, "We're here to see Mr. Madox on official business."

"What is the nature of your business?"

"Are you Mr. Madox?"

"No . . . but—"

"Look, fella, you've got about ten seconds to do something brilliant. Call ahead if you need to, then open the fucking gates."

He looked a little pissed, but kept his cool and said, "Hold on."

He went back to the gate, slipped through the opening, and spoke to the other guy. Then they both disappeared into the log gatehouse.

Kate asked me, "Why do you always need to be confrontational?"

"Confrontational is when I pull my gun. Argumentative is when I pull the trigger."

"Federal agents are trained to be polite."

"I missed that class."

"What if they don't let us in? They can refuse us access to private property if we don't have a search warrant."

"Where's it say that?"

"It's actually in the Constitution."

"Ten bucks says we get in."

"You're on."

The neo-fascist came back to our car and said, "I'm going to ask you to pull up through the gate, and park your car to the right. A Jeep will take you up to the lodge."

"Why can't I take my own car?"

"It's for your own safety and security, sir, and because of our insurance policy."

"Well, we don't want to mess with your insurance company. Hey, you have bears on the property?"

"Yes, sir. Please proceed through the gate and remain in your vehicle until the Jeep arrives."

Did this idiot think I was getting out with bears around?

He signaled to the guy at the gatehouse, and the steel gate slid open.

I drove into the property and turned onto a gravel patch. The gate slid closed behind us, and I said to Kate, "Welcome to the Custer Hill Club. You owe me ten bucks."

She joked, "Twenty says we don't get out of here alive."

A black Jeep with tinted windows approached. It stopped, and two guys wearing holsters and camouflage fatigues got out and came toward us.

I said, "I need odds."

One guy came up to my window and said, "Please exit, and follow me."

This seemed like the kind of place where someone would put a tracking device or a bug in your car, so I had no intention of leaving the car there. I said, "I have a better idea. You lead, I'll follow."

He hesitated, then replied, "Follow me closely and stay on the road."

"If you stay on the road, I'll stay on the road."

He went back to the Jeep and turned around, and I followed him up a hill through a cleared field with big rock outcroppings.

Kate said, "I assume you didn't want them installing unwanted options in the car."

"When you see this level of security, you need to be as paranoid as they are."

"You always know how to handle a bad situation that you've gotten us into."

"Thank you . . . I think."

The road was lined with pole lights and I also noticed a series of utility poles running from the tree line across the open field and into the next tree line. The poles carried five wires, and as we passed beneath them, I saw that three of the wires were actually thick cables that must have been major power lines.

About halfway up the hill, I could see a huge lodge, the size of a small hotel. In the front of the lodge was a tall pole flying the American flag, and below the flag flew a yellow pennant of some sort.

Beyond the lodge at the top of the hill, I saw a tall tower that looked like a cellular relay tower, which explained why we had reception here, and why Harry should have reception if he was alive and well. I wondered if this tower belonged to the phone company, or to Bain Madox.

We reached the lodge, in front of which was a gravel parking space where another black Jeep was parked, along with a blue Ford Taurus, like the one I was driving. But this Taurus had an "e" sticker on the rear bumper, which I knew meant it was an Enterprise rental car. So maybe some weekend guests were still here. Also parked was a dark blue van—probably the same one that Betty had mentioned.

We stopped under the big columned portico, and both guys got out and opened our doors. Kate and I exited, she carrying her briefcase stuffed with airline manifests and car-rental agreements. I made a mental note of the plate number on the Enterprise car, then locked our doors and looked around.

The area surrounding the lodge was clear for about a half mile on all sides, which made for good views and very good security. Harry would have had a tough time getting close enough to this parking field to photograph plates and people, even if he used the rock formations for cover.

Also, I'd counted four security guys so far, and I had a feeling there were more. This place was tight, and I was fairly sure now that Harry had walked into a bad situation.

The Jeep driver said to us, "Please follow me."

I warned him, "No one is to touch this car. If I discover that anyone has added an unwanted feature to this car, he's going to jail. Understood?"

He didn't reply, but he understood.

We climbed a few steps to the covered veranda, where a row of Adirondack chairs and rockers faced out toward the sweeping view down the hill. Aside from the security goons, this was a very pleasant and homey place. I noticed now that the yellow pennant had the number 7 on it.

The security guy said, "Please wait here," and disappeared into the lodge.

Kate and I stood on the porch, and I speculated, "Maybe this place is for sale. Comes with a small army."

She didn't respond to that and instead said to me, "I should check my messages."

"No."

"John, what if—?"

"No. This is one of those rare times when I don't want any new information. We're going to see Bain Madox."

She looked at me and nodded.

The door opened, and the security guy said, "Come in." We entered the Custer Hill Club.

CHAPTER TWENTY-TWO

We walked into a large atrium lobby with a balcony above and a massive chandelier made of deer antlers. The room was paneled in yellow pine and decorated in a rustic style with hooked rugs, hunting and fishing prints, and a few pieces of furniture made of tree branches. I had the feeling that Mrs. Madox, if there was one, had nothing to do with this lodge. I said to Kate, "Nice place."

She replied, "I'm sure there's a moose head around here somewhere."

We heard footsteps coming from a passageway to the left, and a different security guy, this one a middle-aged man dressed in blue, entered the lobby. This must have been one of the palace guards, and he introduced himself to us as Carl. He asked, "May I take your coats?"

We said we'd keep them, and then he addressed Kate. "May I put your briefcase in the coatroom?"

"I'll carry it."

He said to her, "For security reasons, I'll need to look in your briefcase."

"Forget it."

This seemed to put him off, and he asked us, "What is the nature of your business with Mr. Madox?"

I said, "Look, Carl, we're Federal agents, and we don't submit to searches, and we're not checking anything, including our guns, and we don't answer questions, we ask them. You can either take us to see Bain Madox now or we'll be back with a search warrant, ten more Federal agents, and the state police. How do you want to do this?"

Carl seemed unsure, so he said, "Let me find out." He left.

Kate whispered in my ear, "Ten bucks says we get in to see the wizard."

"No, you're not getting your money back after I bullied him into one choice."

I took my cell phone out of my pocket, unhooked the beeper from my belt, and turned them both off. I said to Kate, "These things sometimes spook a suspect, or break up an interview at a critical moment." I informed her, "This is one of the times we're allowed to kill the beeper."

"I'm not so sure about that, but . . ." Reluctantly, she turned off her phone and beeper.

I noticed a large oil painting on the far wall. It was a scene of the Battle of the Little Bighorn, General George Armstrong Custer and his men, surrounded by painted

Indians on horseback, and it looked like the Indians were still winning.

I said to Kate, "Did you ever see that painting of Custer's Last Stand in the Museum of Modern Art?"

"No, did you?"

"I did. It's sort of abstract, and reminds me of Magritte or Dalí."

She didn't reply, wondering, I'm sure, how I knew Magritte or Dalí, or when I was ever in a museum.

I continued, "The painting shows this fish with a big eye and a halo, floating in air, and underneath the fish are all these Native Americans having sex."

"What? What does that have to do with Custer's Last Stand?"

"Well, the painting is titled, Holy Mackerel, Look at All Those Fucking Indians."

No response.

"Get it? Fish, big eye, halo, holy mackerel, look at—"

"That is the *stupidest* joke I've ever heard."

Carl reappeared and said to us, "Please follow me."

We followed him down a hallway into what looked like a library, then continued down a few steps into a huge, cathedral-ceilinged room.

At the far end of the room was a big stone fireplace, logs blazing away, and a big moose head over the mantel. I said to Kate, "Hey, there's your moose head. How did you know?"

Anyway, sitting in a winged chair near the fire was a man. He stood and crossed the big room, and I saw he was wearing a blue blazer, tan slacks, and a green plaid shirt.

We met halfway, and he extended his hand to Kate, who took it. He said, "I'm Bain Madox, president and owner of this club, and you must be Ms. Mayfield. Welcome."

"Thank you."

He turned to me, extended his hand, and said, "And you are Mr. Corey." We shook, and he asked me, "So, how can I help you?"

I remembered my politeness class, and replied, "First, I'd like to thank you for seeing us without an appointment."

He smiled tightly. "What were my choices?"

"Pretty limited, actually."

I took stock of Mr. Bain Madox. He was maybe mid-fifties, tall, fit, and not bad-looking. He sported long gray hair swept back from a smooth forehead, and he had a prominent hooked nose and steely gray eyes that hardly blinked. He sort of reminded me of a hawk, or an eagle, and in fact his head jerked now and then like a bird's.

He also had a cultured voice, as you'd expect, and beyond the outward appearances, I sensed a very cool and confident man.

We looked at each other, trying, I'm sure, to determine who was the real alpha male with the biggest dick.

I said to him, "We need about ten minutes of your time." Maybe a bit more, but you always say ten. I nodded toward the chairs by the fire.

He hesitated, then said, "Well, you must have had a long journey. Come, have a seat."

We followed him back across the room, and Carl tagged along.

I could see lots of dead-animal heads on the walls and stuffed birds, which is not politically correct these days, but I was sure that Bain Madox didn't give a shit. I half expected to see a stuffed Democrat on the wall.

I also noticed a big wooden gun cabinet with glass doors, through which I could see about a dozen rifles and shotguns.

Madox motioned us to two leather wing-back chairs facing him across a coffee table, and we all sat.

Bain Madox, now feeling compelled to be a good host, asked us, "Can I have Carl bring you something? Coffee? Tea?" He motioned toward a glass of amber liquid on the table. "Something stronger?"

Kate, following the procedure for keeping someone sitting longer than they may have wanted to sit and chat, said, "Coffee, please."

I wanted a scotch, and I could actually smell Madox's scotch in his glass, which he was drinking straight up; so maybe there really was a problem with the ice maker.

"Mr. Corey?"

"You know, I'm really dying for a latte. Can you do that?"

"Uh . . ." He looked at Carl and said, "Ask in the kitchen if we can get a latte."

"Or a cappuccino," I said. "Even an Americano will do. Maybe a mocha freezie."

I don't drink this shit, of course, but we needed some time with Mr. Madox.

Carl left, and I now noticed a dog lying on its side between Madox's chair and the hearth, sleeping or dead.

Madox informed me, "That's Kaiser Wilhelm."

"Looks like a dog."

He smiled. "It's a Doberman. Very smart, loyal, strong, and fast."

"Hard to believe." I mean, the stupid dog was just lying there, slobbering on the rug, snoring and farting.

Kate said, "He's a beautiful animal."

Oh, and it had a boner. I wondered what he was dreaming about. Also, Ms. Mayfield doesn't think *I'm* so beautiful when I'm snoring, slobbering, or farting.

"So," asked Mr. Madox, "what can I do for you?"

Normally, Kate and I would have already discussed who was going to lead, and what we were after. However, what we were after—Harry Muller—would tip off Mr. Madox that he was under surveillance, so this limited our questions to the weather and the World Series. On the other hand, maybe Madox already knew he was under surveillance.

"Mr. Corey? Ms. Mayfield?"

I made the decision to follow the example of General Custer and charge ahead, hopefully with better results. I told him, "We're acting on information that a Federal agent by the name of Harry Muller disappeared in the vicinity of this club, and we believe he may be lost on your property or hurt." I searched his face for a reaction, but his only expression seemed to be one of concern.

"Here? On this property?"

"Possibly."

He seemed truly surprised, or he was a good actor. He said to me, "But . . . as you saw, it's not easy to get onto this property."

"He was on foot."

"Oh? But this property is posted, and surrounded by a security fence."

It was my turn to feign surprise, and I replied, "A fence? Really? Well, maybe he got through the fence."

"Why would he do that?"

Good question. "He's a fanatical bird-watcher."

"I see . . . so, you think he may have gotten through the fence and wound up on this property."

"Possibly."

Madox's demeanor remained concerned and perplexed. "But why do you think that? There are millions of acres of wilderness surrounding this property. I have only about sixteen thousand acres."

"Is that all? Look, Mr. Madox, we're acting on specific information, which we need to check out. My question to you is, Have you or your staff seen or encountered anyone on the property?"

He shook his head and replied, "I would have been told." He asked me, "How long has this man been missing?"

"Since Saturday. But it has just come to our attention."

He nodded thoughtfully and took a sip of his scotch. "Well," he said, "I had about sixteen houseguests this weekend, many of whom were hiking or bird-hunting, plus I have security staff, so it's unlikely that this person could have been lost on my property without someone coming across him."

Kate spoke for the first time and pointed out, "Sixteen people divided into sixteen thousand acres is one person per thousand acres. You could hide an army in there."

Mr. Madox thought about the arithmetic and replied, "I suppose if he were hurt and unable to move, it may be possible that he wouldn't have been discovered."

Kate said, "Very possible."

Madox lit a cigarette and blew smoke rings into the air. "What," he asked, "would you like me to do? How can I help?"

I regarded Bain Madox, smoking, drinking, sitting in his leather chair in his big lodge. He looked more at ease than the average suspect. Actually, he looked innocent.

I had the feeling, however, that even if he had something to do with Harry's disappearance, this man would keep his cool. He could easily have told his flunkies to tell us he wasn't in or wasn't available; instead, he'd chosen to meet us face-to-face.

My brief forays into criminal psychology, and my years on the street, taught me about sociopaths and narcissists—incredibly egotistical and arrogant people who thought they could get away with murder by bullshitting.

It was quite possible that Bain Madox had something to hide, and he thought he could hide it under my nose. That wasn't going to happen.

He repeated, "How can I help?"

I replied, "We'd like your permission to conduct a search on your property."

He seemed prepared for that and said, "I can conduct my own search, now that I know there may be someone lost on the property. I have about fifteen staff available, plus all-terrain vehicles and six Jeeps."

I pointed out, "It would take you a month to cover this property. I'm talking about state and local police, Federal agents, and maybe troops from Fort Drum."

He didn't seem to like that idea, but he was boxed in, so he asked me, "Tell me again why you think this man is on *my* property, and not out in the surrounding wilderness?"

That was a really good question, and I had a standard law enforcement answer. "We are acting on information and belief, and that's all I can say." I pointed out, "With the information we have, we could get a search warrant, but that takes time. We'd rather have your voluntary cooperation. Is there a problem with that?"

"No, no problem, but I suggest you begin with an aerial search, which can do the same job more quickly and just as effectively."

Kate said, "Thank you, we know that. We have begun the air search. We're here to get your permission to enter this property with search teams."

"I certainly won't stand in the way of a search for a missing person." He paused. "But I'll need a liability waiver."

Kate was becoming annoyed and said, "We'll have one faxed to you ASAP."

"Thank you. I don't want to sound like a bad citizen, but unfortunately, we live in litigious times."

I couldn't argue with that, and I said to him, "The country is going to hell. Too many lawyers."

He nodded and offered his opinion, saying, "Lawyers are ruining the country. Ruining trust, frightening people who want to be Good Samaritans, promoting a culture of victimization, and engaging in legalized extortion."

I liked this guy and agreed, "In fact, they suck."

He smiled. "They suck."

I thought I should inform him, "Ms. Mayfield is a lawyer."

"Oh . . . well, I apologize if I—"

She said, "I don't practice law."

"Good," he said, then joked, "You look too nice to be a lawyer."

Ms. Mayfield stared at Mr. Madox.

Mr. Madox said, "I assume you'll begin the search in the morning." He pointed out, "It's getting too dark now to send people into those woods."

Clearly Mr. Madox was stalling for time with all the bullshit about liability waivers and so forth. I said, "I think we have about three hours of daylight left."

"I'll have my staff begin a search immediately. They know the terrain."

We looked at each other, and those freaky gray eyes never blinked.

Without taking his eyes off me, he said, "Mr. Corey, please tell me why a Federal agent was on my property."

I already had the answer to that. "The fact that Mr. Muller is a Federal agent is actually irrelevant."

"Irrelevant?"

"Yes. He was on a camping trip. Not on-duty. Was I not clear about that?"

"Perhaps I misunderstood."

"Perhaps." I added, "And since he is a Federal agent, the Federal government is assisting in the search."

"I see. So, I shouldn't make too much of you and Ms. Mayfield being with the Anti-Terrorist Task Force?"

"No, in fact, you shouldn't make *anything* of it." I added, "I should have also mentioned that Mr. Muller is a colleague, so we're here out of personal concern as well as for professional reasons."

He thought a moment, then said, "I haven't experienced that kind of camaraderie since I left the Army. If I were missing, I couldn't think of a single person who would do much more than make a few phone calls to find me."

"Not even your mom?"

He smiled. "Well, maybe her. And maybe my children in good time. Certainly the Internal Revenue would come looking for me after I missed a quarterly payment."

Neither Kate nor I commented on that.

Madox lit another cigarette and blew more smoke rings, saying, "That's a lost art." He asked us, "May I offer you a cigarette?"

We refused his offer.

I glanced around the room and noticed something in a dark corner staring at me with glassy eyes. It was, actually, a huge black bear, standing on its hind legs with its front legs and paws raised in a threatening gesture. I mean, I knew it was dead and stuffed, but it gave me a little jolt. I said to Madox, "Did you shoot that?"

"I did."

"Where?"

"Here, on my property. Sometimes they get through the fence."

"And you shoot them?"

"Well, if it's off-season, we just tranquilize them and relocate them. Why do you ask?"

"I don't like bears."

"Have you had a bad experience?"

"No, I'm trying to avoid a bad experience. Hey, do you think a 9mm Glock will stop a bear?"

"I don't think so, and I hope you don't have to find out."

"Me, too. Do you have bear traps on the property?"

"Definitely not. I have guests on the property, and I don't want them caught in a bear trap." He added, "Also, trespassers. I could get sued." He glanced at his watch and said, "So, if—"

"Just a few more questions while we wait for the latte."

He didn't reply, and I asked him, "So, you're a hunter?"

"I hunt."

"These are all your trophies?"

"Yes. I don't buy them as some people do."

"So, you're a pretty good shot?"

"I was an expert rifleman in the Army, and I can still drop a deer at two hundred yards."

"That's pretty good. How close was that bear?"

"Close. I let the predators get close." He looked at me, and I had the feeling he was being subtly unsubtle regarding yours truly. He said, "That's what makes it exciting." He asked me, "What does this have to do with Mr. Muller's disappearance?"

"Not a thing."

We stared at each other while he waited for me to explain my line of questioning. I said to him, "Just making conversation." I then asked him, "So, this is a private club?"

"It is."

"Could I join? I'm white. Irish and English. Catholic, like Christopher Columbus, but I could switch. I got married in a Methodist church."

Mr. Madox informed me, "There are no such requirements or exclusions, but our membership is filled at the moment."

Kate asked, "Do you accept women?"

He smiled. "Personally, I do. But club membership is restricted to men."

"Why is that?"

"Because that's the way I want it."

Carl appeared carrying a tray, which he set down on the coffee table. He said to me, "Is a café au lait all right?"

"Terrific."

He indicated a small silver coffeepot for Ms. Mayfield, then asked us, "Will that be all?"

We nodded, and Carl disappeared.

Mr. Madox went to the sideboard to refresh his scotch, and I said, "I'll have a small one."

He replied over his shoulder, "You'll have to take it neat." He poured two glasses, turned around, and remarked,

"I seem to be having trouble with my ice maker." He smiled.

Rudy, you old shit, I'm going to shove those rabbit ears up your ass.

More important, Madox *knew* someone was on the way to see him, yet he'd made no attempt to avoid his unknown visitors, even after the gatehouse goons told him we were Federal agents. Obviously, he'd made the decision to check us out while we checked him out.

Madox handed me a crystal glass and said, "Happy Columbus Day." We touched glasses, then he sat, crossed his legs, sipped, and stared at the fire.

Kaiser Wilhelm woke up and snuggled next to his master's chair to get his ears scratched. The stupid dog stared at me, and I stared back. He looked away first, so I won.

Kate sipped her coffee, then broke the silence. "You said you had sixteen guests this weekend."

"That's correct." Madox again glanced at his watch. "I believe they're all gone by now."

Kate informed him, "We may need to speak to them, so I'll need their names and contact information."

Madox didn't see that coming and was momentarily speechless, which I guessed was not usual for him. "Why . . . ?"

"In the event they saw or heard something related to Mr. Muller's disappearance." She added, "Standard procedure."

He didn't seem to like this standard procedure. "That seems totally unnecessary. No one saw or heard anything.

Also, please understand this is a private club whose members wish to remain private."

Kate replied, "I can insure their privacy, and it's up to us to determine if anyone saw or heard anything."

He took a bigger sip of scotch and said to Kate, "I'm not an attorney, as you are, but it's my understanding that unless this is a criminal matter, which it is not, or a civil case, which it is not, then I don't need to give you the names of my houseguests any more than you need to give me the names of *your* houseguests."

I couldn't resist and said, "I had my aunt and uncle, Joe and Agnes O'Leary, over last weekend. Who'd you have?"

He looked at me, and I couldn't tell if he appreciated me or not. Oddly, I liked the guy—man's man and all that—and I think we could have been pals under other circumstances. Maybe if this whole thing was a misunderstanding, and Harry was found in a motel or something, Mr. Madox would invite me up for a weekend with the boys. Maybe not.

Kate said to him, "You're correct that you have no legal obligation to reveal the names of your guests—at least at this point in time—but we'd like your voluntary cooperation now, while a man's life may be in danger."

Mr. Madox considered that. "I'll need to contact my attorney."

Kate reminded him, "You don't like attorneys."

He smiled tightly and replied, "I don't, but neither do I like my proctologist." He continued, "I'll contact the men who were here and see if they'll agree to have their names released."

"Please do that quickly. And while you're at it, I need

the names and contact information of your staff." She added, "Call me tonight. Mr. Corey and I are staying at The Point."

His eyebrows rose. "Are you having trouble spending the anti-terrorist budget?"

Good one. I really liked this guy. I said, "We're sharing a room to save taxpayer money."

He raised his eyebrows again and said, "I won't touch that one." He looked at his watch a third time, and said, "Well, if I'm going to make some calls—"

"By the way," I said, "I noticed that we had good cell-phone reception here, and I saw that tower on the hill. Is that a cell-phone tower?"

"It is."

"You must have some pull."

"Meaning?"

"Meaning, the population of this area is probably less than the population of Central Park on a Sunday, and I don't think a lot of these people have cell phones, yet you have a big, expensive tower right on your property."

"You'd be surprised how many rural people own cell phones," Madox said. "Actually, I had that built."

"For yourself?"

"For anyone who has a cell phone. My neighbors appreciate it."

"I didn't see any neighbors."

"What's your point?"

"Well, the point is, Agent Muller had a cell phone, made and received some calls from this area, and now he's not calling or receiving. This is why we're concerned that he may be injured or worse."

Mr. Madox replied, "Sometimes, because of the distance to surrounding relay towers, service is lost. Sometimes people lose or damage their phones. Sometimes a particular phone company has bad service in an area, sometimes the cell phone is faulty, and sometimes the battery goes dead. I don't make too much of a non-responsive cell phone. If I did, I'd think my children were kidnapped by Martians."

I smiled. "Right. We're not making too much of it."

"Good." He uncrossed his legs and leaned forward. "Anything further?"

"Yeah, what kind of scotch is this?"

"Private label, single malt. Would you like a bottle on your way out?"

"That's very generous of you, but I can't accept a gift. I can, however, *drink* a bottle here and not commit an ethics-code violation."

"Would you like one for the road?"

I answered, "With these roads, I think I'd have trouble finding The Point sober." I suggested, "Ms. Mayfield and I would like to join your security people in the search. Then, maybe we could stay here tonight. Is that possible?"

"No. It's against club regulations. Also, the house staff are all leaving for a well-deserved rest after the three-day weekend."

"I don't need much staff, and Miss Mayfield and I can share a room."

He surprised me by saying, "You're funny. Sorry, I can't extend you an overnight invitation. But if you'd like to stay in a local motel, I'll have one of my staff lead you to South Colton. You may have already been there on your way here."

"Yeah, I think so." I guessed that the scotch had loosened him up a bit, which was why he found me amusing, so I said to him, "I don't want to keep you from making all those calls, but if you've got a minute, I'm curious about this club."

He didn't respond.

"Nothing to do with this disappearance, but this is a really great-looking place. How did it get started? What do you do here? Hunt, fish?"

Bain Madox lit another cigarette, sat back, and crossed his legs again. "Well," he said, "first the name. In 1968 I was commissioned a second lieutenant in the United States Army, and stationed at Fort Benning, Georgia, prior to shipping out to Vietnam. There were a number of officer club annexes at Benning—smaller satellite clubs where junior officers could get together, away from the brass at the Main Club."

"Great idea. I was a cop before joining the ATTF, and I can tell you, I never went to the same bars where the brass hung out."

"Precisely. Well, there was this one club, located in the woods at a place called Custer Hill, and called the Custer Hill Officers Club. The building was a bit basic, and resembled a lodge."

"Ah. I see where this is going."

"Yes. So, several nights a week, a few dozen young officers would get together to drink beer and eat bad pizza, and discuss life, the war, women, and, now and then, politics."

Mr. Madox seemed to leave the room and go back to that place and time. It was quiet except for the crackling fire, which was dying.

He came back and continued, "It was a very bad time for the country and the Army. Discipline had gone to hell, the nation was badly divided, there were riots in the cities, assassinations, bad news from the front, and . . . classmates, people we knew, were dying in Vietnam, or coming home terribly wounded . . . physically, mentally, and spiritually . . . and this is what we talked about."

He finished his scotch and lit yet another cigarette, saying, "We felt . . . betrayed. We felt that our sacrifices, our patriotism, our service, and our beliefs had become irrelevant and detested by much of the country." He looked at us and said, "This is nothing new in the history of the world, but it was something new for America."

Neither Kate nor I commented.

Bain Maddox continued, "Well, we became bitter, then radical, I suppose you'd say, and we took a vow that . . . that if we lived, we'd dedicate our lives to righting many wrongs."

I didn't think that was the exact nature of the vow. The word "revenge" came to mind.

Madox went on, "So, most of us shipped out, some of us returned, and we stayed in touch. Some of us, like myself, stayed in the Army, but most got out when their obligation was completed. Many of us became successful, and we often helped those who didn't, or who needed a career boost, or a job referral. A classic old-boys network, but this one was born in the cauldron of turbulent times, hardened by blood and war, and tested by years of wandering through the wilderness that America had become. And then, as we grew older and more successful, and as our . . . influence grew, and as America began to regain her strength and find her way again, we saw that we counted."

Again he fell silent and glanced around, as though he were thinking about how he'd gotten here in this big lodge, so far from the small officers club in the woods of Georgia. He said, "I built this lodge as a gathering place about twenty years ago."

I said, "So, you guys didn't come up here just for the hunting and fishing. I mean, there's a business angle here, and maybe a little political stuff, too."

He considered his response. "We were . . . engaged in the war against Communism, and I can say truthfully and with some pride that many members of this club were instrumental in the final victory over that sick ideology, and the ending of the Cold War." He regarded us and said, "And now . . . well, we have a new enemy. There will always be a new enemy."

"And?" I asked, "Are you involved?"

He shrugged. "Not to the extent we were involved in the Cold War. We're all older now, we fought the good fight, and we deserve a peaceful retirement." He looked at Kate and me and said, "It's up to people your age to fight this one."

I asked him, "So, the members of this club are all Army veterans from the original Custer Hill Club?"

"No, not really. Some of us have passed on, and some have dropped out. We've added new members over the years, men who share our beliefs and who lived through those times. We've made them honorary members of the original Custer Hill Officers Club, Fort Benning, Georgia, 1968."

I thought about that, and about rich men, and powerful men meeting on a long weekend in a remote lodge, and I thought that maybe there was nothing to this, and maybe the Justice Department was going through one of its many moments of paranoia.

On the other hand . . .

I said to him, "Well, thank you for sharing that with us. It's really interesting, and maybe you should all write your memoirs."

He smiled and said, "We'd all go to jail."

"Excuse me?"

"For some of our Cold War activities. We pushed it a bit."

"Yeah?"

"But all's well that ends well. Don't you agree that to fight monsters, you must sometimes become a monster?"

I replied, "No, I don't."

Kate seconded that. "We need to fight the good fight in a good way. That's what makes us different from them."

"Well," replied Bain Madox, "when someone is aiming a nuclear missile at you, you're perfectly justified in kicking them in the balls."

I could see his point, but arguments like this could go on for days and nights, and I think he'd already had these arguments and resolved these questions many years ago, over beer and pizza.

I'd always thought that people of that generation who came of age in the '60s were somehow different, and maybe scarred, and maybe still carrying one grudge or another. But I don't get paid to think about things like this, or to offer free counseling.

Nevertheless, I said to Mr. Madox, "So, you *do* have comrades who would come looking for you if you disappeared."

He looked at, or through, me for a while, then said, "Do I? I did. When I was young and wore the uniform . . . I think they're all gone now . . . except for Carl . . . He served under me in Vietnam." He added, "Carl and Kaiser Wilhelm are loyal."

Well, if there was a sled named Rosebud lying around, I would have thrown it in the fireplace and faded to black. Instead, I stood and said, "Thank you for your time."

Kate, too, stood and picked up her briefcase.

He seemed almost surprised that he was getting rid of us, and for a moment I thought he looked disappointed. He asked us, "Are you going to join my staff in the search?"

I didn't think that Kate and I would accomplish anything by riding around these sixteen thousand acres with Madox's security staff until nightfall.

"Mr. Corey?"

On the other hand, I wouldn't have minded taking a look around the property. But Kate and I weren't even supposed to be here, and we were already late for our meeting with Major Schaeffer at state police headquarters. I glanced at Kate, then answered, "We'll leave it to your staff to conduct the search. But we'll be back in the morning with search parties."

He nodded and said, "Fine. I'll have my staff begin the search immediately. I'll also make sure tomorrow's search party has terrain maps and the use of my vehicles and staff."

Kate asked, "Didn't you say your staff is going on holiday?"

"The *house* staff is off. The security staff will be here."

"May I ask why you have so many security people here?"

Madox replied, "It's really not that many if you consider they work in shifts to cover a seven-day week, twenty-four hours a day, every day of the year."

"But why do you *need* that kind of security?"

He answered, "A house like this attracts unwanted attention. Besides, the local police are stretched thin and the state police are some distance away. I rely on my own security."

She didn't pursue that, and Bain Madox said, "I'll show you out."

We walked toward the door, and on the way, I asked him, "Will you be here tomorrow?"

"I may be." He paused. "My plans are up in the air."

And so were his two jets. I asked him, "Where do you live full-time?"

"New York City."

"Any other homes?"

"A few."

"How do you get out of here? Car? Plane?"

He replied, "Usually someone drives me to the regional airport in Saranac Lake. Why do you ask?"

"I just want to be sure we can reach you tomorrow.
Do you have a cell phone?"

"I don't give that number out, but if you'll call the security guard number here, someone is on twenty-four hours
a day, and they'll locate me. If we discover anything, we'll
call you at The Point." He gave me the security number.
"But I'll probably see you in the morning."

"You will. Do you have a private plane?"

He hesitated, then replied, "I do. Why do you ask?"

"Can you be reached on the plane?"

"Usually. Why—?"

"Are you planning any flights in or out of the
country?"

"I go when and where business takes me. I'm not sure
why you need to know this."

"I just need to know that I can contact you if there's
any misunderstandings or problems with your security
people, who seem very protective and not particularly
easy to deal with."

"That's what they get paid for, but I'll make sure they
understand that you and Ms. Mayfield can reach me, and
that the search teams can traverse the property freely in
the morning."

"Great. That's all we need."

We passed through the library into the lobby, and I
said, "So, you built this place."

"Yes. In 1982." He added, "As a kid, I always admired the grand lodges up here, and also what were called the Great Camps, built by millionaires at the turn of the last century. In fact, The Point, where you're staying, was a Rockefeller Great Camp."

"Yeah, I know. You have a tux I can borrow?"

He smiled. "I'd opt for room service."

"Me, too. So, why didn't you buy one of these old places which are probably for sale all over?"

He thought a moment, then replied, "Well, I looked at a few, but this private parcel was available in the park, and I bought it for three hundred thousand dollars. Less than twenty dollars an acre. Best investment I ever made."

"Better than oil?"

We made eye contact, and he said, "I suppose you know who I am."

"Well, you're not exactly unknown."

"I try to keep a low profile. But that's not always possible. Thus, the security here."

"Right. Good idea. Nobody's going to get you here."

"I don't think anyone is actually after me."

"You never know." He ignored that, and I asked him, "Hey, what's with the price of oil? Up or down?"

"Your guess is as good as mine."

"That's pretty scary."

He smiled and replied, "Bet on fifty dollars a barrel as we get closer to the war in Iraq." He added, "You didn't hear that from me."

"Gotcha."

He seemed to want to talk, which was fine with me,

and he drew our attention to a wall where about two dozen bronze plaques were mounted, each bearing a name and a date.

He said, "These are some of the men I served with and their dates of death. The earlier dates are those who died in Vietnam, the later ones died in one war or another since then, and some died natural deaths." He moved closer to the plaques and said, "I built this place partly as a memorial to them, partly as a reminder of our beginnings at the Custer Hill Officers Club, and partly as a place to gather on Veterans Day and Memorial Day for those of us still around."

After a few seconds of silence, Kate said, "That's very nice."

Bain Madox continued to stare at the names, then turned to us. "Also, when I built this place, it was the height of the Cold War, and you might remember that the news media was trying to whip the country into a state of hysteria about Reagan leading us to nuclear Armageddon."

I said, "Yeah, I remember that. They had me going for a while. I was buying canned chili and beer by the case."

Madox smiled politely and continued, "Well, I never thought we were going to have a nuclear exchange—not with Mutually Assured Destruction—but the idiots in the media and Hollywood had us all dead and buried." He added, "Basically, they're a bunch of old ladies."

"That's an insult to old ladies."

He went on, "Anyway, I suppose that was on my mind

when I decided to build this place. I know it was on my wife's mind."

"You're married?"

"Not anymore."

"Is she a Democrat or something?"

"She's a card-carrying consumer."

"So," I asked, "you have a fallout shelter here?"

"I do. A totally useless expense, but that's what she wanted."

"Well," I said, "fallout is tricky stuff."

"Fallout is overrated."

I'd never heard radioactive fallout described in quite that way, and for a moment I thought I was speaking to Dr. Strangelove.

Madox glanced at a Black Forest cuckoo clock on the wall and said to us, "I'd show you around, but I'm sure you have other stops to make."

I reminded him, "We'll be back tomorrow at first light."

He nodded and moved toward the door.

I said, "Great painting of the Little Bighorn."

"Thank you. It's very old, artist unknown, and I don't think it's an accurate representation of the final moments of that battle."

"Who would know? They all died."

"The Indians didn't all die."

I wanted to tell him my joke, but I could feel Kate's eyes on me. "Well, they were foolhardy, but brave."

"More foolhardy than brave, I'm afraid." He added, "I was in the Seventh Cavalry. Custer's regiment."

"You don't look that old, or—" I nodded toward the painting.

"In *Vietnam*, Mr. Corey. The regiment still exists."

"Oh . . . right."

He stood by the door, and there was a moment of almost awkward silence. This is where I usually spring something on the suspect, leaving him or her to a bad night's sleep. But in truth, I had no more arrows in my quiver, to use an apt metaphor, and I was really unsure if Bain Madox had anything to do with Harry's disappearance, so I said to him, "Thank you for your time and help."

"I'll send my men out immediately," he replied. "Meanwhile, if the air search comes up with anything, have the state police call that security guard number, and I'll get some people on the ground where the helicopters have lit up the area. If we're lucky, we may find this man tonight."

"I think some prayers might help, too."

Madox commented, "As long as it's above freezing, a person can survive in the woods for weeks if he's not badly hurt."

He opened the door, and we all went out onto the veranda. I noticed that the Enterprise rental car that had been there was gone.

I said to him, "I want to thank you for your service to our country."

He nodded.

Kate said, "Yes, thank you."

Madox replied, "And you're both serving in a different way, in a different war. I thank you for that. This may be the toughest fight we've ever had. Stay with it. We will prevail."

"We will," Kate said.

"We will," Mr. Madox agreed, and added, "I hope I live long enough to see a permanent condition Green."

CHAPTER TWENTY-THREE

We got into our Taurus and followed the black Jeep downhill toward the gate.

We didn't speak while we were inside the property in case there were directional listening devices, but we did turn on our cell phones and beepers, which indicated that Kate had two messages, and I had none.

The dashboard clock said it was 4:58 P.M., so Tom Walsh should still be in his office defending Western Civilization for another two minutes.

At the guardhouse, the Jeep pulled to the side, and the gate slid open. As we exited the property, I could see two guards through a window of the house, and one of them was videotaping us. I leaned toward Kate's window and saluted with my middle finger.

McCuen Pond Road lay in shadow, and I turned on

my headlights so I could spot the bears sooner. I asked Kate, "Well, what are your thoughts?"

She stayed silent awhile, then replied, "He's charming in a spooky sort of way."

One of the more interesting things in life is hearing a woman's thoughts on a man you've both met. Men that I find ugly, she finds good-looking; men I find slimy, she finds sociable; and so forth. In this case, however, I sort of agreed with Kate.

She said, "I think he liked you." She added, "Don't take this wrong, but he sort of reminded me of you."

"How's that, darling?"

"Well, the self-confidence and the . . . for want of a better expression, the male macho bullshit."

"Good expression. More important, does he know more about Harry than he's telling us?"

"I don't know . . . His whole demeanor seemed almost nonchalant."

I replied, "The sign of a sociopath and narcissist."

"Yes, but sometimes the sign of a person who has nothing to hide."

"He has something to hide, even if it's only oil-price rigging. That's why the Justice Department is interested in him."

"True, but—"

"And yet," I said, "he invites us in without his lawyer present."

"What's your point?"

"He wants to know what we know, and he can learn that by the questions we ask him."

"That's one way to look at it."

"And how about that story of the Custer Hill Club?"

She nodded. "What a story. It's really amazing if you think about it . . . I mean, these young officers, staying in touch, some of them getting rich and powerful . . . and Bain Madox building that lodge."

"Yeah. What's more amazing is that he actually admitted to us that this group is or was some sort of secret society that somehow influenced events on the world stage during the Cold War. Including engaging in illegal activities."

She thought a moment, then replied, "He wants to sound important and powerful . . . guys do that . . . but if any of that is true, then it puts a whole different light on the Custer Hill Club." She pointed out, "He raised some suspicions he didn't need to raise."

"He may have thought we already knew about the history of the club."

"Or," Kate said, "it's past history and he's proud of it, like he's proud of his Vietnam service. I don't know . . . but then he said he was a little involved with the war on terrorism."

"Right. That's like being a little pregnant." I said, "As I suspected, there's more to this group than meets the eye. There's a political element here, and in today's world, Mr. Madox's oil mixes well with politics."

"It always did."

I changed the subject back to our immediate concern. "So, did Madox have anything to do with Harry's disappearance?"

She stayed quiet, then said, "The one thing that bothered me was his stalling . . . like he was waiting for Harry to . . . turn up."

I nodded and said, "That would take the heat off him." I added, "I have this bad feeling that Harry is going to turn up soon, and not on Bain Madox's property."

Kate nodded silently, then said, "I need to check my phone messages." She listened to them and said to me, "Tom, twice. He says I need to call him ASAP."

I wondered why Walsh had called her and not me, too.

She checked her beeper and said, "Tom, twice."

"He's a persistent little shit, isn't he?"

"He's not . . . What is your problem with authority?"

"My problem is with supervisors who bullshit me and expect loyalty in return. The essence of loyalty is reciprocity. If you're loyal to me, I'll be loyal to you. Bullshit me, and I'll bullshit you. That's the contract."

"Thank you for sharing that. Now, I'll call our supervisor while you give your undivided attention to the road. Drive slowly so we don't run out of cell-phone coverage."

I eased up on the gas and said, "Put it on speakerphone."

She dialed, and Walsh's voice came through her phone. "Where the hell have you been?" he asked.

Kate replied, without bullshit, "We interviewed Bain Madox at the Custer Hill Club."

"*What?* I specifically told you—was this your idiot husband's idea?"

I cut in. "Hi, Tom. Idiot husband here."

Silence, followed by, "Corey, you have really screwed up this time."

"That's what you said last time."

He was not a happy man and almost shouted, "You totally disobeyed my orders. You're history, mister."

Kate seemed a little ruffled, and said, "Tom, we've gotten permission from Madox to conduct a search on his land at first light. Meanwhile, he promised to begin a search with his security staff immediately."

No reply, and I thought the call was dropped or Tom was having a seizure or something. I said to Kate, "Do you want some of these Cheez-Its?"

Kate asked, "Tom? Are you there?"

His voice came through the phone, and he said, "I'm afraid we don't need to continue the search."

Neither of us responded, and I felt my stomach tighten. I already knew what he was going to say, but I didn't want to hear it.

Tom Walsh informed us, "The state police have found the body of a man that they've tentatively identified by the contents of his wallet and photo ID as Harry Muller."

Again, neither of us said anything, then Tom Walsh said, "I'm sorry to be the bearer of bad news."

I pulled off to the side of the road, took a deep breath, and asked Walsh, "What are the details?"

"Well, about three-fifteen this afternoon, the state police regional headquarters in Ray Brook . . . where you are supposed to be . . . got an anonymous call from a man who said he was hiking in the woods and saw a body lying on a trail. He said he approached the body, determined that the man was dead, apparently from a gunshot wound, then ran back to his vehicle, drove to a park emergency phone, and called the police." He added, "The man would not give his name."

I thought about that, and I thought I knew the man's name. *I was an expert rifleman in the Army.*

Walsh went on, "This man gave a fairly accurate description of the location, and within half an hour, the state and local police, using search dogs, found the body. A further search discovered Harry's camper about three miles south of where the body was found, so it appears that Harry was heading toward the Custer Hill Club, about three miles further north of the trail."

I said, "That doesn't comport with Harry's phone call to his girlfriend."

"Well, I played that message again, and Harry said, quote, 'I'm on-duty, near the right-wing loony lodge.'" Walsh said, "You can't take that to mean he was within sight of or *very* near the Custer Hill property."

This man was obviously not a detective. "Tom," I said, "it doesn't make sense that he'd park his camper six miles away, then call his girlfriend at seven forty-eight A.M., then begin hoofing it through the woods. It would take him almost two hours just to get to the fence, and I assume he was supposed to be at or near Custer Hill at first light. But if we believe this scenario, then he wouldn't have arrived until almost ten A.M. You following me on this, Tom?"

He didn't respond for a few seconds, then said, "Yes, but—"

"Good. And while you're at it, get a triangulation on

Harry's cell-phone call to his girlfriend. That will tell you where he was when he called."

"Thank you, I know that. The phone company is working on it. But other than the cell tower at the Custer Hill Club, there may not be any other towers close enough to get a triangulation."

"How did you know about that cell tower on the Custer Hill property?"

There were a few seconds of silence, then he said, "I just got that from the phone company. We should know more in an hour or so, but I have to tell you, even if he was near the Custer Hill property when he called his girl-friend, it doesn't mean he entered the property. He may have gotten spooked by something and was headed *back* toward his camper when he was shot. You know, there's always two or more ways to look at evidence."

"Really? I'll have to remember that. And by the way, sometimes a little common sense goes a long way."

"Federal prosecutors don't care about common sense. They want the evidence to speak for itself. This evidence does not."

"Well, then, we need more evidence. Tell me about the gunshot wound."

"The gunshot wound entered his upper torso from the rear, and I'm told it probably severed his spinal column, and exited through his heart. No bullet recovered yet. Death was probably instantaneous . . . I spoke to Major Schaeffer, and he assures me there was no indication that Harry lingered . . . he apparently died where he fell." He added, "There was cash in his wallet, and he had his watch, gun, credentials, video camera, digital camera, and so forth, so according to the state police, it appears to have been a hunting accident."

I can still drop a deer at two hundred yards. I replied, "That's what it's supposed to look like."

Walsh didn't comment.

I said, "Obviously we need to look at what's on his cameras."

"Already done. There's nothing on the videotape or the digital disk."

I said, "Get the tape and disks to our lab and see if anything was erased."

"That's being done."

Kate asked him, "How soon can we get an autopsy report?"

"The body is being transported to the county morgue in Potsdam for a positive identification using photo and fingerprints on file from FBI Headquarters. I have instructed that the autopsy not be done there—this is too important to leave to a local medical examiner. I'm having the body flown here to Bellevue tonight or tomorrow."

"Good move. Fax me a copy of the autopsy and toxicology report."

"Toxicology could take four to six days."

"Two or three, on an expedited basis. Also, get word to Bellevue to look for signs of foul play. Drugging, bruises, signs of rope or handcuff marks on the skin, and trauma other than the gunshot wound. Also, the time of death is *very* important."

"You may find this difficult to believe, but the New York City medical examiner, the state police, and the FBI do this for a living."

I ignored that and continued, "Also, have a state police investigator at the morgue ASAP to witness the removal of the clothing and personal effects. He or she needs to look for signs that the clothing or personal effects were tampered with in any way."

"There's someone from the State Bureau of Investigation on their way to the morgue. Plus we have two agents coming from Albany. We're going to get involved with this investigation because it was a Federal agent on assignment who was killed."

"Good. And also make sure the state police and the FBI do a complete crime-scene investigation and look for witnesses. You need to assume a homicide was committed."

"I understand, but it could also be what it appears to be—an accident. This happens all the time up there. Meanwhile, if you were where you were supposed to be, you'd be where you need to be to give your expert advice on how to conduct this autopsy and investigation."

"Tom, fuck you."

"I know you're upset, so I'll ignore that—once."

"Fuck you."

He ignored it a second time and asked, "Where are you now?"

Kate replied, "We've just left the Custer Hill Club."

Walsh said, "Well, not only did you waste your time there but you also tipped off Bain Madox that he is under surveillance."

Kate came to my defense. "John handled it very well. If Madox didn't know he was under surveillance, he still doesn't know. If he already knew, then it's a moot point."

Walsh said, "The real point is, you weren't supposed to be there under any circumstances. What good did you do by going there, John?"

I replied, "I was on a mission of mercy, Tom. I got what I wanted—permission to conduct a search. Okay, we don't need a search anymore, though I'm ready to do it anyway just to mess with Bain Madox."

"That's not going to happen. Now that you've paid him a visit, we are obligated by law to inform him that the person in question has been found off his property."

"Don't be too quick with that information."

"John, I'm not messing around with this timeline. This guy is not your average Joe Citizen. He'll be brought up-to-date by a phone call by a state or local law enforcement officer within the hour."

"Let me discuss that with Major Schaeffer first."

"Why?"

"I just spent forty minutes with Madox, and I got some strange vibes from him—I think that sonofabitch had Harry at his place, grilled him, then murdered him."

"That's . . . that's quite a statement. Think about what you're saying."

"*You* think about it."

Walsh said, "Kate?"

She took a deep breath and said, "It's possible. I mean, it is possible."

"What would be Madox's motive?" Walsh inquired.

I replied, "I don't know, but I will find out."

He stayed silent for a few seconds, then said, "All right. We'll certainly proceed as though it were a homicide. Meanwhile, I need to call Harry's girlfriend, Lori, and Washington is on the other line, so—"

"*Send* someone—a cop from the Task Force—to see Lori Bahnik in person and have a police chaplain along. Also, Harry has kids and an ex-wife. You need to send someone whom the family knows to do the notifications, like his old squad commander or his former partner. Speak to Vince Paresi. He'll know how to take care of it."

"I understand. Meanwhile, drive now to the airport and wait for a helicopter to pick you up. A state trooper will meet you there with Harry's cameras, which you will bring to 26 Fed—"

"Hold on," I said. "We're not leaving here until this investigation is complete."

"You're coming back to Manhattan, tonight. I'll be here—"

"Tom, excuse me, you need *your* people on the scene."

"Thank you. I know that. In fact, two people from this office will be on that helicopter. You, Detective Corey, are off this case, and so is Kate. Return immediately. Meanwhile, Headquarters is on hold, and I don't have the time or patience to—"

"Neither do I. Let me give this to you straight, Tom. Number one, Harry Muller was my friend. Two, you wanted my ass on that assignment, and I could now be lying in that morgue instead of him. Three, I think he was murdered, and four, if you pull me off this case, I'm going to make a stink that they'll smell in the Justice Department."

"Are you threatening me with something?"

"Yes. Five, you sent that man into a fortified camp with no clue about what was there—hell, I just left this place, and a Delta Team couldn't penetrate it, and you either knew that or should have known it. Six, Harry Muller went in there carrying his credentials and no plausible cover story. How long have you been doing this for a living?"

He was really hot and yelled, "Let me tell *you* something—"

"No, let me tell *you* something, Einstein. You totally fucked up. But you know what? I'll go to bat for you when the shit hits the fan. Why? Because I like you? No, because you are right now going to tell me to stay here and stay on the case. If you don't, my next stop after 26 Fed will be Washington. You understand?"

It took him about four seconds to understand, and he said, "You make a compelling argument for your continued work on the case. But so help me God, Corey, if you—"

"You were doing fine until 'so help me God.' Quit while you're even."

"I will *get* even."

"You'll be lucky if you don't get sent to Wichita." I said, "I'll let you and Kate have the last word."

Kate was really shaken up and she said to Walsh, "I have to agree with John that Harry's assignment was not well thought out, and not well handled." She added, "That *could* have been my husband lying in the morgue."

Walsh didn't respond to that and said instead, "I need to speak to Headquarters. Anything further?"

Kate said, "No."

He said, "Get over to the state police in Ray Brook, and call me from there."

He hung up, and we both sat in silence for a while on the side of the road. I could hear birds in the woods, and the sound of the engine idling.

Finally, Kate said, "I was afraid we'd get that news."

I didn't reply, lost in my own thoughts about Harry Muller, who'd sat across from me for about three years; two former cops, working as strangers in a strange land called 26 Federal Plaza. *Body shipped back to New York City for an autopsy, funeral home Thursday and Friday, and Mass and burial on Saturday.*

Kate took my hand and said, "I just can't believe this . . ."

For months after 9/11, I attended wakes, funerals, Masses, and memorial services, day and night, sometimes three in a day. Everyone I knew was on this insane, soul-numbing schedule, and as the weeks went by, I'd run into the same people at funeral homes, churches, synagogues, and cemeteries, and we'd all just look at one another with eyes that were beyond expression; the shock and trauma were fresh, but the funerals started to blur into one another, and the only difference was the grief-stricken family who never looked the same as the last grief-stricken family, and then the widows and kids would show up at some other cop's funeral to pay their respects, and they became part of the crowd of mourners. It was a gut-wrenching and surreal time, black months, with black caskets and black shrouds, and black mourning bands on shiny badges, and black mornings after a night of too much drinking.

I can still remember the shrill of the bagpipe bands, the final salute, and the casket . . . more often than not containing not much more than a body part . . . being lowered into the grave.

Kate said, "John, let me drive."

Harry and I had gone to some of the funerals together, and I recalled that at Dom Fanelli's funeral Mass, out on the steps of the church, Harry had said to me, "When a cop thinks about getting killed on the job, he thinks about some dumb dirtbag who's having a lucky day. Who would've thought something like this could happen right here?"

Kate asked, "John? Are you all right?"

I remembered, too, Dom's mother, Marion Fanelli, conducting herself with great dignity, almost ignored in the crowd as everyone focused on Dom's wife and kids, and Harry said to me, "Let's go talk to her. She's alone."

And that reminded me that Harry's mother was still alive, and I made a mental note to add her to the list of people who should be officially notified with a chaplain in attendance.

Kate had gotten out of the car and opened my door. She took my arm and said, "I'm driving."

I got out and we changed places.

Kate put the car in gear, and we continued on in silence.

The sky above was still light, but the road was in deep shadow, and the forest on either side was black. Now and then, I could see glassy eyes shining in the dark woods, or a small animal scurrying across the road. Around a bend, a deer was trapped in our headlights, and he stood there, half petrified and half shaking in fear before bolting into the woods.

Kate said, "We should be at the state police headquarters in about an hour."

After ten minutes, I said, "Harry's assignment made no sense."

"John, don't think about it."

"He could have seen and photographed cars on this road. One way in, one way out. He didn't have to go onto the property."

"Please don't think about it. There's nothing you can do about it now."

"That's why I have to think about it."

She glanced at me and asked, "Do you really think it was Bain Madox?"

"The circumstantial evidence, and my instincts, say yes, but I need more than that before I kill him."

CHAPTER TWENTY-FOUR

We came to Route 56, which went south, back toward Saranac Lake and the state police headquarters in Ray Brook, or north toward Potsdam and the morgue where Harry should have arrived by now.

Kate started to turn for Ray Brook, but I said, "Turn right. Let's go see Harry."

She reminded me, "Tom said to go—"

"You can't go too far wrong doing the opposite of what Tom Walsh says."

She hesitated, then turned toward Potsdam.

Within ten minutes, we passed the brown sign that said we were leaving Adirondack State Park.

A few miles later, we were in South Colton, where I saw Rudy talking to someone who was pumping his own gas. I said to Kate, "Pull in here."

She turned the car into the gas station. I leaned out the window and called, "Hey, Rudy!"

He came over to the car and asked me, "Hey, how'd you make out there?"

"The ice maker is fixed. I told Mr. Madox what you said about getting the money up front, and he paid me cash."

"Uh . . . you wasn't supposed to—"

"He's very pissed at you, Rudy."

"Ah, jeez, you wasn't supposed to—"

"He wants to see you—tonight."

"Oh, jeez . . ."

"I need to get to the county hospital in Potsdam."

"Uh . . . yeah . . . well, you just follow 56 north." He gave me directions to the hospital, and I said to him, "When you see Madox, tell him John Corey is also very good with a gun."

"Okay . . ."

Kate pulled back onto the road, and we continued toward Potsdam. She said, "That sounded like a threat."

"To a guilty man, it's a threat. To an innocent man, it's an odd statement."

She didn't reply.

The terrain had opened up, and I could see houses and small farms now. The late-afternoon sun cast long shadows over the rolling hills.

Neither Kate nor I said much; there's something about the expectation of seeing a dead body that keeps the conversation subdued.

I kept thinking about Harry Muller, and it was hard for

me to believe he was dead. I replayed my last conversation
with him, and I wondered if I'd had a bad feeling about his
assignment or if what happened since then made me think
that. You never know. But I did know that whether or not
I'd had this feeling of foreboding on Friday, I definitely
had it now.

Within twenty minutes, we drove into the pleasant
college town of Potsdam, where we found the Canton-
Potsdam Hospital at the north end of town.

We parked in the lot and entered the small red-brick
building through the front doors.

There was an information desk in the lobby, and I
identified myself and asked the info lady where the morgue
was located. She directed us to the surgical unit that she
said doubled as the morgue. This did not speak well for the
staff surgeons, and if I had been in a better mood, I'd have
made a joke about that.

We turned down a few corridors and found the nurses'
station at the surgical unit.

There were two uniformed state troopers chatting
up the nurses, and Kate and I showed our credentials. I
said, "We're here to ID Harry Muller. Are you with the
body?"

One of the troopers replied, "Yes, sir. We accompanied
the ambulance."

"Anyone else here?"

"No, sir. You're the first."

"Who else are you expecting?"

"Well, some FBI guys from Albany, and some guys
from the State Bureau of Investigation."

We weren't going to have much time alone with the

body before we had company. I asked, "Is the medical examiner here?"

"Yes, sir. She did a preliminary examination of the body and cataloged the personal effects. She's waiting for the state police and FBI."

"Okay. We'd like to see the body."

"I'll need you both to sign in."

I didn't want to sign in, so I said, "We're not here officially. The deceased was our colleague and friend. We're paying our respects."

"Oh . . . sorry . . . sure."

He led us to a big steel door that was marked OR.

The body of a homicide victim is considered a crime scene that needs to be secured, and the chain of evidence needs to be maintained; thus, the presence of the two state troopers and the sign-in sheet, which led me to conclude that someone other than Kate and I thought this was not a hunting accident.

The trooper opened the door and said, "You first."

I replied, "We'd like to be alone to pay our respects."

The trooper hesitated. "I'm sorry. I can't do that. I need to be—"

"I understand. Can you do me a favor and ask the medical examiner to meet us here? We'll wait."

"Sure."

He disappeared around a corner, and I opened the door. We entered the makeshift morgue.

The big operating room was brightly lit, and in the middle of the room was a steel table on which a body lay covered with a blue shroud.

On either side of the table was a gurney. One held

Harry's clothes, laid out as they would be worn: boots, socks, thermal underwear, trousers, shirt, jacket, and knit cap.

On the other gurney were Harry's personal effects, and I could see the cameras, binoculars, maps, cell phone, wallet, watch, a pair of wire cutters, and so forth. On his key chain were ignition keys for his government vehicle, a Pontiac Grand Am, and his private vehicle, a Toyota. But no key for whatever kind of camper he had been driving. I assumed that the camper key was with the state police or the CSI team so they could move his camper. His gun and credentials would be with the troopers outside.

The room smelled of disinfectant, formaldehyde, and other unpleasant things, so I went over to a cabinet and found a tube of Vicks, which is a standard item in a place where cadavers are cut up. I squeezed some of the mentholated jelly on Kate's finger and said, "Smear this under your nose."

She smeared it on her upper lip and took a deep breath. I don't normally use the stuff, but it'd been a while since I'd been around a stiffening body, so I, too, put some under my nose.

I found a box of latex gloves, we each slipped on a pair, and I said to Kate, "Let's take a look. Okay?"

She nodded.

I went to the table and pulled the blue sheet down from the face.

Harry Muller.

I said to myself, *Sorry, pal.*

His face was dirty because he'd fallen face-first on the trail, and his lips were slightly parted, but I saw no grimace, or any indication that he'd been in agony, so death had come quickly. We should all be so lucky when we're that unlucky.

His eyes were wide open, so I pushed the lids closed.

I pulled the sheet down to his waist and saw a big gauze pad taped over his heart. There was very little blood on his body, so the bullet had stopped the heart almost immediately.

I noticed the lividity of his skin—the pooling of the blood on the front of his body, confirming he'd fallen face-first and died in that position.

I lifted his left arm. Rigor usually sets in within eight to twelve hours, and there was almost no flex in his muscles, but neither was his arm totally rigid. Also, from the appearance of the skin, and the general state of the body, I'd say death had occurred twelve to twenty-four hours ago. To take it a step further, if this was a premeditated murder, it had probably been done at night to minimize the chance of discovery during the commission of the crime. Therefore, it probably happened last night.

Assuming Madox did this, he probably waited for someone to find the body and report it to the police. When that didn't happen by this afternoon, he or an accomplice phoned it in from a park phone, thereby taking the heat off himself before the search of his property began.

In fact, while Kate and I were sitting with him, he was

probably wondering why his phone tip hadn't turned up the body yet, and he was getting nervous.

I examined Harry's wrist and thumb, and saw no evidence of restraints, though often there are no marks.

I took Harry's left hand in mine and examined the palm, fingernails, and knuckles. The hands can sometimes tell you something that the coroner, who is usually more interested in organs and trauma, misses, but I saw nothing unusual, only dirt.

I glanced at Kate, who seemed to be holding up okay, then I came around the table and took Harry's right hand and looked at it.

A female voice said, "Can I loan you my scalpel?"

Kate and I turned to see a woman at the door dressed in surgical scrubs. She was about thirty, petite, with short red hair. As she moved closer, I saw she had freckles and blue eyes. Actually, baggy blue scrubs aside, she was cute. She said, "I'm Patty Gleason, the county coroner. I assume you're the FBI people."

I pulled off my latex glove and extended my hand. "Detective John Corey, Anti-Terrorist Task Force."

We shook, and I introduced FBI Special Agent Kate Mayfield, remembering to add, "Kate is also Mrs. Corey."

Kate further added, "I'm also Detective Corey's supervisor."

Dr. Gleason suggested, "Maybe you can tell him not to handle the body without a medical examiner present. Or maybe not handle it at all."

I apologized but informed her, "I did this for twenty years in New York City."

"You're not in New York City."

We were off on the wrong foot, but then Kate said, "The deceased was a friend of ours."

Dr. Gleason softened. "I'm sorry." She turned to Kate. "What does this have to do with terrorism?"

"Nothing. Harry was also a colleague on the Task Force, and he was up here hiking, and we've come to identify the body."

"I see. And have you made a positive identification?"

"We have," Kate answered. "What's your preliminary finding?"

"Well, from what I can see from the external wounds, a bullet passed through his spinal column, then through his heart, and he died almost instantly. He probably felt nothing, and if he did, it was for only a second or two. He was basically dead before he hit the ground."

I nodded and observed, "In all my years as a cop, I've never seen a perfect shot through the spine and heart that was an accident."

Dr. Gleason didn't comment for a few seconds, then said, "As a surgeon and coroner, I've seen about a hundred hunting-accident wounds, and I've never seen one quite like this either. But it *can* happen." She asked, "You're thinking it was homicide?"

I replied, "We're not ruling it out."

She nodded. "That's what I hear."

Some medical examiners like to play detective, like on TV, but most stick strictly to the facts. Not knowing Patty Gleason, I asked, "Did you find anything that would indicate a homicide?"

"I'll show you what I found, and you can take it from there."

She went over to the supply cabinet, snapped on a pair of gloves, then gave me a fresh glove and said, "I see you've already found the Vicks."

She motioned toward the two gurneys. "I've removed and cataloged everything for placement into evidence bags by the FBI. Do you want to go over the inventory and sign for this stuff?"

Kate replied, "There are other agents on the way who need to list everything on what we call the green sheet."

I said to Dr. Gleason, "Let's look at the body."

She moved beside the gurney and pulled the taped gauze off Harry's chest, removing some hair and revealing a big, gaping hole. "As you can see, this is the exit wound. I used a lighted $7\times$ magnifier and observed bits of bone, soft tissue, and blood, all in minute quantities and consistent with the passage of a high-velocity, large- or medium-caliber bullet through the vertebrae, heart, and sternum."

She went on for a while, clinically describing the end of a human life. She concluded, "As you know, I'm not doing the autopsy, but I doubt there's much more an autopsy is going to show in regard to the cause of death."

I said to her, "We're more interested in the events that led up to the moment of death." I asked, "Did you notice anything unusual?"

"As a matter of fact, I did." She put her finger on Harry's chest, an inch from the edge of the ragged exit wound, and said, "I noticed here . . . can you see that?"

"No."

"Well, it's a small puncture wound. Obviously made before death. I probed it, and it's deep into the muscle tissue. I also examined his shirt and thermal top, and there seem to be corresponding holes, and what appears to be a small bloodstain, so this object—possibly a hypodermic needle—was pushed hard through his clothing and into his pectoral muscle. I can't say if anything was injected, but toxicology should be able to tell us."

Dr. Gleason continued, "And here are two more puncture wounds on his right forearm. No blood or corresponding holes on his clothing. Nor did I find a hypodermic needle in his possession, and I assume he wasn't medicating himself through his shirt."

I asked her, "What do you make of those puncture wounds?"

"You're the detective."

"Right." I thought that the first puncture wound was the one in the chest, through his clothing, which meant it was probably a sedative, administered while he was struggling, or maybe administered from an animal tranquilizer gun. *If it's off-season, we just tranquilize them and relocate them.* The other two, through the bare skin, were hypodermics, given to keep him sedated. I also wondered if it was sodium pentathol, truth serum, but I kept my thoughts to myself, and said, "I'll think about it."

She continued, "I want to show you two more things that lead me to believe there may have been some·other unusual events or incidents leading up to the time of death."

We watched her move around the table toward Harry's head. Little Patty Gleason put her hands under Harry's shoulders and pushed his big torso forward into a sitting position, which caused some gas to escape. Kate drew a startled breath. Coroners, I've noticed, are not gentle with the deceased, and there's no reason why they should be, though I'm always surprised at how they handle a body.

I could see the entry wound now, dead center through his spinal column and in line with his heart. I tried to picture how it happened: Harry was probably still drugged and positioned on the trail, standing or kneeling, by a person or persons while the shooter stood close enough to get a perfect shot, but not close enough for the muzzle blast to leave burns or powder fragments. Or, Harry had been lying down someplace else when he was shot and then moved to the trail. But that was too amateurish, and any CSI team would see that.

In any case, he'd been shot in the back, and all I could hope for was that he didn't know it was coming.

Dr. Gleason was drawing our attention to something else. "Here. Look at this." She put her finger on Harry's right shoulder blade. "This is a discoloration on his skin, which is hard to identify. It's not a contusion, or a chemical burn, and not quite a heat burn. It could be electrical."

Kate and I got closer to the faintly discolored spot, about the size and shape of a half-dollar. It wasn't made by a stun gun, but I'd seen something like this made by an electric cattle prod.

Dr. Gleason was looking at me as I stared at the mark on Harry's shoulder. I said, "I don't know what it is."

She moved to the side of the table and unceremoniously pulled the blue sheet down to the end, exposing Harry's naked body.

She started to say something, but I interrupted. "Would you mind lowering the body?"

"Oh. Sorry." She pushed Harry's stiffening torso down on the table while I held his legs. I mean, I'm used to dead bodies, but they should be lying down, not sitting up. Kate, I could see, was borderline holding it together.

Dr. Gleason made her way down the length of the gurney. "Well-nourished, well-muscled, middle-aged Caucasian male, normal skin, except as noted, and also noted is that he hadn't bathed or shaved in a few days, which is consistent with some time in the outdoors and with his soiled clothing. Nothing I see here is remarkable until we get to his feet and ankles."

The three of us stood at Harry's bare feet, and Dr. Gleason said, "The soles of his feet are soiled, as though he'd been walking barefoot, but this is not outdoor soil or vegetation I see."

I nodded.

She continued, "I found a few fibers that look like rug or carpet fibers, plus you can see what looks like fine dust or dirt that you'd find on a floor. I understand he had a camper, and you should see if he had a rug in there, and take fiber and dirt samples."

I knew another place where I should take fiber and dirt samples, but the chance of getting a search warrant for the Custer Hill lodge was not good at this point.

I moved closer to Harry and said, "There are contusions on both ankles."

"Yes, there are. Plus abrasions. These are very visible, as you can see, and the only thing I can think of was that he was wearing ankle restraints—metal, not tape, or rope, or anything pliable—and that he struggled against them, or tried to run in them. That's why these contusions are so pronounced and so profuse." She added, "The skin is broken in two places." She noted, "I believe his boots and socks were put on after the ankle shackles were removed . . . I believe he was barefoot when he had the shackles on. Look at the location of the skin abrasions and contusions."

Whatever happened to Harry in the hours before his death, it wasn't pleasant. Knowing him as I did, I was sure he wasn't a model prisoner, and thus the cattle prod, the apparent injections, and the ankle restraints. *You did good, buddy.*

Dr. Gleason said, "After I noticed these fibers on his feet, I looked over the rest of his body and found some fibers on his hair, and on his face. They could be from his knit cap, but that's dark blue, and these fibers are multicolored."

I didn't comment, but apparently Harry had been lying down on a rug or a blanket.

Dr. Gleason added, "Also, there are fibers on his trousers and shirt, and his thermal underwear, and they, too, appear to be foreign to anything he was wearing when he was brought here. And I found four black hairs, all about two inches long. One on his shirt, one on his trousers, and two on his thermal underwear. I taped them to the fabric where I found them."

I nodded noncommittally. The less I said, the more Dr. Gleason thought she needed to explain to us, and she continued, "These were not the deceased's hair. In fact, these hairs, under magnification, did not look human."

Kate asked, "Dog hairs?"

"Maybe."

Kaiser Wilhelm?

Dr. Gleason concluded, "That's all that I found on the body that might be unusual."

Kate asked her, "Can you estimate the time of death?"

"Based on what I see, feel, and smell, I believe death occurred about twenty-four hours ago. Maybe less." She added, "The CSI team might find something that could narrow it down, and so might the medical examiner who does the autopsy."

I asked, "Did you remove the clothing and personal effects?"

"I did, with an assistant."

"Other than the animal hair and foreign fibers, did you notice anything else unusual?"

"Such as?"

"Well, unusual."

"No . . . but if you sniff his clothes—especially his shirt—you might still detect a faint odor of smoke."

"What kind of smoke?"

"Smells like tobacco smoke." She noted, "I didn't find any smoking materials among his personal effects."

That's a lost art.

It is an article of faith among homicide detectives, forensic specialists, and medical examiners that the body will give up its secrets. Fibers, hairs, semen, saliva, bite marks, rope burns, cigarette butts, cigarette smoke, ashes, DNA, fingerprints, and on and on. There is almost always a transference between murderer and victim, and victim and murderer. All you have to do is find it, analyze it, and match it to a suspect. The trick was finding the suspect.

I asked, "Anything else?"

"No. But I did only a cursory examination of the clothing and personal effects. I had an assistant present at all times, and I audiotaped my examination of the body and the personal effects. You're welcome to the tape when it's copied."

"Thanks." Apparently she knew this was a hot case.

"What's this all about?"

"You really want to know?"

She thought a moment, then replied, "No."

"Good answer," I said. "Well, you've been very helpful, and we thank you for your time, Dr. Gleason."

"Are you staying with the body?"

"We are."

"Please don't touch the body." She glanced at Harry Muller and said, "If he was murdered, I hope you find who did it."

"We will."

Dr. Gleason bid us farewell and left.

Kate said to me, "Why would a young woman like that want to work in a morgue?"

"Maybe she's looking for Mr. Right." I said, "Let's get to work."

Kate and I moved over to the gurney where Harry's

personal effects were laid out, and, still wearing our latex gloves, we began to examine everything—his wallet, watch, pager, binoculars, video camera, digital camera, compass, wire cutters, bird-watcher's guide, and a terrain map that showed the Custer Hill property outlined in red marker, plus the location of the lodge and a few other buildings that were added to the map. Even with latex gloves, we were careful how we handled the items so we wouldn't compromise a fingerprint.

I examined the contents of Harry's wallet and noticed that there was a spare house key in the change pouch, plus his Toyota key, and the Grand Am key for his government car—but no spare key for his camper. If there had been a spare camper key, someone had taken it, and not the state police, who already had his camper key from the key chain. Therefore, another party may have removed the key from his wallet in order to move the camper away from the Custer Hill property. And who could that be?

Kate said, "Nothing here that looks unusual, out of place, or tampered with, but I'll bet there was something on the cameras that was erased."

I replied, "More likely the disk, tape, and Memory Stick were removed and replaced with spares that Harry would be carrying."

Kate nodded. "So the lab won't be able to pull up any erased images."

"I think not."

I picked up Harry's cell phone and turned it on, then scrolled through his recent incoming calls.

There was his girlfriend Lori Bahnik's call at 9:16 A.M.

Saturday in response to Harry's call to her at 7:48 A.M., followed by ten more calls from Lori beginning on Saturday afternoon after she'd gotten his text message at 4:02 P.M., then all day Sunday, and even today, Monday.

Then there was the duty officer Ken Reilly's call to Harry at 10:17 P.M. Sunday night in response to Lori's call to the ATTF office.

The next incoming call to Harry's phone was at 10:28 P.M. Sunday from a New Jersey number. I said to Kate, "Isn't this Walsh's home number?"

"It is."

"But he said he didn't call Harry until he got to the office this morning."

"Apparently, he lied."

"Right . . . and here's Walsh's call to Harry this morning . . . and before that, Ken Reilly was calling through the night from 26 Fed."

She didn't reply for a while, then said, "It would seem that there is a higher level of concern than Tom Walsh has led us to believe."

"That's an understatement." I added, "The fact that Walsh has been bullshitting us leads me to conclude that this was not a routine surveillance."

"I think we already know that."

I looked again at Harry's cell phone and saw my call to him on Sunday afternoon when I suggested we make hunter's stew, then my final call at 9:45 this morning. After that, there were a few more calls from Lori.

Kate was staring at the cell phone. "This is so sad . . ."

I nodded. I didn't have Harry's password, so I couldn't play any of his messages, but I knew the Tech people would be able to do that.

I scrolled through Harry's recently dialed numbers and saw the call he made to Lori Bahnik at 7:48 A.M. on Saturday morning, then the text message on Saturday afternoon at 4:02 P.M., then nothing.

I was about to shut off the phone when it rang, startling both of us.

I looked at the caller ID and saw that it was Lori Bahnik. I glanced at Kate, and I could tell she was upset.

I considered answering the call, but I wasn't prepared to deliver the news with Harry's body five feet away. I shut off the phone and put it back on the gurney.

I glanced at my watch. It wouldn't be much longer before the state police and FBI agents arrived from Albany. Plus, the two guys from the Task Force must have landed at Saranac Lake airport by now. I wondered who Walsh had sent to replace us. Probably people who followed orders.

I said to Kate, "Let's look at his clothing before the fuzz arrive."

She went to the sink and washed the mentholated jelly off her lip while I took the opportunity to pocket the terrain map. Taking evidence from a crime scene is a felony, but I thought I might need the map and justified it by recalling Walsh's lying to me, and by the fact that I, and not Harry, could have been on that slab.

Kate was at the second gurney now, sniffing at Harry's

shirt. She said, "I'm not sure . . . this could be tobacco smoke . . ."

I couldn't smell anything except the menthol under my nose, but I said, "Who do we know who smokes?"

She nodded.

We went through the clothing, piece by piece, noticing the cellophane tape that Dr. Gleason had used to fix the four animal hairs. We weren't exactly doing anything we weren't allowed to do, but on the other hand, we weren't supposed to be here; we were supposed to be at the state police headquarters in Ray Brook. Also, there's the chain-of-evidence thing, and anyone who handles evidence needs to log in, which we hadn't done. And then you had the FBI and state police investigators who might not take kindly to seeing us when they arrived. In other words, we were in a sort of gray area, which is where I spend a lot of my time. More important, we had a good jump on this, but now it was time to leave.

I said to Kate, "Let's go."

But she said, "Look at this."

I moved closer to her. She was holding Harry's camouflage pants, and she had pulled his right-side pocket inside out. "See this?"

I examined the white pocket lining and saw blue marks that appeared to have been made with a pen.

Kate said, "These could be letters."

Indeed, they could be. As though Harry had written on the white fabric with his hand in his pocket. Or, if Harry was as careless as I was, maybe he'd just shoved an uncapped pen in there.

Kate put the pants on the gurney and we both bent closer, trying to decipher the blue marks, which were definitely ink and did not look random.

I said to her, "You go first."

"Okay . . . there are three groupings of marks . . . the one that is most legible says, M—A—P . . . the next group looks like . . . an N . . . then maybe a U or a V . . . then an asterisk . . . no, a K . . . then the last group looks like . . . E—L—F . . ." She looked at me and said, "Elf?"

I stared at the ink marks. "M—A—P could be M—A—D. I mean, he's writing this blind with his hand in his pocket. Right?"

"Probably . . ."

"Then, NUK . . . and here's another mark almost hidden in the seam . . . so . . . maybe NUKE."

We looked at each other, then Kate said, "Nuke? Like, nuclear?"

"I hope not." I added, "This last one looks clear. ELF."

"Yes . . . what was he trying to tell us? Madox? Nuclear? Elf? What is elf? Maybe he was trying to write HELP."

"No. This is pretty clear. E—L—F."

I glanced at my watch again, then at the door. "We need to get going." I pushed the pocket liner back into the pants and said, "Let them work for this."

We took off the latex gloves and put them in a covered trash can. Then I went to Harry's body and looked at him. Kate came up beside me and took my arm. I'd be seeing Harry again soon at the funeral home, wearing his old uniform. I said to him, "Thanks for the clue, buddy. We're on top of this." I pulled the blue sheet over him and turned toward the door.

We left the OR and walked quickly down the hallway to the nurses' station. I said to the state troopers, "Do you have the deceased's gun and credentials?"

"Yes, sir."

"I need to take his NYPD shield to give to his family."

The guy in charge hesitated, then said, "I'm afraid I can't do that. You know . . . it's—"

"It hasn't been inventoried yet. Who's going to know?"

The other trooper said to his boss, "I'm okay with that."

The man in charge opened an evidence bag that was sitting on the counter, removed the shield from the cred case, and slid it toward me.

I said, "Thanks," and pocketed Harry's shield.

The second trooper asked me, "You think this was a homicide?"

"What do *you* think?"

"Well," he replied, "I saw the body on the trail before they put it in the ambulance, and the only way this guy— your friend—could have been shot square in the back in those thick woods is if the shooter was standing directly behind him on the trail. Understand?"

"Yeah."

"So, this was no accident—unless maybe it happened at night, and the shooter thought he saw a deer on the trail . . . I have to tell you, your friend should have been wearing something reflective or orange. You know?"

"Yeah. Well, it's not hunting season."

"Yeah, but still . . . some locals don't wait for the season to open."

"I understand."

"Yeah. Well, sorry."

"Thanks."

The other trooper also offered his condolences, as did the two nurses behind the counter. I guess they felt badly about the off-season hunting accident, or worse about the possibility of a tourist getting murdered in their nice little corner of the world.

Kate and I walked into the lobby just as two guys in suits were coming through the door. I made them as law enforcement types—FBI or SBI—and they went directly to the information desk and flashed their creds.

The info lady noticed Kate and I leaving as the two guys were talking to her. She seemed to want to draw the guys' attention to their departing colleagues, but we reached the door before the introductions could be made.

We moved quickly to our car, I slid behind the wheel, and we got the hell out of there.

CHAPTER TWENTY-FIVE

We headed back toward the center of town, then followed the signs for Route 56 south. The word "Nuke" was very much on my mind.

Kate said to me, "Whenever I work a case with you, I feel like I'm one step *ahead* of the law instead of *being* the law."

I replied philosophically, "Sometimes the law gets in the way of truth and justice."

"Do you teach that in your class at John Jay?"

"For your information, since 9/11, a lot of people in law enforcement have adopted the Corey Method, meaning the ends justify the means."

"Post-9/11, we've all done a little of that. But this case has nothing to do with Islamic terrorism."

"How could you know that at this point?"

"Come on, John. I don't see *any* connection."

"Well, think about this—Madox has a self-proclaimed history of fighting America's enemies as a private enterprise. Right?"

"Yes, but—"

"Communism is gone; now, enter Islam. He told us he's not too involved in the war on terrorism, which means he's involved. Correct?"

She stayed silent for a while, then answered, "Yes."

"Right. And, of course, you have the oil thing, which is a connection to all of the above."

"*What* is the connection?"

"I'm not sure." But a picture was starting to form in my mind, and it had to do with Bain Madox, nuclear weapons, and terrorism—not a good combination. Kate, however, was not quite ready to deal with that information, so I said to her, "Well, Harry thought someone would understand, so when we think about it, we'll know."

She nodded, then changed the subject. "One thing I'm sure of now is that Madox murdered Harry—or had him murdered."

"He did it himself. Maybe with Carl."

"That may not be easy to prove in a court of law."

Cop killers don't always get to a court of law, but I didn't say that.

Kate read my mind anyway and said, "Please don't do anything stupid. The ends do *not* justify the means."

I didn't respond.

We left Potsdam and headed south on Route 56. It was 6:01 P.M., and the road was getting dark. The windows of the scattered houses were lit, and I could see smoke rising from chimneys. The Columbus Day holiday was coming to an end; dinner was on the stove. Tomorrow was a workday and a school day. Normal people were gathered around the television, or the fireplace, or wherever normal people gathered.

Kate seemed to know what I was thinking and said, "We could buy a weekend house that would eventually become our retirement home."

"Most people don't retire to the snow and ice."

"We could learn to ski and ice-skate. You could learn to hunt and shoot bears."

I smiled, and we held hands.

Her cell phone rang, and she looked at it. "Private. Probably Walsh."

"Take it."

She answered, listened, then said, "We're on our way there, Tom." She listened again, then responded, "We went to the hospital and made a positive ID on Harry."

Whatever Walsh said, it wasn't nice, and Kate held the phone away from her ear in a theatrical gesture. I could hear Walsh fulminating.

I don't like it when someone screams at my wife, so I took the phone from Kate and heard Walsh conclude, "You're his supervisor, so *you* are responsible for him not following my orders. I kept you on this case against my better judgment, and I told you to go directly to the state police headquarters, and I meant it. Are you an FBI agent or are you a nice dutiful wife?"

I replied, "Hi, Tom. Kate's husband here."

"Oh . . . do you take your wife's calls, too? I'm speaking to Kate."

"No, you're speaking to me. If you ever raise your voice to my wife again, I'll take you apart. Understand?"

He didn't answer immediately, then said, "You're going down, pal."

"Then you're going with me."

"I don't think so."

"I do. And by the way, I scrolled through Harry's cell phone, and you forgot to tell us you called him Sunday night, and the duty officer was calling all through the night."

This kept him quiet for a second. Then he asked, "So what?"

I felt that our professional relationship was deteriorating, and that he was contemplating how best to involve me in an involuntary career event, i.e., having me fired. I said to him, "Despite your best efforts, I *will* get to the bottom of this."

He surprised me by saying, "If you do, let me know what you find."

I guess this meant that Washington was not being totally straight with him, which may or may not have been true. In any case, Walsh was following orders, and I was not, which was causing Special Agent in Charge Thomas Walsh some problems. I said, "Eventually, you'll thank me for my extraordinary initiative."

"Your fucking initiative looks a lot like insubordination and failure to follow orders. Also, you're spending a lot of time and energy investigating the Bureau instead of doing your job."

"What's my job?"

"Your job was to find Harry. He's found. You can come home."

"No, now I need to find his killer."

"*You* need to find his killer? *You?* Why is it always *you?*"

"Because I don't trust *you.* Or the people you work for."

"Then resign."

"Tell you what—if I come up empty on this case, you'll have my resignation on your desk."

"When?"

"A week."

"That's a deal. Saves me the trouble of filling out the paperwork to fire you."

"And I don't want to hear any more bullshit about us being taken off this case."

"One week."

I handed the phone back to Kate, who said, "Tom, please call Major Schaeffer and tell him we are the designated investigating agents on this case, and to extend to us all the requisite courtesies and so forth."

Walsh said something, and Kate replied, "No, we don't have any new information or leads, but if we do, we'll certainly share them with you."

I guess she forgot about finding that writing in Harry's pocket, and us speaking to the medical examiner. Selective memory is part of the Corey Method of dealing with the bosses.

She listened for a while, then said, "I understand."

Kate started to say something else, then realized the phone was dead. She shut it off.

I asked, "Understand what?"

"Understand that we have seven days to perform a miracle, and if we don't, we're history."

"No problem."

"And it better be a big miracle. Nothing small like finding a dumb hunter who admits to killing Harry by accident."

"Okay. That's reasonable."

"And if we're going after Mr. Bain Madox for murder, and we fail, Walsh will see to it that we both wind up as security guards at Kmart."

"This is getting challenging."

"Right. Well, you opened your big mouth."

"Thank you for reminding me. What else?"

"Well . . . he said our investigation is limited to a possible homicide. Not to anything else that concerns Madox. That's for the Justice Department to handle."

"Of course. I understand that."

She glanced at me to see if I was being sarcastic. She could have saved herself the analysis. She said, "You were a little rough with him. Again."

"He pisses me off."

"Don't take it personally, and don't fight my battles. I can do that myself at a time and place of my choosing."

"Yes, ma'am."

She took my hand again. "But thank you." She added, "You forgot to tell him to go fuck himself."

"That was implied."

"John, I think he's frightened."

I thought about that and replied, "I think you're right. And you forgot to tell him what we found at the morgue."

She said, "I was just about to when he hung up on me. Fuck him."

We drove in silence awhile, south on Route 56.

My mind kept flashing back to Harry lying dead and naked in the morgue, and I felt sick to my stomach. A good life snuffed out, just like that, because he saw or heard something he wasn't supposed to see or hear.

I was beyond angry—I was filled with homicidal rage against whoever did this to Harry. But I had to keep my cool and work the case until I was sure I had the killer. Then, payback.

We passed through Colton, then South Colton. Rudy's gas station was closed, and I hoped he was on his way to his master's mansion, peeing his pants en route.

I saw the sign welcoming us to Adirondack State Park, and very quickly the trees got bigger and thicker, and the road got darker.

After a few minutes, I said to Kate, "Murder is what we see. But there's something else going on that we don't see."

She didn't reply for a while, then asked, "Such as?"

"The only thing Madox accomplished by staging a hunting accident away from his property was to buy time."

"Time to hide evidence."

"No. Eventually, everything points back to Madox anyway. If buying a little time is what he accomplished, then that's all he wanted."

"Okay, but why?"

I explained, "Bain Madox does not engage in stupid or reckless acts. The only way it makes sense for him to kill a Federal agent whom the FBI knows was on or near his property is if the murder and the subsequent investigation did not concern him. And the only way that makes sense is if something else is going to happen *soon* which is a lot more important to Bain Madox than being a murder suspect." I glanced at her. "So what could that be?"

"All right . . . I get it . . ."

"I know you do. Say it."

"Nuke."

"Yeah. I think this guy has a nuclear weapon. That's what Harry was saying. That's what I believe."

"But . . . why? What . . . ?"

"I don't know. Maybe he's going to nuke Baghdad. Damascus. Tehran."

"I think that's a stretch, John. We need more information. More evidence."

"Right. We might get that sooner than we think."

She didn't reply.

CHAPTER TWENTY-SIX

It was dark when we reached the hamlet of Ray Brook, which was close to the airport where we'd landed that morning.

Close as it was, we'd taken the long way to get there and discovered things on our journey that were not even on our radar screen at 9:00 A.M. when we entered 26 Federal Plaza.

And that was the way some days went in this business. Most days were uneventful; some days, like September 11, 2001, turned on a dime.

Today, Columbus Day, I lost a friend, got into a pissing match with the boss, and met a nut job who might be planning a nuclear surprise.

Next Columbus Day, if there is one, I'll go to a Yankee play-off game.

We found the regional state police headquarters and

troop barracks at the edge of town, and I pulled into the parking lot. I asked Kate, "Are we official, visitor, or morally handicapped?"

"Look for persona non grata."

I couldn't find such a space, so I parked in official parking. We got out and walked toward the large, modern brick-and-cedar building. A sign over the front doors said TROOP "B" NEW YORK STATE TROOPERS.

We entered the lobby and identified ourselves to the duty sergeant, who seemed to be expecting us; in fact, he'd probably been expecting us all day.

He called Major Schaeffer on the intercom and asked us to wait.

There were a few troopers coming and going, dressed in their gray military-style jackets, belted at the waist with a cross strap and holster, and wearing their Smokey the Bear hats. These outfits looked like they hadn't changed since Teddy Roosevelt was governor of New York.

I also noticed that all these guys, and even the women, were tall, and I asked Kate, "Do you think they breed them?"

The place had all the spit and polish of the paramilitary organization that it was, and the only thing it had in common with an NYPD precinct house was a NO SMOKING sign.

There was a stack of brochures on a side table, and Kate, who can't resist informative brochures, took one and read aloud to me, "'Troop B is the northernmost troop, and they patrol the largest geographic area of all the troops—eight thousand, ninety-one square miles—which includes the most sparsely populated counties in the state, marked by great distances and long winters.'"

"Are they bragging, or complaining?"

She read on, "'Patrolling the North Country fosters a special brand of self-reliance, and B Troopers are renowned for their ability to handle any situation with minimum assistance.'"

"The word is minimal. Minimal assistance. Does that mean we're not welcome?"

"Probably, if you're going to correct their grammar." She continued reading, "'In addition to such typical tasks as investigating accidents and crimes, interstate patrol, and special Canadian border details, they often find themselves called on to search for lost hikers, evacuate injured campers, rescue storm-stranded travelers, investigate Fish and Wildlife law violations, and respond to domestic disputes and criminal complaints in remote locations.'"

"But can they walk a beat in the South Bronx?"

Before she could think of a smart reply, a tall, rugged-looking guy in a gray civilian suit came into the lobby and introduced himself. "Hank Schaeffer." We all shook hands, and he said, "Sorry about Detective Muller. I understand you were friends."

I replied, "We are."

"Well . . . really sorry."

He didn't seem to have much else to say, and I noticed that Schaeffer hadn't met us in his office. There's always this problem of turf intrusion, jurisdiction, pecking order, and so forth, but Kate handled it well by saying,

"Our instructions are to assist you in any way possible. Is there anything we can do?"

He informed us, "Your guy Walsh in New York seemed to think you were off the case."

I said, "FBI Special Agent in Charge Walsh has re-thought that. He should have called you." *The prick.* "So, you can call him, or you can believe me."

"Well, you guys work it out. If you'd like, I can have a trooper drive you to the morgue."

He didn't seem to know that we'd been there, done that. I said to him, "Look, Major, I understand this is your show, and you're not happy about having a dead Federal agent on your hands, and you've probably heard more than you want to hear from New York, Albany, and maybe Washington. We're not here to make your life more difficult—we're here to help. And to exchange information." I added, "I have a dead friend lying in the morgue."

Schaeffer thought about that and said, "You look like you could use a cup of coffee. Follow me."

We went down a long hallway and entered a large cafeteria. There were a dozen or so uniformed and civilian-attired men and women scattered around, and Schaeffer found an empty table in a corner.

We sat, and he said, "This is unofficial, in the open, coffee, courtesy, condolences, and no papers on the table."

"Understood."

Schaeffer seemed like a straight guy who would extend a professional courtesy, if for no other reason than to see what he could get in return.

I got right to the point. "Looks like an accident, smells like a homicide."

He gave a slight nod, and asked me, "Who would want to kill this man?"

"I'm thinking Bain Madox. You know him?"

He looked appropriately shocked, then asked me, "Yeah . . . but why—?"

"You know that Detective Muller was here on assignment at the Custer Hill Club."

"Yeah. I found out after he went missing and the Feds needed help finding him." He advised both of us, "It would be nice if I knew about these things ahead of time. You know, sort of a courtesy. Like, this is *my* jurisdiction."

I replied, "I won't argue with you about that."

"Look, you're not the people I need to complain to. But every time I get mixed up with the FBI"—he glanced at Kate and continued—"I feel like I'm getting snowed."

"Right. Me, too. You understand that beneath my Federal credentials, I'm just a cop at heart."

"Yeah, but let me tell you, the NYPD I've worked with are no treat either."

My loyal wife smiled and said, "John and I are actually married, so I'll second that."

Schaeffer almost smiled back. "So, tell me what Harry Muller was supposed to be doing on the Custer Hill property."

I replied, "Surveillance. There was a gathering there this weekend, and he was supposed to photograph arriving guests and get plate numbers."

"Why?"

"I don't know. But I can tell you that the Justice Department is interested in Mr. Madox and his friends. Didn't anyone tell you any of this?"

"Not much. I got the national security baloney."

Baloney? Was that like "bullshit"? Maybe this guy didn't swear. I made a mental note to watch my language. I said, "The Feds are full of baloney, and they're great at snow jobs, but between you and me, there may actually be a national security angle here."

"Yeah? Like what?"

"I have no idea. And to be honest, this is what we call sensitive material, and unless you have a need to know, I can't tell you."

I wasn't sure if he appreciated the honesty or not, so I blew a little snow at him and said, "I fully understand that your troop has a huge area to patrol—like eight thousand square miles—and that you're pretty self-reliant and you need . . . minimum assistance from the outside—"

Kate kicked me under the table as I went on with my snow job, concluding, "We're here to help if you need our help, which I don't think you do. But we really need your help, your expertise, and your resources."

I had more bullshit if I needed it, but Major Schaeffer seemed to sense that I was snowing him. Nevertheless, he said, "Okay. Coffee?"

"Sounds good."

He motioned for us to stay seated and went off to the coffee bar.

Kate said to me, "You are *so* full of bs."

"That's not true. I speak from the heart."

"You speak from a public-relations handout that I just read to you, and that you made fun of."

"Oh . . . is that where I heard that?"

She rolled her eyes, then said to me, "He doesn't seem to know much, and if he does, he's not sharing."

"He's just a little irritated because the FBI is snowing him. And by the way, he doesn't swear, so watch your language."

"*My* language?"

"Maybe he doesn't swear in front of women. I have an idea—he might open up more without a lady FBI agent present. Why don't you excuse yourself?"

"Why don't *you* excuse yourself?"

"Come on—"

Schaeffer returned to the table with a coffee tray and sat.

Kate stood reluctantly and said, "I need to make some calls. Be back in ten minutes." She left.

Schaeffer poured two coffees from a steel pitcher into porcelain mugs. He said to me, "Okay, tell me why you think Bain Madox, a solid citizen with a billion bucks in the bank, and who is probably a registered Republican, killed a Federal agent."

I sensed that Major Schaeffer did not share my suspicion. "Well, it's just a hunch."

"Can you do better than that?"

Not really. "I'm basing this suspicion on the fact that I believe Madox was the last person to see Harry alive."

He informed me, "I was the last person to see my

mother-in-law alive before she slipped on the ice and fractured her skull."

I wanted to question him further about that, but I said, "I was a homicide detective, and you just develop a sense for these things." I told him, "Kate and I went to the Custer Hill Club and spoke to this guy Madox."

"Yeah? And?"

"He's slick. Have you met him?"

"A few times. I actually went hunting with him once."

"No kidding?"

"He wants to keep a good relationship with the state and local police. Like a lot of the rich people up here. Makes their lives easier and safer."

"Right. But this guy's got his own army."

"Yeah. And he doesn't hire any moonlighting or retired cops, which is what most of the rich do. His men are not local, and not involved in law enforcement, and this is a little unusual for somebody who wants to stay tight with the police."

I nodded and said, "That whole place seems a little unusual."

"Yeah . . . but they don't cause us any problems and they keep to themselves. The local police get a few calls a year to pick up a trespasser or poacher who's cut through the fence and been detained. But Madox has never pressed charges."

"Nice guy." Apropos of Harry, I said, "Maybe he kills people who see something they're not supposed to see. Any missing persons? Suspicious accidents?"

"Are those serious questions?"

"Yeah."

He considered his reply, then said, "Well, there are always missing persons, and hunting accidents that seem like they could have been something else . . . but nothing I know about to link to Madox or his club. I'll have somebody check that."

"Good." I asked, "Did you get a search warrant for the Custer Hill property?"

"I did."

"Let's execute the warrant."

"Not possible. The warrant was for a missing-person search. The missing person has been found off the subject property."

"Does Madox know that?"

"How would he even know there *was* a warrant? Or that someone might be missing on his property?" He paused, then said, "I was about to call him and ask for his voluntary cooperation, but then that anonymous call came in that led us to the body. Did you tell him about the missing person?"

"I did. So let's execute the warrant."

Major Schaeffer reminded me, "The person has been *found*."

I thought he might buy into my philosophy, so I said, "The law sometimes gets in the way of truth and justice."

"Not under my command, Detective." He added, "Now that you told him about the missing person, I'll have someone call to inform him that the person has been found."

I was sure this guy had once been an Eagle Scout, and

I didn't want to highlight the differences between a New York City cop and a state trooper, so I said, "Well, we need to think of something to take to a judge for a new search warrant."

"What we need is a link between the body found in the state park and the Custer Hill Club. Without such a link, I can't ask the D.A. to ask a judge for a search warrant." He inquired, "Do you have any proof that Detective Muller had actually been on the property?"

"Uh . . . not conclusive—"

"Well, then, there's no link."

"Well, we have the anonymous phone call about the body. Anonymous is suspicious. Also, there's strong *circumstantial* evidence that Harry was on the property."

"Like what?"

"Like, that was his assignment." I explained about the phone call at 7:48 A.M. on Saturday, Harry's proximity to the property, the suspiciously distant location of his camper from the subject property, and other circumstances that I stretched a little.

Schaeffer listened, then shrugged. "Not enough to place Bain Madox under suspicion and not enough for me to ask for a search warrant."

"Think about it." I had no doubt that the FBI would eventually get a Federal judge to issue a warrant, but that might come too late. It appeared that I'd have to issue myself a Midnight Warrant, meaning breaking and entering. I hadn't done that in a while, and it could be fun, except for Madox's private army, electronic security, and guard dogs.

Schaeffer asked me, "What do you think you'd find on that property?"

"I don't know."

"Judges don't like fishing expeditions. Think of something you're looking for. Did you see anything on his property or in his house that I can take to the D.A.?"

"I saw more security than the president has at his ranch."

"That's not illegal."

"Right. Well . . . I think we just need to work the case." I suggested, "Why don't you stake out the property?"

"What am I looking for?"

"People coming and going, including Madox." I reminded him, "You don't need permission to do a surveillance—only suspicion."

"Thanks for the tip. Yeah, well, the only suspicion I have is what you're telling me." He thought a moment, then asked, "Do you want to spook this guy? I mean, you want an open surveillance or a clandestine surveillance?"

"Clandestine. Like tree cutters watching the road and the perimeter."

"Okay . . . but I need to notify and coordinate that with the county police, and I have to tell you, I think Madox has friends in the sheriff's office."

I considered that, and it seemed as though Mr. Bain Madox, Lord of the Manor, had his tentacles out into the hinterlands, as witnessed by Rudy's call to the Custer Hill Club. I asked Schaeffer, "Does Madox also have friends in *this* office?"

He replied without hesitation, "Not under my command."

"Right." But how would he know? "If you think someone in the sheriff's office is too chummy with Madox, it seems to me that you could in good conscience run a surveillance without notifying the sheriff."

"Nope. I need to solve the problem with the sheriff, not add to the problem."

"You're absolutely right." We weren't even on the same planet. Major Schaeffer ran a clean, tight ship, which was nice, but not convenient at the moment. "We really need that surveillance."

"I'll see what I can do."

"Great." I belatedly informed him, "Kate and I went to the morgue before we came here."

He seemed surprised, then asked, "Did you discover anything new?"

"I spoke to the medical examiner—Dr. Gleason. You should talk to her."

"I intend to. Meanwhile, what did she say?"

"Well, it appears that Detective Muller was subject to some physical abuse before death."

He processed that, then asked me, "What sort of physical abuse?"

"I'm not an M.E." I added, not quite truthfully, "I was just there to make the positive ID and say farewell."

He nodded. "I'll speak to her tonight."

I told him, "She found what appears to be rug fibers and dog hairs." I explained to him what Dr. Gleason had discovered, then said, "If they don't match the rug in his camper, they may match a rug at the Custer Hill lodge. Harry didn't own a dog."

"All right. If we do get a search warrant, we'll check that out."

Major Schaeffer had long-range plans for what was going to be, for him, a short investigation, so I informed him, "You're going to wind up sharing this case with the FBI, and they don't like to share, and they don't play well with others."

He reminded me, "Murder, even of a Federal agent, is a state crime, not a Federal crime."

"I know that, Major. And ultimately, there may be a state trial for murder. But the FBI will be investigating an *assault* on a Federal agent, which *is* a Federal crime. The net result is the same—they're going to be all over this place and this case very soon."

"It's still my case," Major Schaeffer said.

"Right." This was like the local baron telling the invading army that they were trespassing on his land. I said, "For instance, Dr. Gleason is not doing the autopsy. The body is being transported to New York City."

"They can't do that."

"Major, they can do whatever the hell they want. They have two magic words—national security. And when they use those magic words, the state and local police are turned into . . ." I was going to say puppy dogs, but that would piss him off, so I said, "Stone."

He stared at me, then said, "We'll see."

"Right. Good luck."

"What is *your* actual status on this case?" he asked.

"I have seven days to crack it."

"How did you get a whole seven days?"

"I made a bet with Tom Walsh."

"What's the bet?"

"I bet my job."

"And your wife?"

"No, I didn't bet her."

"I mean, did she bet her job?"

"No, she's career FBI. She has to shoot a supervisor before her job is in jeopardy."

He forced a smile. "I don't think you're going to crack this case in seven days, unless someone comes forward."

"Probably not. Are you hiring?"

He smiled again, then said, "I think you're past hiring age for the state police. But the local police are always looking for experienced people from the city." He added, "You'd love it up here."

"Oh, I know I would. I feel like a new man already." I changed the subject. "Where'd you go hunting with Madox?"

"On his property."

"See anything?"

"Yeah. Trees. We met at his house. Big place. Then we went out for deer. Six guys. Me, him, one of my sergeants, and three of his friends from the city." He added, "Lunch was catered in the woods, drinks back at the lodge."

"Did you see anything unusual?"

"No. Did you?"

"No," I replied, "except all that security." I asked him, "Did you see the perimeter fence?"

"Only got a glimpse of it. It's surrounded with floodlights, like a prison camp, except these floods are on motion sensors. Also, Madox has his own cellular relay tower."

"Why?"

"He's rich."

"Right. When was this hunting party?" I asked.

"Two seasons back."

"Like, hunting seasons?"

"Yeah. Up here we have hunting season; ski season; mud, flood, and fly season; then fishing season."

When I left the city, it was the opera and ballet season. "A guy could really keep busy up here."

"Yeah, if you like the outdoors."

"I love the outdoors. By the way, I saw a map of the Custer Hill property, and I saw some outbuildings away from the lodge. What are those buildings?"

He thought a moment, then said, "Well, I know one of them is a bunkhouse. You know, for the guards. There's also a big barn-like building for all his vehicles. Then there's a generator building."

"Electric generator?"

"Yeah. Three diesel generators."

"What's that all about?"

"You can lose power in the ice storms. Most people have some sort of generator backup."

"Right. You've seen these generators?"

"No. They're in a stone building." He informed me,

"The guy in Potsdam who services the emergency generator here also services the ones at the Custer Hill Club."

I recalled the three heavy cables I saw on the utility poles on Madox's property. "Why would this lodge need all that juice?"

He thought about that, then replied, "I'm not sure how much power each generator puts out, and I assume one or two are backups if one fails. But you raise an interesting point. I'll find out how many kilowatts they put out."

"Okay."

"What are you thinking?"

"Quite frankly, I don't know." But this generator thing led me to ask him, "What is the local gossip about the Custer Hill Club?"

He looked at me. "Are you investigating this homicide, or are you picking up where your friend left off?"

"I'm a homicide cop. But I'm also nosy. I like gossip."

"Well, there's the usual gossip. Everything from wild, drunken orgies to an eccentric billionaire sitting around watching his toenails grow."

"Right. Does Madox ever go into town?"

"Almost never. But now and then you get a Madox sighting in Saranac Lake or Lake Placid."

"Did anyone ever see the former Mrs. Madox?"

"I don't know. She's been out of the picture for a long time."

"Girlfriend?"

"Not that I know of."

"Boyfriends?"

"He impressed me as a refined gentleman, but he had a macho side to him. What did you think?"

"Same. I think he's on our team." I asked him, "Do you know how often he comes out to his club?"

"I have no idea. Usually the local or state police are notified when the residents of a big lodge, or a Great Camp, are away so the police can keep an eye on the place—but Madox has full-time, twenty-four/seven security guards. To the best of my knowledge, that place is never left unattended."

I'd guessed that from what Madox himself had told me and Kate, and now it was confirmed. "Did anyone ever suggest that the Custer Hill Club was something other than a private hunting and fishing club?"

He sipped his coffee thoughtfully, then replied, "Well, when that place was being built, about twenty years ago—ten years before I got here—I heard that no local contractors were used. And the rumor was that whoever was building this place was putting in a fallout shelter and sixteen miles of fence, which was true, and radio antennas and perimeter security devices, which was also true. And I guess the diesel generators were installed then, too. The word was that strange people were coming and going, delivery trucks were arriving in the middle of the night, and so forth." He added, "You know, rural people have a lot of time on their hands and good imaginations. But some of this stuff was for real."

"Right. So, what did people think was going on there?"

"Well, I only got this secondhand . . . but this was during the Cold War, so a lot of people assumed this was a secret government facility." He added, "I guess that was a logical assumption given the scale of the project, and what was on people's minds back then."

"I guess. But didn't anyone ask?"

"As I understand it, there wasn't anyone to ask. It was pretty self-contained there. And it wouldn't have mattered much if anyone from the project absolutely denied that it was a government installation. The locals tend to be patriotic, so as long as they thought that place was a secret government facility, they overcame their nosiness and stayed away."

I nodded. Interesting observation. I guess if you're a billionaire looking for security and privacy, you might want to promote the idea that this was a secret government installation disguised to look like a private club. That was as good as sixteen miles of fence. I said, "But now, I assume, everyone understands that this is a private hunting and fishing club."

"There are still a few people who think it's a secret government installation."

I could see the advantage to Madox of keeping the mystique alive.

Major Schaeffer continued, "Look, it's not illegal to surround your property with a fence and security devices, or to hire private guards, or even to hold a Roman orgy. Rich guys do weirder things than that. Paranoia and weirdness are not illegal."

I informed Major Schaeffer, "Paranoia and weirdness are never the endgame."

"I agree. But if Bain Madox is involved in some kind of criminal activity, I don't know about it." He stared at me. "If you know more than you're telling me, now's the time to tell me."

"All I was told is that it has to do with oil-price rigging."

He considered that for a moment, and I could see he was having the same problems with that bullshit that I'd had when I heard it from Walsh. "So," he said, "you think Bain Madox, an oil billionaire, murdered a Federal agent who was doing a routine surveillance of arriving guests who might be involved in an oil-price-rigging conspiracy?" He pointed out, "That sounds a little extreme, don't you think?"

"Yeah . . . well, if you put it that way—"

"What other way is there? And what's the national security angle?"

I was happy to see that he was paying attention, but I was not happy with that question. This guy was hungry and he needed something to chew on, but I certainly wasn't going to offer up nuclear tidbits, so I dissembled a bit and said, "Look, Major, oil is more than black sticky stuff. I mean, Bain Madox is not in the garment business, you know? When oil is involved, anything and everything is possible. Including murder."

He didn't reply but kept looking at me.

I said, "Let's concentrate on the homicide investigation. If we can implicate Madox, that might lead us to some other things."

"All right. Anything else? I need to get to work on this."

I glanced at my watch and said, "I'd like to go out to the crime scene now."

"It's too dark. I'll take you out in the morning."

"Can we light it up tonight?"

"I have the scene secured, and there aren't any CSI people there, and there's no rain or snow in the forecast. Call me here at seven A.M., and we'll work out a visit."

"Maybe just a quick look—"

"You're on overdrive, Detective. Go take your wife to dinner. You got a place to stay?"

"Yeah. The Point."

"You're staying at The Point?"

"Well . . . yeah."

"You guys having trouble spending Federal money? All I got out of Washington were some new radios and a bomb-sniffing dog with allergies."

I smiled. "Well, I don't think terrorism is a big issue here."

"Maybe not Arab terrorism, but we have a few home-grown nuts up here."

I didn't respond.

"Is that what your friend was doing here? Checking out right-wing weirdos?"

"I can't say."

Schaeffer took that as a yes and belatedly informed me, "About ten years ago, when I first got assigned here, some FBI guys came around asking about Bain Madox."

That was interesting. "What did they want to know?"

"They said they were doing a background investigation because Mr. Madox might be appointed to a government job."

That was standard bullshit when you were investigating someone for criminal activity, but it could also be true. In the case of Mr. Bain Madox, I could believe he was being considered for a government appointment, and just as easily believe he was being investigated for criminal activity. These days, one did not necessarily preclude the other. I asked Schaeffer, "Did he get the job?"

"Not that I know of. I think they had something else on their minds." He asked, "So, what's this guy up to?"

"I think he's looking for a presidential appointment to the U.N. commission on global warming."

"Is he for it or against it?"

I smiled politely and said, "Whatever is good for Bain Madox is good for the planet."

Major Schaeffer stood and suggested, "Let's go find your wife."

I stood, and we left the cafeteria and walked toward the lobby. I had a thought and asked him, "Regarding these old rumors, did anyone ever say exactly what kind of secret government facility was being built there?"

"Are we back to the Custer Hill Club?"

"Just for a moment."

"And this will help with the murder investigation?"

"Possibly. You never know."

He went along. "Well, there were lots of wild guesses about what the government was building."

"Like what?"

"Well, let me think—survival training camp, safe house, missile silo, plus a commo school or listening station." He added, "That's because of all the electronics and antennas."

"Do you get a lot of electronic interference around there?"

"Nope. Not a squawk. I think the electronics are dead or never used, or on a frequency that we can't pick up."

I wondered if the National Security Agency ever did an electronic scan on the Custer Hill Club. They should have if the Justice Department was suspicious of something.

Kate was sitting in the lobby, talking on her cell phone, and before we got to her, Schaeffer said, "I'm remembering now that there was a Navy veteran who lived around here, and he was telling everyone that he knew what was going on at the Custer Hill Club, but he wasn't allowed to say."

This sounded like baloney, but I inquired, "Do you remember this guy's name?"

"No . . . but I'll try to find out. Someone will remember."

"Let me know."

"Yeah . . . I think his name was Fred. Yeah, Fred. And he was saying that what was going on there had to do with submarines."

"Submarines? Exactly how deep are these lakes around here?"

"I'm just telling you what I remember. Sounds like some old sea dog pumping himself up."

Kate got off the phone and stood. "Sorry. I was waiting for that call."

There were people in the lobby, including the desk sergeant, so Schaeffer said for public consumption, "Sorry again about Detective Muller. Please be assured we're doing everything possible to get to the bottom of this tragedy."

"We appreciate that," I said. "Thanks for the coffee."

"You need directions to The Point?"

"That would be good."

He gave us directions and asked, "How long will you be there?"

"Until we're fired."

"That won't be long at a thousand bucks a night." He offered, "If there's any local stuff I can help you with, let me know."

"As a matter of fact . . . do you have any problems with bears around here?"

Kate rolled her eyes.

Major Schaeffer informed me, "The Adirondack region is home to the largest black bear population in the East. You are very likely to encounter a bear in the woods."

"Yeah? Then what?"

"Black bears aren't overly aggressive. They're curious, though, and intelligent, and they may approach." He added, "The problem is that the bears equate people with food."

"I'm sure they do, when they're eating you."

"I mean that people—campers and hikers carry food with them, and the bears know that. But they'd rather eat your lunch than eat you. And don't go near their cubs. The females are very protective of their cubs."

"How do I know if I'm near their cubs?"

"You'll know. Also, bears become very active after five P.M."

"How do they know what time it is?"

"I don't know. Just take extra precautions after five P.M. That's when they're foraging."

"Right. The question is, Will my 9mm Glock stop a bear?"

"Don't shoot the bears, Detective." Major Schaeffer noted, "You have intruded into *their* territory. Be nice to the bears. Enjoy the bears."

Kate said, "Excellent advice."

I didn't think so.

Schaeffer concluded his bear talk with, "I haven't had to deal with a fatal bear attack in years—just a few maulings."

"That's reassuring."

Schaeffer told us, "There is a pamphlet about bears on that table over there. You should read it."

If the fucking bears were so intelligent and curious, they should read it, too.

Kate found the pamphlet, then handed Major Schaeffer her card. "That's my cell number."

We all shook hands, and Kate and I left the building and walked through the lit parking lot.

Kate said to me, "I don't want to hear anything more about bears. Ever."

"Just read me the pamphlet."

"*You* read the pamphlet." She shoved it in my coat pocket. "Did Schaeffer say anything interesting?"

"Yeah . . . the Custer Hill Club is a secret naval submarine facility."

"*Submarine?* Is that what Schaeffer said?"

"No. That's what Fred said."

"Who's Fred?"

"I don't know. But Fred knows more than we do."

CHAPTER TWENTY-SEVEN

We got to the car, and I slid behind the wheel, started the engine, and pulled out to the road.

As I drove through Ray Brook, Kate asked, "Tell me what Major Schaeffer said."

"I will. But now I'm thinking."

"About what?"

"About something that Schaeffer said."

"What?"

"That's what I'm trying to remember . . . it was something that made me think of something else—"

"What?"

"I can't remember. Here's an intersection."

"Bear—turn left. Do you want me to drive while you think?"

"No, stop bugging me. I shouldn't have said anything. You always do this."

"No, I don't. If you tell me everything that you and Schaeffer discussed, it will come to you."

"All right." I turned onto Route 86, which was dark and empty, and as I drove, I related my conversation with Schaeffer. Kate is a good listener, and I'm a good reporter of the facts when I want to be. But facts and logic are not the same thing, and I couldn't recall the word associations that had illuminated something in my brain.

When I finished, Kate asked me, "Did it come to you?"

"No. Change the subject."

"Okay. Maybe that will help. Do you think the Custer Hill Club is or ever was a government facility?"

"No. This is Bain Madox's show from beginning to end. Think Dr. No."

"Okay, Mr. Bond, so you think this is more than a hunting lodge, and even more than a place where possible conspirators meet?"

"Yeah . . . there seems to be a whole . . . like, technological level there that is not consistent with the stated purpose of the place. Unless maybe, as Madox said to us, his wife meant it to be a refuge in case of an atomic war."

"I think that was just part of his smoke screen—a logical explanation for what he knew we would eventually hear about the construction of that place twenty years ago." She added, "He's very sharp."

"And you seem especially sharp and bright this evening."

"Thank you, John. And you seem unusually dull and dim."

"This mountain air is clouding my brain."

"Apparently. You should have pressed Major Schaeffer more on some of these points."

I responded with a little edge in my voice, "I was doing the best I could to get his voluntary cooperation. But it's not easy questioning another cop."

"Well, when you sent me out of the room, I just assumed you guys would bond and spill your guts to each other."

The words "fuck you" popped into my mind, but that's how fights start. I said, "You and I will press him a little more tomorrow, darling."

"Maybe you should have told him what we found written in Harry's pocket."

"Why?"

"Well, first, it's the right thing to do, and second, he may know what elf means."

"I doubt it."

"When are we going to share this information?"

"We don't need to. Your FBI colleagues are so fucking brilliant, they'll find it themselves. If they don't, the state police will. If they don't, well then, we'll just ask Bain Madox what mad, nuk, and elf mean."

"Maybe we should. He knows."

"Indeed, he does . . . Wait! I got it!"

She turned in her seat. "What? You know what it means?"

"Yes. Yes, I do. The other words—mad and nuk—were

obviously abbreviations for Madox and nuclear. But elf is an acronym."

"For what?"

"For what Harry thought about Bain Madox—Evil Little Fuck."

She settled back in her seat and said, "Asshole."

We drove on in silence, each of us deep in our own thoughts.

Finally, Kate said, "There *is* that group called Earth Liberation Front. ELF."

"Yeah?"

"Our domestic section deals with them."

"Yeah?"

"ELF has been responsible for what we call eco-terrorism. They've burned construction projects to save the land, they've put steel spikes in trees to destroy chain saws, and they've even planted bombs on the hulls of oil tankers."

"Right. So, you think Madox is going to plant a nuclear device at the next ELF meeting?"

"I don't know . . . but there may be some connection there . . . ELF . . . oil . . . Madox . . ."

"You forgot nuke."

"I know . . . I'm just trying to make a connection, John. Help me with this."

"I don't think Mr. Bain Madox, who claims he helped defeat the Soviet Empire, is now reduced to battling a handful of tree huggers and women with hairy legs."

She didn't reply for a few seconds, then said, "Well, that's better than Evil Little Fuck."

"Not much."

Scattered clouds scudded past a bright orange half-moon, and leaves swirled in the headlight beams.

We were still within the boundaries of the state park preserve, but this area seemed to be a mixture of public and private land, and there were houses scattered along the highway. I noticed a lot of seasonal displays on the front lawns—cornstalks, pumpkins, and so forth. There were also some Halloween displays—witches, skeletons, vampires, and other assorted creepy stuff. Autumn was starkly beautiful and deliciously grim.

I asked Kate, "Do you like autumn?"

"No. Autumn is darkness and death. I like spring."

"I like autumn. Do I need help?"

"Yes, but you know that."

"Right. Hey, I learned a poem in high school. Want to hear it?"

"Sure."

"Okay . . ." I cleared my throat and recited from memory, " 'Now it is autumn and the falling fruit/and the long journey towards oblivion . . . Have you built your ship of death, O have you?' "

She stayed quiet a moment, then said, "That's morbid."

"I like it."

"See someone when we get back."

We drove in silence, then Kate turned on the radio, which was set to a country-western station. Some cowgirl with a twang was singing, "How can I miss you if you don't leave?"

I said, "Do you mind turning that off? I'm trying to think."

She didn't reply.

"Kate? Darling? Hello?"

"John . . . radio communication."

"Say what?"

"There's UHF—ultrahigh frequency, VLF—very low frequency . . . and so forth. Isn't there an extremely low frequency? ELF?"

"Holy shit." I glanced at her. "That's it—that's what I was trying to remember. Radio antennas at Custer Hill . . ."

"Do you think this means that Madox is communicating with someone on an ELF frequency?"

"Yeah . . . I think Harry was saying, Tune in to ELF."

"But why ELF? Who uses the ELF band? Military? Aviation?"

"I really don't know. But whoever uses it, it can be monitored."

She pointed out, "I'm sure if Madox is receiving or transmitting, it's not in the clear. It's voice scrambled or encrypted."

"Right. But the NSA should be able to crack any encryption."

"Who would he be communicating with and why?"

"I don't know. Meanwhile, we need to find out about ELF radio waves. Hey, maybe that's why everyone around here seems so weird. ELF waves. There are voices in my head. Someone is telling me to kill Tom Walsh."

"Not funny, John."

We drove on through the dark night, then I said, "Bain Madox, nuclear, extremely low frequency. I think everything we need to know is contained in those words."

"I hope so. We don't have much else."

I suggested, "Why don't we go to the Custer Hill Club and torture the information out of Madox?"

"I'm not sure the FBI director would approve of that."

"I'm serious. What if this asshole is planning a nuclear event? Wouldn't that justify me beating the shit out of him until he talks?"

"It's the 'What if' that bothers me. And even if we knew with ninety-nine-percent certainty . . . we just don't do things like that. We don't *do* that."

"We will. The next time we're attacked again—especially if it's nuclear—we *will* start beating the shit out of suspects."

"God, I hope not." She stayed quiet for a few seconds, then said, "We need to report everything we've heard, learned, and guessed at. Let the Bureau take it from there." She added, "We don't need to carry this ourselves."

"Okay . . . but we need some time to perfect this."

"Well, all right . . . let's say by this time tomorrow night, we go to Tom Walsh with whatever we have. Agreed?"

I didn't trust Walsh any longer, so I thought I might have to bend the rules and go directly to my NYPD boss on the Task Force, Captain Paresi.

"John?"

"We have a week," I reminded her.

"John, we don't know if the *planet* has a week."

Interesting point. I said, "Let's see what happens tomorrow."

CHAPTER TWENTY-EIGHT

I t was less than twenty miles to The Point, but the place was so secluded that, despite Schaeffer's directions and Max's map, Kate had to call the resort to guide us to the unmarked road.

I put on my brights and proceeded slowly along a narrow, tree-covered lane that looked like a slightly improved Indian trail.

Kate said, "This is so pretty."

All I could see was a tunnel of trees in my headlights, but to be upbeat—and because I'd booked the place—I said, "I feel close to nature." About four feet on each side of the car to be precise.

We reached a rustic gate with an arch made of branches that had been twisted into letters that spelled THE POINT.

The gate was closed, but there was a speakerphone beside it. I lowered my window and pressed the button, and a distorted voice came out of the speaker like at Jack in the Box. "May I help you?"

"I'd like a double bacon cheeseburger, large fries, and a Diet Coke."

"Sir?"

"Mr. and Mrs. Corey, registered guests."

"Yes, sir. Welcome to The Point."

The electric gates began to open, and the voice said, "Please proceed to the first building on your left."

I drove through the gates, and Kate observed, "That was a little more friendly than the Custer Hill Club."

"It better be, for twelve hundred bucks a night."

"This was not my idea."

"Right."

Up ahead was a big wooden structure, and I pulled off the road. We got out, and as we walked up the path, the door opened and a young man waved to us and said, "Welcome. Did you have a good journey?"

Kate replied, "Yes, thank you."

We climbed the steps to the rustic building, and the casually dressed young man said, "I'm Jim." We all shook hands, setting the tone for our stay in this place, which I guessed was friendly, homey, and probably silly. Jim said, "Come on in."

We entered the building, which was the resort office and also a gift shop selling Adirondack artwork and some pricey-looking apparel, which caught Kate's attention.

Women, I've noticed, are easily distracted by clothing stores, and I was certain that the ladies on the *Titanic* stopped at the ship's apparel shop for the Half-Price Sinking Sale on their way to the lifeboats.

Anyway, we got past the clothing, and we all sat in comfortable chairs around a table. Jim opened our file and said, "Here's a message for both of you." He handed me a card on which was written in pen, "Call." From, "Mr. Walsh." Time: 7:17 P.M.

Since I didn't recall either Kate or I telling Tom Walsh where we were staying, I reasoned that Walsh must have recently learned this from Major Schaeffer. No big deal, but I needed to remind myself that Walsh and Schaeffer were in touch.

I gave the card to Kate, then glanced at my cell phone and saw there was no service. I asked Jim, "Are you totally out of the cell service area?"

"It comes and goes. The best service is when you stand in the middle of the croquet field." He thought that was funny and chuckled, informing me, "Sometimes you get service if you stand at the point."

I couldn't resist and inquired, "What's the point, Jim?"

He cleared things up by answering, "Whitney Point on Upper Saranac Lake. It's here on the property." Jim cautioned us, "Actually, we discourage the use of cell phones on the property."

"Why is that, Jim?"

"It detracts from the ambience."

"Figures. Are there phones in the room?"

"There are, but you can't get an outside line."

"Why are they there, Jim?"

"To communicate within the property."

"Am I cut off from the world?"

"No, sir. There is an outside phone in this office, and

one in the kitchen of the Main Lodge, which you may use. If anyone calls here—as Mr. Walsh did—we'll get a message to you."

"How? Smoke signals?"

"By note, or on your room phone."

"Okay." This had an unexpected upside, as well as a downside considering all the calls we needed to make in the next day or two.

Jim continued with the check-in and said, "Two nights. Correct?"

"Correct. Where's the bar?"

"I'll get to all that in a moment." He went through his rap, pushing printed information toward us, along with a souvenir picture book of The Point, a map of the property, and so forth.

Jim asked me, "How will you be settling your account?"

"How about a duel?"

"Sir?"

Kate said to Jim, "Credit card." She said to me, "John, why don't you use your personal card, rather than the corporate card?"

"My credit card was stolen."

"When?"

"About four years ago."

"Why didn't you replace it?"

"Because the thief was spending less than my ex-wife."

No one else seemed to think this was funny. I gave Jim my government R and I Associates corporate card, and he took an imprint.

He marked our map with a highlighter, saying, "If you follow this road, past the warming hut and the croquet field, you'll come to the Main Lodge. Charles will be waiting for you there."

"Where's the bar?"

"Right across from the Main Lodge, in the Eagle's Nest. Right *here*—" He put a big X on the spot. "Enjoy your stay with us."

"You, too."

We left the office and Kate inquired, "Why do you have to be such a boor?"

"Sorry."

"No, you're not. Are we going to call Walsh?"

"Sure. Where's the croquet field?"

We got in the car and proceeded down the road, passing the warming hut, whatever the hell that is, then drawing abreast of the croquet field, at which point I asked, "Do you want me to run out there and call Walsh?"

"No. Charles is waiting."

At the end of the road was a big log structure with a front porch—the Main Lodge—from which another young gentleman, dressed in a tie and jacket, was waving to us. I pulled up, and we got out.

The young fellow bounded down the steps, greeted us, and introduced himself as Charles, adding, "I believe I spoke to Mr. Corey earlier."

"You did."

He made a joke and said, "We've fed the bears."

"Great. Can you feed us?"

I think Charles wanted to feed *me* to the bears, but he said, "In fact, dinner is being served now, and we've set two places for you." He looked at me and said, "Jacket and tie are required for dinner."

"I don't have either, Charles."

"Oh . . . goodness . . . we can loan you a jacket and tie."

Funny that Kate's black jeans passed muster, but I needed a tie and jacket. I said to Charles, "That won't be necessary. Where's the bar?"

He pointed to yet another rustic building about a hundred feet away, and said, "The Pub is right there, sir. There are a number of self-service bars on the property, and all the staff are bartenders, but if you don't see any staff at any of the bars, please help yourself."

"I might like this place."

"Please follow me."

We followed him up the porch steps and into a rotunda-shaped room, all done up in Adirondack style, which was starting to get on my nerves.

Charles said, "This is the entrance foyer to the Main Lodge, which was the home of William Avery Rockefeller."

A nanosecond before I could get off a good one, Kate said, "This is a beautiful room."

Charles smiled. "It's all original."

Clearly Charles enjoyed the finer things in life. In the middle of the room was a round table, on which sat an urn of flowers and a bottle of champagne in a silver ice bucket, with three fluted glasses. Charles popped the cork, poured, and handed us each a glass, then raised his own. "Welcome."

I really don't drink this stuff, but to be polite—and

because I needed the alcohol—I clinked and we all drank.

Charles indicated a small room off the rotunda and said, "Here is a complimentary self-service bar which is open all day and night for your convenience."

It was convenient right now, but Charles continued, "And here"—he motioned toward an arched opening in the rotunda—"is the Great Hall."

I peeked into the Great Hall, which reminded me of the great hall where we'd sat with Bain Madox. Except in this Great Hall, at the far end, were two large, round dining tables in front of a big roaring fireplace. At each table were about ten ladies and gentlemen, eating and drinking, and though I couldn't hear them, I was certain they were engaged in witty conversations that bordered on the banal.

Charles said, "You can access your room, the Mohawk—which by the way was William Avery Rockefeller's master bedroom—through the Great Hall, but since dinner is being served, you may want to go around to your outside entrance, which I'll show you in a moment."

I suggested, "I think we need a drink first."

He nodded. "Of course. If you leave me your keys, we'll take care of your car and put your luggage in your room."

Kate replied, "We don't have luggage," and, apparently concerned that Charles was thinking she and I had just met at a truck stop or something, added, "This trip was sudden, and our luggage will be following tomorrow. In the meantime, can you provide us with some sundries? Toothbrushes, a razor, and so forth?"

"Of course. I'll have some items delivered to your room."

Women are very practical, not to mention concerned about what total strangers think, so, to be a good, loyal husband, I said to Charles, "We're celebrating our wedding anniversary, and we were so excited, we packed the Bentley, then took the Ford by mistake."

Charles processed that, then offered us another champagne, which I declined for both of us. "We'll be in the Pub," I said. "Can you get some food over there?"

"Certainly. If there's anything else you need, just ask anyone on staff."

"How about a room key?"

"There are no keys."

"How do I get in the room?"

"There are no locks."

"How do I keep the bears out?"

"The doors have inside bolts."

"Can a bear—?"

"John. Let's get a drink."

"Right." I said to Charles, "My car has a key. Here it is. I need a wake-up call at six A.M."

"Yes, sir. Would you like breakfast in your room, or in the Great Hall?"

Kate replied, "I'd like breakfast in the room."

We always have this disagreement about room service: I don't like to eat where I sleep, but women, I've noticed, love room service.

Charles asked us, "Would you like to schedule a massage in your room?"

I asked, "During breakfast?"

Kate said, "We'll see what our schedule looks like tomorrow."

"Is there anything else I can assist you with?"

Kate replied, "Not at the moment. Thank you, Charles, you've been very helpful."

I asked him, "Do you have pigs-in-the-blanket?"

"Sir?"

"For the bar."

"I'll . . . ask the chef."

"With mustard. I like the crust a little brown."

"Yes . . . I'll let him know."

"Ciao."

We left the rotunda of the Main Lodge, and I said to Kate, "Wasn't I nice?"

"Not exactly."

She opened the car and retrieved her briefcase, and we walked the thirty yards to the building called the Eagle's Nest, in which was the place called the Pub.

The Pub was yet another rustic room, and a rather nice one at that. It was cozy, with a small fire in the fireplace, and a game and card room that held a pool table, bookshelves, and a stereo system. I noticed there was no television. The pub half of the room had a long bar, behind which were shelves of beautiful liquor bottles, and no bartender. In fact, the place was empty, the guests being at dinner. This was like dying and going to heaven.

I slid behind the bar and said to Kate, "Good evening, madam. May I offer you a cocktail?"

She went along with my silliness. "I believe I'll have a small sherry. No—make that a double Stoli, twist of lemon, two cubes."

"Excellent, madam."

I set two short glasses on the bar, found the ice, the fruit, the Dewar's, and the Stoli and, with a bottle in each hand, filled the glasses to the brim.

We touched glasses and Kate said, "To Harry."

"Rest in peace, buddy."

Neither of us said anything as we each decompressed from a long, eventful, and very sad day.

Finally, Kate said, "Should we call Tom?"

I checked my cell phone again, and there was actually service. "The use of cell phones is discouraged at The Point, madam."

"What if it's important?"

"Then he'll call again."

I freshened our drinks and said, "If the alcohol is free, how do they expect to make any money on us at twelve hundred dollars a night?"

She smiled. "Maybe they're hoping you go to bed early. By the way, you should not have used your government credit card."

I replied, "Look at it this way—if the world is coming to an end, what difference does it make?"

She thought about that but didn't answer.

I continued, "And if we save the world, do you think the government is going to make us reimburse them for this place?"

"Yes."

"Really?"

"Positive."

"Then what's my incentive to save the planet?"

"That's your job this week." She sipped her drink and stared into the fire. "Well, if the world is going to end, this is a good place to be."

"Right. So is the Custer Hill Club."

She nodded.

"Do you play pool?" I asked.

"I have played. But I don't play well."

"Sounds like a hustle." I came around the bar and went to the pool table, where the balls were already racked. I set down my drink, took off my leather jacket, pulled my shirttail out to hide my pancake holster, then I chose a pool stick. "Come on. Let's play."

Kate slid off the bar stool, removed her suede jacket, and pulled her sweater over her holster. She rolled up her sleeves and chose a stick.

I lifted the rack from the balls, and said to Kate, "Since you're such a ball breaker, you break." I actually didn't say that. I said, "After you, madam."

She chalked up, bent over the table, and shot. Good break, but none of the balls went in.

I ran three balls, then missed an easy shot. I think the scotch was starting to affect my hand-eye coordination. Or maybe I needed another scotch.

Kate ran three balls, and I could see she'd played this game before.

I missed another easy shot, and she said, "Are you drunk, or is this a hustle?"

"I'm just not on my game tonight."

She ran another four balls, and I conceded the game and racked up. I said, "Let's play for five bucks a ball."

"We just did."

I smiled and asked her, "Where did you learn to play?"

She grinned mischievously. "You don't want to know."

The second game was closer because she was getting tipsy.

I was actually having fun, playing pool with my wife, who looked good leaning over the table, and listening to the fire crackle in a nice, cozy room in the woods with a free bar.

A young lady entered the Pub carrying a tray of hors d'oeuvres, which I helped her set on the bar. She said, "Hi, I'm Amy. Welcome to The Point. Can I make you a drink?"

"No," I replied, "but make yourself one."

Amy declined my invitation and said, "Here's a breakfast menu. Just pick what you want, and the time you want it delivered to your room, and call the kitchen."

I looked at the tray of sissy hors d'oeuvres and asked Amy, "Where are my pigs-in-the-blanket?"

She seemed embarrassed as she replied, "The chef—he's, like, French—says he's never heard of that." She added, "I don't think we have any hot dogs."

"Amy, this is *America*. Tell Pierre—"

Kate interrupted. "Amy, ask the chef to use breakfast sausage." She explained helpfully, "Saucisses en croûte. With mustard. Okay?"

Amy repeated the French in an upstate accent, promised to return, and left.

I said to Kate, "This country is going to hell."

"John, give it a rest. Try some of these." She handed me a smoked salmon, which I refused.

"I expected real food here. I mean, we're in the woods. You know, like buffalo steaks, or hunter's stew . . ." I recalled my phone message to Harry and poured myself another scotch.

"I know this has been a very tough day for you, John. So, vent, drink, do whatever makes you feel better."

I didn't reply, but I nodded.

We took our drinks back into the game room. I sat at the card table and Kate sat across from me. I opened a fresh deck of cards and asked her, "Do you play poker?"

"I have played. But not well."

I smiled. "Red chips are a buck. Blue are five bucks. You're the bank."

I shuffled as she gave each of us two hundred dollars' worth of chips.

I put the deck in front of her. "Cut." She did so, and I dealt five-card draw.

We played a few hands, and I was doing better at cards than I'd done at pool. I may have lost my hand-eye coordination, but I could play poker in my sleep.

Kate glanced at her cell phone and said, "I have one bar—"

"That"—I cocked my thumb toward the mahogany bar—"is the only bar I'm interested in tonight."

"I think we need to call Tom. Really."

"Whoever loses this hand calls him."

She lost the hand, and twenty-two bucks, but won the right to call Tom Walsh.

She dialed his cell phone, he answered, and she said, "Returning your call." She put it on speaker, then set the cell phone on the table as she gathered up the cards.

I heard him ask, "Where are you?"

Kate said, "At The Point. Where are *you*?"

He replied, "At the office," which I thought was interesting and unusual at this hour. "Can you talk?"

She giggled. "Not very well. I've had four Stolis."

She fan-shuffled the deck near the phone, and Walsh said, "I'm getting static."

"I'm *shuffling*."

He seemed impatient with her. "Where's John?"

"He's here."

I said, "Ante up."

"What—?"

She threw a dollar chip in and said to me, "Cut."

Walsh asked, "What are you doing?"

Kate replied, "Playing poker."

"Are you playing alone?"

She dealt five-card draw and replied, "No, that's solitaire."

"I mean," he said with affected patience, "is anyone there aside from John?"

"No. Are you opening?"

I threw a blue chip in the pot. "Open for five."

She threw two blues in. "Raise you five."

Walsh asked, "Do you have it on speaker?"

"Yes. How many cards do you want?"

"Two."

She hit me with two cards and said, "You better have something better than three of a kind, mister. Dealer stands pat."

"You're bluffing."

Walsh said, "Excuse me—would you mind holding up your game for a minute of business?"

Kate put her hand facedown on the table and whispered to me, "To you."

"You raised my open. It's to you."

"Are you sure?"

Walsh said, "It's to you, Kate. But before you bet, perhaps John can tell me how it went with Major Schaeffer."

I put my hand facedown, sipped my scotch, and said, "Since you know we're at The Point, I assume you've spoken to him—so what did he tell you?"

"He said Kate was not present at the meeting."

"Correct. I did a cop-to-cop with him."

"That's what I was afraid of. And?"

"What did he tell *you*?" I asked.

"He told me that you told him about our bet. I guess you're in a betting mood today."

That was about as witty as Tom Walsh got, and I wanted to encourage him in that direction, so I laughed.

He asked, "Have you been drinking?"

"No, sir. We're *still* drinking."

"I see . . . well—"

"Weren't you supposed to call Schaeffer before we got there to tell him that Kate and I are the designated investigators?"

"Apparently, even drunk, you don't forget an oversight on my part."

"Tom, even if I was *dead*, I wouldn't forget you screwing me around."

Mr. Walsh advised me, "You need to learn to manage your anger."

"Why? It's the only thing that motivates me to come to work."

Walsh ignored that. "Was Schaeffer helpful? Did you learn anything?"

"Tom, whatever Schaeffer told me, he'll tell you. He loves the FBI."

He suggested, "I think we need to continue this discussion when you're less fatigued."

"I'm fine."

"Okay," he said. "Just FYI, Harry's body is being flown by helicopter back to New York for autopsy." He added, "I understand there were signs of physical abuse on the body."

I didn't reply.

Walsh continued, "This is obviously not a hunting accident, and the Bureau is treating it as a homicide."

"What was your first clue?" I added, "Fax me the full autopsy report, care of Schaeffer."

He ignored that. "A team of agents have arrived from New York and Washington, and they'd like to speak to both of you tomorrow."

"As long as they're not here to arrest us, we'll talk to them."

"Don't be paranoid. They just want a full briefing from you both."

"Right. Meanwhile, you need to get a Federal judge to issue a search warrant for the Custer Hill Club property and lodge ASAP."

"That's being discussed."

Kate cut in. "Tom, John and I think that Bain Madox is conspiring to do something that goes beyond oil-price fixing."

There was a silence, then Walsh asked, "Like what?"

"We don't know." She looked at me and mouthed the words "MAD," "NUKE," "ELF."

I shook my head.

"Like what?"

She replied, "I don't know."

"Then why do you think that?"

"We—"

I said, "Let's discuss this when you're sober, Tom."

"Call me in the morning. I know that place doesn't have room phones, and that cell service is not good, but don't fuck with me." He added, "And don't even *think* about submitting a bill for that place." He hung up.

I said to Kate, "It's to you."

She threw three blues in the pot. "Don't even *think* about raising. In fact, don't even call."

"Fifteen, and another fifteen."

She threw in three more blue chips and said, "I'll let you off easy." She fanned out a Jack-high straight flush in hearts, and swept the pot toward her. "What did you have?"

"None of your business."

She gathered the cards and shuffled the deck. "You're a bad loser."

"Good losers are losers."

"Macho, macho."

"You love it."

We played a few more hands, and I was ahead a little on the poker, though still down on the pool. I suggested, "Let's do darts. A buck a point."

She laughed and said, "You can't even get your glass to your mouth. I'm not standing in the same room as you with a dart in your hand."

"Come on." I got up, a little unsteady, and said, "This is like a saloon triathlon—poker, pool, and darts."

I found the darts, stepped back about ten feet from the board, and let them fly. One hit the board, and the others, unfortunately, went astray, the last one pinning a window drape to the wall.

Kate thought that was funny, and I said, "Let's see how *you* do."

She informed me, "I don't play darts. But you can go again." She laughed.

Amy returned with a cloth-covered tray, which she set on the bar. "Here we are. He had apple-smoked turkey sausage."

Before I could tell her what Pierre could do with his turkey sausage, Kate said, "Thank you."

Amy was looking at the darts in the wall but didn't comment, except to ask, "Have you decided on breakfast?"

We perused the menu and ordered breakfast, which even a French chef can't screw up.

I wanted to watch the evening news, and I asked Amy, "Where's the TV?"

She replied, "There are no televisions at The Point."

"What if the world came to an end? We couldn't see it on television."

She smiled, the way people do who know they're dealing with an inebriated person. She addressed Kate, whom she probably thought was sober. "Yeah, like, we had that problem on 9/11. You know? So, they set up a TV here in the bar. So everyone could watch it." She added, "It was really horrible."

Neither Kate nor I commented, and Amy wished us a pleasant evening, stole another glance at the darts, and left.

I uncovered the tray and examined the turkey sausage wrapped in some kind of phyllo dough. "What is this crap?"

Kate said, "We're checking out of here tomorrow."

"I like it here."

"Then stop complaining and eat those fucking sausages."

"Where's the mustard? There's no mustard."

"Time for bed, John." She handed me my leather jacket, put on her coat, gathered up her handbag and briefcase, then led me out the door.

I shoved my Glock in my waistband in case we ran into any bears, and suggested that Kate do the same, but she ignored my good advice.

The air was cold, and I could see my breath, and in the sky were thousands of bright stars against a black sky. I could smell the pines, and the wood smoke coming from the chimneys of the Main Lodge, and everything was very quiet.

I like the noise of the city, and concrete below my feet, and I don't miss seeing the stars at night because the lights of Manhattan create their own universe, and eight million people are more interesting than eight million trees.

And yet, this was undeniably beautiful, and under other circumstances, I might relax here and surrender to the wilderness and be at peace with myself while eating French food with twenty strangers who probably made their money screwing the American public.

Kate said, "It's so serene. Can't you feel the tension and stress just leaving your body?"

"I'm kind of going back and forth on that."

"You need to let go and let nature take over."

"Right. Actually, I'm starting to get in touch with my primitive self."

"John, this may come as a surprise to you, but you're already very in touch with your primitive self. In fact, I haven't yet met the other side of you."

I wasn't sure if that was a compliment or a criticism, so I didn't reply.

We went around the Main Lodge and on to a stone terrace. We could see through the big windows into the Great Hall, and I watched the guests around the two tables, working hard at the game of civilized dinner behavior. None of them were local, of course, and wherever they'd come from, they'd arrived.

I thought of Bain Madox sitting in his great hall—fireplace, dog, hunting trophies, old scotch, a manservant, and probably a girlfriend or two somewhere. For 99 percent of humanity, this would be more than enough. But Mr. Bain Madox, though he should have been very content with his accomplishments and wealth, was being directed by some inner voice into a dark place.

I mean, thinking back on that meeting, I could see something in his eyes and in his demeanor that made me believe he was on a mission, a man of destiny, far above the rest of humanity.

I'm sure he had reasons for whatever he was up to, reasons that he thought were good and which he'd actually hinted at over scotch and coffee. But I didn't care about his reasons, or his inner demons, or his divine voices, or his obvious megalomania; what I cared about was that he was apparently engaged in a criminal enterprise, and that he'd most likely killed a friend of mine on his way toward his larger goal, which itself was undoubtedly beyond criminal.

Kate asked me, "What are you thinking about?"

"Madox. Harry. Nukes. Radio signals. Stuff like that."

"I know we'll figure it all out."

"Well, Kate, the nice thing about this mystery is that even if we don't figure it out, we'll know soon enough what it was that we couldn't figure out."

"I think it would be better if we figured it out before it happens."

We reached the rear of the Main Lodge without encountering any carnivorous wildlife, and I saw a door with a wooden sign that said: MOHAWK.

We entered the unlocked door, and I bolted it, not sure if the door would keep a bear out. Maybe I should move the dresser in front of it.

Kate said, "Oh, this is beautiful."

"What?"

"The *room*. Look at this place."

"Okay." I looked. It was a big cathedral-ceilinged room, paneled in stained pine. There was a king bed that looked like it could be comfortable, but it was so high off the floor, you wouldn't want to fall out of it. On the bed was a wicker basket full of toiletries.

There was a lot of furniture in the room, and lots of throw pillows and blankets lying around, which I know women like.

As Kate went around feeling up the fabrics and smelling the flowers, I checked out the bathroom. I'm a bathroom freak, and this one was okay. I like a good toilet bowl. I washed my face in the sink, then returned to the main room.

Along the far wall was a big stone fireplace, and in the hearth were logs and kindling, to which Kate was holding a match. The fire caught, and she stood and said, "This is so romantic."

Above the fireplace was a huge set of antlers, which reminded me that I was horny. I said, "I'm horny."

"Can't we just enjoy the room?"

"You said it was romantic. So?"

"Romance and sex are not the same thing."

I knew if I argued that point, I wasn't going to get any, so I said, "I'm very sensitive to that. Here, let me put some music on." There was a CD player on the desk and a stack of disks.

- I quickly found an Etta James CD, which I knew she liked, and popped it in. Etta began crooning "At Last."

Kate found a bottle of red wine on a dining table, which she opened. Then she poured two glasses and gave one to me. "To us."

We touched glasses, sipped, and kissed lightly on the lips. I'm not a big wine drinker, but I've discovered that wine equals romance, and romance leads to . . . whatever.

Kate went around and shut off the lamps. We took off our shoes and sat in comfortable upholstered chairs that faced each other in front of the roaring fire.

Kate said, "This was a good idea, except it's too expensive."

"Hey, I got an oil tip from Bain. We're buying oil futures tomorrow as soon as the market opens. Then, I'm calling my bookie with my bet on the start date of the war. Do you think this war has anything to do with what Madox is up to?"

"Possibly."

"Yeah . . . maybe Madox is going to nuke Baghdad and keep us from having to go to war. Could that be his game?"

"I don't know. Why speculate?"

"This is called analysis. This is what we get paid for."

"I'm off-duty."

"Would nuking Baghdad raise or lower the price of oil? And how can I bet on the start date of the war if the war is preempted by a nuclear blast? What do you think?"

"I think you should stop thinking about this tonight."

I looked around the darkened room, lit now by the

fire. The reflection of the flames glowed on the shiny oil paintings along the walls. The wind had picked up, and I could hear it howling in the chimney and saw gusts of leaves blowing past the windows. I said, "This actually *is* romantic. I see the difference now."

She smiled and replied, "You're on the right track."

"Good. Hey, do you realize that William Avery Rockefeller had sex in this very room?"

"Is that all you think about? I mean, here we are in one of the historic Great Camps of the Adirondacks, and all you can think about is that some Rockefeller had sex in this room."

"That's not true. I was about to comment on the pastoral movement among the rich in the early part of the last century that led to the construction of these rural homes as simple refuges from the complexities of urban life, with all its noise, pollution, and teeming humanity."

"That's interesting."

"Also, the Rockefellers were horny. I mean, look at what happened to poor Nelson Rockefeller. Then, you have oysters Rockefeller. Oysters. Get it? So, for me to mention that William Avery—"

"John, you're losing points."

"Right." So we listened to Etta James, watched the fire, and sipped wine. The heat of the fire was making me drowsy, and I yawned.

Kate stood, went to the bed, and removed the comforter and a pillow, which she laid out in front of the hearth.

She then slipped into something more comfortable, meaning nothing, and I watched her as she undressed in the firelight. When she was naked, she lay down on the comforter and looked at me.

I think that was my signal to join her, so I stood and undressed slowly—about five seconds—and we lay on our sides in each other's arms.

She nudged me onto my back and rolled on top of me.

This had been a lousy day, and tomorrow, assuming there was one, wasn't going to be much better. But for now, this was as good as it got.

— PART X —

Tuesday
UPSTATE NEW YORK

The unleashed power of the atom has changed everything, save our modes of thinking, and we thus drift toward unparalleled catastrophe.

—Albert Einstein

Tuesday

UPSTATE NEW YORK

The unleashed power of the atom has
changed everything, save our modes of
thinking, and we thus drift toward unparalleled catastrophe.

— Albert Einstein

CHAPTER TWENTY-NINE

O ur wake-up call came promptly at 6:00 A.M., making me wonder what I was thinking when I asked for it. Little Scotsmen were hurling stones in my head.

Kate rolled over, mumbled something, and buried her head under the pillow.

I found the bathroom in the dark and used the provided sundries, then stepped into the shower, which felt like a million dollars—or at least twelve hundred dollars.

I went back into the bedroom and got dressed in the dark, leaving sleeping beauty to rest.

Actually, we'd both spent a restless night after an overstimulated day. For the first time in a long time, I dreamed I was standing under the burning towers as people jumped from the windows. I also dreamed that Harry and I were at a funeral.

I opened the other entry door to our room and saw

that it led to a short passageway, which opened into the Great Hall.

I went into the Hall, where two round tables were being set for breakfast, and a fire was blazing at each end of the room. If I wasn't a cop, I think I'd like to be a Rockefeller.

The kitchen door was open, and I could hear the sounds of people banging around, preparing for breakfast.

I thought I heard a voice with a French accent saying, "Peegs in zee blanket?" followed by laughter. But maybe I imagined that.

On a side table were coffee and muffins. I poured a cup of black coffee, walked out through the French doors onto the terrace, and took a deep breath of the mountain air.

It was still dark, but I could see that the sky was clear, and it was going to be another nice day in God's country.

There is a belief in law enforcement, reinforced by experience and statistics, that the first forty-eight hours of a criminal investigation are the most critical. Intelligence work and counter-terrorist operations, on the other hand, move at a slower pace. There are good reasons for this, but my instinct and experience as a cop told me that almost everything you need to know, and almost everything you're going to discover, is going to happen in two days. Maybe three.

What you do with that time and information is the difference between a successfully concluded case or a muddled cluster-fuck of meddling bosses, brain-dead prosecutors, lawyered-up suspects, and half-witted arraignment judges. If you give all these people time to think, you're into paralysis by analysis.

As I was having my morning inspirational thoughts, Kate came out on the terrace wearing the guest bathrobe and slippers and carrying a cup of coffee. She yawned, smiled, and said, "Good morning."

"Good morning, Mrs. Rockefeller." Married or not, the morning protocol après sex was a kiss, a compliment, and a reference to the lovemaking that was romantic without sounding wimpy, and explicit without sounding piggish.

I managed to pull all this off, and we stood on the terrace, arm in arm, sipping coffee, looking out at the pines and autumn leaves.

The sun was coming up, and there was a mist lying on the ground, sloping downward toward Upper Saranac Lake, which looked very tranquil. It was quiet, and the air smelled of damp earth and wood smoke. I could see why Harry liked it up here, and I pictured him waking up Saturday morning in his camper to a scene very much like this before he started out for the Custer Hill Club.

Kate said, "Maybe when we finish here, we'll take a week off and rent a cabin on a lake. Wouldn't that be nice?"

I thought that if this case ended badly, we wouldn't have to take a week off; we'd have lots of free time.

Kate added, "I think that might be a fitting tribute to Harry."

"That would be very nice."

Kate was cold, so we went back into the Great Hall. Another couple was on a couch near the fireplace in the sitting area. We refilled our cups and sat on a couch opposite them. My body language clearly indicated that I had no intention of engaging them in conversation. The guy—a bearded, middle-aged gent—gave me the same signals. His wife or girlfriend, however, smiled and said, "Hi. I'm Cindy. This is my fiancé, Sonny."

Sonny did not look sunny. In fact, he looked grumpy. Maybe he just got the bill. Cindy, on the other hand, was happy and friendly, and would probably talk to a goldfish in a bowl.

Kate and Cindy began to chat about The Point, the Adirondacks, and whatever. Grumpy and I stayed silent. The fire felt good.

Cindy and Grumpy were from Long Island, and he was, according to Cindy, "in the publishing business." Cindy was in public relations and that's how they met. Thank God she didn't tell the story, but I was certain one of them must have been drunk.

Kate said she was an attorney, which was partly true, and she told them I was a certified social worker, working in the Muslim immigrant community, which was funny, but Grumpy made a little snorting sound of disapproval.

The subject somehow shifted to shopping, and Cindy informed Kate that there were good shops in the village of Lake Placid. My eyes glazed over, and I thought Grumpy's eyes would do the same, but I noticed he was looking at Kate, whose robe had opened a little at the top. The man was clearly a pig.

On that subject, I couldn't help noticing that Cindy was also very pretty, with long blond hair, hazel eyes, Nordic features, and really great . . . presence, and so forth. She looked about twenty years younger than her so-called fiancé, and I couldn't imagine what she found attractive about him, except for maybe the bulge in his pants. I mean his wallet.

Grumpy broke his silence and said to me, "I have a good idea about immigration. Wherever you were born, stay there." He stood, took a last look at Kate's cleavage from a better angle, and said to her, not me, "Nice meeting you."

Cindy, too, stood and said to us, "We'll see you at dinner. The chef is doing woodcock tonight."

Woodcock? I got to my feet. "I hear that his woodcock is firm and moist."

Cindy smiled tightly.

"John," Kate said, then turned to our new friends. "Have a good day."

Grumpy replied, "I've made other plans."

And off they went.

Kate said to me, "A totally mismatched couple."

"Us or them?"

Grumpy had left a *New York Times* on the couch, and I scanned the front page. One headline read: U.S./ FRENCH SPLIT ON IRAQ DEEPENS. I said to Kate, "See? If these people ate real food like the Irish and the English, they'd have some balls. Who eats snails? Here's another story—a fireworks display at Disneyland outside of Paris caused the nearby French Army garrison to drop their weapons and surrender to a busload of Swedish tourists."

"John, it's really too early for this."

"Woodcock." I read the main headline, which said: BUSH TIES BOMBING AT BALI NIGHTCLUB TO QAEDA NETWORK. I scanned the story and saw that "some Islamic militants were pressing a theory that the United States had masterminded the Saturday attack as a means to manipulate the Indonesian government and to strengthen its argument for a war against Islam."

The Islamic militants had said the same thing about the 9/11 attacks. It was an interesting theory, with just enough plausibility to make some people wonder. I mean, I'm not a conspiracy nut, but I could imagine that there were people in this country, in and out of the government, who wanted an excuse to widen the war against terrorism to include certain Islamic countries. Like Iraq. I thought of something that one of the spookier CIA guys at the ATTF once said: *What we need is one more good attack.*

I think I can do without that, thank you, but I got what he was saying.

Kate said to me, "I'm going to the room to shower. What are you doing?"

I looked at my cell phone and saw I had no service. "I need to call Schaeffer to set up an appointment to see the crime scene, so I'll use the kitchen phone. See you in the room."

"Be nice to Pierre."

"Oui, oui."

She left, and I went into the kitchen. The place was bustling, and no one seemed to notice or care that I was there, so I found the phone, which was on the wall, and dialed the state trooper headquarters. I got the desk sergeant, who put me on hold. The kitchen smelled of frying pork products, and my stomach grumbled.

I opened the *Times* to the obit page, but I didn't see Harry Muller. It might be too soon for an obituary, or maybe it wouldn't run in the *Times*. I scanned the Metro section to see if there was a story about Harry's death, but I didn't see anything. An upstate hunting accident wasn't exactly news, but the murder of a Federal agent was.

Therefore, the FBI and local police would issue a joint statement saying the death was an apparent accident but was still under investigation. Any news organization that called for further information would be asked to hold the story so as not to upset the family and/or tip off a possible suspect. You could usually buy a few days with that.

A waitress walked by, and I said to her, "Do me a favor and check on the breakfast for Corey. Mohawk Room. I could really use a bacon sandwich on rye."

"Now?"

"Please. With coffee."

She hurried off, and Major Schaeffer came on the line. "Morning."

I could barely hear him over the sounds of the kitchen noise, and I said loudly, "Good morning. What's a good time to go out to the crime scene?"

"Be here at eight. I'll meet you in the lobby."

"Thanks. Anything new?"

"I spoke to Dr. Gleason last night."

"Nice lady."

"She said you went a little beyond identifying the body and paying last respects."

"I told you, she showed us the signs of physical abuse."

"Yeah? Did you handle any of the personal effects?"

"Absolutely not." All of them.

He asked, "Find anything, Detective?"

"No." Just the writing in Harry's pocket and the cell-phone calls.

"Remove anything?"

"No." Just the map of the Custer Hill property.

"My troopers say that you and your wife never signed in or out."

"Tell you what, Major, why don't you and I go to the morgue after the crime scene?"

"Too late. The Feds snatched the body last night."

"I told you. You gotta act fast."

"Thank you."

The waitress put a tray on the counter and said, "Your breakfast will be delivered at seven."

"Thanks. Add some of those biscuits that just came out of the oven."

Schaeffer asked, "How's The Point?"

"Great. All the booze is free. How are we doing with the search warrant and surveillance?" I took a big bite of the bacon sandwich. Heaven.

"Forget the search warrant for now. But I did begin the surveillance last night."

·   "Anything?"

"Yeah. At eight-oh-three P.M., two vehicles left the subject property. One was a Ford van registered to the Custer Hill Club. The other was a Ford Taurus registered to Enterprise Rent-A-Car."

I washed down the bacon with coffee and asked, "Where'd they go?"

"They went to Adirondack Regional Airport. The commercial terminal is closed at that hour, and they left the Taurus in an Enterprise spot and put the keys in a drop slot, then both drivers—two males—got in the van and returned to the Custer Hill Club."

"What do you make of that?"

"Looks suspiciously like they were returning a rental car. What do you think?"

Major Schaeffer had a wry sense of humor. I said, "Check the trunk for a body. What was the plate number on the Taurus?"

"I don't have it in front of me." Which was his polite way of saying, "What have you done for *me* lately?"

I said, "I saw a blue Enterprise Taurus at the Custer Hill lodge when I was there." I gave him the plate number from memory and asked, "Is that it?"

"Sounds like it. I'll call Enterprise and find out who rented that car."

I thought I probably had that information from Kate's friend Larry at Enterprise, but I said, "Good. Anything else from the surveillance?"

"No. What are we looking for?"

"You never know. But I'd like to know that Madox is still on the property."

"Okay."

"So, someone needs to call me anytime you see any activity—hold on." Some kid in a dopey psychedelic chef's outfit was trying to get my attention. I asked him, "What do you need?"

"I need to use the phone. I have to place an order."

"What do you have to order? Woodcock? I'm on top of the woodcocks. How many do you need?"

"I need the *phone*, sir."

"Hey, I'm trying to save the world here, pal. Hold on." I said to Schaeffer, "I'm using the kitchen phone. I'll see you at eight."

I hit the cradle and handed the phone to the chef. "If the world comes to an end, it's *your* fault."

A handsome guy in tailored whites, whom I just *knew* was the French chef, came up to me and extended his hand. "Good morning," he said in an accent. We shook. "You are, of course, Mr. Corey."

"Oui."

"Ah, you speak French."

"Oui."

"Bon. I am Henri, the head chef, and I must apologize profusely for the pigs-in-the-blanket."

He got the pronunciation right, if not the recipe. I said, "Hey, don't worry about it, Henry."

"But I do. So, for you, I have ordered the ingredients, and tonight, we serve the pigs for the cocktail hour."

"Terrific. I like the crust a little brown."

"Yes, of course." He leaned toward me and whispered, "I, too, like these little things."

I was sure by now that he was pulling my chain, and I said, "I won't tell. Okay, don't forget the mustard. See you later."

"May I show you my kitchen?"

I looked around. "Looks good."

"You are welcome to place any special order for any meal."

"Great. I've been thinking about woodcock lately."

"Ah, amazing. Tonight is woodcock."

"You don't say? Well, hell, I ought to play the lottery today."

"Yes? Oh, I understand."

I looked at my watch and said, "Well, I—"

"A moment . . ." He pulled a scrap of paper from his pocket and said, "Here is the menu for this evening." He read, "We begin with a ragout of forest mushrooms, followed by a crisp filet of arctic char, served with peppernade and beurre rouge. I think, perhaps, a California chardonnay with that. Yes? Then, the woodcock, which I will serve with an étuvée of local vegetables, and a port wine jus. I am considering a French cabernet sauvignon with the woodcock. What do you think? Mr. Corey?"

"Uh . . . sounds like a crowd-pleaser."

"Good. And we end with an exploration of chocolate."

"Perfect ending."

"With a sauterne, of course."

"Goes without saying. Okay—"

"Will you and your wife be joining us for lunch?"

"No, we have to be at a chipmunk race. Thanks for—"

"Well, I must pack for you a picnic lunch. When are you leaving?"

"Twenty minutes. Don't bother—"

"I insist. You will find a picnic hamper in your car." He extended his hand, we shook, and he said, "We may have our differences, but we can remain amis. Yes?"

Well, jeez, I was really feeling bad now about my anti-French attitude, so I said, "Together, we can kick some Iraqi ass. Right?"

Henry wasn't sure about that, but he smiled. "Perhaps."

"Can do. See you later."

As I made my way out of the kitchen, I heard Henry barking orders for a picnic lunch. Hold the snails, Henry.

I got back to the room and said to Kate, who was in front of the vanity fussing with makeup, "We have to move fast. State police H.Q. at eight."

"Breakfast is on the table. What did Major Schaeffer say?"

"I'll tell you on the way. Where's your briefcase?"

"Under the bed."

I reached under the bed, pulled out her briefcase, and began flipping through the stack of Enterprise rental agreements as I stood at the table and uncovered the basket of hot biscuits.

"What are you looking for?"

"Butter."

"John—"

"Ah, here it is."

"What?"

"The Enterprise rental agreement with the plate number of the car we saw at the Custer Hill Club." I put the agreement on the table and buttered a biscuit.

"Who rented the car?"

"This may be interesting . . ."

"What?"

"This guy's name. It's Russian. Mikhail Putyov."

She thought about that. "Doesn't sound like a member of the club to me."

"Me, neither. Maybe Madox invites old Cold War enemies to the club to reminisce." Still standing, I dug into the omelet and asked Kate, "Do you want breakfast, or do you want to keep painting?"

No reply.

"We have to get going."

No reply.

"Sweetheart, can I bring you your juice, coffee, and a piece of toast?"

"Yes, please."

I'm not that well trained yet, but I'm learning. I brought her juice, buttered toast, and coffee to the vanity table and asked, "Do you have cell service?"

"No."

"I need to make another call from the kitchen."

"Who are you calling?"

"Someone who can get a make on this Russian guy."

"Call our office."

"I'd rather not."

She informed me, "We're already in trouble, John. You understand that, don't you?"

"Here's the way the world works. Information is power. If you give away your information, you give away your power to negotiate the trouble you're in."

"Here's the way my world works," Kate replied. "Stay out of trouble."

"I think it's too late for that, sweetheart."

CHAPTER THIRTY

I went back into the Great Hall, where about a dozen people, including Cindy and Sonny, were now scattered around the two tables having breakfast. Cindy smiled and waved. Sonny was looking for Kate.

I re-entered the kitchen, and the same kid was on the phone again, placing another order. I said to him, "Henry wants to see you. Now."

"Huh?"

"I need the phone. Now."

He got sulky on me but hung up, then stomped off. Young people need to learn patience and respect for others.

I got the number I needed from my cell-phone directory and dialed.

A familiar voice answered, "Kearns Investigative Service."

I said, "I think my dog is an Iraqi spy. Can you do a background check on him?"

"Who is—? Corey?"

"Hey, Dick. I got this French poodle who every Friday night turns toward Mecca and starts howling."

He laughed and said, "Shoot the dog. Hey, how you been?"

"Great. You?"

"Terrific. Where're you calling from? What's The Point?"

"The point of what? Oh, it's the place I'm staying at. Saranac Lake."

"Vacation?"

"Job. How's Mo?"

"Crazy as ever. How's Kate?"

"Great. We're working this together."

We made polite small talk for a minute. Dick Kearns is former NYPD homicide, part of my Blue Network, which I noticed was getting smaller every year as guys retired and moved, or died natural deaths—or, like Dom Fanelli and six other guys I knew, died in the line of duty on 9/11.

Dick was also briefly assigned to the ATTF, where he'd gotten a top secret clearance and learned how the Feds worked, so when he retired he got a gig doing background checks for the FBI on a freelance basis. He's in a growth industry since 9/11, and he's making more money than he ever did as a cop with half the stress. Good for Dick.

The small talk out of the way, I said to him, "Dick, I need some info on a guy."

"Okay, but I'm up to my ears in work. I'll do what I can. When do you need it?"

"Noon."

He laughed. "I have ten background checks I'm doing for the FBI, and they're all late."

"Give them all top secret clearances and send the bill. Look, for now, I just need some public-record stuff and maybe a few phone calls to follow up."

"Noon?"

I noticed that some of the staff seemed interested in my conversation, so I lowered my voice and said to Dick, "It may be a matter of national security."

"And you're calling *me*? Why don't you have your own office do it?"

"I asked, and they referred me to you. You're the best."

"John, are you sticking your nose where it doesn't belong again?"

Apparently, Dick remembered that he'd helped me, unofficially, with the TWA 800 case, and now he thought I was up to my old tricks again. I was, but why trouble him with that? I said, "I'll owe you a big favor."

"You owe me from the last time. Hey, whatever happened with that TWA 800 thing?"

"Nothing. You ready to copy?"

"John, I do this for a living. If I help you, I could go broke, get fired, or get arrested."

"First name, Mikhail." I spelled it.

He sighed, spelled it back to me, and asked, "Russki?"

"Probably. Last name, Putyov." I spelled it, and he confirmed.

"I hope you've got more than that."

"I'm going to make this easy for you. I've got a car-rental agreement, and unless this guy used false ID, I've got all you need."

"Good. Let's have it."

I read him all the pertinent information from the Enterprise rental agreement, including Putyov's address, which was Cambridge, Massachusetts. Dick said, "Okay, this should be easy. What's this guy up to? What is your area of interest?"

"I don't know what he's up to, but I think I need to know what he does for a living."

"That comes with the basic package. Where do I send my bill?"

"To my ex-wife." Dick didn't need any more reason to do this other than to help a former brother in blue, but to make sure he was motivated beyond the national security angle, I said to him, "Do you remember a guy I work with at 26 Fed—Harry Muller?"

"Yeah . . . retired from the job . . . you mentioned him."

"Right. Well, he's dead. Died up here, around Saranac Lake. You may see an obit or a piece in the papers, and the story may say he was killed in a hunting accident. But he was murdered."

"Jeez . . . Harry Muller? What happened?"

"That's what I'm here to find out."

"And this Russian guy is involved?"

"He's involved with the guy who I think did the murder."

"Okay . . . so . . . noon, right? How do I reach you?"

"Bad cell reception here. I'll call you. Be reachable."

"Absolutely."

"Thanks. Best to Mo."

"Hello to Kate."

I hung up and left the kitchen. I needed to find a better place to run this operation.

I made my way out of the Great Hall, into the rotunda, then out the door, where I saw my car with Kate at the wheel.

I jumped in the passenger seat and said, "Okay, we'll know something about Mikhail Putyov by noon."

She put the Taurus in gear and off we went.

I looked at the dashboard clock. "Do you think we can get there in thirty minutes?"

"That's why I'm driving, John."

"Do I need to remind you of your sheer panic in Manhattan traffic?"

"I don't panic . . . I practice tactical evasion techniques."

"So does everyone around you."

"Very funny. Hey, what's in the backseat?"

I glanced over my shoulder. "Oh, I thought ahead and had the chef pack us a picnic lunch."

"Good thinking. Did you meet him?"

"I did. Henry. Henri. Whatever."

"Were you awful?"

"Of course not. He's doing pigs-in-the-blanket during cocktails. Just for me."

I don't think she believed me.

We passed through the gates, down the narrow, tree-lined lane, and turned onto the road. Kate gassed it, and we were off to see the state police unless they saw us first and pulled us over for reckless driving.

Kate inquired, "Anything new with Major Schaeffer?"

"There is. He took my advice and began surveillance on the Custer Hill property."

"And?"

"And, that Enterprise rental car we saw there, which was Putyov's, was returned last night to the airport."

"So, Putyov's gone?"

"If he is, he didn't leave last night from the airport. He . . . or maybe it was someone else driving his car . . . went back to the Custer Hill Club in a van." As she drove, I filled her in, then took the rental agreement from my pocket and perused it. I said, "This guy Putyov rented the car Sunday morning. That means he flew in that day on the flight from Boston or Albany—"

"Boston," she said. "I checked the flight manifests. Mikhail Putyov arrived at Adirondack Regional Airport, Lake Saranac, at nine twenty-five A.M. Sunday."

"Right. He lives in Cambridge." I glanced at the rental agreement. "Putyov rented the car for two days, so he was supposed to turn it in today. Instead, it was returned to the airport parking lot last night." I asked her, "Did you check the flight reservations we got from Betty?"

"I did. Putyov is scheduled to depart today on the twelve forty-five to Boston."

"Okay. We'll check that out." I thought a moment, then said, "I'm wondering why Putyov came in for this gathering later than the others, and why he is apparently still there after everyone else has left."

"That depends on why he's there. Maybe he has oil business with Madox."

"Mr. Madox is a busy man. And a multitasker. A social weekend with old and powerful friends, then he murders a Federal agent, then he winds up the weekend with a Russian from Cambridge, Massachusetts. I don't know how he fit us into his schedule."

Kate commented, "I don't think Harry was part of his weekend plans."

But he may have been.

We headed east on Route 86, and Kate seemed to be having fun passing in the oncoming lane as huge trucks hurtled toward us. I said, "Slow down."

"I can't. The gas pedal's stuck, and the brakes are gone. So just close your eyes and get some sleep."

Kate, raised in a rural area, has a lot of these stupid on-the-road jokes, none of which I find funny.

I kept my eyes open and stared out the windshield.

Kate said to me, "I need to call John Nasseff. Do you know him?"

"No, but he has a nice first name."

"He's NCID, attached to the ATTF."

I replied, "W-H-A-T?"

"Naval Criminal Investigation Division, John. He's a commo guy."

"Ask him about my cell phone."

She ignored that and continued, "I was thinking about

Fred, the Navy veteran. So, if that clue has any relevance at all, then we should ask a Navy commo guy about ELF and see if we hit on something."

I wasn't sure I was completely following this line of reasoning, but Kate might be onto something. On the other hand, I didn't want to be calling 26 Federal Plaza with questions like that. I said, "I'd rather not call our office."

"Why not? That's where we work."

"Yeah, but you know how everyone there gossips."

"They don't *gossip*. They exchange and provide information. Information is power. Right?"

"Only when you keep it to yourself. Let's just go online and learn about ELF."

"*You* go online. I'm calling the expert."

"Okay . . . but make it like a parlor game, like, 'Hey, John, we have this bet going about extremely low frequency radio waves. My sister says they can hard-boil an egg; my husband says they'll fry your brain.' Okay?"

"Do you want him to think we're idiots?"

"Exactly."

"I'm not as good as you are at playing stupid."

"Then I'll call him."

"We'll both call him."

We arrived in the hamlet of Ray Brook, and Kate slowed down. About two blinks later, we pulled into the parking lot of the state police headquarters. It was 8:05 A.M.

Kate took her briefcase, and we got out of the Taurus

and started walking toward the building, but a car suddenly pulled out of a parking space and stopped right in front of us.

I wasn't sure what that was about, but I was on my guard.

The driver's-side window went down, and Hank Schaeffer stuck his head out. "Jump in."

We got in his car, an unmarked Crown Victoria, I in the front, Kate in the back.

I wondered why he was waiting for us in the parking lot instead of the lobby, but he clarified the situation by saying, "I have company this morning."

I didn't need to ask.

He pulled onto the road and said, "Six of them. Three from the New York field office, two from Washington, and one from your shop."

I said, "They're from the government, and they're here to help you."

"They're helping themselves to my files."

Kate, in the back, said, "Excuse me. I'm FBI."

I turned to her. "We're not criticizing the FBI, darling."

No reply.

I asked Schaeffer, "Who's here from the ATTF?"

"Guy named Liam Griffith. Know him?"

"Indeed. He's from the Office of Professional Responsibility."

"What the hell is that?"

"That's Fed talk for Internal Affairs."

"Really? Well, he's looking for both of you."

I glanced back at Kate, who seemed a little upset.

Some people called Liam Griffith the Enforcer, but the younger guys who'd seen *The Matrix* too many times called him the Agent in Black. I called him a prick.

I recalled that Griffith was supposed to be at that meeting in Windows on the World, but he'd been either late or uninvited. In any case, he'd escaped the fate of everyone who'd been there that morning.

Also, I'd had a few run-ins with Mr. Griffith during the TWA 800 case, and my last words to him in the bar at Ecco's had been, "Get the fuck out of my sight."

He took my suggestion, though he didn't take it well.

Now, he was back.

Kate asked Schaeffer, "What did you tell him?"

"I told him you'd probably stop in today. He said he'd like to see you both when you arrive." He added, "I figured you'd want to postpone that."

I said to Schaeffer, "Thanks."

He didn't acknowledge that. "Your boss, Tom Walsh, called right after you left. He asked what we discussed, and I referred him to you."

I replied, "Good. I referred him to *you*. Did you tell him we were staying at The Point?"

"No. Why?"

I glanced back at Kate, then said to Schaeffer, "Well, he left a message for us there."

Schaeffer reiterated, "I didn't mention it."

Maybe, I thought, the FBI guys from the city, or Liam Griffith, had interviewed my friend Max at Hertz. I asked Schaeffer, "Did Walsh say we were assigned to this case?"

"No. But neither did he say that Griffith was here to pull you off the case. But I think he is."

If Kate and I could speak freely now, we'd probably agree that basically we'd been screwed by Tom Walsh. In fact, I couldn't keep that in, and I said to Kate, "Tom reneged on our deal."

She responded, "We don't know that . . . Maybe Liam Griffith just wants to . . . make us understand the terms of our assignment here."

I replied, "I don't think that's why Walsh called the Office of Professional Responsibility, or why Griffith would fly here."

She didn't answer, but Schaeffer said, "Last I heard, you had seven days to crack the case, and until I hear otherwise, you're the investigating team."

"Correct," I said.

Meanwhile, I needed to keep one step ahead of Liam Griffith.

CHAPTER THIRTY-ONE

Less than an hour after we'd left Ray Brook, we turned off Route 56 at Stark Road.

Our cell phones and beepers had been unusually quiet all morning, which would have been a real treat if it wasn't so ominous.

In fact, our usual phone pal, Tom Walsh, was lying low now that the Enforcer, Liam Griffith, was on the prowl. At this point, Walsh and Griffith had chatted a few times, speculating as to the whereabouts of Detective Corey and Special Agent Mayfield, a.k.a. the renegade agents.

I was certain that Griffith had assured Walsh that the miscreants would be along shortly, and that before they got halfway across the lobby of state police headquarters, they'd be in his custody and headed out to the airport, where an FBI helicopter was waiting to take them back to Manhattan.

Well, that wasn't going to happen.

I shut off my cell phone and beeper and motioned for Kate to do the same.

Schaeffer took the same route that Rudy had given us, and within fifteen minutes, we were at the T-intersection where McCuen Pond Road ran north to the Custer Hill Club gatehouse.

Close to the intersection, I saw an orange pickup truck with a state seal on the door parked on the shoulder. Two men in coveralls were clearing brush.

Schaeffer slowed down and said to us, "State police."

He stopped, and the two guys recognized the boss and came up to the car. They looked like they wanted to salute, but they were undercover, so they just nodded and said, "Good morning, Major."

Schaeffer asked, "Any activity?"

One of them replied, "No, sir. Nothing going in or out. Quiet."

He joked, "Don't work too hard. That'll blow your civil service cover."

Both troopers got off good laughs for the boss, and we moved on.

Schaeffer said to us, "If they see a vehicle coming from Custer Hill and turning toward Route 56, they'll radio to an unmarked vehicle who'll pick up the subject vehicle on the highway, as we did last night with the Custer Hill van and the Enterprise car. If the subject vehicle turns this way, into the woods, then the truck here will follow."

Major Schaeffer continued, "Last night, we used a truck from the power company. In a day or so, we're going to run out of excuses to be at that intersection in the middle of the woods."

I asked, "Do you think anyone from the Custer Hill property is even aware of these vehicles?"

"Absolutely. My guys say the Custer Hill security people run a Jeep out to this road at least twice a day, look around, then go back. Sort of like a perimeter recon."

I said, "Bain Madox was an infantry officer."

"I know that. And he knows he has to recon outside his perimeter."

Madox was also paranoid, which was useful when people really were after you.

We continued down the logging road, and Kate said, "John, I see what you meant about Harry's surveillance. It could have been done off the property, back there where Major Schaeffer has his team."

"Right. One way in, one way out." And for those guests arriving in the Custer Hill van from the airport, there should have been a stakeout at the airport to see who arrived on the Boston and Albany flights and who went into the van.

Instead, Walsh sent Harry, alone, onto the property.

This was either a badly conceived surveillance, done on a shoestring budget, or something else. Like someone *wanted* Harry Muller caught. Well, not Harry specifically, but any ATTF cop who got handed this assignment to check out so-called domestic terrorism. Like me, for instance.

As interesting as this thought was, it didn't make much sense. I should just put this under one of the usual categories of piss-poor planning, desk-chair stupidity, or my bad habit of Monday morning quarterbacking.

Schaeffer broke into my thoughts. "I wouldn't dream of criticizing how you people run your assignments, but your friend never had much of a chance to accomplish this surveillance on the property."

Neither Kate nor I replied, and Schaeffer continued, "If you'd contacted me, I'd have given you the lay of the land, offered some manpower, and advice."

I said, "Sometimes, the Feds can be a little arrogant and secretive."

"Yeah. Sometimes."

To change the subject while also taking Schaeffer's advice about using his services, I asked him, "Did you locate Fred?"

"Who? Oh, the Navy veteran. Not yet. I'll ask around."

Apparently, Major Schaeffer hadn't spent too much time on locating Fred the vet. Also, I'm sure he didn't think it was too important. Neither did I, until Kate suggested calling the ATTF Navy commo guy about ELF. You just never know what's going to lead to something, or what might connect two points that weren't even on the same page.

We turned onto a dirt trail that was just wide enough

for the car. Schaeffer said, "This is the trail where we found the body a mile or so from here, then we found the camper about three miles further." He added, "It's almost six miles from the camper to the perimeter fence of Custer Hill. About an hour-and-a-half hike."

Neither Kate nor I responded.

Major Schaeffer continued, "So, you're thinking that Harry Muller originally parked the camper much closer, and that he entered the property about eight A.M. Saturday morning, got picked up by the Custer Hill security, then somewhere along the line he was forcefully interrogated, then maybe drugged, and he and his camper were moved onto this trail, where he was murdered, and his camper was driven a few more miles up the trail. Is that about it?"

I replied, "That's about it."

Schaeffer nodded and said, "Could've happened that way." He asked me, or himself, "But why in the name of God would they murder a Federal agent?"

"That's what we're here to find out."

Kate asked, "Has anyone else had a hunting accident on or around this trail, or near the Custer Hill property?"

Schaeffer kept his eyes on the narrow trail and replied, "I've been thinking about that since Detective Corey brought it up yesterday, so I asked around and the answer is yes, about twenty years ago when the Custer Hill property was being developed." He informed us, "It happened about five miles north of the property. One of my old-timers remembered it."

Kate asked, "What was the outcome?"

"Hunting accident, shooter unknown."

"And the victim?"

"Never identified." He briefed us, "Male, about forty, clean shaven, well nourished, and so forth. Single shot to the head. It was summer, and the victim was wearing shorts, a T-shirt, and hiking boots. No ID, the body was at least two weeks dead when discovered, and some animals had gotten to it. Facial photos were taken but not shown to the general public for obvious reasons. Fingerprints were recovered, but not good ones, and they were unmatchable to any data banks that existed at the time."

Kate pointed out, "Isn't that a little suspicious? I mean, single shot to the head, no ID, no one reported missing, and I assume no vehicle turned up in the area."

"Well, yeah. It's suspicious. But according to my guy who remembered it, there was not a single clue or evidence of foul play, so, to make things simple, the sheriff and the coroner ruled it an accident, awaiting any information to the contrary." He added, "We're still waiting." He paused, then said, "Even now, with this apparent homicide, I wouldn't try to connect that death to the Custer Hill Club, which wasn't even occupied at the time."

I said to him, "Run the fingerprints again."

We drove on in silence. I thought, of course, there could very well be a connection. The victim, if he had been murdered, could be some hiker who saw something he wasn't supposed to see at the Custer Hill construction site—or maybe it was some guy working on the Custer Hill project who saw or knew too much about something. Like ELF. Or something else.

I didn't want to start making Bain Madox into this evil genius who was responsible for everything that went wrong in the world for the last twenty years—floods, famine, war, plague, earthquakes, my extra ten pounds, and my divorce. But this guy certainly fit the part of some sort of global manipulator. I mean, the rule is, If it looks like a duck, walks like a duck, and quacks like a duck, then it's a duck.

Then, I kill the duck.

CHAPTER THIRTY-TWO

Major Schaeffer pulled off the trail onto a recently cleared patch of ground, explaining, "We needed to widen the trail here for a turnaround."

We got out and followed him another twenty yards to where an area was staked out with yellow tape. On the trail itself, they'd used Day-Glo orange to spray paint an outline of Harry's body. In the center of the outline was a blue jay, pecking the ground.

The sun was higher now, and light penetrated the trees and lit up the pleasant woodland trail. Birds were chirping, and squirrels scampered through the trees, dropping acorn husks. A soft breeze rustled the fall leaves, which floated down in a constant flurry. *Now it is autumn and the falling fruit . . .*

There's no good place to die, but I suppose if you

didn't die in your own bed, this was as good a place as any.

On the other side of the taped-off area, I saw a state police SUV on the trail.

Schaeffer said, "Those guys came in from the other direction. They're still looking for a shell casing, but whoever did this did not leave a casing or anything else behind. And we still haven't found the bullet that passed through the victim's body."

I nodded. Assuming the murder weapon was a high-velocity rifle, the chances of finding the bullet in the woods were not good. In fact, there were many spent bullets in the woods, and there was no way that any of them could be identified as the bullet that killed the victim. Even a ballistics match on one of Madox's rifles wouldn't prove anything except that Madox, or a guest, had once gone hunting in the woods. Bottom line—the woods were a good place to commit murder.

Schaeffer continued, "We're keeping the tape out at fifty feet for now, but I'm going to pull it tighter today, then by tomorrow, there's no reason to keep this as a pristine crime scene." He informed us, "Rain forecast for tomorrow." He added, "I think we and the CSI team did all we could. There's nothing here."

Again I nodded, as I kept staring at the Day-Glo orange outline. The blue jay had been joined by its mate.

Schaeffer said, "If you look up the trail, you'll see that it's fairly straight, so it's hard to imagine a hunter on this trail mistaking a man for a deer. And if the hunter was in the woods, it would take a miracle shot to pass through all these trees without hitting one of them."

"Right," I agreed. "Looks like murder."

"Unfortunately, other than the near impossibility of this being an accident, we don't have a shred of evidence that it was murder." He reminded me, "There was no robbery, and the victim had no local ties that might lead to a grudge killing, which sometimes happens up here."

I didn't reply. Major Schaeffer obviously suspected that Harry's assignment was linked to his death, and that the murderer was Bain Madox, but he wasn't going to take that step until he had a good piece of evidence.

Schaeffer asked us, "Do you want to see the photos?"

I didn't, but I said, "Please."

He took a stack of color photos from his overcoat pocket and handed them to me. I flipped through them as Kate stood beside me.

Harry had fallen face-first, as I already knew, and his arms were thrown out from his sides by the impact of the bullet, as shown in the spray-painted outline on the trail.

I could barely see the entry wound in the center of his back, but close-ups revealed a bloodstain in the center of his camouflage jacket.

I stared at a close-up that showed the left side of Harry's face with his eyes open.

I could see the leather strap around his neck that was connected to the binoculars, which had landed clear of his body and were lying close to his left shoulder, near his face.

I asked Major Schaeffer, "Was that the position of the binoculars when you found the body?"

"Yes. These are the photos that were taken before we touched or moved anything." He added, "It may be that he was holding or looking through the binoculars when he was shot, which I think is why they're clear of the body and not under his chest. Or, the impact of the round hitting the body just caused the binoculars to swing on their strap away from the body before it hit the ground."

Possible, but not probable. First, Harry was not looking through his binoculars before he'd been murdered by the people who brought him here. Second, the laws of physics would suggest that the binoculars would swing back to their original position, hanging on Harry's chest, before his body hit the ground. But that was not a certainty.

Major Schaeffer continued, "You saw his personal effects laid out in the morgue, and his video camera was found in the right pouch pocket of his jacket, the camera in his left. In the right cargo pocket of his pants was the bird guide and in the left was the pair of wire cutters."

Major Schaeffer, referring to his notebook, recited the inventory of what was found—key chain, wallet, Glock, credentials, and so forth, and where it was found on the body.

As Schaeffer spoke, I tried to reconstruct how Madox had done this, and I concluded that he'd needed at least one accomplice—probably Carl and maybe someone else, though I doubted that Madox wanted two witnesses to this.

Harry had been drugged, and his ankles had been shackled. They'd put him in the sleeping compartment of the camper and driven him out here. There could have been a second vehicle for a getaway.

Assuming, then, that Madox did not want more than one accomplice, and assuming that Harry was drugged and nearly comatose, Madox was then presented with the problem of how to stand Harry upright so he could be shot in the back as though he'd been walking.

One man could not hold a drugged man upright while the other fired, so the solution was to put Harry on his knees, while Carl—or Madox—held the binoculars and strap tightly around Harry's neck to keep him in the kneeling position. Then, the shooter knelt and put a bullet through Harry's spine and heart.

The accomplice let go of the binoculars as Harry was falling forward, and the binoculars ended up where I saw them in the photo. Then, one or both men unshackled Harry's ankles and moved his arms and legs to simulate the position of a body being hit by a high-velocity bullet and falling forward from a standing position. Then, probably, they'd brushed the trail with pine boughs. The only thing they'd forgotten was that the binoculars would most probably have ended up under the body, and may also have been damaged by the round passing through the body and out the chest.

Otherwise, they did a good job, if I could use that word for a cold-blooded murder.

Schaeffer asked us, "Do you want to see the camper?"

I nodded and handed the photos back to him.

He led us around the yellow tape and through the woods.

We came out on the trail again near the SUV, where the police had also widened the trail for a turnaround. Schaeffer got one of his troopers to drive us the three miles up the trail to where the camper sat parked in a small clearing.

We got out, and I looked at Harry's camper, which I'd never seen before. It was an old Chevy pickup, fitted with a sleeper on the truck bed. Old as it was, it seemed as if it had been kept meticulously clean and in good repair.

Schaeffer said, "We dusted it for prints, did some vacuuming, and got some dirt samples out of the tire treads. This afternoon, we'll tow it out of here to the highway, put it on a flatbed, and send it to the forensic garage in Albany for a thorough going-over. Obviously, we're looking for evidence of other people being in the vehicle."

I said to him, "Sounds like you think it was premeditated murder."

"Let's assume it was."

I pictured Harry drugged and bound in the rear sleeping compartment, and someone, maybe Carl, at the wheel. Driving in front of the camper was Madox in one of his vehicles: a Jeep, a van, or an all-terrain vehicle.

I asked Schaeffer about tire marks on the trail, and he replied, "As you can see, this is hard-packed earth, plus it hasn't rained in two weeks, and then you have all these leaves and pine boughs on the trail. So, no, we didn't get any good tire marks."

Kate asked, "Did the dusting indicate that any surfaces had been wiped clean?"

"No. When you have premeditation, you have gloves. We might get some interesting clothing fibers, but again, with premeditation and smarts, the perpetrators would burn whatever they wore." He added, "There's an open Coke can in the beverage holder, and we'll do a DNA on that, but I don't think our perps were drinking Coke. If we recover DNA, it will probably be Harry's."

Schaeffer looked around at the clearing, then down the trail, and said, "Okay, so here's the camper. What I'm thinking is that there were at least two perpetrators, and two vehicles—the camper and the getaway vehicle— though, as I said, there were no distinct tire marks. They stopped back there, shot the victim, then got back in the vehicles and continued on, putting some distance between themselves and the scene of the crime."

Kate and I nodded, and Schaeffer continued, "If they were locals, they knew about this clearing where a lot of campers and hikers pull off. Then, if you go another mile up this trail, you reach a paved road. So, one guy parked the camper here where you see it, then got into the getaway vehicle, and within a few minutes, they were making their getaway on the paved road up ahead."

Major Schaeffer had done a credible job of reconstructing the crime, partly because he'd already had some time on the scene with CSI people putting their heads together, and partly because he had knowledge of the area.

I said to Major Schaeffer, "I assume you have the key

to this camper, which was missing from Harry's key chain in the morgue."

"I do." He reminded me, "You said you didn't handle the evidence in the morgue."

"Did I say that?" I continued, "I also assume you confirmed that the Chevy truck key you found on the chain was for this camper."

He looked at me. "We're not as smart as you city guys, Detective, but we're not stupid."

Based on my previous experiences with rural and suburban cops, I realized that statement was long overdue. I said, "Just checking," then asked, "How do you think the perpetrators moved this camper three miles from where the body and the ignition key were found?"

"They could have hot-wired the camper, towed it with their other vehicle, or even had a duplicate key made before the crime. But the most likely answer is that the victim had a spare key on his person, or in the vehicle."

"Right." I told him about the apparently missing spare Chevy key in Harry's wallet, and asked him, "Did you notice that?"

He didn't reply directly but informed me, "The absence of a key among other keys is not proof that there *was* a key."

"Right . . . I'm just speculating."

Actually, this was a detective's pissing match, which we all do to keep everyone on their toes, which is good for the investigation, not to mention the detectives' egos.

Kate seemed to sense this and said, "In any case, this was made to appear that Harry left the camper here, and began walking north, toward the Custer Hill Club, and met with an accident three miles from his camper, and about three more miles from the Custer Hill property." She concluded, "Bottom line, he would not have parked six miles from the surveillance property. Plus, the phone call to his girlfriend at seven forty-eight A.M. indicated he was near the subject property, but that's not where he was found. Therefore, we have problems with time, distance, logic, and plausibility, which leads us to conclude that what we see here is not what Harry actually did on Saturday morning, but what someone did *to* him about a day later."

That pretty much summed it up, and neither Major Schaeffer nor I had anything to add.

So we'd done all we could here, which wasn't much, but you had to begin at the scene of the crime, then work backward and forward from there.

The trick was not to become process oriented but to remember the goal, which was to find the killer. The good news was that I had a suspect. Bain Madox. And I had a possible accomplice. Carl. But neither of those names was going to appear on the New York state police homicide report.

I asked Schaeffer, "Are the FBI agents in your office coming out here?"

"I asked them, and they said another team would do that—an Evidence Recovery Team. These guys in my office don't seem particularly interested in the crime scene."

No, I thought, *they were more interested in Bain*

Madox than Harry Muller. And Liam Griffith was only interested in John Corey and Kate Mayfield.

But for me, it was important that I see where Harry Muller had died, and to think about how he'd died: a helpless, drugged prisoner, a police officer, doing his duty, murdered by a person or persons who didn't think as much of Harry Muller's life as they thought of their own self-interests, whatever they were.

I wondered if Bain Madox—assuming it was Madox—had tried to think of another solution to whatever problem Harry Muller posed for him. Surely there must have been a moment when murder was not the best solution, when some other, more clever course of action would have solved whatever problem Madox had with Harry Muller's appearance at the Custer Hill Club.

Most criminals—from the very stupid to the very clever—don't understand the forces they put into motion when they decide on murder to solve a problem. The ones who do understand often try to make it look like an accident, suicide, or natural death. And by doing that, they usually leave more clues than if they'd made it look like an everyday murder and robbery.

The best way to cover up a murder is with the complete disappearance of the body, which, along with the crime scene, holds too many clues. But Bain Madox had a unique problem: he needed to get a soon-to-be-dead Federal agent off his property and onto someone else's property—in this case, state land—where the body could be found before state and local police and Federal agents came around looking for the missing person on Madox's property. Therefore, Madox had something on his property—other than Harry Muller—that he didn't want anyone to see.

This, what we saw here, was Madox's solution, and it wasn't a bad quick fix. It would not, however, survive a full-blown homicide investigation.

If my other theory was correct, however, then time was all Madox wanted before he became a suspect. This bastard had already lit a fuse, and it was burning faster than it would take to find the bomb.

CHAPTER THIRTY-THREE

We returned to Schaeffer's car, turned around, and headed back down the trail. No one had much to say.

We were approaching the T-intersection where the undercover state troopers were still hacking away at the brush. Schaeffer stopped and asked them, "Anything to report?"

One of the guys replied, "The black Jeep did a recon ten minutes ago, and the driver asked us what we were doing."

"What did you tell him?"

"I told him we were clearing brush and leaves, which are potential fuel sources for forest fires started by careless motorists throwing lit smoking materials out the window."

"Did he buy it?"

"He seemed skeptical. Said no one had done that before. I told him the risk of forest fires was very high this year."

"Okay. Tell you what—call Captain Stoner and tell him I want two highway repair crews here filling potholes. Real highway workers, with two troopers along, dressed like road crew and leaning on their shovels like they do."

The trooper smiled. "Yes, sir."

"Then you guys take off."

"Yes, sir."

Schaeffer continued toward Route 56 and said to us, "I think Madox is on to this surveillance by now."

I replied, "He's been on to the fact that he's under surveillance since Harry Muller got caught on his property Saturday morning."

Schaeffer pointed out, "We don't know that Harry Muller got caught on his property." He inquired, "Why was your friend sent here to gather information on Madox's guests?"

"I don't know, and neither did he." I explained, "I spoke to him before he drove up here."

Schaeffer probably thought he was going to get some information from us in exchange for saving us from Liam Griffith and taking us to the crime scene. So, to give him something that he should have had anyway, I said, "Harry was also supposed to check òut the airport. Flight manifests and car rentals. The Feds will, or have already done that. You should do the same before that information disappears."

He didn't reply, so I added, "Kate and I happen to

know that some VIPs from Washington arrived at the airport and may have gone to the Custer Hill Club."

He glanced at me.

When you think you might be pulled from a case because you're stepping on the wrong toes, you need to pass on the info to someone who might run with it—or at least hold it until they decide what to do with it.

I gave Schaeffer another tip. "You should keep the information about your Custer Hill surveillance to yourself for a while."

Again, no reply. I think he'd be a little more chatty without an FBI agent in his backseat. But I'd said what I had to say, and I'd repaid him for his favors. What was written in Harry's pocket was not information that Major Schaeffer needed to know.

Now it was my turn, so I asked Schaeffer, "Do you know this guy Carl? Sort of Madox's right-hand man, or maybe bodyguard."

Schaeffer shook his head. "I don't know anyone at that lodge. As I said, his security people are not local. He has his barracks where he keeps them, and they probably do a week on, then go home, then back for another week or so of duty. As for the house staff, I have the impression they're not from around here either."

That was interesting.

"There's more population north of here, outside the state park, starting with Potsdam, then Massena. In fact, the Canadian border is less than fifty miles from where we are right now, and I know that a lot of Canadians commute to work in the tourist industry here. So, if I was Madox and I wanted staff from out of the area, I'd go whole hog and get them from out of the *country* so that their gossip was not likely to travel back here."

I hadn't met any of the house staff, and I can't tell an upstate accent from a Canadian accent, anyway. As for the security guys, whatever accent they'd been raised with had been replaced by an affected, clipped, military manner of speaking.

Schaeffer informed us, "I made a call this morning and checked that Enterprise plate number, and the car was rented to a guy named Mikhail Putyov."

I didn't reply, so Major Schaeffer said, "Sounds Russian." He added, "And maybe he's still at the lodge. No one has left the Custer Hill Club since last night."

"Right. Aren't you glad you did that surveillance?"

Major Schaeffer ignored that. "The guy I spoke to at Enterprise said two FBI agents, a man and a woman, came around yesterday and got copies of all his rental agreements. Do you know anything about that?"

I asked evasively, "How did he describe them?"

"He said the guy was hitting on Max, the Hertz lady, and the woman was very pretty."

"Who could that be?" I wondered aloud, knowing I was in more trouble from the backseat than from Liam Griffith. Thanks, Major.

Kate spoke up. "I guess that was us."

I asked Schaeffer, "Didn't I mention that when we spoke?"

"No."

"Well, I meant to."

I looked at the dashboard clock and saw it was 10:15 A.M. I said to Major Schaeffer, "By the way, this guy Putyov is booked on the twelve forty-five P.M. flight to Boston. If he's going to be at the airport one hour before departure, as required, he should be leaving the Custer Hill Club shortly—assuming he's at the club."

"How do you know Putyov is booked on the twelve forty-five flight?"

"Didn't I mention that Kate and I did what Harry was supposed to do at the airport? Flight manifests and car rentals."

"No, you didn't." He reached for his radio.

I said, "Madox's security guys are certainly monitoring the police band. Use your cell phone."

He glanced at me, and I couldn't tell if he was impressed with my brilliance or worried about my paranoia. In any case, he used his cell-phone directory and called his surveillance team. "Anything to report?"

He had the speaker on and the trooper replied, "No, sir."

"Well, there may be a vehicle coming from the subject property, heading for the airport. Advise our surveillance vehicle on Route 56."

"Yes, sir."

Schaeffer hung up and glanced at the dashboard clock, then did what I would have done first and called Continental Airlines at the airport. He got our friend Betty on the line and said, "Betty, this is Hank Schaeffer—"

"Well, how are you?"

"Just fine. And you?"

And so forth. I mean, pleasantries are nice, and it's sweet that everyone in RFD land knows everyone else and that they're all related by blood, marriage, or both, but let's get down to business, folks.

Finally, Major Schaeffer asked her, "Could you do me a favor and see if you've got a guy named Putyov"—he spelled it—"on your twelve forty-five flight to Boston?"

Betty replied, "Well, I can tell you without looking it up that we did. But since then, I got a revised manifest out of the company reservations computer, and I saw that he canceled."

"Did he rebook?"

"Nope." Then it was Betty's turn. "Any problem?"

"No, just routine. Call me at the office if this guy Putyov rebooks or shows up. Also, make copies for me of all your flight manifests and reservations for the last six days. I'll pick them up later."

"Okay. Hey, you want to hear something? Yesterday, a guy and a lady from the FBI come around, and *they* want copies of all my flight manifests and reservation sheets. They flew in on an FBI helicopter, so I knew they were for real and they had badges. So I gave them what they asked for."

Betty went on awhile, then added editorially, "The guy had a real smart mouth, and I gave it right back to him."

I didn't recall that I was anything but polite, but even if I was a little smart with her, she hadn't given it right back to me. *Liar.*

Major Schaeffer glanced at me and said to Betty, "Well, thanks—"

She interrupted. "What's happening? This guy said it had something to do with the Winter Olympics." She laughed. "I told him that was in 1980." She added, "The lady was nice, and you could see she was kind of fed up with this crackpot. So, what's this all about?"

"I can't say right now, but I want you to keep this to yourself."

"That's what they said. I would've called you, but I didn't make too much of it at the time. Now, I'm thinking—"

"There's nothing to be concerned about. Call me if this guy Putyov shows up or rebooks. I'll see you later. Okay?"

"Okay. You have a good day."

"You, too." He hung up, glanced at me, and said, "Well, you heard all that."

"I was very nice to her. Kate? Wasn't I nice to Betty?"

No reply.

Schaeffer said, "I meant about Putyov canceling his flight."

"Right. So, possibly he's still at the lodge."

"Yeah. He didn't rebook." He informed us, "These are small commuter airplanes, and the few flights we have are usually full. You can't depend on running out to the airport and finding an empty seat."

Schaeffer had a lot on his plate now, and a lot on his mind, but he had no idea what was going on beyond a homicide investigation. However, he knew something was going on at Custer Hill that interested the Feds and was not supposed to interest him.

We were approaching Route 56, and I said to Major Schaeffer, "Do us a favor and run us up to Potsdam."

"Why?"

"We need to . . . actually, we're trying to avoid Liam Griffith."

"No kidding? What's in it for me?"

"Well, then, just let us out on Route 56. We'll hitch-hike to Potsdam."

"You might see a bear before you see a car."

"Yeah? Well, I'm armed."

"Don't shoot the bears. I'll take you."

"Thanks." I turned around to speak to Kate, but she looked a little frosty. I said to her, "I'll buy you lunch in Potsdam."

No reply.

Then, bigmouthed Schaeffer says, "Max is quite a looker. Funny, too."

"Who? Oh, the Hertz person." A little payback from the good major.

We were at the intersection of Route 56, and Schaeffer stopped the car, and asked, "Potsdam?"

I had a sense of déjà vu from when I was at this cross-roads yesterday and made the decision to go see Harry at the Potsdam morgue rather than go as ordered to state police headquarters.

Now, we had to decide if we were going to face the music with Griffith before we got deeper into trouble, or go up to Potsdam and hide out.

Schaeffer asked again, "Which way?"

I glanced over my shoulder. "Kate? Potsdam or Liam?"

She replied, "Potsdam."

Schaeffer turned right and headed north to Potsdam.

It's tough enough working a homicide investigation when you're out of your jurisdiction. It's even tougher when you're on the lam from the people you're working for, and your partner is pissed at you, and your prime suspect is a buddy of some guys who work for the president.

How do I get myself into shit like this?

CHAPTER THIRTY-FOUR

We chatted a bit about the case as we drove through the park preserve. When we got to South Colton, I asked Schaeffer, "Do you know Rudy who owns that gas station?"

"Yeah, I remember him from when I used to patrol this area. Why?"

"He's Madox's local rat." I explained my brief association with Ratso Rudy.

Schaeffer nodded, and said, "This guy Madox has a lot more going on here than I realized. But as I said, he never caused us any trouble, and I don't think he's here that much. But from now on, I *will* keep closer tabs on him."

I thought that there wasn't going to be much more "from now on," but I didn't reply.

Schaeffer arrived at the same thought. "I guess he's a murder suspect now."

"Well, I think he is."

"Do your colleagues in my headquarters think that?"

"I reported our suspicions to Tom Walsh in New York."

"And what are you two doing in Potsdam?"

I replied, "Just taking a breather."

"Yeah? Why don't you go back to The Point?"

"Well, I think Mr. Griffith may be in our room using Kate's makeup while he waits for us."

"So, you're on the run from your own people?"

"I wouldn't put it quite like that."

"No? How would you put it?"

"Let me think about that. Meanwhile, can we be assured that you won't mention this to anyone?"

"Let me think about that."

"Because, if we can't count on your discretion, you may as well take us back to Ray Brook."

"What's in this for me?"

"You'd be doing the right thing."

"When do I know that?"

"Oh . . . in about two days."

"Yeah? So, you want me to commit a breach of professional responsibility and not mention to Griffith that I took you to the crime scene, and then to Potsdam?"

"Tell you what, Major. Ask him and the other FBI guys what this is all about. If they give you a straight answer, then send them to Potsdam to find us. Deal?"

"I think you'll get the best of that deal. But okay. It's a deal."

"And I'm going to throw in the keys to my Hertz car, which you may want to move out of your parking lot on the off chance that the FBI practices good police procedure and goes through the lot looking for our rental car." I gave him the keys and said, "There's a picnic lunch from The Point in the backseat, and it's yours."

"This deal is getting better. What's for lunch?"

"Probably snails. Also, if you want to cover your tracks a little with the FBI, you should call The Point and ask for us."

Major Schaeffer observed, "You'd make a good fugitive."

Actually, that's what we were at the moment, but there was no reason to remind him of that.

We were on the outskirts of Potsdam now, and Schaeffer asked, "Where do you want to go?"

"Just drop us off at a subway station."

I wasn't sure if Major Schaeffer appreciated or got my humor, but he said, "I guess you need a car."

"Good idea. Is there a rental place around here?"

"There's an Enterprise."

I waited for the rest of the list, but that seemed to be it.

We went through the center of town, then continued up Route 56, past the hospital where we'd seen Harry, and a few minutes later, we arrived at Enterprise Rent-A-Car.

Major Schaeffer parked near the rental office and said to us, "I don't know why you want to avoid Griffith, or what kind of trouble you're in. But if it wasn't for the fact that you lost a friend and partner here, and that your colleagues are freezing me out, I wouldn't be sticking my neck out for you."

I replied, "We appreciate that. Your instincts are good."

"Yeah? Well, I want you to prove to me that they are."

"We'll keep you informed."

"That would be nice for a change." He said to us, "Okay, I'm going to tell Griffith that I *met* you at the crime scene and that I delivered his message to you."

I reminded him, "Get rid of our rental car."

"Let me handle this, Detective."

Kate said to Schaeffer, "Be assured, Major, that John and I will take responsibility for any problems this might cause you."

"The only problem I have at the moment is hosting six Federal agents who are about to pull this case from me."

I informed him, "There are more on the way." Then I said, "Here's the way I think Harry Muller was murdered." I gave him my reconstruction of the murder as I thought it had probably happened. I concluded, "Look for signs that Harry may have been awake enough to kick the sides or roof of his camper."

Major Schaeffer stayed silent awhile, then said, "It could have happened that way. But that doesn't bring me any closer to finding the murderer or murderers."

Actually, his prime suspect was still Bain Madox whether he wanted to believe that or not. I said, "Well, when you find a suspect, you can shake him up with that description of how it was done. It's also good for your report."

He nodded and said thanks, but didn't offer me a job.

We shook hands all around, then Kate and I got out of the car and walked into the Enterprise office. I said to the lady behind the counter, "I'd like to rent a car."

"You're in the right place."

"I thought so. How about an SUV?"

"Nope. I got a Hyundai Accent ready to go."

"What kind of accent does it have?"

"Huh?"

"I'll take it."

I used my personal credit card since my employers had already paid for one rental car. Not to mention that I was on the run from them, and it would take them a while longer to trace my card than it would theirs.

Within fifteen minutes, I was behind the wheel of a little rice burner.

I drove back toward the center of town, and Kate observed, "It really doesn't take that long to rent a car, does it?"

I thought I knew where this was going. "No, especially if I'm not asking for a copy of all their rental agreements for the last four days."

"Not to mention the time you can save by not hitting on the rental lady."

Jeez. Here we were, up to our eyeballs in trouble, and some megalomaniac was about to start World War III or something, and she's busting my balloons about a little kidding around at the Hertz counter a long time ago. Well, yesterday. I refused to play this game and remained silent.

She informed me, "You're not single anymore, you know."

And so forth.

We got into the center of town, and I pulled into a parking space near a coffee shop, and said, "I need coffee."

"John, are you sure you know what you're doing?"

"Yeah. I'm getting a coffee to go. What do you want?"

"Answer my question."

"I know what I'm doing."

"What are you doing?"

"I don't know."

"How long are we going to be doing it?"

"Until we break this case or until our colleagues catch us, whichever comes first."

"Well, I can tell you what's going to come first."

"Coffee?"

"Black."

I got out of the car and went into the coffee shop, a local place, not a Starbucks, where I'd have to visit the ATM machine first.

I ordered two black from the spaced-out young lady behind the counter, and while she was mentally struggling with my request, I noticed a rack of pamphlets and free guides near the door. I plucked a bunch of them out of the rack and shoved them in my pockets.

The space cadet behind the counter was trying to figure out what size lid to use, and I said to her, "I need to make a local call. Can I use your cell phone?"

"Uh . . . ?"

The coffee came to a buck-fifty, and I gave her a five and said, "Keep the change for the phone call."

She handed me her cell phone, and I dialed The Point.

Jim answered, "The Point. How can I help you?"

"This is Mr. Corey. Any messages for me or my wife?"

"Good morning, Mr. Corey. Are you enjoying your stay with us?"

"Hey, Jim, I have to tell you, this is the best twelve hundred bucks a night I ever spent, and that includes the showgirls in Vegas."

Jim was momentarily speechless, then said, "I have two messages for you. Both from Mr. Griffith. He'd like you to call him." He gave me Mr. Griffith's number and asked, "Will you be joining us for dinner this evening?"

"Do you think I'd miss Henry's woodcock? Do me a favor and call Sonny, and remind him that he was going to loan me a jacket and tie. Okay?"

"Yes, sir, that would be Mr. DeMott in the Lookout."

"Right. Deliver the clothes to my room. Okay, see you at cocktails. Henry's doing pigs-in-the-blanket."

"I've heard."

I hung up and handed the cell phone back to Ms. Spacey, who I think thought it was a gift. At least I didn't have to worry about her remembering any of this if the Feds came around making inquiries.

I left the coffee shop, and out on the sidewalk, I had two thoughts. One was that I should stop being reckless and egotistical, and think of Kate's career, and go see Griffith and spill everything to him, including "MAD," "NUK," and "ELF," with the hope that the FBI could figure out what Madox was up to before it was too late.

The other was that I shouldn't do any of those things. And the reason for that was that this case was very strange, and I didn't trust anyone anymore. Except, of course, Kate, who was, in no particular order, my wife, my partner, my lawyer, my immediate supervisor, and an FBI agent.

And although I trusted her, with Kate, you never knew who was going to show up.

I was betting on wife and partner.

CHAPTER THIRTY-FIVE

I got back in the car and handed Kate her coffee and the stack of local travel guides and pamphlets. "We need a place to stay, and not in Potsdam."

"Maybe we should go to Canada and ask for asylum."

"I'm glad you're maintaining your sense of humor."

"That wasn't a joke."

I sipped my coffee as I drove through downtown Potsdam, and Kate flipped through the printed material. I told her about my call to The Point. "Very soon, Griffith will ask the state and local police to begin a missing-persons search for us, if he hasn't already. But I think we can keep ahead of him."

Kate seemed not to hear me and studied the local literature. "This might be a good place to buy a house. Median house value is $66,400."

"I'm just looking for a place to rent for the night, darling."

"Median household income is only $30,782 a year. How much is your three-quarter tax-free disability?"

"Sweetheart, find a place to stay."

"Okay . . ." She flipped through some brochures and said, "Here's a nice-looking B and B—"

"No B and Bs."

"It looks cute. And it looks isolated, if that's what we're after."

"We are."

"It's on twenty-two acres of what used to be the St. Lawrence University riding stables." She read, " 'It offers the privacy of a classic country estate.' "

"How much is this classic country estate?"

"Sixty-five dollars a night. But you can get a cottage for seventy-five."

"That's what we were paying at The Point for an hour."

"Still paying."

"Right. Which way?"

She glanced at the brochure and said, "We need to take U.S. Route 11."

I was beginning my second circuit of downtown Potsdam and knew the place well by now. I drove to an intersection with lots of road markers, and soon we were on Route 11, heading out of town.

I said, "I knew guys on the Fugitive Squad who said that fugitives always seem to be having fun evading capture. It's like, a real high, using your wits, being on the road—"

"I am *not* having fun. Are you?"

"Well . . . yeah. It's a game. Games are fun."

She didn't comment on that and said, "This B and B is about ten miles from here, outside of Canton."

"Canton is in Ohio."

"Maybe they moved it, or maybe, John, there's a Canton in New York."

"We'll see." So we continued southwest on Route 11.

Kate was back to the chamber of commerce pamphlet. "There are a lot of colleges in the area, so the percentage of college-educated people is higher than the national average."

"You'd freeze your college-educated butt off up here."

"The average temperature in January is twenty-seven degrees. That's not too bad."

"Tell me that in January."

"We could stay with your parents in Florida for the winter."

"I'd rather freeze to death." I looked at the dashboard clock, which said 11:47. I needed to call Dick Kearns as soon after noon as possible.

The road was well traveled and cut through open country, farms, and hamlets. We were definitely out of the Adirondack Mountain region and into the Great Lakes plains. Back there in God's country, where the bears outnumbered the people and road traffic was light, Kate and I would attract attention and be remembered. Here, we blended in with the general population. As long as I kept my smart mouth shut.

The little Hyundai handled well, but I'd wanted a four-wheel drive in case we needed to crash the fence at Custer Hill at some point in time. Like tonight.

I asked Kate, "How much ammo do you have?"

She didn't reply.

"Kate?"

"Two extra magazines in my briefcase."

I had one magazine in my inside jacket pocket. I never carry enough ammo. Maybe if I had a briefcase or a purse, I'd carry an extra magazine. "Is there a sporting-goods store in Canton?"

Without answering, she flipped through a local guide, then said, "Here's an ad for a sporting-goods store in Canton."

"Good."

We drove in silence, and within ten minutes, she said, "Turn here onto Route 68. Look for Wilma's B and B."

"Maybe we can open a B and B. You'll cook and clean. I'll shoot at the arriving guests."

No reply.

I saw the sign for Wilma's and pulled into a gravel drive that ran through a rolling field dotted with ever-greens. Up ahead was a Cape Cod–style house with a covered porch.

I stopped the car, and we got out and stepped up to the porch. I looked back toward the highway, which was barely visible.

Kate asked me, "Okay?"

"Perfect. Looks like someplace where Bonnie and Clyde would stay."

She rang the doorbell, and a minute later, a middle-aged gent opened the door and asked, "Can I help you?"

Kate said, "We'd like a room for the night."

"Well, you came to the right place."

That must be the local line. They probably said the same thing when you showed up at the hospital for an emergency appendectomy.

We went inside to a small office space in the foyer, where the proprietor, Ned, said, "You got your choice. Two rooms upstairs, or two cottages."

I said, "We'll take a cottage."

He showed us two photos. "That's Pond House—it's on a pond. And this here's the Field House."

The Field House looked suspiciously like a house trailer. Kate said, "I think the Pond House. John?"

"Right." I asked Ned, "Do you have outside phone lines in these cottages?"

He chuckled. "Sure do. Got electricity, too."

I wanted to tell him we'd just come from a luxury resort without television or phone service, but he wouldn't believe that.

He said, "Pond House has cable TV and VCR, and you got Internet hookup."

"No kidding? Hey, do you have a laptop I could borrow or rent?"

"Got one you can use for free, if you get it back to me by six-thirty. That's when the wife goes on eBay to check her auction. That woman buys junk, then she sells it back on eBay. She says she's making money, but I don't think so."

If I wasn't trying to keep a low profile, I'd tell him that she was probably fucking the UPS guy. But I just smiled.

Anyway, I paid cash for the room, which Ned appreciated, and he didn't seem to need any ID or security deposit. He handed me his laptop, worth about a thousand bucks. I thought about asking him for a six-pack of beer while I was at it, but I didn't want to impose on his hospitality.

Ned gave us a key to the cottage, some basic house rules, and directions to Pond House. "Just follow your nose."

That would have put me in his kitchen, but I think he meant get in the car first.

Kate and I went to the car, and she said to me, "Do you see how nice and trusting people are here?"

"I seem to be missing my wallet."

She ignored that and continued, "This is like where I was raised in Minnesota."

"Well, they did a good job there. Let's discuss relocation later."

I followed my nose for a hundred yards, and we came to a little shingled cottage on a pond.

Kate took her briefcase, and we entered. It was a decent enough place, with a combination sitting room, bedroom, and kitchen decorated in what looked like eclectic eBay. Out back was an enclosed porch that overlooked the pond. Hopefully, there was an indoor bathroom somewhere.

Kate was inspecting the kitchen, and I asked her, "What's in the fridge?"

She opened the door. "A lightbulb."

"Call room service."

She again ignored me and found the bathroom.

I picked up the phone on the writing desk and called Dick Kearns, collect.

He accepted the charges and asked me, "Why am I paying for this call?"

"I'm in jail, and I already used my free phone call to call my bookie."

"Where are you? Who's Wilma on my caller ID?"

"Ned's wife. How'd you make out?"

"With what? Oh, Pushkin. Russian writer. Dead. No further information."

Dick apparently felt the need to jerk me around in lieu of billing me. I said, "Come on, Dick. This is important."

"First, I'm required to ask you, What is your clearance?"

"Five feet, eleven inches."

"Unfortunately, Detective Corey, most of this stuff is not available to people under six feet, but I'll just write here that you've applied for a six-foot clearance."

The old joke out of the way, Dick said, "Okay. Ready to copy?"

"Hold on." Kate had come out of the bathroom and pulled up a kitchen chair near the desk. I said to Dick, "I'm putting us on speaker." I hit the Speaker button, hung up, and said, "Say hello to Kate."

"Hi, Kate."

"Hi, Dick."

"I'm glad you're there to keep this guy out of trouble."

"I'm trying."

"Did I ever tell you about the time—?"

"Dick," I interrupted, "we're on a tight schedule."

"Yeah, me, too. Okay, ready?"

Kate got her notebook, and I took the pad and pencil from the desk and said, "Shoot."

"All right. Putyov, Mikhail. Born in Kursk, Russia, Union of Soviet Socialist Republics, 18 May 1941. Father deceased 1943, Red Army captain, killed in action. Mother deceased, no further info. Subject attended . . . I can't pronounce these fucking Russian words—"

"Spell them."

"Right." He filled us in on Mikhail Putyov's education, and my eyes were glazing over until he said, "He graduated from Leningrad Polytechnic Institute with an advanced degree in nuclear physics. And later, he was associated with the . . . what the hell . . . ? Kurchatov? Yeah, Kurchatov Institute in Moscow . . . This says it's a major Soviet nuclear facility, and this guy did research there."

I didn't comment, but Kate and I exchanged glances.

Dick asked, "Is that what you're looking for?"

"What else?"

"Well, then he worked in a borscht factory, dropping little potatoes in the soup."

"Dick—"

"He worked on the Soviet nuclear weapons program someplace in Siberia . . ." He spelled the name of some town or installation. "This stuff seems to be classified, and from 1979 to the collapse of the Soviet Union in 1991, there's not much info."

"Okay . . . how reliable is this information?"

"Some of it I got directly from the FBI. Putyov is on their watch list. Most of it I got from Putyov's own C.V., which is posted on the website where he works."

"Where is that?"

"Massachusetts Institute of Technology. He's a full professor there."

"What's he teach?"

"Not Russian history."

"Right—"

"I also got some stuff on him online from academic journals. He's well respected."

"For what?"

"Nuclear shit. I don't know. You want me to read this stuff?"

"I'll check it out later. What else?"

"Well, I lucked out with the FBI field office in Boston. I found a guy there who I knew and he was willing to talk off the record. He told me that Putyov was brought here in 1995 as part of our post-Soviet resettling program to neutralize some of this free-floating nuke talent before these guys sold out to the highest bidder. He was set up in this teaching job at MIT as part of the resettling program."

"They should have just shot him."

Dick chuckled and said, "That would have been cheaper. They bought him an apartment in Cambridge, and he still draws a couple of bucks from Uncle Sam. In fact, I did a quick credit check on him, and he comes up triple A. No money or credit problems, which, as we know, eliminates half the motives for half the illegal shit that goes on in the world."

"Right." It was the other half that worried me; the kind of motive for unlawful activities that an oil billionaire might find irresistible. Like power. Glory. Revenge.

Kate asked, "Why is he on the FBI watch list?"

"This guy in Boston told me it was standard procedure for a person like that. The Bureau doesn't have any negatives on him. But they require him to notify them when he leaves the area because, as the guy I spoke to said, Putyov is a walking brain full of things that he shouldn't be sharing with any country that's got an illegal nuke program in the works."

I inquired, "Did Putyov notify the Boston office that he was leaving town?"

"I don't know, and I didn't ask. I was lucky enough to get this guy to talk to me off the record. But my questions were confined to background stuff."

Kate asked, "Wife? Kids?"

"Two grown sons, also brought here as part of the resettling package. Nothing on them. Wife, Svetlana, doesn't speak much English."

Kate asked, "You spoke to her?"

"Yeah. I called the apartment. But before that, I called his office at MIT. His secretary, a Ms. Crabtree, said he e-mailed her over the weekend—Saturday—and wrote that he wouldn't be back until Tuesday—today. But he's not there yet, and no one has heard from him." He added, "I guess he's up there where you are. Right?"

"We don't know." Odd, I thought, that he'd canceled

his 12:45 flight to Boston sometime last night, but hadn't yet contacted his office or the airline to rebook on the next flight to Boston, which I recalled would be 9:55 tomorrow morning, and he wasn't driving back to Boston in his rental car because it had been returned.

Kate asked, "Did his secretary sound concerned?"

"I couldn't tell. She was professional, and I had no reason to push her. So I call Svetlana, and she says to me, 'He not home.' So I ask, 'When he be home?' and she says, 'Tooosday,' and I say, 'Today is Tooosday,' and she says, 'Cool beak,' and hangs up."

"Cool beak?"

"Yeah, that's Russian for call back. So I called back about twenty minutes ago and said, 'I need to reach Mikhail. He won a million dollars in the Reader's Digest sweepstakes, and he needs to claim his prize money,' and she said, 'Moony? Vhat moony?' Anyway, I don't think he's home, or she'd have put him on to claim his money. So, is this guy missing?"

"Maybe. Anything else?"

"No. That's the basic free introductory offer."

"Did you get a cell-phone number for this guy?"

"I asked Svetlana and his secretary. They weren't giving it out, but I'll bet they called it a few times."

"Right. How about the phone company? Or the FBI office in Boston?"

"I'll try the phone company. But I'm not calling my FBI source back. I went as far as I could with him, and he was cooperative, but then he got nosy. We've got to leave that alone unless you want to stir up some shit."

"Okay, leave that alone."

"Kate, why am I doing this? When I worked for the ATTF, they had their own computers, phones, and files."

She looked at me, then said to Dick, "Your friend is pursuing his own theory about something."

"Right. Did you tell him he needs to be a team player?"

"I mentioned that a few times."

By now, I was rolling my eyes.

Dick said, "Well, when John gets fired, I need some help here."

Kate replied, "I think he'll be on the Federal do-not-hire list forever."

"Okay," I interrupted, "let's get back to business. Dick, is there anything else you can think of that might be important or relevant?"

"Relevant to what?"

Good question, and before I could think of an answer, Dick asked, "What's with the nuke stuff?"

"I don't think that's relevant to the homicide investigation."

"Why would an MIT professor be mixed up with a murder?"

"I thought he might be Russian Mafia, but it doesn't sound like it. Okay, I'll—"

"So, did the Arabs snatch this guy?"

"I don't think so. I'll take Putyov's home and work numbers."

He gave them to us, and said, "Okay, guys, the ball is

in your court. Good luck with locating Putyov, and I hope you find the sonofabitch who killed Harry Muller."

"We will."

Kate said, "Thanks, Dick."

"Watch yourselves."

We hung up, and Kate looked at me. "Nuclear physicist."

"Right."

"What's he doing at the Custer Hill Club?"

"Fixing the microwave oven?"

"John, we need to fly to New York today and have Walsh assemble the appropriate people—"

"Hold on. You're overreacting. We don't have any startling information other than a nuclear physicist happened to be a guest at the Custer Hill Club—"

"We have MAD, NUK, ELF, and—"

"Jeez, I hope they found that by now."

"What if they haven't?"

"Then they're stupid."

"John—"

"We can't admit to having evidence that we've hidden . . . well, that we just forgot to mention."

"*We?*" She rose from her chair and said, "*You* didn't report it. *We* have committed a felony. I'm an accessory."

I also stood. "Don't you think I'm going to cover for you?"

"I don't need you to cover for me. *We* need to report everything we have, including Putyov. Now."

"For all we know, the FBI knows everything we know, and they're not sharing it with us—so why should we share it with them?"

"That's our *job*."

"Right. And we *will* share it. But not now. Think of what we're doing as a supplemental investigation."

"No, we're engaged in an *unauthorized* investigation."

"Wrong. Walsh authorized us—"

"Liam Griffith—"

"Fuck him. For all I know, he's here to bring us a week's worth of clean underwear."

"You know why he's here."

"No, I don't. And neither do you."

She moved closer to me. "John, what's your agenda?"

"As always, truth and justice." I added, "Duty, honor, country."

"Bullshit."

"Well, the real answer is we need to save our asses. We're in trouble, and the only way out of that trouble is to bring this case further along toward—"

"And don't forget your ego. This is John Corey, NYPD, trying to prove that he's smarter than the whole FBI."

"I don't need to prove that. It's an established fact."

"I'm going back to New York. Are you coming with me?"

"No. I need to find Harry's killer."

She sat on the bed, sort of staring at the floor. Clearly, she was upset.

I stood there for a full minute, then said, "Kate." I put my hand on her shoulder. "Trust me."

She didn't reply for a while, then muttered, almost to herself, "Why can't we just return to New York and tell

Tom everything we know . . . ? And try to salvage our careers . . . ?"

"Because," I replied, "we're past the point of no return. There is no turning back." I added, "Sorry."

She sat there a bit longer, then stood. "All right . . . what's next?"

"ELF."

CHAPTER THIRTY-SIX

Kate seemed to have calmed down a little, and resigned herself to the fact that the idiot who got her into this mess was probably the only idiot who could get her out of it.

I was feeling a little pressured by that, but I knew if I stayed focused and solved this case—Harry's murder *and* the Madox mystery—then our career problems and personal problems would disappear. And while we were at it, maybe we could also save the planet. As Kate herself said, "Nothing succeeds like success."

The opposite of that was . . . well, disgrace, humiliation, dismissal, the unemployment line, and some sort of nuclear surprise. But why be negative?

To make Kate feel part of the solution, I said to her, "Okay, I'll take your advice, and we'll call John Nasseff."

Kate and I sat at the writing desk and took out our notepads.

I'd rather have used Ned's laptop, but I was pretty certain that John Nasseff, who was a Technical Support guy, was out of the ATTF loop anyway.

She dialed out, using her personal calling card that would not show Wilma's number on a caller ID, then identified herself to the ATTF operator and asked for Commander Nasseff. She put the phone on speaker, and as the call was routed, she said to me, "John Nasseff is an active-duty naval commander, so you may want to initially address him by his rank." She added, "He's an officer and a gentleman, so watch your language."

"And you be careful how you phrase the questions."

She replied, "I think I know how to do this. But why don't you take the lead as you usually do?"

"Yes, ma'am."

Navy Commander John Nasseff came on the line. "Hi, Kate. How can I help you?"

"Hi, John. My husband, John, who works with—works for me—and I need some information about extremely low frequency radio waves. Can you help with that?"

"I think so . . ." He paused, then said, "Can I ask what this is about?"

I chimed in, "Good afternoon, Commander. This is Detective Corey, who works for Special Agent Mayfield."

"Just call me John."

"Same to you. To answer your question, unfortunately, this is a sensitive matter, and we're only at liberty to say it's urgent."

"I understand . . . What would you like to know?"

I asked, "Can ELF waves fry an egg?"

Kate looked pissed, but Commander John replied, "I don't think so."

John Nasseff sounded like the starched Navy guy that he probably was, so I followed up with, "Just kidding. Can you give us some background on ELF waves? And please don't be too technical. I can't even program the buttons on my car radio."

I got him to chuckle, and he replied, "All right . . . it's sort of a technical subject, but I'll try to speak English. First, I am not an expert on ELF signals, but I can certainly give you some basic background."

"We're all ears." I opened my notepad and picked up my pencil.

"Well, to begin . . . I'm pulling up some of this on my computer . . . okay, ELF waves are transmitted at extremely low frequencies . . ." He chuckled to himself and said, "That's why they're called . . . Anyway, these are extremely *long* waves, so say you're transmitting at 82 herz, or 0.000082 megaherz—that's equal to a wavelength of 3,658,535.5 meters, or 3,658.5 kilometers—"

I dropped my pencil and said, "Hold on, John. Hold on. We don't want to send a message on our ELF transmitter. Who uses this wavelength? And what's it used for?"

He replied, "It's only used by the military. Specifically, the Navy. It's used to contact nuclear submarines operating at very low depths."

Kate and I looked at each other. I wanted to ask him

if he knew Fred, but instead I inquired, "Can these ELF waves be monitored?"

"Sure. If you have the right equipment. But you might wait a long time to hear an ELF transmission."

"Why?"

"They have very limited use. And anything you heard would be encrypted."

"Okay . . . take us through this. Who, what, where, when, how, and why?"

"I don't think anything I'm going to say is classified, but I need to ask you if you're on a secure line."

Typical military commo guy. I thought maybe Ned was listening to pass the time of day, but he didn't look like a spy, and Wilma was probably watching the Home Shopping Network. I said to Commander Nasseff, "We're on a regular landline, and it's a one-time use for me at a resort up in the Adirondacks." We weren't actually in the Adirondack Mountains any longer, but that's where Walsh and Griffith needed to think we were if this conversation got back to them. I added, "A resort called The Point. The chef is French, but I'm sure he's not listening in."

"All right . . . as I said, most of this is not classified. So let me explain the practical application of ELF technology. As you know, we have nuclear subs operating at very low depths for extended periods of time—months, sometimes—and most of these subs operate in their regular patrol areas near . . . well, this is a little sensitive, but I'll say near underwater hydro-acoustic stations where they can be in touch with naval operations through normal radio channels. But some of these subs can be out in no-man's-land, too far from these underwater stations, so in an emergency situation, naval operations in Pearl Harbor, for the Pacific Fleet, or Norfolk, for the Atlantic Fleet, need to get in touch with these nuclear submarines that are not near the surface or near an underwater relay station. Follow so far?"

I looked at Kate, who nodded, and I said, "Sure. Go on."

"Well," he continued, "as a for instance, normally used VLF waves—very low frequency—won't penetrate deep into the ocean depths, especially if the water is very saline. Salty."

"I got salty."

"Good. But ELF waves can travel all the way around the world regardless of atmospheric conditions, and they can penetrate anything, including mountains, oceans, and polar ice caps. They can reach a deeply submerged submarine anytime, anyplace. In fact, if it weren't for the existence of ELF waves, we'd have no communication with some of these vessels in our nuclear submarine fleet, and that could lead to a major problem if the balloon went up."

"What balloon?"

"*The* balloon. That's slang for atomic war."

"Right. I like balloon better." Again, Kate and I looked at each other, trying to comprehend this. I didn't know how she was feeling, but thinking of Bain Madox, I was a little worried.

Commander Nasscff made a funny doomsday joke by

saying, "If it wasn't for ELF, we couldn't have a good, all-out atomic war."

"Well, thank God for ELF."

He chuckled. "That's an old Navy commo joke."

"That's a real knee-slapper. Got any more?"

"Well, gee, it's been a long time since the Cold War, but—"

I interrupted. "So, that's the only way . . . the only reason anyone would use an ELF radio—to talk to a submarine."

He replied, "Well, it's not actually a voice radio—it's more of a signal transmitter—like a telegraph—to send encrypted letter-code messages."

"And only to a submarine?"

"Right. A deeply submerged submarine. ELF waves are very long, and therefore the transmissions are *very* slow. But they can *penetrate* anything. Thus, their only practical use is to contact submerged submarines that can't be contacted by normal means."

"Right. Can ELF waves screw up my cell phone?"

He chuckled again. "No. These waves are so far off the chart, they wouldn't interfere with any other radio waves, microwaves, or anything we currently use on a day-to-day basis."

Kate said to him, "So, these ELF transmissions are letter codes."

"Correct."

"And they can only be picked up by submarines?"

"Well, they can be picked up by anyone with an ELF receiver. But unless you know the code, which changes often, it would be meaningless. All you'd hear would be transmitted pulses, which are the letters in encrypted form. From what I understand, a three-letter code is the most common."

Kate asked, "And that tells the people on the sub everything they need to know?"

"Usually, it just tells them that they need to establish normal radio communication." He explained, "An ELF transmission is called a bell ringer. It's to alert a submarine commander that a situation is developing, and he needs to do something to get in touch. But sometimes the three-letter code is self-explanatory. For instance, it could mean 'Surface' or 'Proceed to location A,' which is a pre-designated grid coordinate. Follow?"

Kate replied, "I think so."

"You can't use ELF for long, chatty messages. It can take half an hour for the signal to reach the sub. And I should point out that the submarine can't *send* an ELF signal or message. It can only receive one."

I said, "Like, 'Don't call us, we'll call you.'"

"Correct."

Kate asked, "Why can't a sub send an ELF message?"

"The transmitter and antenna need to be on land. I can explain that later. But meanwhile, if a submarine needs to reply to this one-way message, or if the sub commander needs more data, then the sub would need to get near an underwater hydro-acoustic station—if there's time—or would need to get near the surface and send up a communication buoy to reply or get more information via VLF, or these days via satellite, or other means."

I inquired, "What do you mean, 'If there's time'?"

"Well, for instance, if the other side has already launched ICBMs against us, then there's no time to establish normal radio communication, because by the time the sub receives an ELF signal, which, as I said, can take thirty minutes, all forms of communication in the U.S. have already been vaporized, and the atomic war is all but over." He explained, "If that's what's happening on the surface, then the submarines receive the last and only ELF message they will ever get—a three-letter code that means . . . well, 'Fire away.'"

Kate looked a bit worried, but Commander Nasseff had good news. "ELF waves are not affected by thermonuclear explosions."

I said, "Thank God for that. But let me ask you— what if the guy sending the atomic-launch code sends the wrong letters? Like, he means to type in XYZ, which means 'lunch break,' but he screws up and types in XYV, which means 'Launch your nukes'?"

Commander Nasseff replied with a little amusement in his voice, "That can't happen."

"Why not? Look at the e-mails you get."

"I mean," he explained patiently, "there are safeguards, and all orders to launch need to be verified."

"By *who*? By the time the sub gets the order a half hour after it's sent, as you just said, there's no one left to verify anything."

"This is true. But rest assured that can't happen."

"Why not? I mean, you're talking about three measly letters. Like those monkeys typing King Lear."

"For your information, a three-letter code will yield 17,576 possible letter combinations in the English language alphabet. The Russian alphabet, with thirty-three letters, will yield 35,937 different codes." He explained, "Thirty-three, times thirty-three, times thirty-three equals 35,937. So, what are the chances that a naval radio operator could mistakenly send the code to the submarine fleet to launch their missiles at their predesignated targets?"

Considering the fact that if something could go wrong, it would, I thought the chances seemed pretty good. I said, "Maybe we should use the Russian alphabet. You know? More letters. Less chance of starting a nuclear war by accident."

He found that funny and said to me, "Actually, if you want to know more than you need to know, whoever transmits the message needs to send it as a repeating, error-correcting code, followed by another three-letter verification code. No one can screw that up by accident."

I asked the obvious and more pertinent question, "How about on purpose? Like some nut who wants to start an atomic war?"

He thought about that and replied, "As I said, the codes change frequently."

"But if someone had the code—"

"I can't imagine that any unauthorized person could get the initiating codes and the verification codes, plus getting the current encrypting protocols. Also, the computer encryption software is sophisticated beyond anything you can imagine." He added, "You shouldn't worry about things like that."

I thought of Bain Madox and wanted to say to Commander Nasseff, "*You* should."

Kate asked, "And there is no other possible application for this means of communication? I mean, no other use for ELF waves other than military?"

"Well, that *was* true. But I've heard that since the end of the Cold War, the Russian ELF transmitter has been used for geophysical research. Swords into plowshares." He explained, "The ELF waves can penetrate deep into the Earth's crust and can therefore be used for electromagnetic sounding and monitoring. For instance, seismic research. Earthquake predictions and things of that sort. But I don't know much about that."

Kate said, "So, theoretically, someone outside the military *could* send an ELF transmission. Like scientists."

"Theoretically, but there are only three ELF transmitters in the whole world, and they're all owned by the military." He added, "We have two, they have the other."

Kate thought about that, then asked, "I see . . . but *theoretically* . . . is this top secret, or is it unlawful to build such a transmitter?"

"I don't know about unlawful, and there's nothing top secret about the technology or the physics behind it. The actual problem is that an ELF transmitting station can be expensive to build, and it has no practical application outside of contacting submarines or, recently, in limited geophysical research."

I didn't think that Bain Madox was interested in geophysical research, but he might be, so I asked, "Can these ELF waves detect oil deposits?"

"I would think so."

"So, geologists could use them to find oil."

"Theoretically, but ELF stations can only be built in a few places in the world."

Kate inquired, "Why is that?"

"Well, now that we're talking about the actual transmitter itself, let me explain that. You asked why a submarine can't send an ELF message. One reason is that an ELF transmitter can only be located on land in an area that has very low ground conductivity. And there are only a few places on the planet where this geological condition exists."

I asked, of course, "And where is that?"

"Well, one is where the Russian transmitter, called Zevs, is located—northwest of Murmansk, up near the Arctic Circle. Another place where these necessary conditions exist is here in the U.S. Our two transmitters are the Wisconsin Transmitter Facility—WTF—and the Michigan Transmitter Facility—MTF, and they both share the same geological formation called the Laurentian Shield."

"And that's it?"

"Well, that's it for existing ELF transmitters. But the Brits almost built one during the Cold War for the Royal Navy at a suitable location called Glengarry Forest in Scotland. But for a variety of political and practical reasons, the idea was scrapped."

Neither Kate nor I said anything for a while, then Kate recapped, "So, there are only three ELF transmitters in the entire world."

Commander Nasseff made a little joke and replied, "Last time I counted."

Well, I thought, *count again, Commander.*

Kate and I glanced at each other, but neither of us asked the obvious question about other suitable and perhaps close-by locations. We knew we needed to finesse that question so as not to have Commander Nasseff sitting around the coffee bar telling people that Corey and Mayfield were asking about ELF transmitters in the Adirondack Mountains.

John Nasseff took the silence to mean we were done taking up his time and asked, "Was that helpful?"

Kate replied, "Very. Thank you. One more question. I'm not clear on something. You *are* saying it's *possible* for a private individual to build an ELF transmitter?"

John Nasseff was probably thinking about lunch, but answered, "Sure. Someone can build one in his basement or garage. It's actually fairly basic technology, and some of the components are probably off-the-shelf items, and what's not readily available can be built or bought for the right money. The real problem is the location of the *antenna* and the *size* of the antenna."

"Why is that a problem?"

"Because, this is not a standard vertical antenna. An ELF antenna is actually a long cable, or cables. These cables are strung on telephone-type poles, usually in a big circle, and they run for miles."

That sounded like something I'd seen recently. I asked, "Why is that difficult . . . or expensive?"

"Well, it's expensive," Nasseff replied, "if the government does it." He got off a good laugh, then continued, "As I said, it's all about geology and geography. First, you need to find a location where the rock formation is suitable, then you need to acquire a sufficiently large area of that land."

"Then what?"

"Well, then you string your cables, which are actually the feed for your antenna. These cables may have to run for hundreds of miles—in a circle to save space—or, if the geological conditions are perfect, you could get away with, say, fifty miles or less."

Kate said, "I'm not quite following the geological angle."

"Oh, well . . . let me look this up . . . okay—a necessary ground condition to build an ELF antenna is an area where there are only a few meters of sand, or moraine gravel. Beneath that, you need a rock base of igneous granite, or metamorphic . . . what the hell is this?" He spelled, "G-N-E-I-S-S."

I said, "I hope that's not the code to launch."

He chuckled. "I guess it's a type of rock. Let's see . . . areas of very old Precambrian mountain chains, such as the Laurentian Shield, where our ELF installations are located . . . the Kola Peninsula in Russia, where they have their ELF installation . . . this place in Scotland where the Brits decided not to build an ELF station . . . a place near the Baltic Sea . . . well, you get the picture."

I didn't hear him say, "The Adirondack Mountains," and I was really listening closely.

He continued, "So, if someone wants to build an ELF

station, he goes to one of these areas, buys enough land, then sinks telephone poles in the bedrock and strings antenna wire between them, in a circle. The better the geological conditions, the shorter the wire has to be to provide the same transmitting power. Then the antenna wire is connected to a thick copper grounding cable, which runs down one or more of the telephone poles into a deep borehole in the low-conductivity rock. Then, a powerful electrical generator—and this is a big expense—feeds the antenna cables, and the current runs around the antenna wire, then goes down the copper grounding cables into the rock. And then, the Earth itself becomes the actual antenna. Follow?"

I replied, "Absolutely."

I don't think he believed me and he said, "This is a little technical for me, too. But it seems that if you have enough electrical generating capacity—thousands of kilowatts—and once you get the antenna right, the actual radio transmitter is not that difficult to build, and you can transmit ELF wave signals to your heart's content." He added, "Unfortunately, no one is listening."

I reminded him, "The submarines are listening."

"Only if they happen to be on the frequency that you're transmitting. The Russians are transmitting on 82 herz, and we are transmitting on 76 herz. And even if the submarines are hearing something on the appropriate frequency, their ELF receiver would probably reject the signal."

"Why?"

"Because, as I said, military signals are computer

encrypted. Encrypted when transmitted, and decrypted at the receiving end. Otherwise," he explained, "any nut—as you seem to be suggesting—could theoretically play havoc with the Russian and American nuclear submarine fleets. You know, like start World War III."

I knew exactly what he meant without the explicit example.

Kate was standing now. "Has anyone ever tried something like that?" she asked.

Commander Nasseff was silent on that subject, so I asked the same question.

He came back with a question of his own. "What are you guys on to?"

I knew that was coming, and I didn't want him sending a three-letter code to the Pentagon that meant, "Check out Corey and Mayfield." I said to him, "Well, as you may know, we're in the Mideast Section. That's all I can say."

He thought about that, then responded, "Well . . . these people may have, or may be able to acquire this technology . . . but I don't think there's a suitable geological area in any of those countries."

"That's good news," I said. But this really wasn't about our Mideast friends. I asked him once again, "Has anyone—in the past—ever tried to send a bogus signal to our submarine fleet?"

"I've heard a rumor to that effect."

"When? How? What happened?"

"Well . . . if you can believe this rumor, about fifteen years ago, our nuclear sub fleet was receiving encoded

ELF messages, but the onboard submarine computers weren't able to verify the legitimacy of the encoded messages, so they were rejected." He continued, "And when the sub commanders contacted naval operations in Pearl Harbor and Norfolk by other means, they were informed that no such messages had been sent by them via Wisconsin— Michigan hadn't been built yet." He stayed quiet for a few seconds, then added, "It appeared that some . . . entity was sending bogus messages, but the safeguards worked, and none of the subs took action based on those messages."

I asked, "What action? What did the messages say?"

"Launch."

The room was quiet for a while, then Kate asked, "Could it have been the Russians sending those messages?"

"No. First, the Russians didn't even have ELF transmitting capabilities until about 1990, and even if they did, there was no logical reason for them to order U.S. subs to launch against the U.S.S.R."

I agreed with that and asked, "So, who was it?"

He replied, "Look, this could be one of those apocryphal Cold War stories that submariners or communication personnel make up to impress their girlfriends or their bar friends."

"Right," I agreed. "That story's worth a big hug or a free beer. But it could also be true."

"Could be."

"So," I said, "apparently we have the ELF transmitter count wrong. I'm counting four now."

He stayed silent awhile, then replied, "Actually, about fifteen or sixteen years ago, there was only one ELF station in the world—ours in Wisconsin. As I said, Michigan hadn't been built yet, and neither had Zevs. That's why I think this story has no basis. Who would build and operate an ELF transmitter with the purpose of starting a nuclear war?"

I thought maybe my crazy ex-father-in-law would do that, but he was too cheap to spend the bucks. So I suggested, "The Chinese? You know, telling us to launch against the Russkies, then sitting back and watching us destroy each other."

"Well, that's possible. But if they got caught at it, I wouldn't be surprised if the Russians and Americans agreed to nuke them for that. That is a very dangerous game to play."

It was, and if you were a country with skin in the game, like China or Russia, you'd think twice about it. But if you were a rich, private, and crazy individual sitting in the mountains, you might want to amuse yourself with an ELF transmitter. I pointed out to Commander Nasseff, "You said these ELF waves could be monitored, so I assume the transmission source can also be located."

"That is a good assumption. But the truth is no. Remember, the Earth itself has become the antenna, so the signals seem to emanate from all around you."

"Like a cosmic message?"

"Well . . . it would be more like the ground shaking because of an earthquake. The signal would seem to be coming from everywhere."

"So there's no way to trace the origin of an ELF signal?"

"Not in the sense that you're thinking of. But ELF receivers could get a general idea of where the transmission source was by comparing the effective radiated power that they were receiving at their site. Like all energy sources, the farther away from the origin you are, the weaker the signal becomes. That's how we learned about the Russian Zevs transmitter—we suspected that the Russians had an ELF transmitter to signal their submarines, so we put a receiving station in Greenland, and this station received strong signals. After a while, we were able to home in on its general location in the Kola Peninsula, and spy satellites confirmed. But that was only because the Russians happened to be transmitting continuously while we hunted for the signal source."

I thought about that, then asked, "Was the Navy ever able to figure out where those bogus launch signals were coming from?"

"I have no idea. Although I would suspect not, or everyone involved in naval communication would have heard about it, officially or unofficially. I never heard about it." He reminded me, "But again, these bogus transmissions may never have occurred."

Well, I thought they had, and I suspected that Commander Nasseff thought so, too. I also thought I knew the source.

He switched to a happier thought. "Well, thank God the Cold War is over."

"You can say that again."

But he didn't. "Anything else?" he asked.

I thought of Mikhail Putyov. "Would a nuclear physicist be at all involved in extremely low frequency technology?"

"Not at all. He'd probably know less about it than you do."

"Hey, I'm an expert now. No one's going to try to sell me an ELF wave oven."

"Why," asked Commander Nasseff, ignoring my joke, "would ELF concern the Mideast Section of the Anti-Terrorist Task Force?"

Kate and I exchanged glances, and she wrote on my pad, "You're the bullshitter."

Thanks, Kate. I replied to Commander Nasseff, "Well, as it turns out, based on what you've told us, we may be . . . well, on the wrong wavelength." I chuckled for effect and explained, "We're actually working on a case involving this environmental terrorist group called the Earth Liberation Front. ELF. Wrong ELF. Sorry."

Officer and gentleman that he was, Commander Nasseff didn't dignify that bullshit with a response.

Kate, who knows how not to ask a question that tips off the person being questioned, said to Nasseff, "John, I'm looking at my notes, and I think you said that the only suitable U.S. location for an ELF antenna and transmitter is this geological area in Wisconsin and Michigan called the Laurentian Shield. Do I have that right?"

He could have been snotty and asked what that had to

do with the Earth Liberation Front, but he answered, "I think that's right . . . Hold on . . . here's another place in the U.S. where you can locate an ELF transmitter."

Neither Kate nor I asked where, but John Nasseff informed us, "You're actually standing on it."

CHAPTER THIRTY-SEVEN

We sat on the enclosed porch, which was warmed by the sun coming in the big windows. Outside, leaves fell, ducks swam on the pond, and fat Canada geese waddled across the lawn without their passports.

We were lost in our own thoughts, which were probably similar. Finally, Kate said, "Madox has a big electrical generator, and an ELF antenna on his property, and he probably has a transmitter somewhere in his lodge. Maybe his fallout shelter . . ."

I tried to lighten the moment. "So, you think Madox is exploring for oil?"

She wasn't in the mood for my humor and asked, "Do we think Madox was the person who sent those ELF transmissions to the submarine fleet fifteen years ago?"

"We do."

"But *why*?"

"Let me think. Hey, he was trying to start a thermo-nuclear war."

"Yes, I understand that. But *why*?"

"I guess he was just rolling the dice, crossing his fingers, and hoping for a happy ending."

"That's insane."

"Right. But *he* didn't think so." I said to her, "You may be too young to remember, but there were people in this country in those days—Mr. Madox, I'm sure, among them—who wanted to push the button first and get it over with. They truly believed that the Soviets would be caught napping, and that Soviet technology and weapons systems were faulty, and that we could survive whatever they threw back at us." I added, "Radioactive fallout is overrated."

"Totally insane."

"Well, fortunately, we'll never know." I thought a moment and said, "Madox obviously had some inside information about military ELF codes and decided to use it. The technology to build the transmitter and antenna, as we heard, is not secret, and at some point, about twenty years ago, Madox knew he needed the right piece of real estate, and before you know it, he's shopping for land in the Adirondack Mountains." I added, "Best investment he ever made."

She nodded thoughtfully. "I guess that's what happened . . . but it didn't work."

"No, thank God, it didn't, or we wouldn't be here talking about it."

"Why didn't it work?"

I went over it in my mind and replied, "My guess is

that he underestimated the sophistication and complexities of the computers and the software, which are obviously an integral part of the coded ELF transmissions. And at some point, he was warned by his inside guy that if he kept trying to get the launch code right, the government would make an all-out effort to discover the source of these bogus transmissions, and the FBI would be breaking down the door of the Custer Hill Club. So he gave up on his interesting hobby."

"Or maybe God intervened."

I gave that some consideration and said, "I have no doubt that Bain Madox believed he was on God's side, and God was on his."

"Well, He wasn't."

"Apparently not. Meanwhile, what is the connection between ELF and Mikhail Putyov, former Soviet nuclear weapons physicist, currently a professor at MIT, and houseguest of Mr. Madox?"

Kate thought a moment, then replied, "Maybe . . . maybe this time, Madox is going to try to get our subs to launch against predesignated targets in the Mideast, China, or North Korea."

I processed that and said, "That sounds like the Bain Madox we know. Interesting possibility. But it still doesn't explain Putyov."

Kate thought about that and probably about things she never dreamed she'd be thinking about yesterday. She asked me, or herself, "What the hell is this guy up to?"

"I think he's up to Plan B, and I have no idea what that is, except that it's a version of Plan A, which didn't work fifteen years ago."

I looked at my watch and stood. "Here's what I want you to do, Kate. Go online and see if there's anything else we need to know about ELF waves. Also, Google Mikhail Putyov, and while you're at it, Bain Madox."

"Okay . . ."

"And this is important—get the laptop back to Wilma before six-thirty."

She forced a smile and asked, "Can I go on eBay?"

"No, you may not go on eBay. Okay, then call the FAA and get the continuing flight plans for Madox's two jets. The tail numbers of his aircraft are in your briefcase. That may take a while, knowing the Federal bureaucracy as I do, but be persistent and charming—"

"Why do you think that's important?"

"I really don't know. But I'd like to know where Madox sent those aircraft in case it *becomes* important." I added, "Also, I'd like you to study those flight manifests, airline reservations, and car-rental agreements, and see what else you can come up with. And call Putyov's home and office and see if anyone knows his whereabouts."

"Okay . . . but what are you doing while I'm doing all of this?"

"It's my nap time."

"Very funny."

"Actually, I'm going to run a few errands. I'll get us some food plus some personal items, which don't seem to be included for seventy-five bucks, and whatever else you'd like."

She informed me, "We don't need anything at the store, John. After *we* gather all this information, *we* are heading back to the city." She added, "I'll book a flight from Adirondack Regional Airport, or someplace else around here."

"Kate, I don't think we have enough information yet to buy a get-out-of-jail-free card."

"I think we do."

"No, I think there are people in Washington who know at least as much as we do right now."

"Then why did they send Harry to do surveillance on the Custer Hill Club?"

Good question. And several answers came to mind. "Well, maybe it had to do with this weekend gathering. But beyond that, I don't know."

"John, I think Harry accomplished his assignment. I think they wanted him to get caught."

So did I, and now, so did Kate. I said, "Seems that way."

"But *why* would they want him to get caught?"

"That's the big question. A possible answer is to signal to Bain Madox that he is under the eye. They certainly didn't expect Madox to murder the surveillance person he'd caught."

"Why would the Justice Department and the FBI want Madox to know he was under surveillance?"

"Sometimes, in police work, you use surveillance to shake up a suspect. Sometimes, with rich and powerful people, you use it as a courtesy, or a warning. You know, like, cease and desist before you put us all in a bad situation."

Kate stood and came closer to me. She said, "It could have been you."

Actually, I hope I would have had the brains to scrub

the assignment as soon as I got a close look at the situation. Harry, on the other hand, was a simple soul who always put too much trust in the bosses, and who followed orders.

She asked me, "If you're right, do you think this surveillance has frightened Madox into abandoning whatever he's up to?"

"I think a man like Madox doesn't frighten very easily. He's a man with a mission, and he's already committed at least one murder on his way to completing that mission."

"One that we know of."

"Right. And I'm fairly sure that what happened this weekend had the opposite effect of what Washington hoped for. In fact, Bain Madox's timeline has been shortened to about twenty-four hours, give or take a few hours."

"It may just be that he knows the game is up and he's planning to flee the country. That's what most people would do."

"I'm really convinced he's not like most people. But check out where his jets are."

She nodded and said, "Okay, but if you really think he's going ahead with whatever he's planned, and if you don't want to go back to the city, then we need to get to the closest Federal attorney and ask for a search warrant for the Custer Hill Club."

"Sweetheart, I think the only warrant you're going to find at a Federal courthouse is an arrest warrant for Kate Mayfield and John Corey."

"Then let's go to Schaeffer and see if he can get the local D.A. to get a search warrant."

"Kate, no one is going to issue any warrant with Bain

Madox's name on it based on what you or I tell them. We need to get more evidence."

"Such as?"

"Well, obviously some hair and fibers from the Custer Hill lodge that will match what was found on Harry's body and clothes. That's the connecting forensic evidence that's required to link Madox's lodge to Harry, and Harry to Madox, who was at the lodge."

"All right . . . but how do you get fibers from the Custer Hill Club without a search warrant?"

"The same way I'd do it if I was investigating the murder of John Doe, who I believed was last seen alive at the house of Joe Smith."

"What do you mean . . . ?"

"I'm going to the Custer Hill Club to pay a visit to Mr. Madox."

"I don't want you to go there."

"Why not? This is what I'd do at this stage of any other homicide investigation. We're running out of clues and leads at this point, so I need to go back to the prime suspect and talk to him."

"I'm going with you."

"Actually, you're not. I need you here to work the details that we'll need to build the case . . . the stuff we'll need to get a search warrant." Actually, the time was running out for that, but it sounded good.

"No," she said firmly. "You are not going there alone." She looked at me. "It could be dangerous."

"It's not dangerous. This is not Dracula's Castle. I'm a Federal agent making some inquiries."

"He's already killed one Federal agent."

Good point. But I replied, "And he probably regrets it. If he doesn't, he will later." I walked back into the sitting area and put on my leather jacket.

Kate followed and also put on her jacket.

This was one of those moments that called for just the right combination of firmness and tenderness. I took her in my arms and said, "I need you here. We're a little short on manpower today. I can really handle this myself."

"No."

"I think I have a better chance of getting in to see him if I'm alone."

"*No.*"

"I'll check in with Schaeffer's surveillance team at the intersection. Okay? I'll tell them to give me an hour, and if I'm not out by then, they should send in the cavalry. Okay?"

That seemed to do the trick, and she appeared less insistent that she go with me.

I concluded with, "Keep in touch with Schaeffer. Also, call The Point and see who's looking for us. Tell them we're shopping in Lake Placid; and if Mr. Griffith calls, he should meet us downtown. And remind Jim that Sonny DeMott was going to loan me a tie and jacket for dinner."

"He was?"

"I'm sure he would. Just bullshit them." I added, "Pretend you're me."

She smiled, then said, "I want you to turn on your cell phone."

"Kate, no cell phones. You turn that thing on, and Liam Griffith will be at this door within an hour."

"John . . . this is *not* the way we work."

"Now and then, sweetheart, you have to stretch the rules a little."

"Now and then? You did this on the last case."

"I did? Well, it turned out okay. Meanwhile, see if you can get a pizza delivered."

We went to the door, and Kate said, "Be careful."

"No anchovies."

We smooched, and off I went to Dracula's Castle.

CHAPTER THIRTY-EIGHT

I found a convenience store on the outskirts of Canton. Or maybe it was downtown Canton. Hard to tell.

Anyway, I went in and bought what I needed for my mission, which was a package of Drake's Ring Dings with cream inside, and one of those little sticky lint rollers.

The checkout guy gave me a shortcut back to Colton, a distance of about thirty miles. I also asked him where the sporting-goods store was, and he gave me directions.

I got back in the car and thought about my next move. It was a little after 1:00 P.M., which meant I should be at the Custer Hill gatehouse before 2:00 if I didn't stop to pick up a box of 9mm rounds and a few extra magazines. I mean, if I was going to blow Madox's brains out, I had more than enough ammo in my fifteen-round magazine, plus one in the chamber.

On the other hand, if I needed to shoot my way out of there, I was possibly a few rounds short. Bottom line with ammunition is that it's always better to have more than you need, because if you have less than you need, things didn't usually work out well.

Also, I probably shouldn't have done an ammo check with Kate, who may have been wondering if I was planning an assault on the Custer Hill Club. I wasn't sure about that myself, but it was an option.

Anyway, I decided that my first order of business should be to get to the Custer Hill Club and see what, if anything, Madox was up to. If I needed more ammo, I knew Madox had plenty of guns lying around.

I began driving, and I turned on the radio and listened to a talk show in French, live from Quebec.

I had no idea what they were saying, but everyone seemed really worked up about something, and I could pick out the words "Iraq," "America," "Bush," and "Hussein."

The melodious French language was giving me a headache, so I scanned the channels, trying to find a news channel that might mention the hunting accident, but all I got were DJs and local commercials. I locked in to a country-western station, and Hank Williams was wailing "Your Cheatin' Heart." Why I like this music is a mystery to me and a secret I don't share with many people.

The weather was still good, and the country road was decent and lightly traveled, so I was making good time.

I opened the Ring Dings and sharked the first one, then savored the second. Truly an exploration of chocolate.

I noodled while I drove and listened to Hank singing "Hey, Good Lookin'."

First, Kate was safe enough back in Wilma's B&B if she didn't get an attack of duty, honor, and country, and call Walsh or Griffith.

Ms. Mayfield is a bit more savvy than she seems, and I hoped that she was in her post-9/11 mind-set, and understood that something very odd was going on in New York and Washington, and that she shouldn't be calling anyone about that.

Second, the last time I checked with Major Schaeffer, he was on our side. But that could change very quickly. Or maybe he never really was on our side. If a state trooper pulled me over in my Enterprise rental car, I'd have the answer to that before I got to the Custer Hill Club.

Third, Tom Walsh. He really wasn't clued in to whatever was going on, and now he was probably in trouble for sending the absolutely most wrong agents up here to work the case of the missing Harry Muller. Well, if he was in deep shit, he got what he deserved. On the other hand, he'd originally wanted me here in place of Harry. What was that all about?

Fourth, Liam Griffith, the Enforcer. I recalled that he was a friend of my enemy, the happily departed Ted Nash, CIA officer, so, as the Arabs would say, Any friend of my enemy is my enemy. Especially if they're both assholes. I needed to avoid this guy until I had the power to take him down.

And last but not least, Mr. Bain Madox, who had apparently once tried to start a thermonuclear war to see how it turned out. I mean, this was so far off the chart that I had trouble grasping it. But all the little pieces that I'd seen for myself, including meeting the gentleman, seemed to point in that direction. I thought maybe Madox had watched too many James Bond movies during his formative years, and related too well to the sicko villains.

Bain Madox, however, was not some movie bad guy with a foreign accent; he was an all-American boy, a war hero, and a success story. Sort of like Horatio Alger with a thermonuclear death wish.

But as my therapist would say, if I had one, "John, the thermonuclear-war thing is in the past, and we need to move on." Right. The problem now was to figure out what Bain was doing in that big house to turn his past failure into success.

I got off the back road at Colton, headed south on 56, and entered the sleepy hamlet of South Colton. And there was Ratso Rudy chewing the fat with some guy in a pickup truck.

I couldn't resist, so I pulled into the station. "Hey, Rudy!"

He saw me and ambled over to the car. I said, "I'm lost again."

"Yeah? Hey, how you doin'?" He observed, "You got a new car."

"No, this is the same one."

"You sure? You had a Taurus yesterday."

"I did? Hey, did you see Mr. Madox last night?"

"Well, yeah, I wanted to talk to you about that. He didn't want to see me."

"He told me he did."

"You sure?"

"That's what he said." I added, "Sorry about telling him you said I should get the money up front."

"Yeah . . . I tried to explain that to him, but he thought that was funny for some reason."

"Yeah? What else did he say?"

"Well . . . he said you was pulling my leg. He said you was a wise guy. And a troublemaker."

"Me? Is that the thanks I get for fixing his ice maker?"

"He said there was nothing wrong with his ice maker."

"Who are you going to believe? Me or him?"

"Well . . . it don't matter."

"The truth matters." I asked, "Does he still have houseguests?"

Rudy shrugged. "Didn't see nobody. But there was a car out front of his house, and I thought it was you. Blue Taurus."

"I have a white Hyundai."

"Yeah, *now* you do. But yesterday you had a blue Taurus."

"Right. Hey, did anybody from Madox's place stop in for gas today?"

"Nope. You need gas?"

"No, this thing burns rice wine. Did anybody stop here and ask you for directions to his place?"

"Nope . . . Well, a guy came in from Potsdam, and wanted to check my map."

"Why?"

"He had these directions to the Custer Hill place, and he wanted to check them out. I told him he wasn't going to find it on my wall map, so I checked his directions and gave him some landmarks to look for."

There are different ways to ask nosy questions, and I inquired, "Was he a tall, thin guy with a handlebar mustache, driving a red Corvette?"

"No, he was a repair guy from Potsdam Diesel."

This caught me by surprise, and I was nearly at a loss for words. "Oh . . . right. Charlie from Potsdam Diesel. The generator guy."

"Yeah. But I think his name was Al . . . Yeah. This is the time of year you need to get the generator checked. Last November . . . maybe December, we got this ice storm out of nowhere. Lines down all over the—"

"Right . . . so, is Al still there?"

"Don't know. That was maybe a hour ago. Didn't see him go by. Why? You lookin' for this guy?"

"No . . . just . . ."

"Where you headin'?"

"Huh?"

"You said you was lost."

"No . . ." I asked Rudy, "Did you give Mr. Madox my message? The one about me being a good shot?"

Rudy looked a little uncomfortable. "Yeah . . . he didn't think that was so funny."

"Yeah? What did he say?"

"Not much. Just asked me to say it again."

"Okay . . . good. So . . . I'll see you later."

I got back on the road and headed toward the Custer Hill Club.

Potsdam Diesel.

The generators were about to be fired up, and soon the transmitter would be warming up and the antenna would be humming, sending ELF waves deep into the bowels of the Earth. And someplace on this screwed-up planet was a receiver that was going to pick up those signals.

Holy shit.

CHAPTER THIRTY-NINE

I was driving too fast for the logging road, and the Hyundai went airborne a few times.

Up ahead, I could see where McCuen Pond Road ran north to the Custer Hill gatehouse, but I didn't see anyone leaning on his shovel nor did I see any freshly filled potholes.

I stopped at the T-intersection and looked farther up the logging road, then McCuen Pond Road.

I seemed to be the only one there.

This was like that scene in *The Godfather* where Michael goes to the hospital to see how Pop is doing and discovers that someone pulled the police guard off the job, and the hit men were on the way. *Mama mia*.

I sat there for a minute, waiting for a surveillance guy to pop out of a bush. But I was definitely alone. So, what's up with Schaeffer? Hank? Buddy? Hello?

Well . . . time was wasting, so I turned onto McCuen Pond Road and headed for the gatehouse.

I slowed down, as per the sign, then stopped at the speed bump and pulled my Glock and stuck it in my jacket pocket.

The gate slid open, and a guy in camouflage fatigues walked toward me. As he got closer, I saw he was the same storm trooper I'd dealt with the last time, which was good. Or maybe not. I tried to remember if I'd pissed him off. Kate always remembers who I pissed off, and she briefs me.

I rolled down my window, and the guy seemed to recognize me, notwithstanding my new car. He had the same line as last time: "How can I help you?"

"I'm here to see Mr. Madox."

"Is he expecting you?"

"Look, Junior, let's not go through all this shit again. You know who I am, and you know he's not expecting me. Open the fucking gate."

He definitely seemed to remember me now—maybe because I was wearing the same clothes, but more likely because I'm an arrogant prick. He said to me, unexpectedly, "Proceed to the gatehouse." He added, "He *is* expecting you." Then he smiled.

Well, that was nice. But it wasn't really a *nice* smile. I drove toward the gate, and in my side-view mirror, I saw Junior Rambo on his walkie-talkie.

The gate slid open, and as I drove through, another guy in the gatehouse stepped out and put up his hand. I returned his greeting with an Italian salute, and accelerated up the winding road toward the lodge.

I noticed again the telephone poles and the three heavy wires running between them—and what had looked a little odd yesterday now looked suspiciously like an ELF antenna. Unless, of course, I was totally wrong. I needed a dose of Bain Madox to give me confidence in my suspicions and conclusions.

Coming toward me was a black Jeep, and the driver was waving to me, which was nice, so I waved back and honked my horn as he veered off into the drainage ditch.

Up ahead was the flagpole, flying the Stars and Stripes with the yellow Seventh Cavalry pennant below. I knew, from something I'd read, that the pennant meant the commander was on the premises, so El Supremo was definitely in.

I went around the flagpole, stopped under the portico, got out, locked my car, then stepped up to the porch. The front door was unlocked, and I went into the atrium foyer and glanced up at the balcony.

There was no one around, and I recalled that the house staff was on a break after the three-day weekend, which showed Mr. Madox to be an enlightened employer, or a man who wanted to be alone.

On the wall, General Custer was still making his last stand, and I noticed now, on the paneling above the painting, a fiber-optic fish eye that could see the whole room. In fact, I may have subconsciously noticed it the first time, and maybe that's where my stupid Holy Mackerel joke had come from. Maybe not.

I moved closer to the painting as though studying it,

then closer until I was too near the wall for the eye to see me.

I glanced up at the balcony again, then I pulled my little lint roller out of my jacket, peeled the paper off, and dropped it on the carpet and rolled it with my foot. Then I retrieved it and put it back in my pocket. If that stupid dog was around, I'd have lint-rolled him, too.

I like forensic evidence when other people collect it, analyze it, and report the results to me. But sometimes you have to do this stuff yourself. I didn't think there was much time left to wait for forensics tests, but maybe someone would find the lint roller in my pocket if I wound up having a hunting accident.

I heard a sound behind me and turned to see Carl coming down the staircase. We made eye contact, and I couldn't tell if he'd seen me lint-rolling the rug.

Carl stopped on the last step, stared at me, and asked, "Are you here to see Mr. Madox?"

"I'm not here to see you, Carl."

He didn't respond to that. "You need to be escorted *to* the lodge, and *into* the lodge."

"Yeah. I know. Insurance. Should I try again?"

I don't think he liked me, and he was probably still pissed off about having to make me café au lait.

He said, "Fortunately, Mr. Madox is receiving."

"Receiving what? Cosmic messages?"

"Receiving visitors."

I looked at Carl, who, as I'd noticed on my earlier visit, was a big fellow. He was no kid, but he looked fit, and what he lacked in youth, I was sure he more than made up for in experience. In fact, I could picture him twisting the binocular strap around Harry's neck and holding him upright on his knees while his boss put a bullet through Harry's spine.

I've known a number of tough old combat veterans, and you'd expect them to still be tough, and probably they are, someplace inside. But most of them that I've known have a sort of gentleness about them, as if to say, "I've killed. But I don't want to kill again."

Carl, on the other hand, gave me the impression that he'd add a P.S. to that. "Unless ordered to kill."

He said, "Mr. Madox is in his office. Follow me."

I followed him up the sweeping staircase to a foyer that overlooked the lobby below.

Carl led me to a paneled door and said, "Mr. Madox has fifteen minutes."

"I'll give him longer than that." Unless I kill him before my time is up.

Carl knocked, opened the door, and announced, "Colonel, Mr. Corey to see you."

Colonel? I said to Carl, "*Detective* Corey. Try again."

He looked really pissed, and I thought about asking him for a mocha freezie, but he announced, "*Detective* Corey to see you, sir."

Colonel Madox said, "Thank you, Carl."

I entered the office, and the door shut behind me. I expected to see Colonel Madox all decked out in his beribboned dress uniform, but he was standing behind his desk, wearing jeans, a white polo shirt, and a blue blazer. He said to me, "This is an unexpected pleasure . . . Detective."

I replied, "I had the impression at the gate that I had an open invitation."

He smiled and said, "Yes, actually, I did mention to the security staff that you might drop by again in connection with the missing person—which, I understand, has become moot."

I didn't comment on that, so Madox extended his hand, we shook, and he said, "Welcome."

He motioned me to a chair in front of his desk, and I sat, wondering if Harry had ever been here.

Madox asked me, "Where is Ms. Mayfield?"

"She's at a yodeling class."

He grinned. "So, are you both enjoying your room at The Point?"

I didn't reply.

He said, "I've actually stayed there a few times for a change of pace. I like the lake, which I don't have here. It's a good property, but I find the food too . . . well, Continental for my taste. I prefer simple American food."

I didn't respond, and he asked me, "Do they still have that French chef there? Henri?"

"They do."

"He's a real prima donna, like all of them. But if you talk to him, he'll make you a simple beefsteak, sans mystery sauce, and a baked potato."

Was this asshole trying to tell me something? I knew not to mention that Kate and I were married, but I had broken one of the other cardinal rules when I told him where we were staying, and now he was possibly playing a head game with me.

He seemed to be in a chatty mood, the way a lot of suspects are when the fuzz is talking to them, and he said, "Speaking of the French, what is their problem?"

"They're French."

He laughed. "That's it." He tapped the newspaper on his desk, which I saw was the *New York Times*, and asked me, "Did you see this front-page article? Our loyal French allies are hinting that we're on our own in Iraq."

"I saw that."

"I have a theory that they lost an important part of their gene pool in World War I. A million brave soldiers dead in the trenches. So, who was left to procreate? The mentally and physically unfit, the cowards and the sissies. What do you think?"

I thought he was out of his fucking mind, but I replied, "Genetics are not my strong point."

"Well, it's just my theory. On the other hand, I actually had two former French soldiers in my battalion. One was a Foreign Legionnaire, the other a paratrooper. They joined the American Army to fight, and fight they did. They loved to kill Commies. Great balls."

"There goes your theory."

"No. France doesn't produce enough men like that. But maybe they do, and their feminized society shuns them. They don't respect the warrior ethos any longer. But we do." He said emphatically, "This war in Iraq will be over in less than thirty days."

"When's it starting?"

"I don't know."

"I thought you might have friends in high places."

"Well . . . actually, I do." He hesitated, then said, "Bet on mid-March. Around St. Patrick's Day."

"I say end of January."

"Will you put a hundred dollars on that?"

"Sure."

We actually shook on it, and he said, "When you lose, I'll come looking for you."

"Twenty-six Federal Plaza." We made eye contact and I said, "If you lose, I'll come looking for *you*."

"Call my New York office. It's not far from 26 Fed. Duane Street. GOCO." He mentioned, "I was actually in my office when the planes hit . . . I'll never forget that sight . . ." He asked me, "Were you in your office? Did you see it?"

"I was about to walk into the North Tower."

"My goodness . . ."

"Let's change that subject."

"All right." He asked me, "So, will Ms. Mayfield be joining us?"

Odd question, considering I said she was at a yodeling class, plus I had only fifteen minutes with His Majesty. Maybe he liked her looks, or maybe he wanted to know if this was a bust. "It's just me today."

"All right . . . so, I've been running off at the mouth, and I never asked you the purpose of your visit."

The purpose of my visit was a homicide investigation, but I didn't want to jump right into that. That's usually a showstopper, and you might be asked to leave. So I said, "I just thought I'd stop by and thank you for offering your assistance with the missing person."

"You're quite welcome. Sorry to hear the bad news."

"Yeah, me, too." At this point, we'd talk a bit about that, and I'd thank him again for being a good citizen, and I'd leave. But I left that subject alone for now and asked him, "Mind if I take a look at your view?" I nodded toward the window.

He hesitated, then shrugged. "If you wish."

I stood and went over to the window. The view directly behind the lodge was of the continuing slope of the hill, at the top of which was his relay tower, which sprouted all sorts of electronic arms, and I wondered if that had anything to do with his ELF antenna.

In the distance, I could make out several telephone poles, and I saw birds landing and taking off from the three big cables. They didn't seem to be glowing, smoking, or flying backward, so I took that as a good sign.

Off in the distance, I saw a big prefab barn. Its doors were open, and inside I could see a few vehicles—a black Jeep, a blue van, and a lawn tractor. Outside the barn were parked a few all-terrain vehicles, which I assumed were used to patrol the property. I expected to see that Colonel Madox also had a few Abrams tanks, but there was no sign of tread marks.

To the right, about a hundred yards from the lodge, I saw two long buildings. From Harry's map, which I had in my jacket pocket, I identified the white wooden structure as the barracks, and it looked like it could hold about twenty men. The other structure was the size of a house, and it was built of solid bedrock, with a sheet-metal roof and steel shutters closed over the windows. Three chimneys belched black smoke, and near the open door of the building was a step van whose painted sign said POTS-DAM DIESEL.

Madox came up beside me and said, "Not a spectacular view. The view out the front is better."

"I think this is interesting." I asked him, "Why do you have all these telephone poles and cables running around your property?"

We made eye contact, and he didn't flinch. "Those poles and wires were installed to connect the call stations around the property."

"Really?"

"You remember when you were a cop on the beat, and you had police call boxes?"

"Right. We also had two-way car radios since the 1950s, which are a lot cheaper than a few hundred telephone poles in the bedrock."

Mr. Madox did not respond. In fact, he was probably thinking hard right now, wondering if these were just idle questions, or leading questions.

He said to me, "As I discovered in combat, radios are not reliable. In any case, the call boxes are rarely used now that we have cell phones and high-quality walkie-talkies. He informed me, "The poles are also used to mount and power the security lights."

"Right." And the listening devices and video cameras. "Hey, what's that white building?"

"The barracks."

"Oh, right. For your army. And I see your motor pool out there. This is a hell of a place."

Nelson DeMille

"Thank you."

"And that stone building?"

"That's where my electrical generator is."

"I see *three* chimneys blowing smoke."

"Yes, three generators."

"Do you sell power to Potsdam?" I asked.

"I'm a big fan of redundancy."

"Redundancy."

"Yes. And so is God. That's why we have two balls."

"But only one dick. What's that about?"

"I've often asked myself that very question."

"Me, too." He was now supposed to ask me why I was asking all these questions, but he didn't. Instead, he said, "Well, thank you for stopping by. Again, sorry about . . . I'm sorry—what was his name?"

"Harry Muller."

"Yes. People need to be careful in the woods."

"I see that."

"Is there anything else?"

"I just need a few more minutes of your time."

He smiled politely and reminded me, "That's what you said the last time, and you stayed awhile."

I ignored that and moved away from the window, then looked around the office. It was a big room, paneled in light pine with oak furniture. On the floor was an oriental rug.

Above Madox's desk was a framed photograph of an oil tanker with the words GOCO BASRA on the bow. Another framed photograph showed a burning oil field.

Madox said to me, "The Gulf War. Or, should I say, Gulf War One?" He added, "I hate to see good oil burning, especially if no one is paying me for it."

I didn't reply.

Usually, my routine of short questions and shorter responses shakes up a suspect, but this guy was cool as a cadaver on ice. I did sense, however, a little uneasiness in his manner. In fact, he lit a cigarette but blew no smoke rings this time.

Neither of us spoke, then I moved toward a wall filled with framed certificates and photographs.

They were all military—awards, citations, an honorable discharge, his commission as a second lieutenant, his promotions, and so forth, plus a number of photographs, mostly of Madox in various uniforms, about a half dozen taken in Vietnam.

I looked at one that showed his face close-up. His skin was painted in camouflage, plus it was dirty, and there was a fresh cut over his right eye from which ran a trickle of blood. His whole face was shiny with sweat, and his eyes peered out from his blackened features, looking more hawk-like and piercing.

He said to me, "These photographs remind me of how lucky I am to be here."

Well, I thought, *let's see how lucky you are.* "I see three Purple Hearts."

"Yes. Two minor wounds, but the third Purple Heart was nearly posthumous."

I didn't ask for any details, and he didn't offer any, except "An AK-47 round, through my chest."

Obviously, it hadn't hit any vital organs but may have caused blood loss to his brain.

He said, "I was on my third tour of duty, and I was pushing my luck."

"Right." Harry hadn't been so lucky.

"But you know what? I'd do the same thing again."

I thought I should remind him that the definition of crazy was doing the same thing over and over again and expecting different results.

The odd thing, of course, was that, as Ms. Mayfield suggested, Bain and I had connected, and if he hadn't apparently killed a friend of mine, and if he wasn't trying to take over or fuck up the planet, I'd probably like him. In fact, he seemed to like me, despite my nosy questions. But then, I hadn't killed any of *his* friends, and I hadn't yet messed up his plans to nuke the planet, or whatever he was working on. So he had no reason not to think I was an okay guy.

As I studied the remainder of his photos, he asked me, "Have you ever been wounded in the line of duty?"

"I have."

"Military or police?"

"Police."

He informed me, "As you know, then, it's traumatic. It's so far removed from your normal, everyday experience that you can't quite grasp what happened."

"I think I got it."

"What I mean is, if you're in combat—or doing police work—you expect you may be wounded—or killed—and you think you're prepared for it. But when it actually happens, you can't believe it's really happened to *you*." He asked me, "Wasn't that your reaction?"

"I really think I got what happened."

"Did you? Well, maybe people react differently." He

expanded on his subject and said, "Then, after you comprehend what's happened, you go into another state of mind." He explained, "To paraphrase Winston Churchill, There's nothing as satisfying as getting shot and surviving."

"Right. The alternative is getting shot and dying."

"That's the point. It's a near-death experience, and if you survive, you're never the same again. But I mean that in a positive way. You feel very . . . euphoric . . . powerful. Almost immortal. Was that your experience?"

I recalled lying in the gutter on West 102nd Street after two Hispanic gentlemen popped off what sounded like a dozen rounds at me, managing an unimpressive three hits at twenty feet, and I remembered seeing my blood running into a storm drain in front of my face.

"How did you feel?" he asked.

"I think I felt fucked up for a few months."

"But *afterward*. Didn't it change your life?"

"Yeah. It ended my career."

"Well," he said, "that's a big change. But I mean, did it change how you *looked* at life? How you felt about the future? Like, God had something big planned for you."

"Like what? Getting shot again?"

"No . . . I mean—"

"Because I got shot again."

"Really? In the line of duty?"

"Well, yeah. I wasn't on vacation."

"I thought your career was ended."

"I'm on career number two." I added, "Libyan guy. I'm still looking for him."

"I see." He seemed stuck on this subject. "Apparently, you take these attacks on you personally."

You let the suspect talk because he may be headed somewhere. And even if he's not revealing something about the crime, he's revealing something about himself. I replied, "When people shoot at me, I tend to take it personally, even if it they don't know me."

He nodded and said, "That's interesting because, in combat, you never take it personally, and you never think about finding the actual person who was shooting at you. That's the last thing on your mind."

"So, you weren't pissed at the little guy who plugged you?"

"Not at all. He was just earning his pay. Same as I was earning mine."

"That's very forgiving. And you don't strike me as the forgiving type."

He let that slide and continued, "What I mean is, soldiers don't see the enemy as individuals. The enemy is one big amorphous threat. So, it doesn't matter who individually is trying to kill you, or whom you kill in return, as long as the guy you kill is wearing the same uniform as the guy who tried to kill you." He explained, "You're shooting at the uniform, not at the man. Understand?"

"Well . . . I never saw the Libyan, but the two Hispanic guys who tried to kill me were wearing tight black chinos, purple T-shirts, and pointy shoes."

He smiled and said, "I guess you can't go around shooting everyone who's dressed like that. But I could shoot anyone who looked like the enemy."

"That's a treat."

He informed me, "Revenge is very healthy, but it doesn't have to be personal revenge. Any enemy combatant will do."

"That may not be as healthy as you think."

"I beg to differ. Revenge brings closure." He added, "Unfortunately, that war ended before I could return to duty and even the score."

I had the sudden thought that if I could pin Harry's murder on this guy, his lawyer would plead insanity, and the judge would say, "I agree, Counselor. Your client is out of his fucking mind."

It occurred to me that this guy had probably been lost in limbo after the Soviets went belly-up, and there were no major-league enemies left that were worth his attention, or who needed to be killed so that Bain Madox could save the nation.

Then came September 11, 2001. And *that*, I was sure, was what this was all about.

He changed the subject abruptly and asked me, "Have you gotten into the woods at all?"

"A little this morning. Why?"

"I was wondering if you'd seen any bears."

"Not yet."

"You should try to see a bear before you go back to the city."

"Why?"

"It's an experience. They're fascinating to watch."

"They don't look that interesting on the National Geographic Channel."

He smiled and said, "You can't *smell* them on television. The thrill is being face-to-face with a wild animal that you know can kill you."

"Right. That's a thrill."

"But if you're armed, that's cheating. The interesting thing about black bears is that you can actually interact with them. They're dangerous, but they're not dangerous. Follow?"

"I think I lost you after the first 'dangerous.'"

"Well, think of a lion on one hand, and a lamb on the other. With those animals, you know exactly where you stand. Correct?"

"Right."

"But a bear—a black bear—is more complex. They're intelligent, they're curious, and they will often approach a human. Ninety-five percent of the time, they're just looking for a handout. But five percent of the time—and it's hard to tell when that is—they're looking to kill you." He took a step closer to me and said, "*That* is what makes it interesting."

"Right. That's interesting."

"You see my point? The *potential* for death is there, but the likelihood of death is low enough so that you are drawn into the encounter for the thrill. Your heart races, your adrenaline shoots out of your ears, and you're stuck right there, between fright and flight. You see?"

I mean, I didn't *smell* alcohol on his breath, but

maybe he was drinking vodka, or snorting something, or he *was* nuts. Or maybe this was a parable, about John and Bain.

He concluded with, "Now, a brown bear or a polar bear is a different story. You know exactly what's on their minds."

"Right. What are those colors again? Brown is . . . ?"

"Bad. Grizzly."

"So, black is—"

"Not bad." He added, "The white ones are polar bears. They'll rip you apart." He informed me, "We only have black bears here."

"Good. And they know they're black?"

He thought that was funny, then looked at his watch. "Well, again, thank you for stopping by. If . . . well, if there's some sort of . . . fund established for Mr. Miller . . . please let me know."

I totally lost it, but I took a breath and got myself under control. I really wanted to gut-shoot him, and watch him die slowly as I explained that me shooting him was very personal, and not at all professional and not what I was paid to do.

He seemed to be waiting for me to say good-bye, but I just stood there, and he said to me, "By the way, a mutual friend of ours, Rudy, stopped by last night."

Or maybe I could explain to him that I shot him for God and country. I didn't know what he was up to, but I was fairly certain that he had to be stopped, and if I didn't stop him right now, then whoever tried to stop him later might be too late. Bain Madox would understand that.

He said, "Rudy. From the gas station in South Colton."

I put both my hands in the pockets of my leather jacket and felt the butt of my Glock in my right hand.

Madox continued, "He seemed confused about something. He was under the impression I'd asked you to let him know that I wanted to see him."

"Didn't you?"

"No. Why did you tell him that?"

But if I shot him right here and now, only he would know why. And maybe that was enough.

But maybe I needed to know more. For sure, the police and the FBI would want to know more.

"Detective?"

And maybe, to be honest with myself, I couldn't just pull my gun and shoot an unarmed man. And to be even more honest, Mr. Bain Madox intrigued me . . . no, he impressed me. And he'd already been shot—he'd survived a war, and he was, or believed he was, a patriot continuing to do his duty, and if I told him he was actually a psychopathic killer, he'd be shocked.

"Mr. Corey? Hello?"

We made eye contact, and I thought he guessed what was on my mind. In fact, his eyes focused on where my right hand was gripping the gun in my pocket.

Neither of us spoke, then he said to me, "Why did you tell him to tell me that you were a good shot?"

"Who?"

"Rudy."

"Rudy?" I took another breath and brought my hand

out of my pocket, empty. I said, "Rudy. Rudy, Rudy. How is Rudy?"

He seemed to sense a pivotal moment had passed, and he dropped the subject of Rudy. "I'll have Carl show you out." He walked to his desk, picked up a walkie-talkie, and was about to hit the Send button.

I said, "I'm here to investigate a homicide."

He hesitated, then put down the walkie-talkie. He looked at me and asked, "What homicide?"

I moved closer to his desk and replied, "The murder of Harry Muller."

He appeared appropriately surprised and confused. "Oh . . . I was told that it was an accident. The body had been found . . . I'm sorry, I should have expressed my condolences to you. He was a colleague of yours."

"A friend."

"Well, I am *very* sorry. But . . . I had a call from the sheriff's office, and the person said this man's body had been found in the woods and that it was ruled a hunting accident."

"It hasn't been ruled anything yet."

"I see . . . so . . . there's a possibility of foul play."

"That's right."

"And . . . ?"

"I was hoping you could help me."

"No . . . I'm sorry. What would I know about . . . ?"

I sat in the chair in front of his desk and motioned for him to have a seat.

He hesitated, aware that he didn't have to sit and talk

about this, and that he could ask me to get out of his chair, his house, and his life. But he wasn't going to do that. He sat. Technically, I had no jurisdiction here to investigate a homicide—that was still the job of the state police. But Madox didn't seem to know that, and I wasn't about to give him a lesson in constitutional law.

We did the old eye-lock thing, and the guy never blinked. Amazing. How did he do that? Even guys with glass eyes blink.

He asked me, "How can I help you, Detective?"

"Well, it's like this, Mr. Madox. Harry Muller, as you may know, was not here to watch birds."

"You said he was."

"He wasn't. Actually, he was here to watch *you*."

He didn't feign shock or surprise. He seemed to think about that, nodded, then said to me, "I understand that the government is interested in me. A man in my position would be surprised if the government *wasn't* interested in him."

"Yeah? Why do you think the government is interested in you?"

"Well . . . because of my dealings with foreign powers. Oil pricing." He informed me, "I'm a personal friend of the Iraqi oil minister."

"No kidding? How's he taking this war thing?"

"I haven't spoken to him recently, but I imagine he's not very positive about the imminent invasion of his country."

"I guess not. So, you think the government is interested in you because . . . why?"

"Because my interests and the interests of the United States government don't always coincide."

"I see. So, whose interests come first?"

He smiled a little, then answered, "My country always comes first, but my country is not always well represented by my government."

"Yeah. I can buy that. But let's say for argument's sake that the government doesn't give a rat's ass about your dealings with foreign powers. That maybe you're wrong about that. So, why else would they be interested in you?"

"I have no idea, Mr. Corey. Do you?"

"No."

"And why would Detective Miller from the Anti-Terrorist Task Force be sent to spy on me? Does the government think I'm a terrorist?"

"I don't know. Who said that Detective Muller was from the Anti-Terrorist Task Force?"

He hesitated a second, then replied, "He's a colleague of yours. You're on the Task Force."

"Right. Good detective work."

He lit a cigarette, but again blew no smoke rings. "So, what you're saying is that this man Miller—"

"*Muller*. Detective Harry Muller."

"Yes. Detective Harry Muller was sent here to . . . spy on me—"

"And your guests."

"*And* my guests, and you don't know—"

"It's called surveillance, by the way. Spying is a negative word."

He leaned toward me. "Who gives a shit what it's called?" He finally lost his cool, slammed his desk, raised his voice, and said, "If this man—Detective *Muller*—was sent here to . . . *observe* me and my guests, then I am damn pissed off about that! The government has no right to intrude on my privacy, or the privacy of my guests, who have lawfully assembled on private property for—"

"Right. Right, right, right. That's another issue. The issue here is murder."

"*You* say it is. The sheriff says it was an accident. And if it *was* murder, what does that have to do with me?"

If you tell the guy he's a suspect, then you have to read him his rights, and I didn't have the damn card with me, and if I did, and I read it, he'd say, "You got the wrong guy, Detective. Excuse me while I call my lawyer."

So I said, "I didn't say it had anything to do with you."

"Then why are you here?"

"To tell you the truth"—which I had no intention of doing—"I think it might have something to do with one of your security people."

He really wasn't buying that, but it was good enough so that we could both pretend we were on to something, and continue our cat-and-mouse routine for a while.

He leaned back and said to me, "That's . . . that's incredible . . . but . . . I mean, do you have any evidence of this?"

"I can't discuss that."

"All right. But do you suspect anyone in particular?"

"I can't say at this point." I explained, "If I name a suspect, and I'm wrong, there's hell to pay."

"Right. But . . . I'm not sure, then, how I could help."

"Well, the standard procedure is for the FBI to ask you for all your personnel files, then we begin to question your entire security staff, and also your house staff, to try to determine everyone's location, movements, and so forth at around the time of the death."

I went on a bit, and he listened, then said, "I still don't understand why you think one of my staff may have committed a murder. What would be his or her motivation?"

"Well, I'm not sure. Maybe it was a case of overenthusiasm."

He didn't reply.

"Let's call it going beyond the call of duty. Maybe there was an altercation. Maybe what happened could be ruled involuntary manslaughter, or some other lesser offense, like justifiable homicide."

He thought about that and said, "I'd hate to think one of my men could do this. They're well trained, and there's never been an incident before." He looked concerned. "Do you think, as an employer, I could be sued for wrongful death?"

"That's not my area of expertise. You should ask your lawyer."

"I will." He reminded me, "As I said yesterday, lawsuits are ruining this country."

I thought he'd said *lawyers,* but now that he needed

one, they weren't so bad after all. I suggested helpfully, "I'll ask Ms. Mayfield about that."

He didn't reply but put out his cigarette, then said, "Well, I'll provide whatever personnel files you or anyone may need." He asked me, "When do you want all of this?"

"Probably tomorrow." I informed him, "There's an FBI Evidence Recovery Team on the way."

"All right . . . I'm not sure the files are kept here. They may be in my New York office."

"Let me know."

"How can I reach you?"

"The Point. How can I reach *you*?"

"As I said, through my security staff."

"That may not work out in this case," I reminded him.

"Then through my New York office."

"How about your cell phone?"

"My office has a twenty-four-hour operator. *They* will call my cell phone."

"Okay. How long will you be staying here?"

"I'm not sure. Why?"

"One day, two days, a year? When are you leaving?"

He obviously wasn't used to being grilled, and he replied with impatience, "Two or three days. How long will *you* be staying here?"

"Until the case is solved." I asked him, "Where are you going when you leave here?"

"I . . . probably New York."

"Okay. I have to ask you to notify the FBI in New York if you plan to leave the country."

"Why?"

"You may be a material witness in a homicide investigation."

He didn't reply.

"Also, I'll need you to provide me with a list of your weekend guests."

"Why?"

"They may also be material witnesses. You know, they may have overheard something, or be able to give us information about security staff or house staff who were acting strangely. Or about the movements of other guests." I said to him helpfully, "It's like a murder-mystery weekend in a big country house. You know, like, did Mr. . . . say, Wolf, who was reading in the library, notice that . . . let's say, Carl the butler was missing for two hours and came home with blood on his clothes. That sort of thing."

No answer.

I continued, "Also, I'll need any surveillance tapes that may have been taken on your property, or in this lodge. And I'll need the security log, which I'm sure you, as a former Army officer, insist be kept. Who was on-duty, when they came on-duty, got off-duty, what security rounds they made, any unusual incidents, and so forth." I reasserted, "I'm sure that log and those security tapes exist."

He neither confirmed nor denied the existence of a logbook or security tapes.

I pulled out my notebook and said to him, "I wonder if you could give me the names of your weekend guests off the top of your head." I reminded him, "I think you said there were about sixteen."

By now, Mr. Bain Madox was feeling a little hemmed in, like George Custer. There didn't seem to be any way out of this encirclement, but he found one. "I'm afraid I have to cut you short, Detective." He explained, "I need to make some important phone calls to the Mideast, and it's getting late there. And I have other pressing business to take care of." He reminded me, "I run a business, and to-day is a workday."

"I know that. I'm working a homicide."

"I appreciate that, but . . . I'll tell you what. I have an idea."

"Good. What's your idea?"

"Why don't you come back this evening? We can mix business and pleasure. Let's say cocktails at seven, and if you'd like to stay for dinner, that would be fine."

"Well, I don't know about dinner. Henry is doing woodcock tonight."

He smiled and said, "I think I can do better than that, and I'll also have a list of my weekend guests for you."

"Terrific." I couldn't drop my lint roller on the rug without explaining why I was playing with a lint roller, so I slipped off my shoes and rubbed my socks over the fuzzy oriental rug, which is always easy to match.

I really had the strong sense that Harry had been here, and in about two days, I might know. Then, I could come back here with an arrest warrant for Mr. Bain Madox for murder, or better yet, since that charge might not stick, I could, in good conscience, gut-shoot him. Unless, of course, by that time, he was in Iraq or someplace playing poker with the oil minister.

I asked him, "Who's cooking tonight?"

"I'll work something out." He added, "I can do the cocktails. Scotch, correct?"

"Right. Well, that's very nice of you."

"And of course bring Ms. Mayfield."

"I'll see if she's back from her yodeling."

"Good. Dress is casual." He added with a smile, "No tux."

"Tux is tomorrow night."

"That's right. Wednesdays and Saturdays." He prompted, "Please talk Ms. Mayfield into coming, and tell her not to worry about how to dress." He said to me, man-to-man, "You know how women are."

"I do? When did that happen?"

We both got a little chuckle out of that, and we were bonding again. Great. Meanwhile, I wondered if Kate and I would get out of here alive. "Will anyone be joining us?"

"Uh . . . I'm not sure yet. But you and I can retire to the library if we need to take care of some business."

"Good. I hate to talk about murder at dinner." I asked him, "Are any of your weekend guests still here?"

"No. They've all left."

Maybe he forgot about Mikhail Putyov.

He stood and said, "So, seven for cocktails, then some business, then dinner if you can pull yourself away from the woodcock."

"That's a tough call." I slipped on my shoes, stood, and said, "Hey, what's étuvée of vegetables?"

"I'm not sure." He gave me some advice. "Don't eat anything you can't pronounce, and never eat anything whose name has an accent mark over any of the letters."

"Great advice."

"Again, sorry about Detective Muller. I hope to God it had nothing to do with any of my staff, but if it did, you can be assured of my complete cooperation." He added, "I'll see about the information you asked for."

"Thanks. Meanwhile, mum's the word. We don't want to spook anyone."

"I understand."

We shook, I left his office, and there was Carl standing a few feet from the door. He said to me, "I'll show you out."

"Thanks. You could get lost in this place."

"That's why I'm showing you out."

"Right." *Asshole.*

We descended the stairs, and I asked Carl, "Where's the restroom?"

He motioned to a door off the hallway. I went in and took the hand towel from a ring and wiped some surfaces, collecting hair, skin cells, and whatever other DNA the forensic people liked to play around with. I wished I could have gotten Madox's cigarette, but short of asking him if I could keep his butt for a souvenir, that wasn't possible.

I stuffed the hand towel in the small of my back and exited.

Carl showed me to the front door.

I said to him, "See you at six."

"Seven."

Not too bright. But loyal. And dangerous.

CHAPTER FORTY

U p ahead, the steel gate wasn't opening as I approached the gatehouse, and I started honking.

The gate began to slide open, and as I reached the gatehouse, the two storm troopers gave me mean stares as they stood there with their thumbs hooked into their gun belts. If that was the best they could do, I wouldn't bother to flip them the bird, but I did accelerate, veer close to them, then cut the wheel, and squeezed the Hyundai through the half-opened gate.

In my side-view mirror, I saw them kicking the gravel and stomping the ground. I think they were pissed off.

Maybe I didn't have to be such a prick. But you need to establish who the alpha male is right up front. People like knowing their place in the pecking order.

Also, I had no doubt that one or both of these guys

had grabbed Harry on the property. And if not them, then some guys wearing the same uniform. Right, Bain?

There was still no surveillance team visible, and I wondered what the hell Schaeffer was up to.

I drove out to Route 56 and headed north.

I replayed my conversation with Bain Madox, which made for some interesting side thoughts. Bottom line on that, Bain and John knew that Bain and John were playing head chess with each other.

Anyway, Madox asked me to dinner, and, of course, Ms. Mayfield was invited. And Madox deduced from my unchanged clothes that Ms. Mayfield and I had come here on short notice. So he went out of his way to make sure Ms. Mayfield would feel comfortable at the club in whatever she was wearing. That was very thoughtful of him—not to mention observant. Bain Madox would make a good detective.

I knew Kate was worried about me, and you can get away with a three-minute cell-phone call before it's traced, so I turned on my phone and dialed the Pond House number. Kate answered, "Hello?"

"It's me."

"Thank God. I was starting to worry—"

"I'm fine. I can only talk for a minute. I need to run some errands, and I'll be back in about an hour."

"Okay. How did it go?"

"Good. I'll fill you in when I get back. Did you get some of those things accomplished?"

"Yes, I—"

"Did you speak to Schaeffer?"

"I couldn't reach him."

"Okay . . . hey, did you get a pizza?"

"No. You can pick up something."

"Hungry?" I asked.

"Famished."

"Good. I swung an invitation for us for dinner at the Custer Hill Club."

"What?"

"I'll tell you about it when I see you." I informed her, "Dress is casual."

"Are you kidding?"

"No. It's casual. Seven for cocktails."

"I mean—"

"I have to hang up, see you later."

"John—"

"Bye. Love you." I hung up and shut off my phone. Did I say we were going to dinner at the Custer Hill Club? Am I crazy?

Anyway, I was approaching Rudy's gas station, and there was Rudy, talking to another self-service customer. I pulled in and called out, "Rudy!"

He saw me, ambled over, and said, "You back?"

"From where?"

"From . . . ? I don't know. Where'd you go?"

"I tried to smooth things over for you with Mr. Madox."

"Yeah . . . ? I told you, I talked to him. He's okay."

"No, he was still pissed at you. Well, I got good news and bad news. What do you want first?"

"Uh . . . the good news."

"The good news is that he's not pissed at you anymore. The bad news is that he's opening a GOCO gas station across the street."

"Huh? He's *what*? Oh, jeez. He can't do that."

"He can and he is."

Rudy looked across the street at the empty field, and I'm sure he could picture it: eight gleaming new pumps, clean restrooms, and maps of the park.

I said to him, "Competition is good. It's American."

"Oh, shit."

"Hey, I need a favor. Rudy?"

"Huh . . . ?"

"I gotta go pick up a deer carcass. You got something bigger I could swap for this Korean lawn mower?"

"Huh?"

"Just for tonight. And I'll throw in a hundred bucks for your trouble."

"Huh?"

"And I'll fill your tank."

"You need gas?"

I drove the Hyundai around the back of his station, out of view, and within five minutes I did a deal with Rudy, who was still acting like he'd been kicked in the head by a mule. In fact, he didn't notice that the Hyundai keys were not in the ignition as I said they were.

My parting words to him were, "Don't call Madox about this. That'll make it worse. I'll talk to him."

"He can't do that. I'll go to court."

Anyway, Rudy's bigger vehicle turned out to be a beat-up Dodge van whose interior looked like it had suffered a fuel explosion during a food fight. But it ran like a champ.

I continued on, and in Colton, I passed up the turn for Canton and took the long route, via Potsdam.

When you're running from the posse, you need to change horses often, shoot your last horse, and never ride the same trail twice.

I reached Canton and found Scheinthal's Sporting Goods, where I bought a box of .40-caliber rounds for Kate and a box of 9mm for myself. Everyone in law enforcement should be using the same caliber handgun, like in the military, but that's another story. I also got us four spare Glock magazines. The proprietor, Ms. Leslie Scheinthal, needed ID for the ammo purchase, and I showed her my driver's license, not my Fed creds.

I needed to change my socks, which had recently become forensic evidence, so I bought a pair of wool socks that would be good for collecting more rug fibers and hairs in Mr. Madox's dining room and library.

Of course, all this investigative technique stuff would become moot if Madox slipped a Mickey Finn in our drinks, or shot us with a tranquilizer dart, and we woke up dead, like Harry. Also, there was the possibility of good, old-fashioned gunplay.

On that subject, I had the thought that a situation could arise where Kate and I might be relieved of our weapons. I had no intention of letting that happen without a fight, but the fact was, we were walking into an armed camp, and it's hard to argue with ten guys who have assault rifles pointed at you. I was sure that Harry had encountered a similar situation.

So I looked around the sporting-goods store for something that wouldn't set off a metal detector and might pass a frisk, and at the same time would be more useful in a tight situation than, say, a pair of wool socks.

Ms. Scheinthal, who was a pretty young lady— though I didn't notice—asked me, "Can I help you with anything?"

"Well . . . this is kind of a long story . . ." I mean, I really didn't want to get into the whole thing about my dinner host and his private army holding me up at gunpoint and taking my pistols, then me needing a hidden weapon to kill them, and so forth. So I said, "I'm . . . I need some survival gear."

"Like what?"

"I don't know, Leslie. What do you have?"

She walked me to an aisle and said, "Well, here's some stuff. But all camping gear is really survival gear."

"Not the way my ex-wife camped, with a house trailer and a cleaning lady."

Leslie smiled.

I looked over the stuff and tried to figure out what the hell I could smuggle into the lodge that wouldn't set off a metal detector. Stun grenades have almost no metal, so I asked her, "Do you have stun grenades?"

She laughed. "No. Why would I carry stun grenades?"

"I don't know. Maybe to fish. You know, like dynamite fishing."

She informed me, "That's illegal."

"No kidding? I do it all the time in Central Park."

"Come on, John."

She seemed to want to help, but I wasn't being very

helpful myself. She said, "So, you're camping out. Right?"

"Right."

"So, do you have winter gear?"

"What's that?"

She laughed. "It gets *cold* out there at night, John. This isn't New York City."

"Right. That's why I bought these wool socks."

She thought that was funny, then said, "Well, you need winter camping gear."

"I really don't have a lot of cash, and my ex-wife stole my credit card."

"You got a rifle, at least?"

"Nope."

"Well, you need to watch out for the bears. They're unpredictable this time of year."

"So am I."

"And don't think you're safe with those peashooters you got. Last guy I knew who tried to drop a bear with a pistol is now a rug in a bear den."

"Right. Funny."

"Yeah. *Not* funny. Well, if a bear comes around your camp, looking for food, you have to bang pots and pans—"

"I don't have pots and pans. *That's* why I need stun grenades."

"No. You know what you need?"

"No, what?"

"You need a compressed gas horn."

She took a tin canister off the shelf, and I asked her, "Is that a can of chili?"

"No—"

"Compressed gas. You know?"

"John—*jeez*. No, this is like . . . an air horn." She explained, "This usually scares them off, and you can also use it to signal you're in trouble. Two longs and a short. Okay? Only six bucks."

"Yeah?"

"And this . . ." She took a box off the shelf and said, "This is a BearBanger kit."

"Huh?"

"This is like a signal flare launcher with cartridges. Okay? See, here, it says the flare fires one hundred thirty feet high and can be seen nine miles away during the day, and eighteen miles at night."

"Right . . ." A little flare went off in my head, and I said, "Yeah . . . that could do it."

"Right. Okay, when you fire this cartridge, it puts out a one-hundred-fifteen-decibel report. That'll scare the you-know-what out of the bear."

"Right. So the bear will make doo-doo in the woods."

She chuckled. "Yeah. Here." She handed me the box, and I opened it. It seemed to consist of a launcher, not much bigger than a penlight and similar in appearance, plus six BearBanger flares, the size of AA batteries. This little thing packed a wallop.

Leslie said, "You just put the cartridge in here, then push the pen-like button, and the flare fires. Okay? But try not to point it at your face." She laughed.

Actually, it wasn't *my* face that it was going to be pointed at if and when I needed to fire this thing.

She continued, "And don't point it *at* the bear. Okay?

You could hurt the bear or start a forest fire. You don't
want to do that."

"No?"

"No. Okay, you'll get a bright light, equal to . . . what's
this say? About fifteen thousand candlepower." She smiled.
"If I see it, or hear it, I'll come looking for you." She added,
"This is thirty bucks. Okay?"

"Okay."

"So, take the air horn and take the BearBanger.
Right?"

"Right . . . actually, I'll take two BearBangers."

"You got company?"

"No, but this would make a nice birthday gift for my
five-year-old nephew."

"No, John. No. This is not a toy. This is a big flash
bang for adults only. In fact, you need to sign an ATF
form to buy this."

"Adult-in-training form?"

"No. Alcohol, Tobacco and Firearms."

"Really?" I took another BearBanger kit, and as we
walked to the checkout counter, I silently thanked the
fucking bears for helping me solve a problem.

Leslie gave me a form from the Bureau of Alcohol,
Tobacco and Firearms, in which I stated that I hereby
certified that the BearBangers were to be used for legitimate wildlife pest control purposes only.

Well, that was very close to my intended use, so I
signed the form.

There was a box of energy bars on the counter, and I
took one for Kate. I would have taken two, but I wanted to
keep her hungry for dinner.

Leslie asked me, "Is that it?"

"Yup."

She rang up the ammunition, air horn, socks, energy bar, and two BearBanger kits.

I paid her with the last of my cash, and I was two bucks short, so I was going to give up the energy bar, but Leslie said, "Owe it to me." She gave me her business card and suggested, "Stop back tomorrow and let me know what else you need. I'll take a check, or there's a few ATMs in town."

"Thanks, Leslie, see you tomorrow."

"I hope."

Me, too.

I got back in Rudy's van and headed toward Wilma's B&B.

Bears. Madox. Nuke. ELF. Putyov. Griffith.

Asad Khalil, the Libyan terrorist with a sniper rifle, was looking good right now.

CHAPTER FORTY-ONE

At 4:54 P.M., I pulled into the long driveway to Wilma's B&B.

I could see a woman peering through the window of the main house, and it was undoubtedly Wilma, waiting for her UPS lover, and she was probably wondering who the guy was in the van.

I stopped at Pond House, gathered my plastic shopping bags from Scheinthal's Sporting Goods, got out, knocked on the door, and announced, "It's your mountain man."

Kate opened the door, and I went inside. She asked me, "Where did you get that van?"

"Rudy." I explained, "It's important to switch vehicles when you're a fugitive."

She didn't comment on that. "How did it go? What's in those bags?"

"It went well, though Bain still doesn't have his meds right. Let me show you what I bought."

I emptied the contents of the two bags on the kitchen table. "Clean socks for me, some extra ammo and magazines for us—"

"Why—?"

"An air horn, and two BearBangers—"

"Two *what*?"

"Scares away the bears, *and* signals that you're in trouble. Pretty neat, huh?"

"John—"

"Hey, you should have seen this sporting-goods store. I never knew so many things came in camouflage. Here's an energy bar for you."

"Did you get anything to eat?"

"I had a granola bar." Or was that a Ring Ding?

I sat on the kitchen chair and pulled off my shoes, then my socks, which I could see had rug fibers on the soles, and at least one long dark hair, which I hoped belonged to Bain Madox, Kaiser Wilhelm, or Harry Muller. I said, "This is from Madox's office, and I have a hunch—really a hope— that Harry was sitting in the same chair that I sat in."

She nodded.

I put the socks in a plastic bag, then took a page from my notebook and wrote a brief description of the time, date, method, and place of collection, signed it, and put it in the bag.

I then took the lint roller out of my pocket, removed the protective paper, peeled off the first layer of sticky paper that was coated with fibers, and explained to Kate, "This was from the foyer carpet."

I carefully pressed the sticky paper to the inside of the plastic bag and said, "One time, I swiped a murder suspect's ham sandwich from his kitchen"—I began writing up the lint-paper description and continued—"I got enough DNA to link him to the crime . . . but his lawyer argued that the evidence was improperly obtained—*stolen,* without a warrant—and therefore not admissible, and I had to swear that the suspect *offered* me the half-eaten sandwich . . ." I rolled the bag up and asked Kate, "Do you have any tape?"

"No. But I'll get some. So, what happened?"

"To what? Oh, the evidence. So, the defense attorney grills me about why the accused would offer me a half-eaten ham sandwich, and I'm on the stand for twenty minutes, explaining how this happened, and why I shoved the sandwich in my pocket instead of eating it." I smiled at the memory of that testimony. "The judge was impressed with my bullshit, and ruled the ham sandwich as admissible." I added, "The defense attorney went bonkers and accused me of lying."

"Well . . . but it was a lie. Wasn't it?"

"It was a gray area."

She didn't comment on that, but asked, "Did they get a conviction?"

"Justice was done."

I found the hand towel in the bottom of the second bag and said to Kate, "This is from the downstairs pee-pee room, and I used this to wipe some surfaces." As I wrote a note about the hand towel, I said, "This comes under the category of the ham sandwich. Was I *offered* the hand towel to keep, or did I take it without a search warrant? What would you say?"

"It's not for me to say. It's for *you* to say."

"Right . . ." I wrote on the note and said aloud, "Offered to me by Carl, an employee of the suspect, when he noticed it was . . . what? Stuck in my zipper?"

"You may have to think about that."

"Right. I'll finish this later. Okay, so with any luck, some of these hairs and fibers from Custer Hill will match those found on Harry, and similarly, maybe some of Harry's hair and clothing fibers were left at Custer Hill, and they'll be mixed in with this stuff."

Kate had no comment, except to say, "Good job, John."

"Thank you." I informed her, "I was a good detective."

"You still are."

Shucks.

She said, "I think we have enough forensic and other evidence now to call Tom Walsh, then get back to New York, ASAP."

I ignored that suggestion and showed her my new wool socks. "We have another shot at collecting evidence from the lodge." I asked her, "What kind of socks do you have on?"

She didn't reply to my question, and instead asked me, "Are you serious about that dinner invitation?"

"I am." I put the lint roller back in my pocket. "How many times does a murder suspect invite you to dinner?"

"Well, the Borgias used to do it all the time."

"Yeah? They were . . . ? Gambino family. Right?"

"No, they were Italian nobility who used to poison their dinner guests."

"Really? And the guests kept coming? That's pretty stupid."

"Point made."

She unwrapped the energy bar, and I asked her, "Do you want me to take a bite to see if it's poisoned?"

"No, but if you're hungry, I'll share this with you."

"I'm saving my appetite for dinner."

"I'm not going there."

"Sweetheart, he specifically invited you."

"And you're not going either." She said to me, "Tell me what you and Madox talked about."

"Okay, but first, call Wilma."

"Why?"

"Tell her you'll get her laptop back to her before six-thirty, and ask her for a roll of tape."

"Okay." She moved to the desk, and I walked barefoot to the couch, not wanting to taint my new socks with Wilma's B&B.

Kate picked up the phone, and I said to her, "Also, ask Wilma to call you immediately if your husband drives by in the white Hyundai."

I thought Kate would tell me I was an infantile idiot, but she smiled and said, "Okay." She had an odd sense of humor.

Kate called and got Wilma on the phone and thanked her for the laptop and promised to return it before 6:30. Then Kate said, "Could I impose on you for two more favors? I need a roll of tape—masking tape or duct tape. I'm happy to pay you for it. Thank you. Oh, and if you see my husband drive by in the white Hyundai, could you call me immediately?" Kate smiled as Wilma said something. Kate explained, "It's just a friend, but . . . well . . . yes—"

"Tell her you need enough tape for your wrists and ankles, and see if she has whipped cream."

"Hold on, please—" She covered the phone and, suppressing a laugh, said to me, "John—"

"And call us if any other vehicle is headed for Pond House."

Kate looked at me again, nodded, and said to Wilma, "My husband may be driving another vehicle. So, if you see *any* vehicle coming toward Pond House—yes, thank you."

Kate hung up and said to me, "Wilma suggests that my friend move his van, and reminded me that there's a back door off the porch."

We both got a good chuckle out of that, which is what we needed. Kate said, "As if I don't know how to get rid of a guy out the back door."

"Hey."

She smiled, then said, seriously, "I guess Wilma is now our lookout."

"She's motivated."

Kate nodded. "Sometimes, you think good."

"*I'm* motivated."

Anyway, we belatedly hugged and kissed, then Kate informed me, "I booked us a flight to LaGuardia from Syracuse at eight-thirty A.M. tomorrow. That was the first available flight I could get."

I didn't want to argue about that at this point. "I hope you didn't use your credit card."

"They weren't taking checks over the phone."

"Well, when you get to the airport, tell Liam Griffith I said hello."

"John, they can't get credit-card information that fast . . . well . . . we can drive to Toronto tonight. There are lots of flights to New York and Newark from Toronto."

"We are *not* crossing an international border." I asked, "Okay, how'd you make out?"

She opened her notebook on the desk. "All right. First, as I said, I couldn't reach Major Schaeffer. I called twice and left messages that I'd call him again. But I don't think he wants to talk to *me*. You may have better luck."

"I'll call him later." I lay on the couch and said, "There was no visible stakeout team at McCuen Pond Road."

"Maybe they were concealed."

"Maybe. But maybe Schaeffer pulled the plug on us."

"But you went in anyway."

"I carved a note on a birch tree."

She continued, "I went through the flight manifests, airline reservation sheets, and car rental agreements. There were no startling names that popped out, except Paul Dunn and Edward Wolffer. And, of course, Mikhail Putyov." She glanced at her notes and continued, "There were a few other names that *sounded* familiar, but maybe that's because I'm reading into these names." She added, "For instance, James Hawkins. Does that sound familiar to you? And don't tell me he played third base for the Yankees."

"Okay, he didn't. Hawkins. Did you Google him?"

"I did. There *is* a James Hawkins on the Joint Chiefs

of Staff. Air Force General. But I can't tell if this is the same guy."

"Well . . . if he went to the Custer Hill Club, it probably is. Did he rent a car?"

"No. He arrived from Boston on Saturday, at nine twenty-five A.M., and departed on the twelve forty-five P.M. flight back to Boston on Sunday, connecting to Washington."

"Okay . . . if he went to Custer Hill, he was probably picked up by the van." I added, "It's interesting that Madox didn't send his corporate jets for any of these VIPs. But I guess he and they probably didn't want that direct connection between them. And that's always a little suspicious."

Kate replied, "Often, it's just a matter of government officials not accepting costly gifts or favors from rich people. It's an ethical issue."

"That's even more suspicious." I said, "So, Madox may also have had a member of the Joint Chiefs of Staff at his gathering. Air Force general."

"I wonder if these guests knew Harry was there, and what happened to him . . ."

I couldn't imagine that people like that would be complicit in a murder. On the other hand, if the stakes were high enough, anything was possible. "What else on the airport info?"

"That's it. As for the dozens of other names, we'll need a team to work that list to see who these people are, and what, if any, connection any of them might have to Bain Madox."

I said, "I hope our colleagues are already working on that. But we'll never know the results."

She didn't comment on that and said instead, "Then, I went online and Googled Mr. Bain Madox, and there's surprisingly little on him."

"That's not so surprising."

"I guess not. Most of what I found were corporate facts—his position as CEO and principal shareholder of Global Oil Corporation. And not much on that. Also, very little in the way of biography, almost nothing personal—no mention of his ex-wife or children—only a half-dozen quotes from published sources, and not a single unpublished quote or comment from anyone."

"Apparently, he's able to get blogs and other third-party information deleted."

"Apparently." She glanced at her notes and went on, "The only thing vaguely interesting is that about fifty percent of his oil and gas holdings, and half his tanker fleet, are owned by unnamed interests in the Middle East."

I thought about that, and what Madox had just said about his Iraqi oil-minister buddy during my chat with him. This meant that, like most Western oil executives, he had to kiss some ass in Sandland. But since Bain Madox did not seem like the ass-kissing type, he might be planning a way to eliminate his partners, forever and ever. Maybe that's what this was about.

Kate continued, "I then went online and researched ELF." She informed me, "There's not much more than what John Nasseff told us, except that the Russians use their ELF system differently than we do."

"Right. They have more letters in their alphabet." I yawned and listened to my stomach growl.

"There's another difference." She looked at her notes again. "Listen to this—the U.S., as we discovered, sends ELF messages to the nuclear sub fleet as a bell ringer, but the Russians, during times of heightened tensions, send a continuous message to their nuclear submarines that, in effect, says, 'All is well.' When the positive message stops, that means there's a new, urgent message on the way, and if that message doesn't arrive within the time it would take for an ELF signal to reach the submarines, then the silence is taken to mean the ELF station has been destroyed, and the subs are then authorized to launch against their predesignated targets in the U.S., or China, or wherever."

"Jeez, I hope they're paying their electric bills on time."

"Me, too." Kate continued, "This is why our ELF receiver in Greenland was able to home in on the Russian ELF signal on the Kola Peninsula—because they were using this continuous 'All is well' signal during a period of heightened tensions, which, according to this article, *we* precipitated in order to get the Russians to switch to their continuous-message system, which, in turn, enabled us to find their ELF transmitter on the Kola Peninsula."

"Wow. Aren't we clever? And talk about nuclear brinkmanship. Aren't we glad the Cold War is over?"

"Yes. But this got me thinking that Madox, who had once obtained American ELF codes, may have obtained the Russian ELF codes." She informed me, "According to this article—written by a Swede, incidentally—Russian encryption software is not as sophisticated or impenetrable as ours, so it could be that Madox has changed his ELF frequency to the frequency used by the Russians, and he's going to try to send false signals to the Russian sub fleet to nuke . . . China, or the Mideast, or whoever he doesn't like these days."

I thought about that. "I guess if the Russian codes are easier to penetrate than ours, that's a possibility." I added, "Same Custer Hill ELF transmitter, different nuclear submarines. Any more interesting ELF stuff?"

"Just that the Indians are looking to build an ELF station."

I sat up on the couch and asked, "What the hell do they need that for? Launching tomahawks? They have the casinos, for God's sake."

"John, the *India* Indians."

"Oh . . ."

"They're developing a nuclear submarine fleet. So are the Chinese and the Pakistanis."

"That sucks. Next, it'll be the postal workers. Then we can kiss our asses good-bye."

Kate informed me, "Actually, the world is becoming a far more dangerous place than it was during the Cold War when it was just us and them."

"Right. What's the median price of a house in Potsdam?"

She didn't seem to recall and sat at the desk, lost in thought. Then she said, "I also discovered some . . . not good news."

"Like, bad news?"

"Yes."

"What?"

"I'm still trying to sort it out. Let's finish the rest of what we need to discuss first so we have a context."

"Is your mother coming to visit?"

"This is not a joke."

"All right. What's next?"

"Mikhail Putyov."

CHAPTER FORTY-TWO

Mikhail Putyov," I said. "No sign of him at Custer Hill. How about his home or office?"

"I called his office first, and his secretary, Ms. Crabtree, said he wasn't in, so I said I was a doctor and this concerned a serious health matter."

"That's a good one. I never used that."

"It works every time. Anyway, Ms. Crabtree loosened up a bit and told me that Dr. Putyov hadn't shown up at work, hadn't called, and that her calls to his cell phone went right into voice mail. She had also called Putyov's wife, but Mrs. Putyov did not know where her husband was." Kate added, "Obviously, Putyov never told anyone where he was going."

"Did you get Putyov's cell-phone number?"

"No. Ms. Crabtree wouldn't give it to me, but she gave

me hers for after hours, and I gave her my beeper number." Kate added, "Ms. Crabtree sounded concerned."

"Okay, so Mikhail is AWOL from MIT. How about home?"

"Same. Mrs. Putyov was on the verge of tears. She said that even when Mikhail is with his mistress, he calls and makes an excuse for not coming home."

"He's a good husband."

"John, don't be an asshole."

"Just kidding. So, Mikhail is not just AWOL, he's missing in action."

"Well, he is as far as his wife and secretary are concerned. But he's probably still at the Custer Hill Club."

I shook my head. "If he was, he'd have called. A man in his situation, with FBI chaperones, doesn't disappear and put his wife, family, or office in a position to think about calling the FBI. That's the last thing Putyov wants."

Kate nodded, then asked, "So . . . ?"

"Well," I said, "apparently, not everyone who walks into the Custer Hill Club leaves in the same condition as when they arrived."

"Apparently not." She pointed out, "You've been there twice. Want to try again?"

"Third time's a charm."

She ignored that and continued, "So, I Googled 'Putyov, Mikhail,' and pulled up some published articles and unpublished pieces that other physicists had written about him."

"Do they like him?"

"They respect him. He's a star in the world of nuclear physics."

"That's nice. Then why is he hanging around Bain Madox?"

"There *could* be a professional relationship. Although, for all we know, it could be some sort of personal relationship. Maybe they're just friends."

"Then why didn't he tell his wife where he was going?"

"That's the question. Anyway, all we know for sure is that a nuclear physicist named Mikhail Putyov was a guest at the Custer Hill Club and is now missing. Anything beyond that is speculation."

"Right. Hey, did you call The Point?"

"Yes. There were two new messages from Liam Griffith saying it was urgent that we contact him."

"Urgent for who? Not us. Did you say we were shopping for moose heads in Lake Placid?"

"I told Jim at the front desk to tell anyone who calls that we are expected back at The Point for dinner."

"Good. That might keep Griffith cooled off until he shows up at The Point and discovers he got snookered." I asked, "Did Walsh call?"

"No."

"See? Our boss cut us loose. Nice guy."

"I think we cut him loose, John, and now he's returning the favor."

"Whatever. Screw him. Who else called?"

"Major Schaeffer called The Point, as per your suggestion. His message to you was, 'Your car has been returned to The Point. Keys with front desk.'"

"That's nice. He forgot to leave the stakeout team in place, but he didn't forget to cover his butt with the FBI."

"Did anyone ever tell you that you were cynical?"

"Sweetheart, I was an NYPD cop for twenty years. I'm a realist." I reminded her, "I think we've been through this before. Okay, what else?"

She dropped her favorite subject and continued, "A man named Carl—sounds familiar—called and left a message that said, 'Dinner is on.' Jim asked for the details, but Carl said that Mr. Corey already had the details and please bring Ms. Mayfield, as discussed." She added, "So, Madox wasn't leaving his name, or anything that could connect our disappearance to him or his lodge."

"*What* disappearance?"

"*Our* disappearance."

"Why are you so suspicious of people?"

"John, fuck off." She continued, "We also had three voice-mail messages in our room."

"Griffith and who else?"

Kate referred to her notes. "Liam Griffith, at three forty-nine, said, cheerily, 'Hi, guys. Thought I'd see you earlier. Give me a call when you get this. Hope all is well.'"

I laughed and said, "What an asshole. How stupid does he think we are?" I quickly added, "Sorry. That sounded cynical—"

"Second voice mail asking if we'd like to schedule a massage—"

"Yes."

"Last voice mail from Henri, who sounds cute, asking what type of mustard you'd like with your . . . pigs-in-the-blanket."

"See? You didn't believe me."

"John, we have more pressing matters to deal with than—"

"Did you call him back?"

"I did, to keep up the pretext that we were returning to The Point."

"What did you tell Henry? Deli mustard, right?"

"I did. He's very charming."

"He wanted to show me his woodcock."

She ignored that. "I also made a massage appointment for both of us tomorrow morning."

"Good. I'm looking forward to that."

"We're not going to be there."

"This is true. Well, I'm sorry to disappoint Henry after all the trouble he went to, but I'm not sorry to miss cocktails with Liam Griffith."

Kate looked a little fatigued, or maybe worried, and I needed to give her a pep talk, so I said, "You did a great job. You're the best partner I've ever had."

"I'm your boss."

"Right. Best boss I've ever had. Okay, so, the FAA—"

The phone rang, and I said to Kate, "You expecting a call?"

"No."

"Maybe it's Wilma. Your husband is on the way."

She hesitated, then answered the phone. "Hello?" She listened, then said, "Thank you. Yes . . . I'll tell him. Thanks."

She hung up. "It *was* Wilma. Duct tape is outside our door. She says my friend should move his van."

We both laughed, but clearly we were on edge. I went to the window, checked out the terrain, then opened the door and retrieved a big roll of duct tape.

I sat at the kitchen table and began wrapping the makeshift evidence bags, as per rules and regulations. I said to her, "Tell me about the FAA."

She didn't reply and instead asked me, "Why don't we just get the Hyundai back from Rudy, take those evidence bags, and drive to New York?"

"Do you have a pen? I need to sign this tape."

"We could be at 26 Fed at about . . ." She looked at her watch and said, "About three or four in the morning."

"You can go. I'm staying here. This is where it's happening, and this is where I need to be. Pen, please."

She handed me a pen from her bag. "*What* is happening?"

"I don't know, but when it happens, I'll be here." I signed the tape and said, "Actually, we *should* split up in case . . . Okay, you drive Rudy's van to Massena, rent *another* car, and drive to New York."

She sat on the chair beside me, took my hand, and said, "Let me finish telling you what I've learned, then we'll decide what to do."

This sounded like she had an ace up her sleeve, which was probably the bad news. Whatever it was, it was pressing on her mind.

I said, "The FAA. Bad news?"

"The good news is that I was able to get some information. The bad news is the information."

CHAPTER FORTY-THREE

The FAA," Kate began. "As you predicted, this was a challenge. But, finally, someone at the FAA clued me in to call the regional Flight Service Station—the FSS—in Kansas City, where these two GOCO aircraft arrived Sunday afternoon from Adirondack Regional Airport."

"Good. What did the FSS in KC say?"

"Well, they said these two aircraft landed, refueled, and filed continuing flight plans, then departed." She glanced at her notes. "One Cessna Citation, piloted by Captain Tim Black, with tail number N2730G, flew to Los Angeles. The other, piloted by Captain Elwood Bellman, with tail number N2731G, flew to San Francisco."

"Really?" That sort of surprised me. I was sure that one or both of Madox's jets would fly back here to Adirondack Regional Airport, where Madox could hop aboard and go wherever he needed to go in a hurry. "And those were their final destinations?"

"As of about an hour ago. I called the FSS in LA and San Francisco, and no new flight plans have been filed."

"Okay . . . but why did they fly to Los Angeles and San Francisco?"

"That's what we need to find out."

"Right. We also should find out where the pilots are staying in these cities so we can talk to them."

"I had the same thought, and I discovered that private aircraft use what's called Fixed Base Operations—FBOs—to take care of arriving and departing aircraft. At LAX, I discovered that GOCO aircraft use Garrett Aviation Service as their FBO, and at SFO, GOCO aircraft use a company called Signature Flight Support. So, I called these FBOs and asked if they knew where the GOCO pilots and co-pilots might be. I was told that sometimes a pilot leaves a local number, usually a hotel, where they can be contacted if needed, or their cell-phone numbers. But not this time. The only contact information that these FBOs had on the pilots was the GOCO flight department at Stewart International Airport in Newburgh, New York, where GOCO has its base operations, maintenance hangar, and dispatch office."

"And? You called these people?"

"Yes, I called the GOCO dispatch office at Stewart, but, for obvious reasons, I did not identify myself as FBI, and no one would give me any information on the two crews."

"Did you tell them you were a doctor and that both pilots and co-pilots are legally blind?"

"No, but I'll let you call and see what you can find out."

"Maybe later." I asked, "What are the names of the co-pilots?"

"Oddly, the flight plans don't ask for the name of the co-pilot."

I could see that the Federal Aviation Administration hadn't tightened up its act regarding private aviation since 9/11. But I already knew that.

Kate said, "The flight plan does show the number of persons on board, and both aircraft had two. Pilot and co-pilot."

"Okay . . . so these aircraft landed at LAX and SFO, no passengers, and they've been parked there since Sunday night, and there are no new flight plans filed, and I assume Captain Black and Captain Bellman and their unidentified co-pilots are enjoying the sights of LA and San Francisco as they await further instructions."

"It would seem so."

I thought about all of this and concluded that maybe it had no meaning, and was perfectly normal. Just four pilots jetting across the continent without passengers, burning jet fuel at the rate of several hundred gallons per hour, while their boss transported more fuel into the country in his tankers. I asked Kate, "Does this seem strange to you?"

"In and of itself, maybe yes. But we don't know this world." She informed me, "One of the FBO employees in San Francisco, for instance, suggested that maybe these aircraft had been chartered by someone for a pickup in San Francisco."

"Do you think a man like Madox charters his personal jets to make a few bucks?"

"Apparently some rich people do. But there's more."

"I hoped there was."

Kate continued, "I spoke to a Ms. Carol Ascrizzi, who works for Signature Flight Support in San Francisco, and she told me she was asked to transport the pilot and co-pilot in the courtesy van to the taxi line at the main terminal."

This didn't seem unusual or important, but I could tell by Ms. Mayfield's tone of voice that it was. "And?"

"And, Ms. Ascrizzi said that GOCO, like most bigger companies, almost always books a car and driver ahead of time to take the flight crew wherever they need to go. Therefore, she found it odd that this pilot and co-pilot needed to take a taxi from the main terminal. So, Ms. Ascrizzi, wanting to be nice to good customers, told me she offered to drive the two guys to their hotel." Kate informed me, "Apparently, these crews usually stay in some place with corporate rates near the airport. But the co-pilot told her, thanks, but they were going downtown, and they'd take a taxi."

"Okay . . . did she know where they were going?"

"No, they didn't say."

Which, I thought, could be why they were taking a taxi and not the offered courtesy van, and why there was no livery car waiting for them. "All right. Anything else?"

"Yes, she told me that these two guys—pilot and co-pilot—had two large black leather trunks with them. The trunks were padlocked, and they were on wheels, and they were very heavy, and it took both men to get each trunk into the van."

"Okay. Big and heavy. Padlock and wheels." I said, "I guess that was the cargo that Chad saw at the airport here. Now, it's been off-loaded in San Francisco, and I assume LA also." Kate wasn't bringing this information to any point, so I mentioned helpfully, "Maybe the men had their wives or girlfriends on board as stowaways, and these big, heavy trunks held two days of clothes for the ladies."

She inquired, "How did you manage to get a sexist remark into a conversation about aircraft cargo?"

"Sorry." It wasn't easy. "I was just speculating." I further speculated, "So . . . gold? Two dead bodies? What?"

"You should think about it."

"Okay. What did Carol Ascrizzi say? Was she suspicious? Did the pilot and co-pilot act suspicious or nervous?"

"The pilot and co-pilot, according to Ms. Ascrizzi, were perfectly normal, and joked about the weight of the trunks and the fact that GOCO hadn't booked a car and driver for them. The co-pilot flirted with Ms. Ascrizzi and told her he hoped he'd see her Wednesday when they returned to the airport for their departure."

"Okay . . . departure to where?"

"The co-pilot said their final destination was LaGuardia, but he didn't say what stops they'd make en route. The pilot left instructions at Signature Flight Support to have the aircraft ready for a noon departure on Wednesday with full fuel.".

"All right . . . so, the pilot and co-pilot, according to Ms. Ascrizzi, seemed normal, but the cargo did not." I thought about that and said, "So, the cargo was flown to LA and San Francisco in *two* private jets, rather than one jet, making two stops in those nearby cities."

"That's correct."

"And there was no car and driver to take the crew and this cargo to where they needed to go."

"Correct."

"And the pilot instructed Signature Flight Support in San Francisco to have the aircraft ready for a noon Wednesday departure with the final destination of LaGuardia, but from what you said, they hadn't yet filed a flight plan with the FAA."

"Correct. But that's not unusual. Flight plans, I discovered, need to be filed near the time of departure, to take into account current weather, airport traffic, and so forth."

"That's logical."

"Sorry I couldn't feed your paranoia."

"Oh, don't worry about that. I got more where that came from. In fact, here's one—the pilot and co-pilot's secret destination in San Francisco."

"Why secret?"

"Well, there was no hired car and driver, which would leave a paper trail, plus they passed up the opportunity to take the courtesy van into town after loading these trunks full of bricks or something into the van, which then had to be off-loaded at the taxi line, then loaded into *two* taxis, because of the size of the trunks, for the trip into town. Does that make sense?"

"No. So, I called Garrett Aviation Service at LAX and got a guy named Scott on the phone who asked around while I was on hold, and he got back to me with pretty much the same story—two big black trunks, and the courtesy van only to the taxi line."

"Ah. So, apparently these four guys had the *same* instructions—to take *taxis* to wherever they were going with those trunks."

"It would seem that way."

"So, quite obviously, these two flight crews had a *secret* destination or destinations in LA and San Francisco, and that's why they each took a *taxi*, which would take a lot of luck to trace. Now, the question is, Does this have anything to do with Bain Madox's insane plan to become Emperor of North America, or whatever the hell he's up to? Or, is it not relevant?"

"I think it's relevant."

"Is this the bad news?"

She replied, "We need more context. Now, you tell me about your conversation with Madox."

"Okay. Then I get the bad news?"

"Yes. Unless you can figure it out yourself before we're finished with the other items on the agenda."

"That's a challenge. Okay, do I have everything I need to figure out the bad news?"

"You're at the point where I was when I figured it out. Then I found one more piece of information that confirmed what I was afraid of."

"Okay. Wow."

I thought about that, and there was something coming together in my brain, but before it fell into place, Kate said, "You're on. Custer Hill. Bain Madox."

All roads lead back to Custer Hill and Bain Madox.

CHAPTER FORTY-FOUR

I sat back on the couch, and Kate sat in an easy chair. I said, "All right. First, Bain Madox was half expecting me." I added, "Great minds think alike."

I love it when she rolls her eyes. It's so cute. I continued, "The house staff seems to be gone, but the security guards are there, and so is Carl."

I gave Kate a short briefing of my time with Bain Madox, including the tangential discussions about being wounded in the line of duty, and Madox's odd obsession with bears. I said to her, "But maybe these topics were not tangential. Madox may have been speaking allegorically."

"Sounds more like macho bullshit to me."

"Right. That, too. More important, I put Mr. Bain Madox on official notice that he was a material witness in a suspected homicide." I explained my bogus suspicions about one of his security guards being Harry's killer. "So, now we have him in a tight spot."

Kate reminded me, "Murdering a Federal agent is not a Federal crime."

"Well, it should be."

"But it's not." She informed me, "New York State has the jurisdiction. That means Major Schaeffer." She asked, "Don't you teach that in your class at John Jay College of Criminal Justice?"

"Yes, I *teach* it. I don't practice it. Actually, I covered myself by using the word assault, which *is* a Federal crime." I added, "Madox is not a lawyer. He's a suspect."

"But he *has* a lawyer."

"Don't sweat the small stuff."

She looked a little exasperated with me, but conceded, "I guess that was a good move. Is that about the time he asked you to dinner?"

"Actually, it was." I added, "He'll have some of the information that I asked for tonight."

"Yeah, right. Well, now you need to officially notify Major Schaeffer and Tom Walsh of what you did."

"I will."

"When?"

"Later." I continued to fill in more of what Madox and I spoke about, but I didn't mention that a moment had come when I considered a classically simple solution to a complex problem. I wanted to say to my wife and partner, "Just as Madox had solved his Harry Muller problem with a half ounce of lead, I could have resolved the entire Madox problem in less time than it took to pick the lint off the rug." But I didn't say that.

I did say, however, "Madox expressed his condolences about Harry, though he couldn't remember Harry's name."

Kate looked at me.

I said, "Madox wanted to know if there was a fund he could contribute to."

She kept looking at me, and I think she suspected that I'd thought about expedited justice, used now and then in cases of cop killers.

Kate said to me, "I called Harry's girlfriend, Lori Bahnik."

This took me by surprise, but I realized I should have done that by now. "That was nice of you."

"It wasn't an easy conversation, but I assured her we were doing everything possible to get to the bottom of this."

I nodded.

"Lori said to say hello to you. She's glad that it's you on the case."

"Did you tell her I wasn't on the case any longer?"

"No, I did not." Kate stared at me and said, "Last I heard, you and I were on the case."

We made eye contact and exchanged brief smiles. I switched subjects. "Well, bottom line with Bain Madox is that he is now feeling pressed, and he may do something stupid, desperate, or clever."

"I think he's already done all three by inviting you to dinner."

"*Us*, darling. And I think you're right."

"I *know* I'm right. So, why don't you just play right into his hands and show up? *Or*, do something more clever like *don't* show up." She asked, "May I call Tom Walsh now?"

I ignored that and continued my briefing. "I also got a good look at Madox's back lot from his second-story office window." I informed her, "There's a barracks there big enough to hold twenty or thirty men, but I imagine not more than half are on duty at any time. Plus, there's a stone building with three chimneys belching smoke, and a diesel generator service truck parked outside."

She nodded and said again, "It may be time to share this information. I'll call Tom, you call Major Schaeffer."

"All right. I'll call Hank Schaeffer first, so we'll have more things to chat about with Tom Walsh."

I stood and went to the desk phone, and using my phone debit card, I called state police headquarters in Ray Brook.

Major Schaeffer was in for Detective Corey, and he asked me, "Where are you?"

I hit the Speaker button and replied, "I'm not sure, but I'm looking at a menu in French."

Major Schaeffer wasn't amused. "Did you get my message that your Hertz car was at The Point?"

"I did. Thank you."

He informed me, "Your friend, Liam Griffith, is not happy with you."

"Fuck him."

"Should I pass that on?"

"I'll do it myself. By the way, I went to the Custer Hill Club, and there was no visible stakeout there."

"Well," he replied, "they were there. I pulled them back to Route 56 because this black Jeep kept snooping around. I have another team on the logging road in case anyone comes in or out from the back roads."

"Okay." I inquired, "Anything new with your surveillance team?"

"No one has arrived at the Custer Hill Club, except you in a white Enterprise rental Hyundai, and also a diesel service truck." He gave me the details of my arrival and departure, and asked me, "What the hell were you doing there?"

"I'll get to that. Has the diesel service truck left yet?"

"Not as of five minutes ago. No one else has left the subject property, so I guess this guy Putyov is still there." He asked me, "Did you see any sign of him there?"

"No, I didn't." I asked him, "Was I followed after I left the Custer Hill Club?"

"No."

"Why not?"

"Because I was called directly by my surveillance car, who told me it was an Enterprise rental, and the renter was a Mr. John Corey, and I told them you were on the job."

"Okay." So, if that was true, then the state police hadn't seen the vehicle switch at Rudy's gas station. If it wasn't true, then I was driving around in a hot van. But that only mattered if I didn't trust Major Schaeffer, and the jury was out on that. Bottom line, I really think I would have noticed if I'd been followed.

Major Schaeffer inquired again, "What were you doing there?"

"I was sizing up the suspect and collecting forensic evidence."

"What kind of forensic evidence?"

"Hairs and carpet fibers." I explained what I'd done.

Major Schaeffer listened, then asked, "Where is this evidence now?"

"In my possession."

"When are you giving it to me?"

"Well, I think there's a jurisdictional question that needs to be resolved first."

"No, there isn't. Murder is a state crime."

I reminded him, "You haven't classified it as a murder."

There was silence as Major Schaeffer contemplated the consequences of his fence-straddling. Finally, he said, "I could arrest you for withholding evidence."

"You could, if you could find me."

"I can find you."

"No, I'm really good at this." I said, "I'll think about what's best for this investigation, and best for me and my partner."

"Don't think too long." He asked me, "What did Madox have to say?"

"We talked about bears." I informed Major Schaeffer, "I put Bain Madox on notice that he was a material witness in a possible homicide investigation." I explained how I did that, and concluded, "Now, he needs to cooperate, voluntarily, or involuntarily, and that also puts some heat on him."

Schaeffer replied, "Yeah. I understand how that works, Detective. Thank you." He asked me, "When did murder in New York State become a Federal crime?"

"When did Harry Muller's death become a murder?"

Clearly, Major Schaeffer was not happy with me or my methods, so he didn't answer my question, but informed me, "Madox may now have to cooperate in the investigation, but you'll never see him again without his lawyer present."

I wondered if Madox's lawyer was coming to dinner. On that subject, I decided not to tell Schaeffer about Madox inviting me to dinner until I was well on my way to Custer Hill. I mean, I needed him to know where I was, in case there was a problem. But I didn't want him to know about it *too* early in case he or Griffith became part of the problem by arresting me.

He said, "Okay, I've done you some favors, and you've done me some favors. I think we're even on favors."

"Actually, I have a few more favors to ask of you."

"Put them in writing."

"And then I'll owe you a favor."

No reply. I think he was pissed. Nevertheless, I said, "Speaking of diesels, did you ever find out how big those diesel generators are at Custer Hill?"

"Why is that important?"

"I don't know that it is. I'm sure it's not. But I saw that building there—"

"Yeah. I saw it, too, when I was hunting there."

I let a few seconds pass, then he said, "I had one of my men call Potsdam Diesel, but my guy got the information wrong, or their office person didn't read the file right."

"Meaning?"

"Well, my guy said they told him the generators put out two thousand kilowatts." He paused, then said, "*Each.* Hell, that could power a small town. It must be twenty kilowatts—maybe two hundred, tops. Or maybe twenty thousand *watts.*"

"Is there a difference?"

"There is if you stick your dick in a light socket." He dropped that subject and said to me, "Let me give you some advice."

"Okay."

"You're not in business for yourself. This is a team effort. Rejoin the team."

Kate raised her hand in a seconding motion.

I said to Major Schaeffer, "It's a little late for that."

"You and your wife should get over to headquarters *now.*"

It's always nice to be invited home again, and it's tempting, but I didn't trust my family any longer, so I said, "I think you have all the Federal agents you need there."

He offered, "I'll meet you someplace that'll make you feel . . . safer."

"Okay. I'll let you know where to meet us later."

Before he could respond, I hung up and looked at Kate, who said, "John, I think we should go to—"

"End of discussion. New topic. Potsdam Diesel." I picked up the phone and dialed Potsdam Diesel, whose phone number I recalled from their service truck.

A young lady answered, "Potsdam Diesel. This is Lu Ann. How can I help you?"

I hit the Speaker button. "Hi, Lu Ann. This is Joe, the caretaker at the Custer Hill Club."

"Yes, sir."

"I have Al here servicing the generators."

"Is there a problem?"

"No, but could you pull the sales and service files for me?"

"Hold on."

The speaker started playing Muzak and I said to Kate, "I'm not current on watts—no pun intended—but Schaeffer wasn't believing six thousand . . . what were they called? Megawatts?"

Kate replied, "Kilowatts. A thousand watts is a kilowatt. Six thousand kilowatts is six *million* watts. A lightbulb is usually seventy-five watts."

"Wow. That's a lot of—"

Lu Ann was back. "I have it. How can I help you?"

"Well, if I lost power and the generators kicked in, could I make toast and coffee in the morning?"

She laughed and said, "You could make toast and coffee for Potsdam."

"Yeah? So, how many *kilowatts* do I have?"

"Okay, you have three Detroit brand, sixteen-cylinder diesel engines, each capable of driving its matching generator to two thousand kilowatts."

Kate and I exchanged glances.

I said to Lu Ann, "No kidding? How old are these generators? Is it time to replace them?"

"No. They were installed in . . . 1984 . . . but they should last forever with service."

"But how much is a new one?"

"Oh . . . I'm not sure, but the cost of these in 1984 was $245,000."

"Each?"

"Yes, each. Today . . . well, a lot more." She asked me, "Is there a problem with the service?"

"No. Al's doing a great job. I can see him sweating from here. When is he going to be finished?"

"Well . . . we only have Al and Kevin . . . this was called in Saturday afternoon, and we're real busy . . . You know you're paying on an expedited basis?"

Kate and I again glanced at each other. I said to Lu Ann, "No problem. In fact, add a thousand dollars to Mr. Madox's bill for Al and Kevin."

"That's very generous of you—"

"So, what do you think? Another hour?"

"I don't know. Do you want me to call them, or do you want to go talk to them?"

"You call them. Look, we're having a big dinner party, so maybe they can come back another time."

"When would you like to schedule that?"

"November thirty-first."

"Okay . . . oh . . . I see here there's only thirty days in—"

"I'll call you on that. Meanwhile, give these guys a holler, and tell them to knock off. I'll hold."

"Hold on, please."

The phone started playing "The Blue Danube Waltz" for some reason, and I said to Kate, "I should have done this an hour ago."

"Better late than not at all." She added, "Six *thousand* kilowatts."

"Right. Why am I listening to 'The Blue Danube Waltz'?"

"You're on hold."

"Do you want to dance—?"

Lu Ann came back on the line and said, "Well, I have good news. They're finished, and they're packing their tools."

"Great." *Shit.*

"Is there anything else I can do for you?"

"Pray for world peace."

"Okay . . . that's nice."

"Lu Ann, you have a good evening."

"You, too, Joe."

I hung up and said to Kate, "In the history of the world, this is the first time a service crew finished ahead of schedule."

"Madox wasn't going to let those guys leave anyway. So, if we weren't convinced that we were looking at an ELF antenna, that information should convince us."

"I was already convinced. This is the clincher." I added, "If you notice the silverware glowing tonight, let me know."

"John, we are not going—"

"What is the downside of going there for dinner?"

"Death, dismemberment, disappearance, and divorce."

"We can handle that."

"I have a better idea. Let's get in that van and drive to Manhattan. *Now.* We'll call Tom on the way—"

"Forget it. I am not going to be on the fucking Thruway talking to Tom Walsh on my cell phone, while the shit is hitting the fan right here. In fact, the real reason we're going to the Custer Hill Club tonight is not dinner, or to gather more evidence, but to determine if we can and should place Mr. Bain Madox under arrest for the murder of—sorry, the assault on—Federal Agent Harry Muller."

She thought about that, then replied, "I don't think we have enough evidence, or probable cause to—"

"Fuck the evidence. We *have* the evidence. It's in those bags. And the probable cause is the sum total of everything we've seen and heard."

She shook her head and said, "An arrest on *any* Federal charge—especially of a man like Bain Madox—would be premature, and could get us in *real* trouble."

"We're already there." I added, "We need to arrest this bastard *tonight*. Before he does whatever he thinks he's going to do next."

She didn't say anything, and I thought I'd made my point. "All right, let's have the bad news." I added, in a nicer tone, "Then I can make a rational decision about what to do next."

She said, "I thought you might have figured it out by now."

"I would have mentioned it if I did. Hold on." I thought

for ten full seconds, and something was trying to connect in my brain, but I had too many things on my mind, so I asked, "Animal, mineral, or vegetable?"

She moved to the desk and, still standing, pulled the laptop closer. "Let me show you something."

CHAPTER FORTY-FIVE

K ate hit a few keys on the laptop computer, and a page of text came up on the screen. She said, "That's an unpublished piece about Mikhail Putyov, written ten years ago."

I glanced at the screen. "Yeah? And?"

She turned the computer toward me and said, "The writer is a fellow named Leonid Chernoff, another Russian nuclear physicist, also living in the U.S. This piece is in the form of a letter to fellow physicists, in which he praises Putyov's genius."

I didn't respond.

She continued, "And here"—she scrolled—"Chernoff writes, and I quote, 'Putyov is quite content now in his teaching position, and finds his work challenging and rewarding. Though one must ask if he is as challenged as when he worked at the Kurchatov Institute on the Soviet miniaturization program.' " She looked at me. "End quote."

"Miniaturization of *what*?"

"Nuclear weapons. Like nuclear artillery shells, for instance, or land mines. Also, nuclear suitcase bombs."

It took me half a second to get it, and I felt like I'd been kicked in the stomach. "Holy shit . . ." I stared stupidly at the illuminated laptop screen, my mind racing through everything we'd heard, discovered, knew, and suspected.

"John, I think there are two nuclear suitcase bombs in Los Angeles, and two in San Francisco."

"Holy *shit*."

"I don't know the final destination of those weapons, or if Madox's two aircraft are going to be transporting those suitcases to their ultimate destination or destinations, or if they're going to be put on a ship, or—"

"We need to ground those aircraft."

"Done. I called my friend Doug Sturgis, who's the ASAC in the LA field office, and told him to put those two aircraft under surveillance in case the pilots show up, or have the planes impounded as evidence in a Federal case that was urgent and of the highest priority."

I nodded. Her "friend" Doug was, I think, an old boyfriend from when she'd been posted in LA some years ago. I'd had the pleasure of meeting this pin dick when Kate and I had chased down Asad Khalil in California—and I had no doubt that this wimp would jump through his ass for his old pal Kate.

Still, I didn't see how Kate could kick off a major case with a single phone call to some assistant special agent in charge in LA. I mean, the workings of the FBI remain a mystery to me, but I seem to recall a chain of command.

I asked her about this, and she replied, "What I did—to avoid going through Tom Walsh—was to ask—plead with Doug—to treat this as an anonymous terrorist threat tip." She informed me, "That will actually get the ball rolling faster, if Doug says that the tip sounded legitimate."

"Right. And he's doing this?"

"He said he would." She added, "I explained that I . . . and you . . . were having some credibility problems with the ATTF, but that I had this extremely reliable information, and it was *urgent,* and it was in *his* jurisdiction, and—"

"Okay. I got it. And he's your pal, so he stuck his neck out for you."

"He wouldn't stick his neck out for anyone. But he does have to respond to a credible terrorist threat."

"Right. I guess he knows you're credible."

"Can we move on?"

"Yeah. I just needed to know that this is in the right hands, and it's not sitting in someone's tomorrow box."

She moved on. "I also gave Doug the names Tim Black and Elwood Bellman, and I told him that Black was probably staying in a hotel in Los Angeles, and Bellman in San Francisco, and that we needed to find these pilots ASAP." She added, "I told him my suspicion that they could be transporting suitcase nukes."

I nodded. That was the right move, obviously. "Did that get his attention?"

She ignored that and continued, "He promised to begin a manhunt in LA immediately, and to call the San

Francisco field office, and also to put this out to all local law enforcement agencies in both cities and suburbs. He will also speak to his boss in LA, and both of them will call the Directors in Charge in New York and Washington, and report this tip. Doug will affirm that he believes it is a credible tip, based on the specific nature of the information and so forth, and he'll describe the actions he's taking."

"Good. But if this turns out to be four suitcases filled with porn magazines for Madox's Arab friends, will Doug take the rap? Or will he mention your name?"

She looked at me and asked, "Do you think I'm wrong on this?"

I thought a moment, then replied, "No. I think you're right. Four suitcase nukes. I'm with you."

"Good. Thank you." She continued, "I told Doug to ask for an elevated domestic terrorist threat level."

"That should get the LA office off their surfboards." I reminded her, "This is not actually a domestic threat."

"No. And Bain Madox is not a terrorist . . . well, maybe he is. But I couldn't figure out how to classify a plot to send four suitcase nukes overseas, so I said to Doug, 'Treat it like an elevated domestic threat, as long as we believe the suitcases are still in LA and San Francisco.'"

"Good move."

"The FBI in both cities are contacting all the local cab companies to see if any of their drivers remember picking up a male passenger at the taxi line at LAX and SFO, carrying a large, black leather trunk. But I think that's a long shot because, as you know, many of those cabbies are foreigners, and they don't like to talk to the police or FBI."

That was not a politically correct statement from a Federal employee, but when the pressure was on, even the Feds had to retreat into reality.

She continued, "We have a better description of the trunks than of the pilots and co-pilots. So, I asked Doug to call the FAA and get Black and Bellman's license photos e-mailed to the FBI in LA and San Francisco ASAP. Then, I learned, to my amazement, that pilot licenses don't have photos on them."

"Unbelievable. Another incredible example of FAA post-9/11 stupidity."

"So I used the FAA addresses for the pilots to get their state *driver's* licenses with their photos. Black lives in New York, Bellman lives in Connecticut."

"I see you were busy while I was gone."

"I got real busy after I realized we may be dealing with suitcase nukes."

"Right. And how is Doug?"

"I was too busy to ask him. But he did send you his regards."

"That's nice." Fuck him. "Did he appreciate you telling him how to do his job?"

"John, I had the information, and I'd been thinking about this, and he was . . . well, stunned. So, yes, he appreciated my input."

"Good." Also, I recalled he seemed dim-witted.

I thought about this new and exciting development, and my mind was trying to compute all the angles, equations, and possibilities. I said to Kate, "If these pilots went to hotels, and if this is some kind of secret Madox mission, which it seems to be, then these four guys probably checked in under false names."

She nodded. "But we have the real names of the two pilots, so the FBI will have their driver's license photos very soon, if not already." She informed me, "Doug is asking the Kingston regional office in New York to send an agent to the GOCO dispatch office at Stewart Airport to find out who the co-pilots were."

"Good thinking." It seemed that this end of the problem was covered, but I thought that finding those four pilots would not be easy, especially if Madox had instructed them to lay low, not answer their cell phones, stay in their hotel rooms, and use false ID.

Kate said, "Unfortunately, the suitcase nukes—if that's what they were transporting—could very well be out of their hands by now."

"They *are* suitcase nukes. Just call them what they are."

"Okay, okay. Madox is going to ship them someplace out of the country. My guess is the Mideast, or another Islamic country." She went on, "I called Garrett Aviation Service back and got a guy on the phone who said that the Cessna Citation could not make a Pacific crossing unless it went up the West Coast to Alaska, then the Aleutian Islands, then Japan, and so forth." She pointed out, "This would involve many refueling stops, not to mention customs checks along the way. So, I think we can rule that out."

I nodded and processed all this. Madox's Cessna Citations had landed Sunday night in LA and San Francisco. The pilots and co-pilots had left no local address, but had indicated that they were flying out Wednesday—tomorrow—and heading back to New York. And I was sure that the pilots thought they *were,* and maybe they really were. Meanwhile, where was their cargo? Most probably it was not with them any longer.

I said to Kate, "I'm thinking that Madox is going to use—or has already used—one of his own oil tankers to transport these nukes someplace. *That* is why his aircraft landed in seaport cities."

Kate nodded. "I came to the same conclusion, and I asked Doug to begin a search of ships and containers at both ports, beginning with GOCO-owned ships." She said unnecessarily, "This is a big job. But if they get the NEST teams activated soon, and the port security people, who also have gamma-ray and neutron detectors, we might get lucky."

"Right . . . but they need to sweep not only ships and containers but also warehouses and trucks . . . and for all we know, those nukes are going to be shipped by commercial air carriers."

"They're also checking all area airports."

"Okay. But this really is like looking for a needle in a haystack."

"These needles are radioactive, and we have a good chance of finding them."

"Maybe, if they're still in LA and San Francisco. But here's a more likely scenario—those nukes are already on their way by sea or air to their final destinations. I mean, it's been almost two days since they arrived on the West Coast."

"You may be right, but we need to search for them in these cities in case they're still there." She added, "It will be easier to find the pilots, especially if they turn up at LAX and SFO tomorrow."

"Right. Okay, here's the bottom line on those pilots. It would be nice to find them, but I don't think the FBI will find them with their suitcases. The pilots will, however, know where they delivered the suitcases, or maybe who picked them up. But the trail will probably end there." I pointed out, "Unfortunately, we're about forty-eight hours late on this, and the next time those suitcase nukes are seen, it will be in the form of four mushroom clouds over Sandland."

Kate stood silent and motionless for a while. "God, I hope not."

"Yeah." Well, it seemed that Kate and what's his name in LA had done all they could on short notice, and they'd done a good job—though this was not rocket science, or nuclear physics for that matter. It was standard police and FBI work, and it would yield the four pilots, and maybe even some information about the suitcase nukes. The problem, however, was—as it had always been with this case—time. Madox had started the game before the visiting team had even shown up, and he had points on the board before his opponents took the field.

But there was, possibly, good news. A weak link in this nuclear chain. I said to Kate, "The ELF transmitter. *That* is how he is going to detonate those bombs."

She nodded. "*That's* what ELF was about. Each bomb must have an extremely low frequency receiver connected to the detonating device. The ELF waves, as we discovered, can travel around the world and penetrate anything. So, when the bombs are where Madox wants them to be, he sends a code from here, and within an hour, the signal reaches the receivers in the suitcases, wherever in the world they are."

"Right. So it seems as though this asshole built this elaborate ELF station almost twenty years ago to send bogus messages to the U.S. nuclear submarine fleet in order to start World War III. But that didn't work out, so now he's figured out another way to make his investment pay off."

Kate nodded and said, "It all makes sense now."

"Right . . . and Putyov was the guy who did whatever he had to do with those suitcase nukes to make them detonate by way of an ELF wave."

"Also, I discovered online that miniature nuclear weapons need periodic maintenance, so that was also Putyov's job."

"The late Dr. Putyov."

Kate nodded.

I asked, rhetorically, "Where the hell did Madox get these nukes?" Then I answered my own question. "I guess they're for sale from our new friends in Russia—which is why Madox hired a Russian. Shit, I couldn't even find a good Swedish mechanic to fix my old Volvo, and fucking Madox has a Russian nuclear physicist to tune up his atomic bombs." I added, "It's all about money."

"Money and madness are not a good combination."

"Good point. Okay . . . so, I guess four cities someplace are in trouble in a few days . . . or a few hours—Islamic cities. Right?"

"Right. What else makes sense?"

I thought about who might be in Madox's crosshairs. But the potential targets were too numerous to count. And it depended to some extent on if those nukes were being transported by air or sea or some combination of air, sea, and land. I wouldn't put it past this guy to nuke Mecca or Medina, but maybe this was purely a business deal, and he'd picked oil-shipment points in countries that had pissed him off. Bottom line—what difference did it make?

Kate said, "Well, I think I did everything I could, and Doug is going to do everything *he* can."

"Yeah . . ." I glanced at my watch. "This will give the LA field office something to do before their evening aerobics classes."

"John—"

"But on the subject of who knows what, and when—Washington *does* know something about this. It's just that they forgot to tell us about it."

No comment from FBI Special Agent Mayfield.

"That's the only way Harry's assignment makes any sense." I continued, "The Justice Department and therefore the FBI in Washington know what Madox is up to. Right?"

"I don't know. But, as I told you, this was something a lot bigger than you realized when you started sticking your nose into a Justice Department investigation."

"I think we both understand that." I said to Kate, "Here

are two conspiracy theories for you: one, the government knows what's going on at Custer Hill, and Harry was the sacrificial lamb sent to give the FBI an excuse to bust down Madox's doors and arrest him. But here's a better one—the government knows what's going on at Custer Hill, and Harry was the sacrificial lamb sent to get Madox and his friends off their asses so that they'd pull the trigger on those nukes."

Kate shook her head. "That is insane."

"Yeah? Do you see FBI SWAT teams descending on the Custer Hill Club?"

"No . . . but . . . they may be waiting for the right time—"

"If that's true, they may have waited a little too long." I reminded her, "Harry was at Custer Hill Saturday morning. Madox's meeting with his friends was Saturday and Sunday. Putyov showed up on Sunday morning to tune up the nukes. Madox's aircraft landed on the West Coast Sunday night. Monday was probably the day the nukes were making their way to Sandland. Today is Tuesday, and Potsdam Diesel is finished tuning up the generators." I concluded, "Sometime tonight or tomorrow is detonation day."

Kate didn't reply.

"And Madox is not acting alone. It was not a coincidence that his weekend guests included two, possibly three, and maybe more high-ranking men in the government. Hell, for all we know, the directors of the FBI and the CIA are in on this." I added, "Maybe it goes higher than that."

She thought for a few seconds, then said, "Okay . . . but does it matter at this point who else may be involved with Madox, or who knows about this? The point is, if this is what it seems to be, then I've done the right thing by calling the FBI field office in LA—"

"I assume you didn't tell your friend about Madox, ELF, or where you were calling from, or—"

"No . . . because . . . I wanted to speak to you first. What if I'm wrong about all of this? I mean, if you think about it, there *could* be another explanation for everything—"

"Kate, you're *not* wrong. *We* are not wrong. *Harry* was not wrong. It's all very clear. Madox, nuke, ELF. Plus, Putyov."

"I know. I know. Okay, so now we have to contact Tom Walsh and have *him* officially notify FBI Headquarters as to the source of this information, meaning me . . . and you, and what we're basing this—"

"Right." I looked at my watch again and saw it was 6:10 P.M. "You do that. Meanwhile, I have a dinner date."

She stood and said, "No. There's no reason to go there."

"Sweetheart, Madox is tuning up his ELF transmitter, awaiting some sort of message that his four suitcase nukes are where they're supposed to be. Then, an ELF wave will be making its way slowly across the continent, and the Pacific Ocean—or the other way across the Atlantic— until it's picked up by the ELF receivers in those four suitcases." I added, "Millions of people will die, and a radioactive cloud will blow across the planet. The least I can do is try to stop this at its source."

She thought about that, then said, "I'm going with you."

"No, you're going to call out the cavalry and get them to the Custer Hill Club—without a fucking search warrant or probable cause or any of that crap—by telling them truthfully that a Federal agent is on the property and is in danger."

"No—"

"Call Walsh, call Schaeffer, call the local sheriff if you have to, and call Liam Griffith and tell him where he can find John Corey. But give me a thirty-minute head start."

She didn't reply.

I went to the kitchen table and got my act together by loading my two Glock magazines with 9mm rounds and clipping the two BearBanger launchers in my shirt pocket alongside my pen, and finally putting on my new socks, which didn't seem so important any longer. Also, I couldn't think of a use for the air horn, but I took it anyway, in case Rudy's van horn didn't work.

While I was doing this, Kate was banging away at the laptop, and I asked her, "What are you doing?"

"I'm sending an e-mail to Tom Walsh, telling him to contact Doug in LA, and revealing that I was the source of the information."

"Don't send it until you hear from me." I added, "I hope Walsh is checking his e-mail tonight."

"He usually does."

On that subject, the FBI still has only internal, "secured" e-mail, so, as unbelievable as it sounds, Kate could not e-mail Walsh's FBI account, and couldn't reach or copy anyone in the office, such as the after-hours duty agent. Therefore, she was e-mailing to Walsh's personal account, hoping he checked it regularly. And this is a year after 9/11.

I said to her, "Okay, I'll call you on my cell phone when I get close to the Custer Hill Club."

"Hold on. Okay, I sent it to a service. Delayed send for seven P.M." She unplugged the laptop, placed it on the kitchen table, then put on her suede jacket. "Who's driving?"

"Since I'm the only one going, I guess I'll drive."

She put the box of .40-caliber ammo in her purse along with the two magazines, then picked up the laptop and walked to the door. I held her arm and asked her, "Where do you think you're going?"

She reminded me, "You said Madox *specifically* asked for me, darling. You wanted me to go. So, I'm going."

I informed her, "The situation has changed."

"It certainly has. I've done all I can here." She pointed out, "You put me through two days of shit to get where we are—now, I want to be in on the action. And you're wasting time." She pulled away from me, opened the door, and walked outside. I followed her.

It was dark now and cold. As we walked to the van, I said to Kate, "I appreciate your concern for me, but—"

"This has more to do with me than you, for a change."

"Oh . . ."

"I don't work for you. You work for me."

"Well, technically—"

"You drive."

She got in the passenger seat of the van, and I got in the driver's seat and drove toward the main house.

Kate said, "Also, I *am* concerned about you."

"Thanks."

"You need supervision."

"I don't know—"

"Stop here."

I stopped at Wilma and Ned's house, and Kate said, "Here. Return Wilma's laptop. She has ten minutes before her auction closes."

I had no idea what that meant, but it sounded important, so I took the laptop, got out, and rang the bell.

The door opened, and Wilma stood there. She looked like a Wilma, and I wouldn't want to arm wrestle her for the laptop.

She looked me over, then glanced at the van and saw Kate. She informed me, "I don't want no trouble here."

"Me, neither. Okay, here's your laptop. Thanks."

"What do I say if the husband comes looking for her?"

"Tell the truth." I said to her, "Do me a favor. If we're not back by morning, call Major Hank Schaeffer at the state police headquarters in Ray Brook. Schaeffer. Okay? Tell him John left some stuff for him at the Pond House." I added, "Good luck with the auction."

She glanced at her watch, said, "Oh . . . God . . . ," and shut the door.

I got back in the van, and off we went.

Kate was loading her two magazines and commented, "This van is gross."

"You think?" I related my brief conversation with Wilma, and Kate responded, "We'll be back before morning."

That was optimistic.

The dashboard clock said 3:10, which may have been wrong. My watch said 6:26, and we'd be fashionably late for cocktails.

I had this sense that somewhere, someplace, another clock was ticking.

CHAPTER FORTY-SIX

As I drove, I asked Kate, "What did you put in that e-mail to Walsh?"

"I told you."

"I hope you didn't mention that we were on the way to the Custer Hill Club for cocktails and dinner."

"I did."

"You weren't supposed to do that. Now, the posse may intercept us—or be there ahead of us."

"No, they won't. I told you, I sent the e-mail to a service that will send it later. Delayed send, at seven P.M."

"I never heard of that."

"It was specifically invented for situations like this, and for people like you."

"Really? That's neat."

She explained, "You want to be inside the Custer Hill lodge before anyone knows we're even going there. And by the time Tom Walsh reads my message, we are, hopefully, resolving some issues there. Correct?"

"Right."

"And, we'll be heroes."

"Right."

"Or dead."

"Now, don't be thinking negative thoughts."

"Do you want to turn around now?"

I looked out the windshield. "Why? Did I miss my turn?"

"John, do you think this might be a good time for you to come to your senses?"

"No, this is not a good time for that. Did you come along to bug me, or help me?"

"To help you. But if you drive to the state police headquarters, I'd think you were very smart."

"No, you'd think I was a chicken-livered, yellow-bellied, ball-less wimp."

"No one would ever call *you* that. But sometimes, like now, discretion is the better part of valor."

"Some wimp made up that expression. Look, I'm not stupid. But this is *personal*, Kate. This has to do with Harry. Plus, there's a time element here." I explained, "The ELF station is, or will be, up and running, and I don't know if anyone in law enforcement could get on the Custer Hill property faster than we, who have been *invited*."

"That may or may not be true."

"What is true is that I want a piece of that sonofabitch before anyone else gets to him."

"I know that. But are you willing to risk a possible nuclear incident to satisfy your personal vendetta?"

"Hey, *you* sent that e-mail on a delay."

She pointed out, "I *can* call Major Schaeffer and Liam Griffith right now."

"We're going to do that right before we get to Custer Hill. For now, we need to get there without interference."

She didn't reply to that but instead asked me, "Do you think Madox is going to send that ELF signal tonight?"

"I don't know. But we have to assume that our invitation to dinner has something to do with his timeline." I suggested, "Turn on the radio and see if we hear a breaking news story about nuclear blasts somewhere. If we do, I can slow down and not worry about being late for dinner."

She switched on the radio, but nothing happened. "It doesn't work."

"Maybe the ELF waves knocked out AM and FM. Try the ELF channel."

"Not funny."

I was on Route 56 now, heading toward South Colton, and I took the Hyundai keys out of my pocket and put them in her hand. I said, "I'm stopping at Rudy's gas station, and you're taking the Hyundai and driving to state police headquarters."

She opened the window and tossed out the keys.

"That's going to cost me fifty bucks."

"All right, John, we'll be there in about twenty minutes. Let's take this opportunity to discuss what to expect, and what we need to say, and do. Plus, we should discuss some contingency plans, and what our objective is in going there."

"You mean a game plan?"

"Yes, a game plan."

"Okay. Well, I thought we'd play it by ear."

"I don't think so."

"All right . . . well, first, don't allow a metal scan. And certainly not a frisk."

"Goes without saying."

"I mean, I doubt he'd try that, unless all pretense of us being dinner guests is dropped."

"And if that happens?" Kate inquired.

"Well, if they ask for our guns, then we'll show them our guns *and* our shields."

"What if there are ten of them with rifles?"

"Then, we go into our Federal agent mode and tell them they're all under arrest. And let's not forget to mention to Madox that the entire B Troop barracks of the New York state police knows where we are. That's our ace in the hole."

"I know that. But actually, no one yet knows where we're going. And what if Madox doesn't care who knows where we are? What if Hank Schaeffer is in the kitchen cooking, and the sheriff is making drinks? What if—?"

"Don't make Madox ten feet tall. He's smart, rich, powerful, and ruthless. But he's not Superman, sweetheart." I added, "*I* am Superman."

"All right, Superman, what else do we need to think about to keep ourselves alive and healthy?"

I advised her, "Don't ask for a frozen daiquiri or anything that can be drugged. Drink what he's drinking. Same with the food. Be careful. Remember the Borgias."

"*You* remember the Borgias. I swear, John, you'd eat chili and hot dogs even if you *knew* they were poisoned."

"What a way to go." I continued my briefing. "Okay, our demeanor. This is a social occasion, mixed with the unpleasant business of a Federal investigation. So, act accordingly."

"Meaning what?"

"Meaning, just the right combination of being polite, but firm." I continued, "Madox likes his scotch. Try to gauge his sobriety. If he's not drinking much, take that as a sign of trouble."

"I understand."

We discussed a few more fine points of etiquette that might not be addressed by Emily Post.

When we finished with etiquette class, Kate returned to survival school. "Tell me about the BearBangers."

"Hey, these are neat." I gave her one and told her how to load it and fire it, and went over its possible use as a weapon of last resort if we were relieved of our hardware. I said, "It might pass a frisk since it looks like a penlight. But you might want to stick it in your crotch."

"Okay. Can I tell you where to stick yours?"

"This is serious."

We went through some possible scenarios, some contingencies, and some Plan Bs.

I said to her, "My original plan—which I still like— was to bust in there, through some point in the fence, and take out one or two of the antenna poles, and/or take out the generators."

She didn't respond to that.

I continued, "That's a very direct solution to the ELF problem. That is the weak link in Madox's plan to detonate these suitcase bombs. Right?"

"What if there are no suitcase bombs? What if that's not an ELF station?"

"So, we apologize for the damage and offer to pay for the poles and generators."

I let that sit there awhile as we drove, but Kate wasn't talking, so I pulled out my map of the Custer Hill property and put it on her lap.

She looked at it. "Where did you get this?"

"Harry gave it to me."

"You *took* this from the morgue?"

"It wasn't inventoried—"

"You *took* evidence?"

"Cut the FBI crap. I *borrowed* it. It's done all the time." I tapped the map on her lap, and said, "There's an old logging road there on the east side of the property which runs right up to the fence, then beyond. Okay, we take that road, crash through the fence, then about a hundred yards later, we intersect with this perimeter road that connects all the poles. See it?"

She wasn't looking at the map, but at me.

I continued, "So, we run along that road, line up a pole with the front of the van, and hit it. Okay? The pole goes down, the wires snap, and the ELF station is off the air. What do you think?"

"Well, aside from this being insane, I don't think this van would knock one of those poles from the bedrock."

"Sure it will. That's why I borrowed it."   *

"John, I grew up in rural Minnesota. I've seen vans and even pickup trucks hit utility poles, and the pole usually wins."

"Yeah? Hard to believe."

"And even if the pole cracks, the wires usually hold, and the pole hangs there."

"No kidding? I should have spoken to you before I got myself excited about this."

"And if the wires *do* snap, and hit this van, we'll be toast."

"This is true. Bad idea." I went on, "Okay, so, if you look at the map, you'll see the generator house. See? Right there."

"Watch the road."

"Okay, now this is a challenge, because the house is made of stone, with steel doors and steel shutters. But the weak link is the chimneys—"

"Wasn't this in the story of the three little pigs?"

"Yeah. But we don't go down the chimney. We get on the roof from the top of this van, then we stuff our jackets into the chimney pots, which is what the stupid wolf should have done, and the smoke backs up, and the generators conk out."

"I see three chimneys and two jackets."

"There's a blanket in the back of the van, plus enough other crap to fill six more chimneys. What do you think?"

"Well, technically, it sounds feasible. Did you factor in ten or twenty security guards with all-terrain vehicles and assault rifles?"

"Yeah. That's why I bought extra ammunition."

"Of course. So, let's say this works, or doesn't work. Do we still show up at the front door for dinner?"

"That depends on the results of the shoot-out with the guards. We'll play that by ear."

"Sounds like a plan. Where is this logging road?"

I think she was being sarcastic. There are advantages and disadvantages in having a female partner. The ladies tend to be practical and cautious. The guys tend to be stupid and reckless, which may account for the fact that there are fewer men than women in the world.

I said, "Well, it was just an idea." I added, "I thought of it before we were invited to dinner."

"I don't know how you lived long enough for me to meet you." She added, "I had hoped that evolution and natural selection had solved the problem of people like you."

I certainly didn't reply to that.

She continued, "But you bring up an important point. The ELF system. The weakest link in the ELF station is not the poles, wires, or the generator. It is the transmitter."

"This is true."

"I'm assuming the transmitter is in the lodge itself."

"Most likely. It would be safe and secure there, and hidden from view."

"Right. It may be in the basement. The fallout shelter."

I nodded. "Probably."

"So, if you want to shut down Madox's ELF station, then *that* is where we shut it down."

"Absolutely." I suggested, "You excuse yourself to go to the ladies' room—which Madox will know takes fifteen to twenty minutes—find the transmitter, and smash it."

"Okay. And you can cover me by sticking the Bear-Banger up your ass and firing it."

Ms. Mayfield was in a strangely humorous mood tonight. It must be her way of dealing with stress.

I said to her, "As I mentioned earlier, the real purpose of this visit is not social—it is to place Bain Madox under arrest for . . . give me a Federal crime that fits."

"Kidnapping. He had to kidnap Harry before he assaulted him."

"Right. Kidnapping and assault. The state tries him for murder."

"Correct."

Actually, if Madox provoked me in any way, he wouldn't have to worry about *any* trial. I said to Kate, "It's good to be married to a lawyer."

"You *need* a full-time lawyer, John."

"Right."

"Also, to make an arrest, you need something aside from your suspicions."

"If we *don't* arrest him tonight," I said, "do you want to be responsible for four nuclear explosions tomorrow? Or *tonight*?"

"No . . . but, legalities aside, an arrest is not that easy at the Custer Hill Club." She pointed out, "There are only *two* of us, and many of them."

"We are the law."

"I know that, John, but—"

"Do you have that little card to read him his rights?"

"I think I can recite that without a card by now."

"Good. Do you have handcuffs?"

"No. Do you?"

"Not on me." I said, "We should have brought the duct tape. Maybe Madox has the shackles he used on Harry. Or, maybe I'll just kick him in the nuts."

"You seem very confident."

"I am very motivated."

"Good. By the way, why do we need these Bear-Bangers? We have guns and shields. Right?"

"Well . . ."

"Yeah, well. Okay, John, I'm with you. But don't get us into something you can't get us out of."

I may already have done that, but I said, "Just be alert, aware, and ready—like any other tricky arrest. We are the law, he is the criminal."

She had two words for me: "Remember Harry."

I looked at her and said, "Kate, that's why we're doing this alone. I really want to make this bust myself. Just me. And you, if you want."

We made eye contact, and she nodded. "Drive."

Kate seemed a little anxious about the evening, but she also seemed to be looking forward to it. I know this feeling very well. We're not in this business for the money. We're in it for the excitement, and for moments like this.

Duty, honor, country, service, truth, and justice are good. But you can do that from behind a desk.

In the end, you carry the gun and the shield out into

the field for the sole purpose of confronting the bad guys. The enemy. There is no other reason to be on the front lines.

Kate understood that. I understood it. And, in about an hour, Bain Madox would also understand it.

CHAPTER FORTY-SEVEN

We passed Rudy's darkened gas station and continued on into the state park preserve.

We approached Stark Road and saw a power-company truck parked on the side with its lights flashing, and I was sure this was the state police surveillance vehicle. I slowed down to be certain he saw us turning onto Stark Road.

As we continued on through the tunnel of trees, I said to Kate, "Okay, give the state police a call, and tell them that I need to speak to Major Schaeffer, and it's urgent."

Kate took her cell phone out of her bag, turned it on, and said, "I have no service."

"What do you mean? Madox's relay tower is only about four miles from here."

"I have no service."

I took my cell phone out and turned it on. No service. "Maybe we need to get closer." I gave her my phone.

I turned onto the logging road, and Kate, holding both cell phones, said, "Still no service."

"All right . . ." McCuen Pond Road was coming up, and I slowed down and hit my brights, hoping to see a stakeout vehicle, but there was no one at the T-intersection.

I made a left onto McCuen Pond Road and looked at my watch. It was 6:55 P.M. A few minutes later, we approached the lights and warning signs of the Custer Hill gate. I asked Kate, "Service?"

"No service."

"How could that be?"

"I don't know. Maybe Madox's tower is having a problem. Or maybe he shut it down."

"Why would he do that?"

"Let me think."

"Oh . . . yeah. He really is a paranoid asshole."

"A smart paranoid asshole." She asked me, "Do you want to turn around?"

"No. And leave the phones on."

"Okay, but no one will be able to pick up our signal here unless the cell tower at Custer Hill comes back on the air."

"It could just be a temporary glitch." But I doubted that. Now that we wanted to be located, we were electronically silent. Shit happens.

I slowed down at the speed bump, then stopped at the stop sign. The gate slid open a crack, and I could see my favorite security guard in the floodlit entrance to the property. He came toward us, and I stuck my Glock in my waistband. I said to Kate, "Be alert."

"Right. Ask him if you can borrow his landline phone

to call the state police to tell them we're at the Custer Hill Club."

I ignored the sarcasm and watched the security goon coming toward us at a leisurely pace. I said to Kate, "Anyway, I'm sure we were spotted by the state police stakeout."

"I'm sure you were, Rudy."

"Oh . . . oh, shit. That was pretty stupid."

She could have been angry or critical, but she patted my hand and said soothingly, "We all have stupid moments, John. I just wish you hadn't picked this particular time to have one."

I didn't reply but gave myself a mental slap on the face.

The neo-Nazi got to the van, and I rolled down the window. He seemed surprised to see me in what he probably knew to be Rudy's van. He looked at Kate, then said to us, "Mr. Madox is expecting you."

"You sure about that?"

He didn't answer but stood there, and I wanted to smash his idiotic face. I noticed his name tag. Mom and Dad had christened their little boy Luther. They probably couldn't spell Lucifer. I asked him, "Is anyone else coming to dinner, Lucifer?"

"Luther. No. Just you."

"Sir."

"Sir."

"And ma'am. Let's try again."

He took a deep breath to show me he was trying to control his temper, then said, "Just you, sir, and you, ma'am."

"Good. Practice that."

"Yes, sir. You know the way. Sir. Please drive slowly and carefully this time. *Sir.*"

"Fuck you." I proceeded to the gate, which was now fully open.

Kate asked, "What did he mean by 'this time'?"

"Oh, he and his buddy there"—I slowed down at the gatehouse and blasted the air horn out the window at the other guard, which caused him to jump about five feet—"tried to throw themselves under the wheels of my car this afternoon." I drove on.

"Why did you do that? You scared the hell out of me."

"Kate, these two bastards, and their pals, were the guys who grabbed Harry on Saturday. And for all I know, one or two of them helped murder him on Sunday."

She nodded.

"We'll see every one of these guys in court."

She reminded me, "We may see every one of them in the next half hour."

"Good. I'll save the taxpayers some money."

"Calm down."

I didn't reply.

As we proceeded up the long winding drive, motion sensors turned on the lamppost lights.

Under one of the lampposts, I saw what looked like a big wood chipper on the lawn, which reminded me of the Mafia expression about putting their enemies through the wood chipper. I always got a laugh out of that for some reason, and I smiled.

Kate asked, "What's funny?"

"I forgot." Less funny was that there weren't any trees or dead branches on the lawn.

Normally, you don't go into situations like this without backup. But this situation was anything but normal. The irony here was that we'd been hiding from the ATTF, Liam Griffith, the FBI, and the state police—and now that I wanted everyone to know where we were, only Bain Madox knew.

When I get really paranoid, like now, I start to imagine that the CIA is involved. And considering what this was all about, why would they *not* be involved?

Kate asked me, "What are you thinking about?"

"The CIA."

"Right. This, as it turns out, would also involve them."

"It would." Yet, you rarely *see* them or hear from them. That's why they're called spooks, or ghosts, and if you see them at all, it's usually at the end. Like about now.

I said to Kate, "In fact, I see Ted Nash's hand in this."

She looked at me. "Ted Nash? John, Ted Nash is dead."

"I know. I just like to hear you say it."

She didn't think that was so funny, but I did.

Up ahead in the turnaround circle was a flagpole, and flying from the pole was the American flag and the Seventh Cavalry pennant, illuminated by two spotlights.

I informed Kate, "A pennant or banner means the commander is on the premises."

"I know that. Didn't you ever notice my pennant on the bedpost?"

I smiled, and we held hands. She said to me, "I'm a little . . . apprehensive."

I reminded her, "We are not alone. We have the full power and authority of the United States government behind us."

She looked over her shoulder and said, "I don't see anyone else here, John."

I was glad to see she was maintaining her sense of humor. I gave her hand a squeeze and stopped the van under the portico. "Hungry?"

"Famished."

We got out and climbed the steps to the porch. I rang the bell.

CHAPTER FORTY-EIGHT

C arl answered the door and said to us, "Mr. Madox has been expecting you."

I replied, "And good evening to you, Carl."

I'm sure he wanted to say, "Fuck you," but he didn't, and showed us into the atrium foyer. He said, "I'll take your coats."

Kate responded, "We'll keep them."

Carl seemed unhappy about that, but said, "Cocktails will be in the bar room. Please follow me."

We went through the door near the staircase and walked toward the rear of the lodge.

The house was quiet, and I didn't see, hear, or sense anyone around.

I still had my Glock in my waistband, but it was covered by my shirt and jacket. My off-duty .38 was in my ankle holster. Kate had slipped her Glock in her jacket pocket, and, like most, if not all, FBI agents, she had no second weapon—except the BearBanger somewhere in her jeans. My BearBanger was clipped like a penlight in my shirt pocket. My two extra magazines were in my jacket, and Kate's four were in her handbag and her jacket. We were loaded for bear, or Bain.

I wasn't expecting any funny business while we were in motion—also, I figured that Madox wanted to at least say hello and size up the situation before he made a move.

On that subject, I wondered if he would opt for a macho move, like an armed confrontation. Or, would he take the less confrontational approach, like a Mickey Finn in our drinks, followed by a short trip through the wood chipper?

If Madox was going to go military on us, then I was playing the odds that not all of his security guards were trusted killers, so maybe we'd have to deal with only Madox, Carl, and two or three other guys.

A more positive but probably unrealistic thought was that there wasn't going to be a poisoning or shoot-out at the Custer Hill Club, and that Bain Madox, when confronted with our evidence and placed under arrest, would realize that the game was up and admit to murdering Federal Agent Harry Muller, then lead us to the ELF transmitter. Case closed.

I glanced at Kate, who looked calm and composed. We made eye contact, and I smiled and winked at her.

I also got a look at Carl's face. Usually, you can tell by the face and body language if a guy knows that something unpleasant is about to happen. Carl didn't seem tense, but neither was he relaxed.

Carl stopped in front of a set of double doors, one of which had a brass plate that said BAR ROOM. He knocked, opened one door, and said to us, "After you."

"No," I said, "after *you*."

He hesitated, then entered and motioned to the left, where Mr. Bain Madox stood behind a mahogany bar, smoking and listening on the phone, which I noticed was a landline, not a cell.

Across the dimly lit room was a burning fireplace, to the right of which was a set of drawn drapes that may have covered a window, or a set of double doors leading outside.

I heard Madox say, "All right. I have company. Call me later." He hung up, smiled, and said, "Welcome. Come in."

Kate and I gave the place a quick look, then took different paths around the furniture to the bar. I heard the door close behind us.

Madox put out his cigarette. "I wasn't sure you'd gotten Carl's message at The Point, and I hoped you hadn't forgotten."

Kate and I reached the bar, and I said, "We've been looking forward to the evening."

Kate added, "Thank you for inviting us."

We all shook hands, and Madox asked, "What can I get you?"

I was glad he didn't say, "Name your poison," and I inquired, "What are you drinking?"

He indicated a bottle on the bar and replied, "My private-label single malt, which you enjoyed yesterday."

"Good. I'll take it straight up." In case you drugged the soda water or ice cubes.

Kate said, "Make it two."

Madox poured two scotches into crystal glasses, then refreshed his own drink from the same bottle, which may have been his polite way of showing us that the scotch wasn't going to kill us.

True to his word, Madox was dressed casually in the same outfit he'd worn this afternoon—blue blazer, white golf shirt, and jeans. So Kate and I would feel comfortable when we arrested him.

He raised his glass and said, "Not a happy occasion, but to happier times."

We clinked glasses and drank. He swallowed. I swallowed. Kate swallowed.

I could see the darkened room in the bar mirror, and there was another set of open doors at the far end of the room that led into what appeared to be a card room or game room.

Also, behind the bar, to the left of the liquor shelves, was a small door that probably led to a storage area or wine cellar. In fact, there were too many doors in this place, plus drapes drawn across what could be doors leading outside. And I don't like standing at the bar with my back to a room, with a guy behind the bar who could suddenly drop out of sight. So I suggested, "Why don't we sit by the fire?"

Madox said, "Good idea." He came around the bar as Kate and I walked to a grouping of four leather club chairs near the fireplace.

Before he could seat us, Kate and I took the chairs facing each other, leaving Madox to take one of the chairs facing the fireplace, with his back to the closed double doors. From where I sat, I could see the open doors to the card room, and Kate could see the bar where the small side door was.

Having claimed my seat, I stood and went to the drapes to the right of the fireplace and said, "Do you mind?" as I pulled them open. There was indeed a set of French doors there, which led to a dark terrace.

I came back to my chair, sat, and noted, "That's a nice view."

Madox did not comment.

Basically, all bases were covered, and I was sure that Bain Madox—ex–infantry officer—appreciated our concern about fields of fire.

Madox asked us, "Would you like to take your jackets off?"

Kate replied, "No, thanks. I'm still a little cold."

I didn't answer, and I noticed he wasn't taking off his blazer, probably for the same reason we weren't taking off our jackets. I didn't see a bulge, but I knew he was packing something, somewhere.

I surveyed the room. It was more in the style of a gentlemen's club rather than an Adirondack lodge. There was an expensive-looking Persian carpet on the floor, and lots of mahogany, green leather, and polished brass. There was not a dead animal in sight, and I hoped it stayed that way.

Madox said, "This room is an exact replica of the one in my New York apartment, which in turn I copied from a London club."

I inquired, "Isn't that a little confusing after you've had a few?"

He smiled politely, then said, "So, let's get rid of some business." He turned to me. "I have the duty roster of my security staff who were here over the weekend, and I'll see that you have it before you leave."

"Good. And your house staff?"

"I have a complete list of the staff who were working on the weekend."

"And the security log and the security tapes?"

He nodded. "All copied for you."

"Terrific." And this left the sticky question of his rich-and-famous weekend guests. "How about the list of your houseguests?"

"I need to think about that."

"What's to think about?"

"Well, obviously, the names of these people are not everyone's business." He added, "Which I guess was why the government sent Mr. Muller here to get these names by . . . devious means. And now you want me to give you these names, voluntarily."

I reminded him, "Harry Muller is dead, and this is now an investigation into his death." I added, "You said this afternoon that you'd have those names for us."

"I'm very aware of that, and I've called my attorney, who will get back to me tonight. If he tells me to turn over those names, I will give them to you tonight."

Kate said, "If he doesn't, we could subpoena that information."

Madox replied, "That may be the best way for me to

give you those names." He explained, "That would take me off the hook with my guests."

Basically, this was all bullshit to make us think he had some serious issues to consider. Meanwhile, all he was really thinking about was his ELF signal to Sandland, and how best to get Corey and Mayfield into the wood chipper.

He informed us, "My attorney tells me that the Federal government has no jurisdiction in a state homicide case."

I let Kate handle that one, and she said, "Any murder charges that come out of this investigation will be brought by New York State. In the meantime, we're investigating the disappearance of a Federal agent, and his possible kidnapping, which is a Federal crime, as well as a possible criminal assault on the deceased agent." She asked Madox, "Would you like me to speak to your attorney?"

"No. I'm sure the United States government can find a Federal law to fit any crime these days, including jaywalking."

Special Agent Mayfield replied, "I think this is a bit more serious than that."

Madox let that slide, so I changed the subject to put everyone at ease. "Good scotch."

"Thank you. Remind me to give you a bottle before you leave." He said to Kate, "Not many women are single malt drinkers."

"Around 26 Fed, I'm just one of the boys."

He smiled at her, and responded, "I think they need eyeglasses at 26 Fed."

Good old Bain. A man's man, and a ladies' man. A real sociopathic charmer.

Anyway, Madox figured we were finished with business and continued to charm Ms. Mayfield. "So, how was your yodeling class?"

Kate seemed a little confused by the question, so I said helpfully, "*Yoga* class."

"Oh . . ." said Mr. Madox. "I thought you said *yodeling* class." He chuckled and admitted to Kate, "My hearing is not what it used to be."

Kate glanced at me. "It was a good class."

Madox asked her, "How are you enjoying The Point?"

"It's very nice."

"I hope you're staying for dinner. I promised Mr. Corey I could do better than Henri."

Kate replied, "We'd planned to stay for dinner."

"Good. In fact, since there's no one here, and no one would know, you're welcome to stay overnight."

I didn't know if that included me, but I replied, "We may take you up on that."

"Good. It's a long trip back to The Point—especially if you've been drinking, which you're not doing enough of." He smiled at me and expanded on the subject by saying, "Also, you're not driving a vehicle that you're familiar with."

I didn't reply.

He continued, "Let's see—yesterday, you had a Taurus; this morning, you had a Hyundai; and tonight, you have Rudy's van. Have you found something you like?"

I hate wiseasses, unless they're me. I said to him, "I was just about to ask you to loan me a Jeep."

He didn't respond to that but inquired, "Why are you changing vehicles so often?"

To confuse him with the truth, I replied, "We're on the run from the law."

He grinned.

Kate said, "We've had problems with our two rental vehicles."

"Ah. Well, I'm sure they would have given you another one—but that was good of Rudy to loan you his van." He returned to the investigation. "I've made some inquiries, and this suspected homicide hasn't even come to the attention of the sheriff's office." He informed us, "They're still ruling it an accident."

I noted, "This investigation is Federal and state, not local. What's your point?"

"No point. Just an observation."

"I think you should leave the jurisdictional aspects of this case to the law."

He didn't answer, and neither did he seem annoyed at the rebuke. Obviously, he wanted us to know that he knew more than he should know—including, possibly, that Detective Corey and FBI Agent Mayfield were not in close contact with their colleagues, and wanted to stay that way by switching vehicles every twelve hours.

I didn't know if Bain Madox knew that for sure, but he definitely knew that we hadn't made a cell-phone call within ten or fifteen miles of here.

So we sat in neutral for a minute—logs blazing, scotch

and crystal glistening in the fire—then Madox said to Kate, "I expressed my condolences to Mr. Corey, and I'd like to do the same to you. Was Mr. Muller a friend of yours, also?"

Kate replied, "He was a close colleague."

"Well, I'm truly sorry. And I'm very upset that Mr. Corey believes that one of my security staff may have been involved in Mr. Muller's death."

"I also believe that. And on the subject of upset, you can imagine how upset Detective Muller's children are to learn that their father is not only dead but was probably murdered." She stared at our host.

Madox returned the stare but did not respond.

Kate continued, "And the rest of his family, and his friends and colleagues. When it's murder, the grief turns to anger very quickly." She informed our host, "I'm damned angry."

Madox nodded slowly. "I can understand that. And I sincerely hope that none of my security people were involved, but if they were, I also want to see this person brought to justice."

Kate said, "He will be."

I opened a new possibility and said, "It could even have been one of your house staff . . . or your house-guests."

He reminded me, "You thought it was one of my security guards. Now, it sounds as though you're on a fishing expedition."

"A hunting expedition."

"Whatever." He asked me, "Can you be more specific

about why you think one of my staff—or houseguests—was involved in what you believe is a homicide?"

I think we all knew that we really meant Bain Madox—and somehow, I didn't think he really gave a shit.

Nevertheless, I thought that some inside information about the case might shake him up, so I said to him, "Okay, one, I have solid evidence that Detective Muller was actually on your property."

I looked at Madox, but he had no reaction.

I continued, "Two, we believe through forensic evidence that Detective Muller was actually *in* this house."

Again, no reaction.

Okay, asshole. "Three, we have to assume that Detective Muller was detained by your security people. We also have evidence that his camper was originally close to your property, then moved." I explained all of that in detail.

Still no reaction, except a nod, as though this were interesting.

I outlined some of the case to Mr. Bain Madox, describing how the murder was done by at least two persons—one driving the victim's camper, the other in a separate vehicle that I said could have been a Jeep, or an all-terrain vehicle, based on two separate sets of tire marks, which we actually didn't find, but he wouldn't know that for sure.

I lied that the initial toxicology report showed strong sedatives in the victim's blood, then I described how I thought the actual murder took place with the victim drugged, and held in a kneeling position with the binocular strap, and so forth.

Madox again nodded as though this were still interesting but somehow abstract.

If I expected some reaction—like shock, disbelief, discomfort, or amazement—then I was going to be disappointed.

I took a sip of scotch and stared at him.

The room was silent, except for the crackling fire, then Madox said, "I'm impressed that you could gather so much evidence in so short a time."

I informed him, "The first forty-eight hours is the critical period."

"Yes. I've heard that." He asked me, "How did forensic evidence point back to this lodge?"

"If you really want to know, I collected rug fibers, plus human and dog hairs when I was here, and they matched what was found on Detective Muller's clothes and body."

"Did they?" He looked at me and said, "I don't recall giving you permission to do that."

"But you would have."

He let that alone, and said to me, "That was very quick lab work."

"This is a *homicide* investigation. The victim was a Federal agent."

"All right . . . so, from these fibers . . . ?"

I gave him a quick course in fiber analysis. "The fibers on the victim match the ones I found here. The dog hairs will probably match the hairs on your dog, what's-his-name—"

"Kaiser Wilhelm."

"Whatever. And the human hairs found on Detective Muller's body, plus whatever other DNA turns up on the victim's clothes or body, will lead us to the killer or killers."

We made eye contact, and he still wasn't blinking, so I said, "With your help, we can make a list of everyone who was here over the weekend, then get hair and DNA samples from them, and some fibers from clothing, such as those camouflage uniforms your security people wear. Understand?"

He nodded.

"Speaking of your army, where and how did you recruit these guys?"

"They're all former military."

"I see. So, we have to assume they're all well trained in the use of weapons, and other types of force."

He informed me, "More important, they're all well disciplined. And as any military man will tell you, I'd rather have ten disciplined and well-trained men than ten thousand untrained and undisciplined troops."

"Don't forget loyal, and motivated by a noble cause."

"Goes without saying."

Kate asked our host, "How many security guards are actually here this evening?"

He seemed to read the subtext, and smiled slightly, the way Count Dracula would do if his dinner guest inquired, "So, what time does the sun rise around here?"

Madox answered, "I think there are ten men on-duty tonight."

There was a knock on the door, and it opened, revealing Carl wheeling in a cart, atop which was a large covered tray.

Carl carried the tray to the coffee table, set it down, and removed the cover.

And there, on a silver tray, were dozens of pigs-in-the-blanket, the crust slightly brown, just the way I like it. In the center of the tray were two crystal bowls—one holding a thick, dark deli-style mustard, and the other, a thin, pukey yellow mustard.

Our host said to us, "I have a confession to make. I called Henri and asked him if either of you had expressed any food preference, and—voilà!" He smiled.

That wasn't the confession I was hoping for, and he knew that, but this wasn't bad either.

Carl asked, "Is there anything else?"

Madox replied, "No, but"—he looked at his watch—"see how dinner is coming along."

"Yes, sir." Carl left, and Madox said, "No woodcock tonight—just plain steak and potatoes." He turned to me. "Have one of these."

I caught Kate's eye, and clearly she didn't think I could resist a little piggy, drugged or not. And she was right. I could *smell* the aroma of the crust and the fatty beef hot dogs.

They all had toothpicks stuck in them—red, blue, and yellow—so all I had to do was guess which color marked the safe piggies. I chose blue, my favorite color, and picked one up, then dipped it in the deli mustard.

Kate said, "John, you should save your appetite for dinner."

"I'll just have a few." I popped the pig in my mouth. It tasted great—hot, firm crust, spicy mustard.

Madox said to Kate, "Please help yourself."

"No, thank you." She shot me a concerned look and said to him, "You go ahead."

Madox also picked a pig with a blue toothpick, but chose the yellow mustard. So maybe I picked the wrong mustard.

Actually, I felt fine and had another, this one with the yellow mustard, just to be on the safe side.

Madox chewed, swallowed, and said, "Not bad." He chose a red toothpick and offered the piggy to Kate. "Are you sure?"

"No, thank you."

He ate it himself, this time with deli mustard. So I had another.

Hot dogs made me think of Kaiser Wilhelm. His absence at his master's side was a case of The Dog That Did Not Fart in the Night.

Dogs alert their masters, and everyone else, that someone is approaching—and I had the strong feeling that Madox did not want Kate and I to know if anyone was outside those doors.

Also, if Kaiser Wilhelm was here, I'd feed him about twenty pigs to see if he keeled over, or if Madox stopped me.

On the other hand, maybe I was over-analyzing this, as I tend to do when my bloodhound instincts are aroused.

I thought it was time to increase the discomfort level,

so I said to Madox, "I, too, have a confession to make. You know about the Borgias. Right?"

He nodded.

"Well, after you invited us here, we got this toxicology report on Harry Muller showing high levels of sedatives in his blood. And, Kate has been . . . well, concerned about . . . you know."

Madox looked at me, then Kate, then back at me, and said, "No. I don't know." He added in a curt tone, "And perhaps I don't want to know."

I continued, "I guess this comes under the category of being bad dinner guests, but Kate . . . and I guess I . . . are a little concerned that you may have . . . a staff member who has access to powerful sedatives, and this could be the person who used them on the deceased victim."

Mr. Madox did not comment on that, but he did light a cigarette without asking if anyone minded.

I made eye contact with Kate, and she seemed more uncomfortable than Bain, who actually appeared offended.

To make him feel better, I took another pig-in-the-blanket—blue toothpick, yellow mustard—and popped it in my mouth. "On the other hand," I went on, "it appears that Detective Muller was sedated by means of a tranquilizer dart, followed by two hypodermic injections to keep him sedated." I looked at Madox, but there was no reaction. "So, maybe we can rule out a Mickey Finn in the scotch or knockout drops in the mustard tonight."

Madox sipped his scotch, drew on his cigarette, then asked me, "Are you suggesting that someone here is trying to . . . sedate you?"

"Well," I replied, "I'm just extrapolating from the

evidence at hand." I made a little joke to lighten the moment. "A lot of people say I need sedating, and maybe it would do me some good—if it wasn't followed by a bullet in my back."

Madox sat quietly in his nice green leather chair, blowing smoke rings, then he glanced at Kate and pointed out to her, "I think if you believe that, then dinner is not going to be much fun."

Good one, Bain. I really liked this guy. Too bad he had to die, or if he was lucky, spend the rest of his life in a place less comfortable than this.

Kate decided to take the offensive. "I'm interested in Carl."

Madox stared at her, then said, "Carl is my oldest and most trusted employee and friend."

"That's why I'm interested in him."

Madox replied sharply, "That's almost the same as an accusation against me."

"Perhaps Detective Corey and I should have informed you that no one who was on this property this weekend is above suspicion. And that includes you."

At this point, Madox should have told us to forget dinner and asked us to leave his house. But he wasn't doing that because he was no more through with us than we were with him.

In fact, this is the point where you've crossed the threshold, and now you begin the transition from the unknown suspect to the person you're speaking to. Hopefully, the suspect has already said something incriminating, or will when you start to bully him. Lacking that, you need to rely on the existing evidence and good hunches. It all ends with me saying something like, "Mr. Madox, I'm placing you under arrest for the murder of Federal Agent Harry Muller. Please come with us."

Then, you take the guy downtown and book him. Or, in this case, I'd have to take him to state police headquarters, which would make Major Schaeffer happy.

On that subject, I was starting to think that Schaeffer's surveillance team hadn't seen us going to the Custer Hill Club, or if they had, and reported it, Schaeffer was not doing anything about it. And why would he? More important, I pictured Tom Walsh having dinner or watching TV instead of reading Kate's e-mail to him. Actually, I had the feeling that the cavalry would not be arriving soon, or ever. So, it was up to us to make the arrest.

This case, however, had some unique problems, like the suspect's private army, and some familiar problems, like the suspect's status as a rich and powerful man.

And, of course, aside from the homicide, there was the suspicion that the suspect was involved in a conspiracy to nuke the planet. And that was my more immediate concern, and my and Kate's jurisdiction.

So, with that in mind, it was time to go nuclear, and I said to Bain Madox, "Speaking of houseguests, you had a guest who arrived Sunday, and has apparently not left yet. Will he be joining us for dinner?"

Madox stood suddenly, then walked to the bar. As he poured a short one, he remarked, "I'm not sure what—or who—you're talking about."

I didn't like him being behind me, so I, too, stood, and motioned for Kate to stand. As I turned toward the bar, I said to Madox, "Dr. Mikhail Putyov. Nuclear physicist."

"Oh. Michael. He's gone."

"Gone where?"

"I have no idea. Why?"

"Well, if he's not here," I said, "then he seems to be missing."

"Missing from where?"

"Home and office." I informed him, "Putyov's not supposed to leave home without telling the FBI where he's going."

"Really? Why is that?"

"I think it's in his contract." I asked, "Is he a friend of yours?"

Madox leaned back against the bar with his glass in his hand, and seemed to be in deep thought.

I asked, "Was that a tough question?"

He smiled, then said, "No. I'm considering my reply." He looked at me, then at Kate. "Dr. Putyov and I have a professional relationship."

It sort of surprised me that he'd say that, but I guess we all realized that it was time to be honest, open, and sensitive to one another's needs and feelings. Then we could all hug and have a good cry together, before I arrested or shot him.

I inquired, "What *kind* of professional relationship?"

He waved his hand in dismissal. "Oh, John—can I call you John?"

"Sure, Bain."

"Good. So, what *kind* of professional relationship? Is that the question? Okay, how can I describe this . . . ?"

I suggested, "Start with nuclear weapons miniaturization."

He looked at me, nodded, and said, "Well, that's a good start."

"Okay. Can I also say suitcase nukes?"

He smiled and nodded again.

Well, this was easier than I expected, which might not actually be a good sign, but I continued, "Two more houseguests—Paul Dunn, adviser to the president on matters of national security, and Edward Wolffer, deputy secretary of defense."

"What about them?"

"They were here—correct?"

"They were." He added, "You can see why I don't want people snooping around."

"You're allowed to have famous and powerful friends over for the weekend, Bain."

"Thank you. The point is, it's no one's business."

"But in this case, it might be my business."

"Actually, John, you may be right."

"I *am* right. Also, James Hawkins, Air Force general and member of the Joint Chiefs of Staff. He was here, too. Right?"

"Right."

"Who else?"

"Oh, about a dozen other men, none of them important to the business at hand. Except Scott Landsdale. He's the CIA liaison to the White House." He added, "That's secret information, so it can't leave this room."

"Okay . . ." I didn't have that name, but I'd be disappointed if there wasn't a CIA guy involved in . . . whatever. I said, "Your secret's safe with us, Bain."

Madox explained to Kate and me, "Those four men make up my Executive Board."

"What Executive Board?"

"Of this club."

"Right. So, what did you guys talk about?" I asked.

"Project Green and Wild Fire."

"Right. So, how's that going?"

"Fine." He looked at his watch, so I looked at mine. It was 7:33, and hopefully Walsh was getting around to reading his personal e-mail. Hopefully, too, the state troopers would be arriving soon. But I wasn't counting on that.

Madox said, "Well, now I have some questions for *you*. Are you alone tonight?"

I did a good imitation of a laugh. "Sure."

"Well," he said, "it doesn't matter at this point."

I didn't want to hear that.

He asked, "How did you figure this out?"

I was happy to reply, "Harry Muller. He wrote us a note on the lining of his pants pocket."

"Oh . . . well, that was smart."

I said to him, "Fuck you."

He completely ignored that and asked me, "Have you ever heard of Wild Fire?" He gave me a hint. "Highly sensitive government protocol."

"To be honest with you, Bain, I don't read all my memos from Washington." I glanced at Kate, who was standing with her back to the fireplace, her hand in her gun pocket, and asked her, "Kate? You ever hear of Wild Fire?"

"No."

I turned back to Madox, shrugged, and said, "I guess we missed that memo. What did it say?"

He seemed impatient with me and responded, "It wouldn't be in a *memo*, John. I think you have most of what you need, so don't be intellectually lazy and expect me to put it all together for you."

I said to Kate, "He's calling us lazy. After all the work we've done."

Madox admitted to both of us, "Actually, you seem to have solved the homicide case, and you're closer to the other thing than I'd thought. But you need to put it together."

"Okay." I went to the French doors and opened them.

It was a nice night, and a bright half-moon was almost directly overhead, lighting up the clearing behind the lodge.

Off in the distance, I could see the metal roof of the generator building, and the three chimneys belching smoke into the air. Also, there were two all-terrain vehicles and a black Jeep prowling around back there, as though they were guarding the building.

I said to Madox, "I see the diesel engines are running."

"That's right. I just had them serviced."

I turned from the double doors and walked back to where Madox was still leaning against the bar. "Six thousand kilowatts."

"Right. Who told you that? Potsdam Diesel?"

I didn't answer his question. "Where's the ELF transmitter?"

He didn't seem surprised and replied, "I'm not overly impressed that you figured out this was an ELF station. It's all there for anyone to see—the generators, the cables, the location here in the Adirondacks—"

"Where's the transmitter, Bain?"

"I'll show it to you. Later."

I said to him, "Now would be a really good time."

He ignored that, and we eyeballed each other. He didn't look like a man with a serious problem. He asked me, "So, have you come to any startling conclusions?" He turned to Kate. "Kate? A eureka moment?"

Kate said to him, "Four suitcase nuclear weapons were flown on your two aircraft to LA and San Francisco."

"Correct. And?"

She continued, "And your ELF transmitter will send a signal to detonate those devices when they reach their final destinations."

"Well . . . close."

I was getting a little tired of this bullshit, so I said to Madox, "The game's over, pal. I'm placing you under arrest for the murder of Federal Agent Harry Muller. Turn around, put your hands on the bar, and spread your legs." I said, "Kate, cover me." I stepped toward Madox, who wasn't doing what I told him to do.

I heard Kate say, "John . . ."

I glanced back and saw Carl at the door with a raised shotgun directed at Kate.

Across the room, another man stood at the open doors of the game room with an M16 rifle raised and pointed.

A third man walked in through the doors from the terrace, aiming an M16 at me.

As they both moved closer into the room, I saw that the guy who'd come from the game room was Luther, and the guy from the terrace was the guard at the gatehouse, whom I'd blasted with my air horn.

I glanced back at Madox and saw he was holding a big Army Colt .45 automatic, pointed at my face.

Well, I couldn't say I hadn't seen this coming, but it still seemed unreal.

Then Madox said to us, "You knew you weren't getting out of here alive."

CHAPTER FORTY-NINE

Kate and I made eye contact, and she didn't look frightened; she looked pissed off about something. Maybe me.

Madox said, "All right, both of you, facedown on the floor." He added, in case we didn't know, "One false move and you're both dead." He further added, "No kidding."

So we got facedown on the floor, which was the correct police and military procedure for disarming prisoners. Obviously, we were dealing with people who knew how this was done.

I heard Madox say, "Kate, you first. Weapons. Slowly. John, keep your face in the carpet, and don't even *breathe*."

I couldn't see what was going on, but I heard what I thought was the sound of a boot or shoe kicking Kate's

Glock across the carpet, and Madox said to her, "Do you always carry your gun in your pocket?"

She didn't reply, and Madox continued, "A lot of good it did you." Then, he asked her, "Any more weapons?"

"No."

"Where's your holster?"

"Small of my back."

He ordered, "Take her holster, and take off her watch, her shoes, socks, and jacket, then wand her."

I heard the sounds of these items being removed and tossed aside, then Madox said, "Frisk her."

Next, I heard Kate say, "Get your fucking hands off me."

Madox retorted, "Do you want a strip search, or a frisk and wanding?"

No reply. Then Luther's voice said, "Clean."

Madox ordered, "Turn over."

I heard her turn over, then a few seconds later, the wand made a hit, and Carl asked, "What's that?"

Kate replied, "My fucking belt and zipper. What's it look like?"

Madox said, "Take your belt off."

I didn't know if they wanded her again, but I didn't hear a buzz, so the BearBanger hadn't been detected.

Madox instructed, "Carl, pat her down."

I couldn't see where he patted her, but she said to Carl, "Having fun?"

A few seconds later, Carl said, "Clean."

I didn't know *where* that BearBanger was on Kate's body, but either it had escaped detection or they had it and didn't know what they had.

Madox said to the other security guy, "Derek, put the shackles on her."

I heard metallic sounds as the shackles were clamped and locked, then Madox said, "Your turn, John. You know the drill. Gun first."

Still lying facedown, I brought my hand under my chest as though reaching for my gun, and I pulled the Bear-Banger out of my shirt pocket, then laid it on the carpet under my stomach.

Madox had apparently moved behind me, near my feet. "Don't even *think* about being a hero, or your wife is dead." He added, "Yes, I know she's your wife."

"Fuck you." I pulled my Glock from my belt and slid it across the carpet.

"What else? No lie, John, or I put a .45 slug in your ass."

"Ankle holster. Left side."

Someone pulled up my pants leg and took my holster and .38 revolver.

Then, two guys pulled off my shoes and socks, and my leather jacket and watch. Madox said, "Wand him."

One guy, I think Luther, walked around me with the wand, but nothing set it off.

Madox continued, "Frisk him."

Someone patted down my legs, took my wallet, then patted down my back. Luther reported, "Clean."

I said, "Bain, Luther was squeezing my ass."

Luther wasn't amused and said, "Shut your fucking mouth, *sir*."

"You're supposed to *pat*, not *squeeze*."

I felt a heavy boot smashing into my right rib cage as Luther shouted, "Asshole!"

Madox warned Luther, "Don't ever do that without my permission."

After I caught my breath, I couldn't resist pointing out, "Not *that* well disciplined, Bain."

Madox said, "Shut up." He informed me, "I really don't like your sarcasm." He snapped, "Roll over!"

I needed to roll over without exposing the Bear-Banger on the carpet under my stomach. So, instead of doing a simple sideways roll, I made a pretense of being in pain from the kick in the ribs and did a passable imitation of a beached whale flopping around so that I wound up in the same place on the carpet with the BearBanger under my back.

I could see Madox now, standing near my feet, and Carl standing near Kate, pointing the shotgun at her.

Luther was off to my right side, holding the wand, which he was slapping into his hand, as though it were a billy club that he was thinking about swinging at my head.

The other security guy, Derek, was someplace I couldn't see from where I was lying, but I figured he'd repositioned himself behind my head with his M16 pointing down at me.

The only good news here was that Madox, for some reason, hadn't just opened fire.

He seemed to sense what I was thinking and said to me, "If you're wondering why I'm taking all this time and trouble with you two, the answer is I need some information from you. Also, I don't want blood on this Persian carpet."

Both those reasons sounded good.

Madox instructed, "Take off your belt."

I unbuckled it, pulled it through the loops, and tossed it aside.

He said to Derek, "Shackle him," and Derek ordered, "Raise your legs."

I raised my legs, and Derek slapped the ankle bracelets on and locked them in place. I was surprised how heavy they were, and I dropped my legs, causing the shackles to rattle.

Luther pulled the pen out of my shirt pocket, then passed the wand over me. My zipper also set it off, so Luther stuck the wand down my pants and said, "No brass balls, Colonel."

Everyone got a little chuckle out of that, except me and Kate.

It occurred to me that I'd pissed off everyone in this room—maybe including Kate—and that though they'd been mostly professional so far, it could get very personal very quickly. So I thought, for my wife's sake, I should try to keep my mouth shut.

I looked over at Kate, who was lying about ten feet from me, also on her back, and also wearing shackles. We made eye contact, and I said to her, "It's going to be okay when they get here."

"I know."

Of course, it wasn't a matter of "when" but a matter of "if."

Madox barked, "Shut up. Speak only when spoken to." He said to Luther, "Frisk him again."

Luther did a rough frisk, going so far as to stick his thumb in my testicles, then said, "Clean."

Madox moved to the bar and started going through our jackets, credentials, shoes, and belts, then he dumped the contents of Kate's handbag on the bar and rummaged through the items. He said to us, "I count six fully loaded magazines. Did you think you were going to have a fire-fight?"

The other three idiots laughed.

I couldn't resist saying, "Fuck you."

Madox informed me, "That's what your friend Harry kept saying. Fuck you. Fuck you. Do you have anything *intelligent* to say?"

"Yeah. You're still under arrest."

He thought that was funny and said, "So are you."

Madox was still going through our things on the bar, and I saw him take the batteries out of our cell phones, then examine my pen. He still hadn't found Kate's BearBanger, so I hoped she still had it.

Madox said, "Well, here's Detective Muller's credential case. John, why do you have that?"

"To give it to his family."

"I see. And who's going to give *your* badge to your family after you're dead?"

"Is that a rhetorical question?"

"You wish it was."

He had our notebooks now, and I knew he couldn't read my notes because no one, myself included, can read my handwriting. But he said to Kate, whose handwriting is very neat, "I see you have a logical mind. Rare for a woman."

She replied, of course, "Fuck you."

He ignored that as he flipped through her notebook. "Kate, does anyone know you're here?"

"Just the FBI and the state police, who are on their way."

"If there was anything like that happening at state police headquarters, I'd know about it."

That was not what we wanted to hear.

He asked me, "John, what do they know at 26 Fed?"

"Everything."

"I don't think so."

"Then don't ask."

"You were seen speaking to Harry, Friday afternoon as you both got on the elevator at 26 Fed. What did you speak about?"

I really didn't want to hear that Bain Madox had a source inside 26 Federal Plaza.

"John?"

"We didn't talk business."

"All right . . . I'm a little pressed for time, John, so we can continue this later."

"Later is good."

"But I'm not going to be so nice later."

"You're not so nice *now*, Bain."

He laughed and said, "You ain't seen nothing yet, *pal*."

I advised him, "Go fuck yourself."

He was standing directly over me now, with those hawk eyes staring down at me like he was in flight and he'd spotted an injured animal on the ground.

He said to me, "There are two kinds of interrogations. I don't know about you, John, but I actually prefer the kind without blood and broken bones, and screams for mercy." He turned from me and said, "Kate? How about you?"

She didn't reply.

He continued on that subject. "Also, there are two ways to go through the wood chipper—dead or alive." He informed us, "Putyov went through dead because that was just a killing of convenience. But you two piss me off. However, if you cooperate, I'll give you my word of honor that you'll have a quick, merciful death by a gunshot to the head before you go through the wood chipper and become bear food. Okay? Deal? John? Kate?"

I couldn't quite see what was in that deal for me, but to buy a little time, I said, "Deal."

"Good." Madox said, "All right, you asked to see my ELF transmitter. So, I'll show it to you."

"Actually," I said, "I'll just take those lists of your houseguests and staff, and we'll be on our way."

"John, this is not funny."

It was Madox speaking, but it could just as well have been Kate.

I could see and hear all four men moving around the room, then Madox said, "Okay, Mr. and Mrs. Corey, you can stand now. Hands on your heads."

I began to sit up and grimaced from the pain in my ribs, which was not imaginary anymore. I put my hand behind my back to push up, palmed the BearBanger, and stuck it in the back of my tightie whities, then got to my feet. So far, so good.

I turned toward Kate, who was standing and looking at me. I said to her, "You're going to have to bear up later."

She nodded.

Madox reminded me, "Shut up." He glanced at his watch, then said to Carl, "Let's move out."

Carl ordered, "Follow me. Ten-foot intervals."

Carl headed toward the open doors of the card room, and Madox said to us, "Move. Hands on your heads."

We followed Carl.

I had never walked in shackles, and even though there was some slack in the chain, it wasn't easy to put one foot in front of the other, and I found myself shuffling, like the men on the chain gang. Plus, the metal was already chafing my bare ankles.

Also, my beltless pants were dropping, and I had to hitch them up a few times, which caused Luther to shout, "Hands on your head!"

I could see that Kate, ahead of me, was having a lot of difficulty walking, and she almost stumbled. But her tight jeans held up, and she kept her hands on her head.

I didn't know who was following, so I glanced over my shoulder and saw Madox about ten feet behind me, his Colt .45 in his hand, swinging at his side.

Luther was bringing up the rear with his M16 rifle at the ready. Derek, the air horn victim, had stayed back in the bar, and he was collecting everything that was taken from us.

Madox said to me, "The next time you turn around, you'll be sprouting a third eye in the middle of your forehead. Understand?"

I think I understood what he was saying.

So, as it turned out, Mr. Bain Madox was not so charming, well mannered, or even civilized. Goes to show you. Actually, I think I liked him better this way—gloves off, all pretenses dropped, and, more important, he was taking us to the ELF transmitter.

Carl halted in the middle of the card room, and Madox said, "Stop."

Kate and I did as we were told, and I looked around. On one wall was a big dartboard whose target was a full-color photo of Saddam Hussein's face.

Madox reminded me, "You asked when the war was going to start. Well, the operational date is March 15—the ides of March—give or take a day or two for glitches. But I'm starting it early. In less than an hour."

"Are we getting dinner first?"

Luther, at least, thought that was funny.

Madox, who was ahead of me now, seemed a little tense, or maybe preoccupied, and didn't reply to my question.

Anyway, Carl had slung his shotgun over his shoulder, and I got a good look at it. It was a Browning automatic shotgun, probably 12-gauge, and it would fire five rounds as quickly as you could pull the trigger and stay on your feet. For Carl, that would be no problem.

Madox's Colt .45 automatic held seven rounds in the clip and one in the chamber. The gun was notoriously inaccurate, but if a blunt-nosed .45 slug hit you anyplace, you'd go airborne, and as my ex-military buddies liked to say, "It's the fall that kills you."

Luther's M16 was another animal altogether. Very accurate at medium distances, and if Luther was carrying the fully automatic version, it could spray twenty steel-jacketed rounds at you in less time than it took to say, "Holy shit, I'm dead."

In any case, we'd lost Derek, the air horn guy, who probably had an appointment with an ear doctor, and now Kate and I had to contend with only three guys. But they weren't your normal run-of-the-mill street scum—like my Hispanic friends who sort of closed their eyes when they fired at me, or the Mideastern gentlemen who, I honestly believe, can't be trying to hit anyone when they fire their AK-47s.

Anyway, not only were these three guys paramilitary but Kate and I were shackled, beltless, barefoot, and in a tight spot.

Bottom line, this was not the time to go BearBanger. And I hoped Kate understood that.

Also, we needed to get to the ELF transmitter.

I noticed that Carl was reaching under the big, round card table. Then he stepped back. As I watched, the table began to lift, and I could hear the humming of an electric motor as the table continued to rise along with the round rug beneath it and the circular section of the floor beneath

he rug. I could see now the hydraulic piston that was lift-
ng everything, and when the table legs, rug, and floor
ection were about five feet from floor level, it stopped,
eaving a hole in the floor about four feet in diameter.

Carl sat on the floor with his legs dangling into the
ole, then disappeared. Soon, a light came out of the dark
pace.

Madox said, "Kate, you first."

She hesitated, and he moved quickly toward her,
grabbed her arm, and propelled her forward toward the
opening in the floor.

She almost fell because of the shackles, and I said to
Madox, "Take it easy, asshole."

He looked at me and said, "One more word out of
you, and *she* will be sorry. Understand?"

I nodded.

Madox held Kate's arm and maneuvered her to the
edge of the opening, saying, "It's a spiral staircase. Hold the
ails and move quickly."

Kate sat on the floor and grabbed a rope handle hang-
ng from the underside of the elevated floor, then de-
cended into the hole.

Madox motioned me toward the opening. "Let's go."

I felt Luther give me a shove, and I realized that this
half-wit was too close for his own safety, and Madox
yelled at him, "Get back, you idiot!"

I said to Madox, "I won't hurt him."

As I started toward the hole, Madox, who was no idiot,
moved away from me and aimed his Colt .45. "Stop."

I stopped.

A few seconds later, Carl's voice called out, "Clear."

Madox informed me, "Kate is on the floor, and Carl has his shotgun aimed at her head. Just so you know." He pointed to the opening. "Go."

I sat on the floor and lowered myself, feet and shackles first, into the hole until I felt the first step. I knew that once Kate and I were down in this subterranean area, no one on the ground was going to find us.

Madox said, "Let's go, John. I'm on a tight schedule."

I descended the spiral staircase, which wrapped around the hydraulic piston. It was not that easy to move in shackles, but my hands were free, so I held both rails and mostly slid down.

On that subject, if Madox intended to handcuff us at some point, then I'd have to make a move before that happened. I knew Kate also understood that.

It was about twenty feet to the floor below, the height of a two-story building, and I guessed without too much thinking that this was the fallout shelter.

At the bottom of the spiral staircase was a round, concrete room, lit with bare fluorescent bulbs.

Opposite the last step, about ten feet away, was a shiny steel bank-vault door embedded in the concrete wall.

Behind me, Carl said, "Facedown."

I turned and saw Carl at the other end of the round space, pointing his shotgun at Kate, who was lying facedown on the floor.

This might have been a good time to make a move, but before I could decide, Carl aimed his shotgun close to Kate's head and shouted, "Three! Two—!"

I got down on the cold concrete floor, and Carl yelled, Clear!"

I heard Madox scrambling down the spiral staircase s though he'd practiced this a few times.

He said, "John, I think one of you has to go."

I didn't reply.

A few seconds went by, and I heard Luther's boots on he stairs, then the hissing sound of the hydraulic piston, nd finally the table and floor dropping into place.

Luther was down the spiral stairs, and Madox said to im, "Open the door."

I heard the vault wheel click, then a small squeak as he heavy door swung open.

Madox told me, "John, no matter what move you nake, or try to make, Kate is the first to get shot." He said o Carl and Luther, "You got that? If Corey makes a move, ou shoot Kate. I'll take care of Mr. Corey."

Carl and Luther both replied, "Yes, sir."

Then, Madox warned, "You're trying my patience, nd I'm running almost ten minutes behind schedule. o, you either behave and do what you're told, quickly, r I shoot one of you so we can get back on schedule. Jnderstand?"

"I understand."

"Good. You're never a hero to your wife, anyway, so on't even try."

"Good advice."

The next thing I heard was Madox saying, "Kate. tand. Hands on head."

She stood, and Madox instructed, "Follow Carl." Then

to me, "John. Stand. Hands on head. Follow at twenty feet."

I stood, put my hands on my head, and noticed now a big canvas bag on the floor. It was partly unzipped, and I could see the sleeve of my leather jacket peeking out. Apparently, Derek had given Luther all our things, and the last trace of our being at Custer Hill—except for Rudy's van, which they'd get rid of—was now gone.

Madox saw what I was looking at and said to me, "They won't even find your DNA in the bear shit." He motioned toward the door. "Go."

I went through the vault door, which was embedded in about three feet of concrete.

Madox, behind me, said, "Welcome to my fallout shelter."

Luther brought up the rear, and I could hear the vault door closing and locking.

I had the sense that we were under the back terrace, deep in the bedrock, and not connected to the basement of the house. I also had the sense that there wasn't anyone on the surface who could ever find us.

CHAPTER FIFTY

We were now in a wide corridor whose concrete walls were painted a light green that changed into sky blue about a third of the way up the ten-foot height. The ceiling was covered with frosted glass panels, behind which were bright violet lights that, I guessed, were grow lights, though I didn't see any vegetation, unless you counted the horrid 1980s Astroturf on the floor.

I suppose someone was trying to create the illusion that you were outdoors in a sunlit meadow that happened to look like an underground concrete corridor.

Madox said, unnecessarily, "You're supposed to think you're aboveground."

I asked, "Aren't we?"

He didn't answer my question. "My idiot ex-wife's idea." He added, "She had an irrational fear of atomic war."

"Silly woman."

He seemed in a better mood, and he motioned to an open door to the right, which I could see was a children's playroom. "The children were young then, and she thought they'd thrive down here."

I commented, "The grow lights might help, but their playdates might be somewhat limited."

He wasn't paying any attention to me, and he actually seemed to be talking to himself. "She saw *On the Beach* and *Dr. Strangelove* about twenty times, and I don't think she realized one was a serious film, and the other was gallows humor." He added, "Nuclear Armageddon movies sent her to her therapist for months."

I had the impression that Bain Madox had some issues with his ex-wife's obsession with nuclear holocaust, and maybe what he was trying to do now was work through that by starting a nuclear war of his own. I was sure that Mrs. Madox would be one of the first people he called after it was over.

Anyway, Kate and I moved slowly down the passage in our shackles, and every time I hitched up my pants, Luther yelled, "Hands on your head," and I replied, "Fuck you."

I could hear the vents blowing, but the air smelled damp and slightly unpleasant.

On either side of the passage were open doors that revealed furnished rooms—bedrooms, a sitting room, a kitchen, and a long dining room with paneled walls, heavy drapes, a coffered ceiling, and plush carpets. Behind one closed door, I distinctly heard talking, then I realized it

vas a radio or television—so maybe someone else was
lown here.

Madox, again talking to himself, said, "She spent a
'ortune decorating this place. She wanted to sit out the half-
ife of radioactive fallout in the style to which she'd be-
:ome accustomed."

He was on a roll, so I didn't comment.

He continued, "On the other hand, I find this space
useful. First, for my ELF transmitter—and also as a place
o store a fortune in art treasures, gold, and cash." He made
a joke. "The last IRS agent who came snooping around is
still locked in a room down here."

Good one, Bain. Actually, this place looked like the
Führerbunker, but this might not be the right time to make
hat comparison.

We reached the end of the passageway, which must
have run for fifty yards, and Carl unlocked a steel door,
opened it, and turned on the lights.

Madox said, "Kate, follow Carl. John, stop."

Kate disappeared into the doorway, and I stood
here.

Carl called out, "Clear."

Madox said, "John, follow."

I was getting a little tired of these doggie commands,
but it wasn't worth mentioning now that we were so close
o . . . the end.

I entered the room and saw that Kate again was on the
floor, and Carl stood against the far wall, covering her and
me as I entered.

Madox instructed, "John, down."

I lay facedown on a plush blue carpet. On a professional level, I appreciated Carl and Bain's military precision, and their textbook handling of two prisoners who, though shackled, unarmed, and outnumbered by three armed men, they understood to be potentially dangerous.

On the downside of that, these guys weren't giving me an inch to wiggle out of this.

Using shackles instead of handcuffs was a judgment call, and I could see why Madox had gone with the shackles up to this point.

The only real mistake they'd made so far was not finding the BearBangers, which was why the police stripsearched prisoners and examined the body cavities. Now that we were in the dungeon, that might very well be Madox's next move, along with handcuffs—and that would be our signal to act.

Meanwhile, Madox and Carl seemed to be busy with something other than us, but I caught a glimpse of Luther near the door with his M16 raised and pointed, and the muzzle sweeping back and forth between me and Kate. I didn't see the canvas bag, which Luther had apparently stowed somewhere along the way. Therefore, the only weapons in this room were the ones we saw pointed at us.

On the subject of weapons, Carl's choice of an automatic shotgun in confined quarters was also very professional—bullets from high-powered rifles have a tendency to pass through people and hit other people you don't necessarily want to hit, then ricochet and become dangerous to the shooter and his friends.

In fact, down here, Luther's M16 was almost as dangerous to him as it was to us. Nevertheless, I didn't want him firing it at us.

As for Madox's Colt .45, it was okay in confined quarters with masonry surfaces. It would put a big hole in you at close range, and its exit velocity wasn't usually fatal to anyone on the other side of the intended victim. Also, if it hit a concrete wall, its blunt-nosed bullet was more likely to splatter than ricochet.

Having analyzed all that, my conclusion was that Kate and I were basically fucked. In fact, the BearBangers were getting smaller and smaller in my mind.

Madox said, "On your knees. Hands on your heads."

I lifted myself into a kneeling position, with my hands on my head, and I saw Kate do the same. We were about ten feet apart in the dimly lit room, and we made eye contact. She dropped her face and eyes down toward where the BearBanger was stuck, somewhere in her jeans or panties, and probably behind her zipper. She glanced at me, and I gave a slight shake of my head. *Not the right moment,* I wanted to say. *You'll know when.*

I looked around the room as my eyes adjusted to the dim light.

Madox was sitting with his back to us at some sort of electronic console that was against the far wall. I assumed that was the ELF transmitter. Eureka. Now what?

Luther was still standing near the door, covering Kate and me with his rifle.

Carl wasn't visible, but I heard him breathing behind us.

The room itself was a sparsely furnished and functional-looking office. This was obviously Bain's atomic-war headquarters, where he could spend the day making phone calls to see if anyone was alive out there after the Big One. He probably had a ticker tape, too, to see how his defense and oil stocks were doing.

I never understood, during the '70s and '80s, why people wanted to survive a nuclear holocaust. I mean, other than some cans of chili and a case of beer, I never made any long-range, post–nuclear war plans.

But to be fair to Bain, this was mostly his ex-wife's idea. I wondered what became of her. Wood chipper?

Anyway, I noticed, too, that mounted on the paneled wall to the right of the electronic console were three flat screen television monitors on swing arms. They looked new and out of place in this 1980s time capsule.

To the left of the console was a bank of six older television sets, and they were all lit, but it was hard to see the black-and-white images on them, which kept shifting. I realized these were security monitors, and I made out the gatehouse on one screen, then an image of the lodge taken from the gatehouse, which then shifted to an image of the generator building, and so forth.

Therefore Madox would know if the cavalry arrived, and so would Kate and I. But so far, everything out there in Custer Hill land looked normal, peaceful, and quiet.

A recurring unhappy thought was that even if the state police and the FBI busted through the gate and kicked in the doors of the lodge, no one would find us down here.

And even if Schaeffer remembered that there was

supposed to be a fallout shelter somewhere, he'd probably be looking in the basement of the lodge itself, and he might very well mistake some room down there for a fallout shelter.

For damned sure he wasn't going to find the hydraulic floor under the card table, and even if by some miracle he did, it would take hours or longer to get an explosive ordnance team down here to blast open that vault door.

Wow. We were double fucked. There was only one way out of this mess, and that was the way I should have chosen this afternoon—this bastard and his buddies had to die, here and now, before they killed us, and before Madox detonated those four nukes in Sandland.

Madox swiveled around and asked me, "Do you understand what's happening? John?"

"I think we established that you're going to send an ELF wave to four receivers that are attached to nuclear detonators in four suitcase bombs."

"Correct." He added, "I've actually begun the transmission."

Shit.

He said, "Come closer. On your knees. Come on."

Kate and I moved on our knees closer to the console, then Carl, behind us, ordered, "Stop."

We stopped.

Madox asked, "Can you see these three little windows?"

We looked to where he was pointing to a black box on top of the console. The first window in the box was spinning a dizzying array of red LED letters, and Madox said, "I've sent out the first letter of the three-letter code that will detonate the four devices." He explained, "I could have put a time clock in each of the nuclear suitcases, but then the detonation time would be preset, and out of my control. So I chose a command-detonation mode, meaning my ELF radio, which is perfect for this task, and foolproof." He added, "I finally got my money's worth out of this ELF station."

I told him, "You know, Bain, you can explore for oil with ELF waves."

He smiled and said, "I see you've done some homework." He informed me, "I don't need to explore for oil. I already know where it is, and the present owners are about to be nuked."

"Why are you doing this?"

He looked at me and replied, "Ah, the 'why' question." He lit a cigarette. "Why? Because I'm fucking sick and tired of a succession of ball-less presidents kissing Arab ass. That's why."

I figured he'd kissed a little Arab ass himself, and this was payback. I figured, too, I'd go along with him, and said, "You know, Bain, Kate and I see this shit every day in our job. Illegal Muslim immigrants being treated like they were constitutional lawyers, suspected terrorists all lawyered up and threatening to sue for false arrest." I went on with my litany of problems on the job, but oddly, Madox didn't seem that interested. I concluded with, "I understand your frustrations, but exploding four nuclear weapons in Sandland is not going to solve the problem. It'll make it worse."

He laughed, which I thought was strange.

Then, he swiveled around again and punched a few keys on his keyboard. He explained, "Each letter needs to be encoded with a four-letter code group."

"Right," I agreed. "Can we talk about this?"

He didn't seem to hear me, and he appeared intent on reading his dials and listening to something on a set of headphones that he held briefly to his ear.

I noticed that the first window in the black box had stopped spinning letters, and it was locked into a bright red "G."

Kate spoke up. "When the state police and FBI get here, they're going to knock out your generators, and the antenna poles."

Madox was still playing with his electronics, and replied without turning around, "Kate, first, they haven't even left police headquarters yet, which is over an hour from here. Second, they really don't know what's happening here. Third, even if they got here in the next thirty minutes, they'd be too late." He explained, "This will all be over in less than twenty minutes."

I noticed now that the second window in the black box was spinning red letters.

Madox swiveled in his chair and said to us, "The second letter is sent, and the four receivers in the suitcase nukes will pick it up in about fifteen minutes."

I thought maybe he was juking and jiving us about how much time we had left, so to show him we'd done our homework, I said, "About thirty minutes."

"No, fifteen. That's how long each repetitive ELF

wave will take to reach San Francisco and Los Angeles, and have its signal decoded in the receiver."

"The Mideast," I corrected. "Thirty minutes."

"*No,*" said Mr. Madox impatiently. "You still don't get it—which is good news for me."

Kate asked, "Get what?"

"Get Project Green and Wild Fire."

Madox swiveled around again and read his electronic dials, commenting, "The generators are maintaining six thousand kilowatts." He put his hand on the keyboard. "Now, all I have to do is type the encryption for the last letter in the three-letter code."

As he said that, the second letter on the black box froze at "O." So now it read "G-O."

He noticed it and said, "We have a G and O. So, what's the code word? I can't remember. G-O-B? G-O-T?" He laughed over his shoulder at us. "G-O-C-O? No, too many letters. Help me. John? Kate? Please, God, let me remember . . . ah! That's it. G-O-D."

The man was clearly having fun, while losing his marbles.

He typed on his keyboard, and the last window began spinning letters.

He swiveled back to us and said, "So, what's happening is that my encryption software has successfully sent the letters G and O via ELF wave toward the four receivers, which is confirmed by the G and O on the black box. But, as you know, it takes a while for these repetitive waves to actually reach the receivers and for them to properly decode. Understand?"

I didn't think he really gave a shit if we understood, unless he was trying to see what we knew, so I said, "We understand."

"Really?" He informed us, "I've used a repeating, self-correcting code, which is continuously transmitted until the initiating sequence is received. In other words, D-O-G won't work. Only G-O-D can make an explosion. Follow?"

I reminded him, "Don't forget to activate your isotopes."

"To . . . what?" He looked at me like I was crazy, then continued, "This is the same software system that the Navy uses for their nuclear submarine fleet. But maybe you knew that. Do you know about my little experiment back in the 1980s?"

Kate replied, "We do. And so does everyone in the FBI."

"Really? Well . . . that's too bad. But not relevant now. In any case, when that black box spells G-O-D, about fifteen minutes later, the four receivers will have the entire three-letter code in proper sequence. GOD. Then, after two minutes, if there's no change in the continuous transmitted signal, the four receivers will send an electronic pulse to the four detonators, which are attached to the receivers, and we have four nice nuclear explosions, thanks to Dr. Putyov."

Neither Kate nor I responded to that.

Madox lit another cigarette and watched the black box as the last window kept spinning letters. Then, the window read "D," and the box read, "GOD." Madox, who thought that meant him, said, "So, all three letters are now being sent across the country in a continuous pattern."

I still wasn't understanding why he was saying "across the country," but maybe I did understand, and I didn't want to know.

Madox pushed a few buttons on the console, and four green LED numbers—*15:00*—appeared on a big screen, then he hit another button, and the numbers began to count down. He told us, "It's hard to say exactly how long the ELF wave will take to get properly decoded by the receivers, but about fifteen minutes is a good guess. Then, as I said, the receivers need to hold these letters for precisely two minutes to be certain they're reading the continuous, self-correcting code correctly. Then"—he slapped his hands together—"BOOM!"

I saw that coming, but poor Luther almost wet his pants.

Madox thought that was pretty funny, so he did it three more times. BOOM! BOOM! BOOM! But the surprise was gone, and no one jumped.

I mean, this guy was out of his fucking mind, and I hoped that Carl and Luther were getting it. I was sure that Harry had gotten it at some point, and maybe Carl and Luther would remember what happened to Harry.

I focused on the countdown clock, which now read *13:36,* then *:35,* and so forth, on the way to nuclear ecstasy for Bain Madox.

Madox chain-lit another cigarette, looked at his watch and then the countdown clock, then checked some of his instruments, then glanced at the six security monitors.

Madox seemed to be in a manic state, and I could understand that this was his payoff moment for years of work and planning.

I, on the other hand, didn't have much to do except kneel with my hands on my head, watching and listening. I mean, I wasn't exactly bored observing a nuclear event unfolding, but I'm more of an action guy.

On that subject, Carl was still behind us, so going for the BearBanger, which had dropped a bit south in my tightie whities, was not an option. I might get the Bear-Banger out, but I'd be dead before I could figure out which way was up and press the button on the other end of it.

Kate had a better chance of reaching into the front of her jeans and pulling the thing out before Carl or dim-witted Luther noticed. And I could see she was getting tense just thinking about it.

She was watching Luther as much as she could get away with it, but we couldn't watch Carl, and I had no idea how closely he was focused on us. Plus, just when Luther's dim brain seemed to be wandering, Madox would suddenly swivel around and chat with us.

In fact, he now turned toward us. "You probably think I'm crazy."

I replied, "No, Bain, we *know* you're crazy."

He started to smile, but then realized his troops were present, and he didn't want to put any ideas into their heads, so he got serious, like he was sane, and said to me, "There's not one major figure in the history of the world who has not been called crazy. Caesar, Attila, Genghis Khan, Napoleon, Hit—. Well, maybe he was a little unbalanced. But you understand what I'm saying."

"I understand that if you think you're Napoleon, you may need to speak to someone."   ,

"John, I don't think I'm anyone except who I am."

"That's a good start, Bain."

He informed us, "I don't think you appreciate what I'm doing." He thereupon went into a whole riff about great men who changed the course of history, including some guy named King John of Poland, who saved Vienna from the Turks and didn't get anything out of it. I mean, who gives a shit, Bain?

Meanwhile, the countdown clock read *11:13*, and counting.

Kate took advantage of Madox's pausing to light a cigarette and asked him, "What is Wild Fire?"

He blew a few smoke rings, then answered, "It's a top secret government protocol that goes into effect if and when America is attacked with a weapon or weapons of mass destruction. It's the only good and sane thing we've ever done since MAD—Mutually Assured Destruction."

Kate followed up with, "What does that have to do with . . . with what's happening now?"

He looked at her through his smoke and asked, "So, you really *don't* know, do you?"

I had the impression that if we answered some of these questions wrong—if he thought we were really clueless—then we'd be joining Putyov and the IRS guy sooner rather than later, so I replied, "We were briefed, but—"

"Good. Tell me."

"Okay . . . well . . . Wild Fire is a secret government protocol that goes into effect—"

"John, you're such a bullshitter." He said, "I'll tell *you*." He launched into an explanation of Wild Fire, which I found scary but at the same time strangely reassuring. The scariest thing was that Bain Madox knew the intimate details of a secret that was right up there with the most sensitive national secrets in the country, including where the Roswell aliens were hidden.

Meanwhile, the countdown clock read *9:34,* and as I watched while Madox spoke, it went to *9:00,* then *8:59.*

I was catching most of what Madox was saying, and when he began to recite the cities in the world of Islam that were going to be nuked if Wild Fire was ever triggered, I thought the guy was going to have an orgasm.

I mean, he was in total ecstasy, and I sort of hoped he would swoon or something.

When he got to the part of the Wild Fire plan about nuking the Aswân High Dam, he became animated, threw his arms into the air, and said, "Billions of gallons of water. The entire Lake Nasser and the Nile will sweep away Egypt and deposit sixty million bodies in the Mediterranean."

Jeez. Bain. Tell me you're not nuts.

As riveting as this was, I did notice two things: one, Madox had his Colt .45 stuck in the inside pocket of his blue blazer, and two, Luther was looking a little concerned, as though this were all new to him. In fact, he lit a cigarette, which you're not supposed to do on-duty. Especially if it means leaving your rifle dangling by its sling over your shoulder while you screw around with your cigarettes and lighter.

Meanwhile, the room was getting smoky, and I was

going to point out that secondhand smoke was not healthy for any of us, but then Bain would point out that neither Kate nor I should be thinking long-range.

The countdown clock read *7:28.*

A phone rang somewhere in the room, and it was actually Madox's cell phone, which he pulled out of his pocket. He said, "Madox," then he listened and confirmed, "Project Green is go," followed by, "Kaiser Wilhelm," who must be in on this, or more likely that was a code word that meant everything was fine, and he—Madox—was not under duress.

Madox listened again, then responded, "Good." He glanced at the countdown clock and said into his cell phone, "About five or six minutes, give or take, then the two minutes for the lock-in. Yes. That's good. What are they having for dinner?" He listened, laughed, and said, "I may be saving you all from a fate worse than death. Okay. Good. Thanks, Paul." He added, "God bless us all." He hung up and told me, "You'll appreciate this, John. The president and his guests are having French cuisine— poached truite saumonée with sauce relevée for dinner. So, where was I?"

I said, "Excuse me, Bain. I must not have been paying attention, but—"

"Oh, sorry. That was Paul Dunn. The special assistant to the president on matters of national security." He explained, "They're having a small, intimate dinner at the White House tonight. This is good because the president and first lady can be quickly evacuated from Washington. Along with Paul."

"Is the food that bad?"

Madox laughed and said, "You actually *are* funny."
He put the cell phone back in his pocket. "FYI, I have a
cell antenna down here, and my relay tower is again activated, but unfortunately for my non-paying customers in
the vicinity, the system is now voice scrambled." He asked
me, "Where was I?"

"Sixty million bodies floating down the Nile."

"Right. The biggest single loss of life in the history of
the world. Plus, don't forget another hundred million or
more of our Muslim friends incinerated in a hundred
more nuclear explosions."

I still wasn't quite following this. I understood what
Wild Fire was—which sounded a little extreme as a retaliation for a terrorist nuke going off in America—but who
was I to judge? What I didn't understand was how Madox,
by nuking four Islamic cities, was going to trigger Wild
Fire . . . then I got it. It wasn't four *Islamic* cities. It was
two *American* cities. The cities where the nukes were right
now—LA and San Francisco. *Holy shit.* I looked at Kate,
who I could see was white as a ghost.

Madox grabbed a remote clicker from his console
and turned on the three flat screen televisions.

The first one brightened, and I could see a news studio,
and a weather lady was pointing at a national weather map.
Madox said, "Washington," then he hit the Mute button as
the sound came up.

The second screen showed another news studio and
some guy was giving a sports roundup. Madox noted,
"San Francisco," then muted that TV as well.

The third screen showed two news anchors yakking it

up with a daytime skyline behind them, and it took me a few seconds to recognize it as downtown Los Angeles. Madox listened for a few seconds, then looked at his watch. "Okay, it's seven fifty-six here, so on the Left Coast, it's four fifty-six P.M." He looked at his countdown clock that read *4:48, :47, :46, :45—.*

He said, "So, we have five or six minutes for the last letter—D—to reach the receivers. Then, two minutes for lock-in." He paused. "GOD."

I cleared my throat and said to him, "Are you . . . ? I mean, are you . . . ?"

"Spit it out, John."

"What the *fuck* are you doing?"

"What's it *look* like I'm doing?"

I didn't reply, and neither did Kate.

He sat back in his swivel chair, crossed his legs, and lit yet another cigarette. "Project Green. That's the name of my plan to trigger Wild Fire. Get it? Four suitcase nukes—two in LA, two in San Francisco." He added, "They cost me ten million bucks, plus maintenance."

Madox glanced back at the countdown clock. "They'll all blow in less than six minutes." He turned toward us and said, "Then, the Wild Fire retaliatory response kicks in, and we blow those Islamic sons of bitches off the face of the Earth for what they did to Los Angeles and San Francisco—" He stopped abruptly, as though something just dawned on him, then said, "I forgot. *I'm* blowing up San Francisco and Los Angeles." He laughed.

Holy shit. I said to him, "Bain, for God's sake, you can't—"

"John, shut up. You sound like Harry now. And while you're shutting your mouth, think about how beautiful this is. Project Green. Wild Fire. Why green? Because . . ." He looked at the flat screens. "See that ribbon running across the bottom on the LA channel? What's that say? Alert Level Orange. Do you know what it's going to say in the very near future? Green. Permanent Green. Get it? You'll never again be wanded at an airport . . . well, actually, you'll never again be *at* an airport. But think of all our fellow Americans who are inconvenienced at the airport."

He rambled on a bit, and I looked at the news shows from LA and San Francisco, hoping I'd see some indication that some dangerous plot had been uncovered in those cities. But the anchors were starting to wrap it up. I hoped—prayed, actually—that both pilots and co-pilots in both cities had been found. But the chances of all four of those guys being found by now, along with the suitcase nukes, were not good.

I said to Madox, "Bain, the government will know it was *you* and not the terrorists who—"

"John, even if they did figure it out, it would be too late. Wild Fire is hardwired and on a hair trigger."

"Bain, they'll be here looking for you—"

"You know what? I don't give a shit as long as I know that the world of Islam is lying in nuclear ruin. I don't mind being a martyr for my country, my faith—"

"Are you out of your fucking mind? You're going to murder millions of Americans, millions of innocent Muslims—"

"John, shut the fuck up." He glanced quickly at Carl and Luther, then said to me, "The ends justify the means."

"No, they do *not*—"

He raised his voice. "They do! This is a whole New World we're talking about. Are you too stupid to understand—?"

"I have to pee."

Madox looked at Kate. "What?"

"I have to pee. Please, I can't hold it in. I don't want to . . . to wet myself here—"

Madox seemed annoyed, thought a moment, then said, "Well, I don't want you wetting yourself here either, considering the lousy job the air-purification people did." He instructed Carl, "Watch her."

Carl ordered Kate, "Down on all fours. Turn around."

Kate did as she was told, then Carl said, "Over there."

I lost sight of her, but I heard Carl move across the floor, and then I heard a door opening behind me.

Madox watched what was happening, as did Luther, who again took out his cigarettes.

Carl said to Kate, "Go ahead. I'm not closing the door."

The moment had arrived. Carl was watching Kate with his back to me, and Madox was dividing his attention between his countdown clock, which now read *3:26*, his security monitors, which still showed no problems, and his flat screen TVs, where news shows were still wrapping up their hours.

Luther was fixated on the open bathroom door.

I turned my head and looked behind me. Carl was standing at the door with his shotgun at his hip, pointed at Kate, whom I could see standing in front of the toilet bowl, unbuttoning her jeans, then unzipping her fly.

I don't know what Carl thought he was going to see, but he was about to see something else.

Madox said, "John, you don't need to watch your wife peeing. Turn this way."

I turned away from what was going to be a very bright light, held my breath, and shut my eyes. I was prepared for it, but when it happened, I almost peed my pants myself.

There was a deafening explosion that filled the room as if the noise were solid. Simultaneously, the room was lit with a blinding light, which I could actually see through my closed eyelids, and I heard Carl screaming in pain.

I was flat on the floor now, with my BearBanger in my hand, but the room was full of smoke, so I couldn't see Madox or Luther, and I hoped they couldn't see me. I'd already decided that Luther presented the biggest threat with his M16, so I pointed the BearBanger at where I could see movement near the door and fired.

Another huge explosion filled the room as the flare shot out of the BearBanger like a red laser beam and exploded on the wall—or on Luther.

It didn't matter if I hit him or not because by now everyone was half blind, deaf, and definitely fucked up.

I spun around and lunged across the floor where I saw Carl lying on his back. I reached around for his shotgun but couldn't find it.

Then Kate shouted something, but I couldn't hear her.

I looked at her and saw she already had the shotgun.

There were small fires on the carpet from the Bear-Banger flares, and I also noticed a couch blazing.

I caught a glimpse of Carl's face—or what used to be his face—then I got into a crouch and charged at Madox, whom I could now see on the floor near his swivel chair, moving around, obviously disoriented, but nowhere near out of action. I took too long a stride for the shackle chain, and I fell forward, then scrambled on my hands and knees toward him.

Before I could get to Madox, Luther stood and brought his rifle up to his shoulder and was about to fill me with holes when a shotgun blast filled the room, and Luther seemed to defy gravity as he lifted off his feet and slammed into the wall.

Before he dropped, Kate fired a second time, and Luther's lower jaw disappeared.

I again lunged at Madox, who was now on one knee, facing me with his Colt .45 in his hand.

He started to raise his gun, and Kate shouted, "Freeze! Freeze! Drop it! Drop it or you're dead!"

There was this long moment while Bain Madox considered his options. Kate helped him decide by blowing a hole in the ceiling above his head. Before the plaster even hit him, he dropped his gun.

Time sort of hung there for a while, with Madox and I both on our knees facing each other from about five feet away. Kate was standing about ten feet away, the shotgun pointing at Madox's head.

The room smelled of burned explosives, and a blue smoke hung in the air. My eyesight was returning, but black specks danced around wherever I looked. As for my hearing, I'd heard the shotgun blasts, but they'd sounded far away, and if there was any other noise in the room, I couldn't detect it.

I stood slowly and got my footing, then grabbed Madox's .45 off the carpet and went over to Luther, who was sitting against the wall near the door. He was not dead but would wish he was if he survived without a lower jaw. Kate's first shot had shredded his arm, but his rifle was still hanging by its sling across his chest, so I pulled it away from him and set the selector switch from full automatic to safety, then I slung the rifle over my shoulder.

Kate had motioned Madox onto the rug, where he was lying with his face buried in the thick, blue plush carpet, which I could tell him firsthand was not comfortable.

I glanced at the countdown clock and saw we had two full minutes before *00:00*.

I needed to do this by the book, to be sure there was no one left who presented a danger to Kate or me. So I went over to Carl, who was still alive, and who also had some parts of his face where they didn't belong.

I started to frisk him, but amazingly, he sat up, like Frankenstein on the laboratory table, and I backed off.

I watched him get to his feet. Clearly he was blind— not temporarily blinded, but, judging from the burns around his eyes, permanently blind. Nevertheless, he put his hand inside his jacket and brought out a Colt .45 automatic.

I was going to say, "Drop it!" but then he'd know where to fire, so with time running out, I made a difficult decision and put a .45 bullet through his forehead.

He was too big to be lifted off his feet, and he fell backward, like a huge tree toppling.

Kate said, "Fifty-eight seconds."

I walked over to Madox, who was staring at Carl's body, and asked him, "How do I stop this?"

He turned his head toward me and replied, "Fuck you."

"Do you have anything intelligent to say? Come on, Bain. Help me. How do I stop this?"

"You can't. And why do you want to? John, *think* about this."

I have to be honest and admit that I had been thinking about it. I mean, God help me, but I did think about letting it happen.

Kate called out, "Forty seconds."

I got my head back on straight and remembered what Madox had said about the ELF signal, and I seemed to recall something about a continuous signal, and a lock-in period, so I thought that if I stopped the ELF wave, right here at the transmitter, the receivers wouldn't or couldn't lock in and send a signal to the nuclear detonators. Electronics is not one of my strong points, but destruction is, and there was nothing to lose, except two cities, so I stepped back and told Kate to do the same.

The countdown clock read :15 seconds, but I recalled from Bain that the ELF wave and the decoding could be a minute or two faster or slower in reaching the receivers, and for all I knew, the two-minute lock-in time was already running—or finished.

I glanced at the three flat screen TVs, but there was nothing unusual happening in San Francisco, Los Angeles, or Washington.

Kate said, "John."

I looked where she was staring and saw that the countdown clock read *00:00*, and the black LED box was now flashing "GOD—GOD—GOD."

I raised the Colt .45 and pointed it at the ELF transmitter.

Madox had gotten up and was on his knees now, in front of the transmitter, as though he were protecting it. He held his hands up and shouted, "John! Don't do it! Let it happen. I beg you. Save the world. Save America—"

I fired three rounds over Madox's head into the transmitter, and three more into the rest of the electronic console, just to be sure. Then Kate blasted the last two shotgun rounds into the smoking electronics.

The lights, dials, and instruments blinked off, and the big metal console smoked and sparked. The word "GOD" blinked out.

Madox had turned his head and was looking at the dying ELF transmitter, then he turned to me, then Kate, then back to me, and said in almost a whisper, "You ruined everything. You could have let it happen. Why are you so stupid?"

I had a few good replies for him about duty, honor, and country, and also about "If I'm so stupid, why do I have your gun?" but I got right to the point and said, "This is for Harry Muller," and fired my last bullet into his brain.

CHAPTER FIFTY-ONE

We found the key in Carl's pocket and removed our shackles. We also found his Colt .45 on the floor, and Kate stuck it in her waistband.

Kate and I stood side by side in the smoky room, as mute as the three televisions that we were watching. My heart, and I'm sure hers, was thumping.

After a few minutes of commercials—with no urgent bulletins or screens going black in LA or San Francisco—I said to Kate, "I guess everything is okay."

She nodded.

I asked her, "Are *you* okay?"

"I'm fine . . . I'm just . . . stunned."

I let a few minutes go by, then said to her, "You did a good job."

"*Good?* I did a fucking excellent job."

"Excellent job." I asked, "Hey, where did you hide the BearBanger?"

"You don't want to know."

"Right."

After another minute of silence, she asked me, "Do you believe this? Do you *believe* what Madox was going to do?"

I looked at the electronic console and said, "Desperate times call for desperate measures."

She didn't respond for a second, then said, "John . . . for a minute there . . . I thought you were . . . wavering a little."

I thought about that. "Honestly?"

"Don't answer."

But I had to say something, so I said, "It's going to happen anyway."

"Don't say that."

I tried a joke. "Why don't we stay down here for a few years?"

She didn't reply.

I glanced at Bain Madox, who was still in a kneeling position, but now with his head thrown back, resting on the edge of his electronic console table. Those gray hawk eyes were wide open, as unblinking and emotionless as ever. And, except for the red hole in the middle of his forehead, I could hardly tell he was dead, which was creepy.

Kate saw me staring at him. "You did what you had to do."

Which we both knew was not true. I did what I *wanted* to do.

I looked away from Madox and watched the six security monitors, but I didn't see anyone, except for a shadow moving around in the gatehouse, and I guessed that was Derek. Then I saw a Jeep pass in front of the generator house.

I said to Kate, "They're still out there, and no one has arrived from state police headquarters."

She nodded. "So, we'll stay here awhile."

I really didn't feel like hanging around this room much longer with two stiffs on the floor, and a smoldering carpet and couch, plus the smell of burnt electronics.

Also, Luther was gurgling, and I recognized that sound. There wasn't much I could do for him, but I thought maybe I should try, so I looked around for a land-line phone to call state police headquarters to get an ambulance, not to mention some state troopers to arrest Derek, and whoever else needed to be arrested, and get us the hell out of there.

Kate kept staring at the three television sets, and glancing at a clock on the wall. "I really think it's okay."

"Yeah." I couldn't find a phone, and I thought about trying another room, and that reminded me of the room with the closed door where I'd heard a television.

I mean, I was still a little punchy from the Bear-Bangers, but I should have been more alert.

Also, my hearing had not fully returned, and neither had Kate's, so we never heard anyone coming down the corridor, and the first I knew that we weren't alone was when I heard a voice say, "Well, I didn't expect this."

I spun around, and standing by the door was the ghost of Ted Nash. I was speechless.

Kate, too, stood across the room, staring, and her mouth actually dropped open.

Finally, I said, "You're dead."

He replied, "Actually, I'm feeling fine. Sorry to upset you."

"I'm not upset. I'm disappointed."

"Be nice, John." He looked at Kate and asked her, "So, how are you?"

She didn't answer.

I *knew* I saw the hand of the CIA in this, but in my worst nightmare, I never thought I'd see Ted Nash again. Or, maybe I did.

Nash scanned the room, but didn't comment on the destruction, the blood splattered all over, Luther dying a few feet from him, or Carl lying dead in the middle of the floor. Ted was a cool guy. He did, however, look at Bain Madox and said, "That's a real shame."

Apparently, we had different opinions of the deceased.

Nash said, not to us but to himself, "Well, there are going to be a lot of disappointed people in Washington."

Neither Kate nor I responded, but I thought about getting the M16 unslung from my shoulder and into the firing position.

I wasn't being totally paranoid because Ted Nash is probably a killer, and for sure not a big fan of John Corey. Plus, he was wearing a sport jacket, and he had his right hand stuck inside, like the pretty-boy fashion models in the catalogs. This was the nonchalant, gun-in-my-pocket look.

Kate finally spoke. "What are you doing here?"

"I'm working."

"You . . . you were in the North Tower . . ."

"Actually, like you, John, and other people, I was late."
He said philosophically, "Isn't it funny how fate works?"

I replied, "Yeah. Fate is a barrel of laughs. What's the deal, Ted? Are you going to tell me you're here to stop Madox, but once again you were a few minutes late?"

He smiled and replied, "I'm not here to stop Madox." He glanced again at the late Mr. Madox. "But apparently you were."

"I was just here for dinner."

Then, before we could engage in any more witty repartee, he pulled his pistol, which was a Glock similar to my own, and said, "You guys *really* fucked things up."

"No, Ted. We just saved San Francisco and Los Angeles." I said, to be sure he understood, "We're heroes. The bad guys are dead."

He was getting a little pissed, the way he always does with me, and now that he had his gun out, and we all knew where he stood on this issue, he said, "You have *no* idea how you've fucked things up." He stared at me, and glanced at Kate. "The world as we know it was about to be forever changed. Do you understand that? *Do* you?"

He was getting himself all worked up, so I didn't answer his stupid question.

He went on, "This was the best, most ingenious, most daring and courageous plan we have ever come up with. In one fucking day—one day, John—one fucking day, we could have wiped out a major threat to America. And *you*—you and this *bitch*, here, fucked it up."

"Hey, I'm *really* sorry."

Kate took a deep breath and said sharply, "First of all, Ted, I'm *not* a bitch. Second, if this government wants to destroy Islam with atomic weapons, or threaten to destroy them, then they should have the *balls* to do that without faking a fucking terrorist attack on two American cities, and killing millions of Americans—"

"Shut the *fuck* up! Who gives a shit about Los Angeles and San Francisco? Not *me*. Not you, either. Don't take the moral high ground with me, Kate. We had a chance here to bring this Muslim shit to a happy conclusion, but you and this fucking clown you're married to—" He glanced at me, and for the first time noticed the sling on my shoulder, and the black muzzle of the M16 peeking up from behind my back. He pointed the Glock at me. "Get that fucking rifle off your shoulder. Don't touch it. Don't touch anything. Let it slide to the floor. *Now!*"

I leaned left so that the sling started to slide off my shoulder and down my arm, while trying to figure out how to get a grip on the rifle, click off the safety, aim from the hip, and get off one good shot.

Apparently, Mr. Nash was tired of my slow response and said, "Don't bother. Just stand there and die." He aimed his Glock at my chest. "Just so you know, I pulled some strings to get you sent here, and hopefully killed, instead of poor Harry Muller, who you will be joining in about three seconds. Also"—he nodded toward Kate—"I *did* screw her—"

I heard a loud blast but didn't see his muzzle flash. He did, however, toss his gun into the air. Or so it seemed. His body went straight back, as though he'd been kicked in the chest, and he slammed into the wall next to Luther. As he was sliding to the floor, Kate emptied Carl's Colt .45 into Ted Nash's body, which jerked violently each time another bullet hit him.

I watched her get off the last three shots, and there was nothing hysterical or frenzied about the way she was shooting. She was holding the big automatic with both hands in the correct grip, knees bent, arms straight, aim centered, squeeze, fire, breathe, hold it, squeeze, and so forth. Until the slide locked in the empty position.

I went over to her to take the pistol, but she threw it aside.

I said, "Thanks."

She kept staring at Nash's body, covered now with blood and gore from a head wound.

She said, "*Not* a bitch, Ted."

I'd have to remember not to use that word when we argued.

CHAPTER FIFTY-TWO

I found a landline phone and called Major Schaeffer, who, as it turned out, was totally clueless about where we were or what was going on.

I gave him a very edited, need-to-know briefing, mentioning murder and mayhem, and requesting troopers, an ambulance, a CSI team, and his presence.

Kate and I, carrying Luther's fully loaded M16 and Nash's thankfully fully loaded Glock, explored and secured the other rooms in the subterranean living quarters, which could have been featured in *Better Homes and Fallout Shelters*.

We found the canvas bag with our stuff in it, and got ourselves back together.

There's nothing interesting or educational about being a helpless prisoner, especially if your jailers are psychotic and homicidal, so I never quite understood the Stockholm syndrome thing where the prisoner starts to identify with his or her captor and begins to sympathize with whatever bullshit the captor is using as an excuse for his bad behavior.

Now and then, however, what the psycho is doing or saying actually does appeal to what the prisoner already believes, or has thought about himself in the dark parts of his mind.

But enough about that.

Kate and I found Mr. Madox's barroom, which was actually a smaller version of the one upstairs, and she liberated a bottle of Dom Pérignon, vintage 1978, which she opened and drank from a water tumbler.

I found some warm bottles of Carlstadt beer, which doesn't improve with age, and, in fact, had gotten a little cloudy since 1984. But it hit the spot.

Regarding Mr. Ted Nash, this was his second and hopefully last time back from the dead. I counted seven— count 'em, seven—holes in him, which was not bad for eight shots. In fact, I felt silly feeling for a pulse, and Kate asked me what the hell I was doing. But I needed to be really sure.

Also regarding Ted Nash, in less than three minutes, he'd managed to totally piss me off. First, I'm not a clown, Ted, and my wife is not a bitch. As for the other thing . . . well, it happened. Even Kate can make a mistake with men. I'm sure not all of her boyfriends were John Coreys.

She must have guessed what I was thinking about,

and she finished another glass of champagne and said, "It never happened. He was lying."

Well, I couldn't ask Dead Ted, so I let it go. "CIA guys lie," I said.

"Believe me."

She had Ted's Glock, so I said, "I believe you, sweetheart."

Being a lawyer and an FBI agent, she informed me, "I can explain the first and second shot as self-defense. I can't explain the other six shots."

I suggested, "Let's say Ted challenged you to hit him eight times." I added, "Actually, I'd be happy to take the rap—or the credit—for killing him."

"Thanks, but . . . I'll handle it."

We moved back into the ELF room to check the security monitors, and we saw Schaeffer's guys arriving in marked and unmarked cars, with an ambulance, all lined up on McCuen Pond Road behind the closed gate.

Oddly, the gate wasn't opening, and the lead car smashed through it.

Then, two uniformed troopers went into the gatehouse, and a few minutes later, two EMS guys from the ambulance carried a body on a stretcher out of the gatehouse and back toward the ambulance.

Kate asked me, "What's that about?"

"I'm pretty sure Derek is dead."

"Dead?"

"Yeah. Madox needed him to tidy up the lodge and get rid of the van I borrowed from Rudy. But Madox didn't want Derek talking about that, or talking about where everyone was in the fallout shelter . . . so he got someone to get rid of Derek."

Kate commented, "Bain Madox seems to think of everything."

"Not everything, and not anymore."

We gave it fifteen minutes to be sure that the right people were in charge upstairs, then made our way to the spiral staircase, found the hydraulic switch to raise the card table, and ascended into the card room, where the air was fresh.

We had our creds out, and we were passed from one state trooper to another, until we found ourselves in the great room, where Major Schaeffer had set up his command post with a radio and a few troopers. Kaiser Wilhelm was sleeping and farting near the hearth.

Schaeffer asked us, "What in the name of God is going on here?"

I replied, "The murder of Harry Muller is solved. Bain Madox and Carl the butler did it."

"Yeah? Where's Madox?"

"In the fallout shelter."

"We searched the whole basement."

I explained how to find the fallout shelter and added, "You got three dead down there, and one seriously wounded."

"Who's dead?"

"Madox, Carl, and some other guy."

"Madox is dead? How did he die?"

I answered, evasively, "Get your CSI team there and let them get to work. Also, the wounded guy needs help fast."

Schaeffer picked up his radiophone and gave instructions regarding the fallout shelter.

I also advised Schaeffer, "You should disarm and restrain the security guards."

"They're disarmed and confined to their barracks under guard."

"Good."

"What do we have on them?"

"Accessories or witnesses to Harry's murder. Tell them the boss is dead, and see if they'll start talking."

He nodded, then said to us, "Those three diesel engines and generators were running at full capacity and we shut them down. Do you know anything about that?"

I replied, "Well, as it turned out, Fred was right. Submarines."

"What . . . ?"

Kate said, "Sorry, Major, this comes under the category of national security."

"Yeah?"

I changed the subject back to homicide and informed Schaeffer, "Don't bother looking for Putyov here."

"Why not?"

"Well, according to the late Mr. Madox, he murdered his houseguest Dr. Putyov, then put the body through the wood chipper."

"What?"

"If it matters, Putyov got what he deserved. But I can't get into that." I suggested, "You may want the CSI guys to pay special attention to the wood chipper. If they don't find anything there, you might think about collecting some bear shit and see if you can find a little of Dr. Putyov's DNA there."

Schaeffer said, "I'm not quite following—"

"Hey," I asked, "what happened to the guy in the gatehouse?"

"He's dead."

"Derek. Right?"

"That's what his name tag said." He informed us, "The EMS guys thought it looked like poisoning. Maybe a neurotoxin. The guy was twitching like an epileptic before he died."

I said to Kate, "Jeez, I hope it wasn't the pigs-in-the-blanket."

Schaeffer replied, "We didn't find any pigs-in-the-blanket, but there was a fresh pot of coffee in the guard-house, and this guy had a spilled coffee mug on his desk. So, we're thinking the coffee. We'll test it and do the toxicology."

Kate said to me, "Madox does plan ahead."

"Not anymore."

Kate asked Schaeffer, "Are the FBI here?"

"Oh, yeah. They set up their own command post." He jerked his head upward and said, "In Madox's office. Your buddy Griffith is there, and he's still looking for you."

Kate suggested, "Let's go say hello."

"Okay." I said to Schaeffer, "See you later."

He looked at us and said, "You smell like smoke, and you look like hell. What happened?"

I replied, "It's like a really long and very weird story. Let me get back to you on that."

He reminded us, "You must remain on the scene to assist with the investigation."

"See you later."

I took Kate's arm, and we left the great room.

There were about a dozen uniformed state troopers going through the house, obviously without knowing what they were supposed to be doing. I flashed my creds and asked one of them, "Where's the kitchen?"

"Kitchen? Oh . . . you just go down this hallway."

"Thanks." I headed for the kitchen, and Kate said to me, "We need to see Liam Griffith."

"Schaeffer said he was in the kitchen."

"In Madox's *office*."

I tapped my ear. "Come again?"

We found the kitchen, which was unoccupied. I noticed that there was no sign of dinner preparations, and I pointed this out to Kate, who replied, "I think dinner was a ruse, John."

"Yeah? No steak and potatoes?"

"Why are we here?"

"Because I'm hungry."

"Can I get you a cup of coffee from the gatehouse?"

"Sure, and get one for yourself." I opened the big, industrial-size refrigerator and found some cheese and cold cuts.

"How can you eat?" she asked me. "My stomach is churning."

"I'm hungry." I threw the cheese and cold cuts on the counter, then went to the kitchen sink and washed up. I think I had some of Madox on me.

As I was doing this, Mr. Liam Griffith entered the

kitchen and asked us, "Where the hell have you two been?"

I looked up from the sink. "Could you hand me that dish towel?"

He hesitated, then handed it to me. "What are you doing here?"

I dried my face and replied, "We've been saving the planet from nuclear destruction."

"Really? Then, what did you do for an encore?"

I handed the towel to Kate, who went to the sink to wash up.

I said to Griffith, "Well, then we killed a buddy of yours." I unwrapped the cheddar cheese and said, "Ted Nash."

Mr. Griffith did not reply, but I could see from his face that he wasn't understanding me. Finally, he said, "Ted Nash is dead."

"That's what I said. Doesn't that sound great?"

He still wasn't comprehending what I was saying, so I was pretty sure that Liam Griffith, prick though he was, had no clue about any of this.

Kate dried her hands and face. "He didn't die in the North Tower. But he's dead now." She added, "I killed him."

"What?"

I said, "We will not say anything else on that subject at this time. Do you want some cheddar cheese?"

"Huh? No." Finally, he said to us, "As you know, you're both in major trouble. I have orders to escort you back to the city as soon as I locate you, which I've done. I have the pleasure to inform you that you are both the subject of possible disciplinary action, and hopefully worse."

And on and on.

I must have eaten a half pound of cheese and cold cuts while he was rambling on, and I looked at my watch a few times as a hint that he should wrap it up.

When he was through, he asked us, "What exactly happened here?"

I replied, "Kate and I found Harry Muller's killer."

"Who is it?"

Kate answered, "It was Bain Madox, the owner of this lodge."

"Where is he now?"

I said, "In the fallout shelter. Dead." I added, "I killed him."

No reply.

"And that's all you need to know, and all we're saying."

"All right . . . then I need you to come with me."

"Where're you going, Liam?"

"I told you. Back to the city. There's a helicopter waiting at the airport."

I informed him, "We really can't leave a crime scene. Major Schaeffer—"

"All right. The three of us will spend one hour here with the state police so you can explain what happened. Then, I need to insist that the police release you into my custody."

I looked at Kate, and she nodded. I said to Griffith, "Kate and I will confine our statements to the subject of Harry Muller's murder. Everything else that you and the state police see here is a matter of national security, which will not be discussed until we're back at 26 Fed. Understand?"

"Maybe you can give me a hint about how national security plays into Kate killing a CIA officer."

Kate responded, "Liam, I don't think your security clearance is high enough for me to tell you about that."

He looked a little pissed, but got off a smart remark. "Ted always spoke highly of you, Kate."

"Not the last time we spoke."

Liam Griffith is no idiot, and said, "You're both either in deep trouble or you're going to get a commendation. So I'll just shut up until I find out which it's going to be."

I commented, "Today must be your annual smart day."

So we spent an hour with Major Schaeffer, the state detectives, and the crime scene investigators, during which Kate and I danced around the central issue of what the hell was going on in the Führerbunker. Then, after a pissing match between Schaeffer and Griffith, Kate and I got in Liam's rental car and began our drive from the lodge, which took us past the flagpole where the American flag still flew, illuminated by the spotlight; and below the stars and stripes was Bain Madox's Seventh Cavalry regiment pennant.

Yeah, I had mixed feelings about the guy, mostly negative, but . . . well, if he hadn't killed Harry, and if he hadn't been prepared to kill a few million other Americans, including Kate, me, and anyone else who got in his way, plus a couple hundred million innocent men, women, and children . . . well, he was a complex man, and it was going to take me a while to figure him out.

We also passed by the wood chipper, and that sort of brought me back to reality. The big things—like nuclear Armageddon—were a little abstract. It's the small things, like the wood chipper, that make you understand evil.

Well, we helicoptered back to New York City, and by the time we got to 26 Federal Plaza, there were about a dozen people there from the office, including, of course, Tom Walsh, and another dozen from Washington, all waiting for us with open notebooks and tape recorders.

Tom Walsh greeted us warmly by saying, "What the fuck was I thinking when I sent you two up there?"

I replied, "What were you thinking when you sent Harry up there?"

He had no answer for that, so I asked him, "Whose idea was it to send *me* up there alone on that assignment?"

No response.

I informed him, "I'll tell you. It was Ted Nash's idea."

"Nash is dead."

"He is now, and I'm not."

Kate said to Walsh, "But it could have easily gone the other way."

Walsh looked at both of us, and I could see he was trying to figure out if he was supposed to be clueless, angry, or blameless. He couldn't seem to decide, so he went to the men's room.

I could see that there was still a lot of confusion about what had happened and what our status was—heroes or felons—but I also sensed that one or two guys from Washington knew exactly what this was all about, but kept it to themselves.

We were debriefed in Walsh's office by two-man relay teams for hours, but Kate and I held up pretty well as we gave the interviewers an hour-by-hour, blow-by-blow account of everything that had happened since we walked into 26 Federal Plaza on Columbus Day morning and spoke to Tom Walsh—including talking to Betty at Continental CommutAir and Max and Larry at the car-rental desks, then checking out Madox's jets at the general aviation office, then the decision to go to the Custer Hill lodge instead of state police headquarters, and on and on.

I could see that the FBI people were partly impressed by our initiative and good investigative techniques, and somewhat troubled by our total failure to follow orders and becoming fugitives. I hoped they were learning something.

Also, I could sort of tell, as the night wore on, that Kate and I were the only ones there who weren't worried about something.

Interestingly, most of the FBI interviewers seemed unhappy that Bain Madox—the mastermind and prime witness to this conspiracy—was dead, and that I killed him. I said, of course, it was self-defense, though it was actually self-gratification. I mean, it was a stupid thing to do, and by whacking him, I complicated the investigation into the conspiracy. I wish I had it to do over again; of course, I'd do the same thing, but I'd first remind myself that I wasn't acting professionally.

Also, unless I was imagining things, at least two of

the FBI guys from Washington did not seem that unhappy that Madox was not able to talk.

On the subject of Kate killing CIA officer Ted Nash, none of the FBI guys commented or pressed the questioning, which was odd but understandable. They weren't going to touch that subject unless or until they heard from someone higher up.

I had a little fun watching Tom Walsh squirm, and more fun sitting in his office with my feet on his conference table as Kate and I were debriefed. At about 3:00 A.M., I expressed a strong craving for Chinese food, and an FBI agent went out and found an open place. Hey, it's not every day you're the center of attention, and you have to milk it a little.

There was a lot to unravel here, and I had no idea where this was going to go, or how high up the Project Green conspiracy reached. And, of course, neither Kate nor I would ever know.

At dawn, two FBI agents drove us back to our apartment and told us to get a good night's sleep, even though it was morning.

Back in our apartment, we stood on the balcony and watched the sun rising over lower Manhattan, both remembering the morning of September 12, 2001, when we'd watched the black smoke blocking out the sun not only for us, and New York, but for the whole country.

I said to Kate, "As we know in this business, every act of violence, and every murder, is revenge for the murder before it, and the excuse for the murder after it."

She nodded and said, "You know . . . I wanted to get out of this business . . . go someplace else . . . but now, after this, I want to stay here and do what I can . . ."

I looked at her, then back at lower Manhattan, where we could once see the Twin Towers rising into the sky. I said to her, or myself, "I wonder if we'll see the alert level go to Green again in our lifetime."

"I doubt it. But if we keep working at it, we can keep it from going Red."

Bottom line, the FBI in Los Angeles and San Francisco found the pilots and co-pilots, and found the suitcase nukes in their hotel rooms. In fact, one of the co-pilots was sitting on one of them, watching TV, when the FBI opened the door to his room.

Bottom, bottom line, I got stuck with a three-thousand-dollar bill from The Point, and as Kate predicted, the accounting office didn't want to hear any explanations, plus, Walsh wouldn't go to bat for us, so Kate and I are eating out less often for a while.

We need to go to FBI Headquarters in D.C. to be fully, fully debriefed, give statements, and write reports.

Regarding the Executive Board of the Custer Hill Club, the only news so far—reported in small items in the print media—is that the deputy secretary of defense, Edward Wolffer, has taken a leave of absence; Paul Dunn, the presidential adviser on matters of national security, has resigned his position; and General James Hawkins has retired from the Air Force.

These three events, taken by themselves, did not seem

remarkable, and caused no stir in the ever-vigilant news media. Meanwhile, Kate and I are waiting for more startling news about these guys, such as their arrests. But so far, Dunn, Wolffer, and Hawkins have not made the front page, or the 6:00 news, and I wouldn't be surprised if we never heard another thing about them, despite what Kate and I told the FBI. Maybe they lost those notes.

As for the fourth member of Madox's Board, CIA officer Scott Landsdale, no news is not necessarily good news. This guy is still out there somewhere, and Scott is either going to go scot-free or, if he's in big trouble, no one is ever going to hear about it. I mean, should we trust an organization that gets paid to lie?

On another, perhaps related subject, the war with Iraq seems on track, and I'm taking Madox's inside information and betting on the week of March 17, which my bookie says is a long shot at three-to-one odds. If I can triple my thousand-dollar bet, I can cover The Point. As for oil futures, my broker says that post-war Iraqi oil will flood the market, and prices are going down—not up, as Madox said. I have to think about who to trust—my stockbroker or Bain Madox. That's a tough call.

One thing we did not have to do in Washington was explain how or why Kate killed a CIA officer. On that subject, the head CIA guy in the ATTF told us that the dead man found in the Custer Hill lodge remained unidentified, and that the CIA officer named Ted Nash, whom we once knew, had died in the North Tower on September 11, 2001.

I wasn't about to argue with them about that, and neither was Kate.

I do think about Madox's Project Green a lot, and I'm pretty sure that what almost happened—an attack on an American city or cities with weapons of mass destruction—is going to happen, sooner or later. But now, I'd have to wonder where the attack actually came from.

And on that subject, without sounding too paranoid, I think that Kate and I probably saw and heard more than some people are comfortable with. I mean, I'm not suggesting that the CIA is planning to whack us because we know too much, or because we know about Scott Landsdale, or because Kate killed CIA officer Ted Nash. But you never know, so maybe we'll buy a dog, and check under the hood before we start the car.

You can't be too careful in this business, and you have to know who your friends are, and who your enemies are, and if you can't figure that out, keep your gun oiled, loaded, and close.

Acknowledgments

As in past novels, I want to thank US Airways captain Thomas Block (retired), contributing editor and columnist to many aviation magazines, and co-author with me of *Mayday,* as well as being the author of six other novels. Tom's assistance with technical details and editorial suggestions was, as always, invaluable, although he put a value on it and sent me a bill, which I was, of course, happy to pay. Tom and I met about fifty-five years ago, and the only person I've known longer is myself.

Thanks, too, to Sharon Block (Tom's wife), former Braniff International and US Airways flight attendant, for her careful reading of the manuscript, and her excellent suggestions.

I wish to thank my good friends Roger and Lori Bahnik for keeping me company in the North Country wilderness and for being such excellent guides through the bear-infested woods.

Once again, many thanks to my friend Kenny Hieb, retired NYPD Joint Terrorism Task Force detective, for his expert advice and assistance.

Also, thanks again to my longtime friend John Kennedy, deputy police commissioner, Nassau County Police

Department (retired), labor arbitrator, and member of the New York State Bar, for his advice and suggestions.

When verisimilitude and literary license clash, license usually wins, so any errors regarding legal or police procedural details are mine alone.

Special thanks go to Bob Atiyeh, a private pilot with an instrument rating, who shared with me his knowledge of general aviation procedures, flight plans, SBOs, FBOs, and everything else I needed to know and had no clue about.

Thanks always to my excellent assistants, Dianne Francis and Patricia Chichester. There is a special place in Heaven for authors' assistants, and truly Dianne and Patricia have earned it.

And last, but always first, my fiancée, Sandy Dillingham, whom I thank for giving me the gift of a new life. I love you.

There is a new trend among authors to thank very famous people for inspiration, non-existent assistance, and/or some casual reference to the author's work. Authors do this to pump themselves up. So, on the off chance that this is helpful, I wish to thank the following people: the **Emperor of Japan** and the **Queen of England** for promoting literacy; **William S. Cohen,** former secretary of defense, for dropping me a note saying he liked my books, as did his boss, **Bill Clinton; Bruce Willis,** who called me one day and said, "Hey, you're a good writer"; **Albert Einstein,** who inspired me to write about nuclear weapons; **General George Armstrong Custer,** whose brashness at the Little Bighorn taught me a lesson in judgment; **Mikhail**

Gorbachev, whose courageous actions indirectly led to my books being translated into Russian; **Don DeLillo** and **Joan Didion,** whose books are always before and after mine on bookshelves, and whose names always appear before and after mine in almanacs and many lists of American writers—thanks for being there, guys; **Julius Caesar,** for showing the world that illiterate barbarians can be beaten; **Paris Hilton,** whose family hotel chain carries my books in their gift shops; and last but not least, **Albert II, King of the Belgians,** who once waved to me in Brussels as the Royal Procession moved from the Palace to the Parliament Building, screwing up traffic for half an hour, thereby forcing me to kill time by thinking of a great plot to dethrone the King of the Belgians.

There are many more people I could thank, but time, space, and modesty compel me to stop here.

On a more serious note, the following people have made generous contributions to charities in return for having their names used for some of the characters in this novel: James (Jim) R. Hawkins, who contributed to Canine Companions for Independence; Marion Fanelli and Paul Dunn—Cradle of Aviation Museum; Carol Ascrizzi and Patty Gleason—Make-A-Wish Foundation; Gary Melius, on behalf of his friend, John Nasseff, and Lori Bahnik—Boys & Girls Club of Oyster Bay–East Norwich; and Leslie Scheinthal—Variety Child Learning Center.

Many thanks to these caring and public-spirited men and women. I hope you've enjoyed your alter egos and that you continue to support worthwhile causes.